THE PROVIDER

JOANNA MARGOT

The Provider

A totally gripping psychological thriller with a shocking twist

ISBN: 9798336174007

Copyright © Joanna Margot, 2024

https://joannamargot.com

THE PROVIDER

A totally gripping psychological thriller with a shocking twist

JOANNA MARGOT

Sherri Luna Myers is reading Scarlet Temptation
Yesterday at 22:45pm · 🌐

OMG OMG OMG I just finished Scarlet Temptation!! Damon Crux is my new book boyfriend!!! So hands off ladies! Just kidding we can share!

But seriously how dreamy would it be to be snatched away by a mafia prince and locked up in his luxurious basement with food and books and kinky s*x and be ordered to not lift a finger for the rest of your life!!!!!!!

 121   60 Comments

👍 Like   ↪ Share

View more 54 Comments

 **Donna Krib** Girl same!!!!
🙂 10
Like · Reply · 3h

Kelly X Give me Damon Crux and the library in Beauty and the Beast!!
🙂 8
Like · Reply · 3h

Lily N 🌸OMG you have to read Scarlet Sin now! It's even better!
🙂 12
Like · Reply · 4h

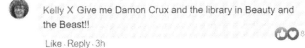 **Eveline Grace Davis** Damon Crux can cuff me to his bed anytime #relationshipgoals
🙂 17
Like · Reply · 4h

Jean Fox I can share no problem!
🙂 14
Like · Reply · 5h

Kayla Lowe-Darling Best book I read this year!!
🙂 25
Like · Reply · 5h

 Write a comment...

Chapter One

The One

The first thing I notice is that my hands are cuffed to the bed frame. I'm not sure I can open my eyes. A headache pounds mercilessly between my temples, and it feels like my eyelids are glued together. I want to rub them, but when I try to lift my right hand, I hear the rattle of the chain and feel the bite of metal on my wrist. My heart sinks, and I must snap my eyes open even if it hurts, because I need to see, I need to wake up and discover it's all just a weird episode of sleep paralysis, and my hands aren't actually cuffed.

I get that sometimes. Sleep paralysis. It hasn't happened in a while, but that doesn't mean it went away. It's a normal thing, really, and up to fifty percent of people experience it at least once in their lives. Five percent of people have regular episodes, so maybe I can say I'm part of that five percent.

But no, this is not sleep paralysis, this is real. Because I have my eyes open now, I'm lying on my right side, and I'm trying to pull my hands free once more. The chain rattles, the metal cuffs chafe my skin. As my heart sinks deeper and deeper, seemingly beating in my bowels now,

I sit up as best as I can, leaning on my right elbow, and I look around the room. Unfamiliar. And so very different from my bedroom.

There are dim overhead lights, the ceiling is low, and the walls are covered in gaudy gold and pink wallpaper. There's a table and two chairs, both painted pink, and a closet – pink as well. Every inch of the floor is covered in a plush pink carpet. It looks new. Everything looks new, in fact, and so pink that it makes my stomach turn.

I look at the bed, and the sheets are not pink, but they're gold, which is just as bad. Gold sheets. I didn't even know it was a thing. The bed is large, the mattress is just right – not too hard, not too soft – and the pillows are... Why am I even thinking about the pillows? What is wrong with me? Who cares about the carpet, and the mattress, and the pillows, when there are no windows in this place? When there are two closed doors visible from where I'm sitting, and a third one, made of shiny metal, with a keypad next to it?

I've been kidnapped.

The headache, the dry eyes, dry mouth, the sluggishness in my limbs... I've been drugged and kidnapped.

My heart is truly beating in my bowels now, and I squeeze my legs together. This is not the time to need the toilet. It happens to me when I'm nervous or scared, or both. In college, I got a stomachache before every exam, and I made sure I got there early enough to have time to calm myself. Waiting in the hall helped, because at first,

I was nervous, and then I slowly got bored and irritated that I had to wait so long, but that meant the nerves were gone, and the stomachache too. By the time my classmates showed up and we were let into the classroom, I was ready to ace the exam.

"Okay," I whisper to myself, letting out a long, trembling breath. "Okay."

It's not okay. Oh God, it's so far from being okay! How is this happening to me? Me! I am... so uninteresting. Basic, a loner, a bookworm. I live in the crappiest one-bedroom apartment in New York, because it's all I can afford, and my books occupy more space than my furniture. I don't dress nicely, and I don't wear makeup. An old pair of jeans, a faded T-shirt, and a messy bun – those are my go-tos. On the street, you wouldn't even notice me. Am I pretty? Maybe. I guess. I have... potential?

This isn't happening to me. This can't be happening to me.

"Okay..."

I shoulder off the duvet and inspect the handcuffs. They're tight around my wrists. I can barely move my hands a few inches, then the chain – which isn't long at all – stops me with a rattle. It's wrapped around the bed frame underneath, and I see no way of freeing myself. I pull and move my hands to the right, then to the left, but the chain doesn't budge much.

My vision blurs for a second, and I blink a few times. Good God, this headache will be the death of me – if something else doesn't kill me first. Like the man who drugged and kidnapped me.

It has to be a man, right? Okay, deep breaths. What's the last thing I remember?

Last night, around midnight, I went to the convenience store one block away, like I always do. Two things: I get hungry around midnight – hungry for ice cream, that is – and I prefer to do my shopping late, when there are fewer people I can bump into. I'm not a fan of chatting with the neighbors. The more serious food, I order online. There's nothing wrong with that. There's nothing wrong with me. I just don't like people very much. Not because I think I'm better than them, or anything like that. I just think... I don't fit in. I suck at making small talk, and I always feel awkward just making eye contact.

Okay, so I went out to get ice cream and microwave popcorn. After finishing a huge project for a client, I felt like I deserved to indulge in bad snacks that don't go together. Yes, I like to put my popcorn in the ice cream box and mix it all together. I added a bottle of cheap wine, paid, and the cashier slid the paper bag over to me. He's a kid, not even in his twenties, obsessed with his phone, and that's why I'm loyal to his parents' convenience store – when I pay for my stuff, he doesn't even look at me, let alone say hi. There was another late shopper in the store, a middle-aged woman, and when I walked out, the street was quiet. I barely saw anyone on my way back home.

I reached my building and walked up the few steps to the door. I was humming, lost in thought, and bumped into someone who was getting ready to go in. I yelped, took a step back, and almost dropped my paper bag.

"Sorry." A man's voice.

"No, I'm sorry," I said. "I wasn't looking."

He opened the door and moved slightly aside. "Here."

"Um... thanks." I slipped inside, and I remember trying to steal a glance at him.

Again, I'm awkward when it comes to making eye contact. The light in the hallway flickered, like always. That bulb has been dying for a month now, and no one seems to care enough to change it. All I could see as I walked in was that he was tall and lean, with dark hair and black-framed glasses, handsome in a way.

He followed me inside, and I immediately lowered my gaze. "Um... are we neighbors?" I asked.

"Something like that," he said.

I hadn't seen him around before, but I didn't think much of it. It's not like I know my neighbors. Except for the lady living right below me, who once knocked on my door to complain about my habit of moving my furniture all the time. I explained to her that I had not moved my furniture once, only for her to yell at me that she'd call the police and stomp away. I racked my brain for hours trying to figure out what she was talking about, then when I sat down with a cup of tea to work on a new article for one of my clients, I realized my desk chair was the problem.

I ordered a special mat for it, and the lady didn't bother me again.

I dug out my keys from my back pocket as I headed for the stairs. I live on the third floor.

"Good night, then," I said.

"Good night." He sounded like he was close to me. Too close.

A prick in my neck. That's the last thing I remember.

I want to touch my neck now. The spot where he stabbed me with the needle is itching, triggered by the memory.

They say most times, it's a non-stranger. If a woman gets assaulted or kidnapped, usually it's by someone she knows. I furrow my brows and think hard, but it's near impossible with this headache. Do I know the guy who opened the door for me last night? Tall, dark hair, glasses. That stupid bulb that no one changes!

The door across the room begins to emit an electric whirr, and I tuck my legs as close to my body as I can. I pull at the chain. I can roll onto the floor, but how would that help me? With wide eyes and my heart pounding harder than ever, making me ill and sweaty, I watch as the door slides inside one of the walls.

The moment of truth. Do I know the man who kid-napped me?

Chapter Two
The Other One

Sydney Murphy struggles with her suitcase as she's trying to fish her keys out of her oversized bag, and press the button to the ninth floor at the same time. The elevator doors close, and her hand brushes against her smartphone. That's not what she's looking for, but she pulls it out anyway, just to check her messages. Nothing. It's 7 AM, the last text she sent to Finneas was at 1 AM, and he still hasn't checked his phone. He must've gone to bed early the night before, she thinks, though it's not something he does often. She's not mad or anything. It would've been nice if he could've picked her up from the airport, but it's not his fault. It was all last minute, and she didn't even have time to call him before she had to take a red-eye flight back home.

She drops her phone back in the bag and finally finds her keys. The elevator stops, the doors open, and she hurries down the corridor to the apartment she and Finneas have been sharing for the past two years. They've been engaged for two and a half, and the wedding will happen any time now, this year or the next, or when one of them finally gets off their ass and starts planning it. It will probably have to be her. She'll have to get off her ass, but at the moment, work keeps her busy. She and Finneas are working for the same IT company, but for some reason, she's the one being sent on business trips. It's a mystery to her, because between the two of them, Finneas is better with people.

The key turns in the lock, and she pushes the door open with the weight of her body. The familiar scent of home fills her nostrils, and she lets out a groan as she shrugs off her jacket and toes off her shoes. She hazards a glance in the hall mirror. Her short brown hair is a mess, the pixie cut having lost its shape, and her green eyes are sunken in. If she is to survive today, she needs coffee. She has five minutes to make it and pour it into a thermos, and then she needs to call a cab and run to her mom's place in White Plains. Normally, she would take the train, but she's exhausted, and a cab will be faster.

That is the emergency. Sydney's mother called her the night before in tears, saying that her chest hurt, and she was scared. A simple cold? Pneumonia? An impending heart attack? With Syd's mom, it could be anything, but ninety-nine percent of the time, it's nothing. Still, when she calls, Syd drops everything.

She makes a beeline for the kitchen, vaguely registering the mess in the living room. Finneas sometimes leaves his clothes all over the couch and floor, especially when she's away for a few days. It's fine. She'll pick them up while the coffee brews. What's important is that he's neat when she's around. She sets the coffee maker and goes back into the living room.

A blue T-shirt, a pair of washed-out jeans, a silk blouse, a bra... Wait, what?

Sydney freezes with her hand in the air, the bra dangling from her index finger. It's red, lacey, sexy, and not one of hers. She knows this bra. She has seen it before. But it's not hers.

She drops the rest of the clothes and walks to the bedroom door, which is closed. Before she turns the knob, she hesitates for one second. One second in which she closes her eyes, draws in a breath, releases it. She wonders if there's any chance she won't be greeted with the sight she expects. There must be a perfectly valid, perfectly innocent explanation. She opens her eyes, and she believes it. What awaits behind the door won't shatter her world today, because these people... these two people are the most important, most special people in Syd's life.

She opens the door. Her eyes scan the room gradually, starting with the floor at her feet, the grayish carpet that covers a massive scratch on said floor, the pair of red panties on said carpet – which, again, are not hers – and finally, to the king-sized bed where her best friend, Abbi, lies draped over her fiancé, Finneas. Since their clothes are strewn all over the apartment, of course they're naked.

Syd takes a few breaths. Abbi and Finneas must have had one hell of a night, seeing how they're snoring softly, even with her standing in the doorway. Not that she's made a lot of noise since she got in, but she can't understand how some people can sleep through anything. She herself is a very light sleeper. Emphasis on very.

She bangs the door hard against the wall. Her best friend and her fiancé jump up at the same time, so violently that Finneas smacks his head against Abbi's. She lets out an "ouch!", but instead of checking to see if she's okay, Finneas pushes her off him and pulls at the sheets, trying to cover himself and Abbi with them.

"Let me guess," Syd says. "It's not what I think it is."

There's heavy silence for a long moment, and it's odd, but it makes Syd feel uncomfortable. Like she's the one in the wrong.

Finneas and Abbi exchange a look. Then Finneas does check Abbi's nose and makes sure it's not broken. He takes her hand, and it's like they're communicating telepathically.

Syd's heart drops. Abbi looks up, and when their eyes meet, Syd knows she's about to get more than an apology. She'll get the truth.

"Syd, I'm so sorry," Abbi says. "We're both sorry. We didn't know what to do, how to tell you... My heart breaks that you had to find out this way. Finneas and I have been seeing each other for a while now. We're in love. We can't help it. I am so sorry, but please... You have to know that we never meant to hurt you. We love you so much."

The room starts spinning. Syd braces herself on the doorframe, and her eyes fall to the bra she's still holding. She blinks and shakes her head, trying to clear her mind, trying to put the world back in order. She lets the bra fall to the floor, finally, but when she raises her gaze, her best friend and her fiancé are still there, still looking at her like she's the third wheel in her own apartment, in her own relationship.

"This isn't happening," she says.

Finneas has the decency to let go of Abbi's hand and get out of the bed. He finds his boxer briefs and puts them on.

"Syd, I'm so, so sorry. We wanted to tell you so many times."

"Three years," says Syd. It's two and a half, but a round number makes a better point. "We've been engaged for three years. We're getting married this year. Or the next."

He shakes his head. "This is the worst way to find out. I... I don't understand. You left the conference two days early?" He reaches for his phone.

Syd's eyes widen at the implication she hears in his tone. She straightens her back and forces herself to stand on her own, without the help of the doorframe.

"I texted you a dozen times," she says. "It's not like I wanted to drop in out of the blue and see if you're cheating on me. My mom called... She's..." But she stops herself and purses her lips. Why the hell is she explaining herself? She's not the bad guy here. "Never mind." She touches her temple with her fingertips as she turns to leave. "I can't deal with this right now."

"Syd!"

She ignores him as she crosses the apartment and grabs her coat and shoes. Coffee forgotten, she struggles to get her shoes on as she jumps on one foot and then the other towards the elevator. Her fingers shake as she orders a cab on her phone. First, she needs to make sure her mother is all right, and then she can figure out the mess that's her relationship. She can't believe this is happening to her. What has she ever done to these people – or to anyone, for that matter – to deserve this? It's not a "woe is me" kind of situation. It's a genuine, honest question, and something that she'll probably have to explore later in therapy. As if she can afford it...

For the entirety of the cab ride, she tries very hard not to cry. By the time she gets to her mother's house, she's feeling better. Putting distance between herself and the two people who have betrayed her helps, which means that she will have to cut them off completely, or she will never heal.

Her mom opens the door and stares at her in slight confusion, as if she doesn't understand why she's there. Syd scans her from head to toe. She looks fine to her.

"Are you going to let me in?"

"Oh. Oh!"

The middle-aged woman steps aside, and Syd gets into the house. It smells of fried eggs and bacon. Her mother has been making breakfast.

"I didn't know you were coming," she says. "I would've made two portions."

"It's fine, Mom. I can't eat."

"Too early? I guess it's too early for you."

What does that even mean? Syd chooses to ignore her comment.

"So, what's wrong? You said you're having chest pains?"

Her mother stalks into the kitchen, and Syd follows her. They sit down at the table, and her mom touches her chest gingerly.

"I'm feeling better now," she says. "It was really bad last night, Syd. I thought I was having a heart attack."

"And now?"

Her mom shrugs. "Who knows? It could've been heartburn, because it's gone almost completely."

Syd places her elbows on the edge of the table and drops her head in her hands. She doesn't know what to say to that. She's at a loss for words. Her mother starts telling her some boring story about the neighbor next door. They've had a bone to pick with each other for years.

"She never trims those trees, her garden is overgrown, which is a hazard, right? It has to be. I don't think it's legal! And that son of hers! He's been banging away inside, like he's remodeling each room at a time, and I have a feeling it will never end. These people who love to bang, and hammer, and tinker... they never stop. It's an addiction."

As she goes on and on, Syd wonders...

If something happened to her, something really bad... Would these people even care?

Chapter Three

The One

"Good morning, Evie."

"I don't know you," I whisper, more to myself than anything.

He ignores me, takes out his phone, and taps the screen a few times. The lights, which were dim before, brighten to their full power, and I can see him clearly now. He slips his phone into the pocket of his gray slacks and studies me for a moment. I study him in turn.

He is tall and lean, but not skinny. He's wearing a polo shirt, and I can see his arms are strong, the muscles taut, like he works out, maybe not obsessively, but enough to easily overpower someone who doesn't work out at all. Like me. His hair is dark brown, and his eyes are blue behind his glasses. I recognize him as the guy from last night, and now I know for sure he's not a neighbor. But have I seen him before? On the street, in the convenience store, or in a café? I don't know. I don't remember. He's handsome but not remarkable, and anyway, every time I go out, I keep my head down and rarely look around me.

"How are you feeling, Evie?" He pulls out a blister pack. "I got you Ibuprofen. I figure your head must be killing you."

"I... I don't know who you are," I say again. It seems like my mind is stuck. I can't get over the fact that this guy is a stranger. But he knows my name.

He smiles. "Oscar. Sorry, I should've introduced myself. How rude of me."

He takes a few steps towards me, and I cower against the metal headboard, trying to make myself as small as possible. The chains don't allow me to move much.

"This is a misunderstanding," I say.

He stops and cocks an eyebrow, as if he's interested in hearing more.

"I don't know you, and you don't know me, and I think you got the wrong person."

"Is your name not Eveline Grace Davis?"

I swallow heavily. My throat feels like sandpaper. "Yes, but I... I have nothing to do with you. Nothing to do with anything." I rattle the chain. "Why are you doing this to me?" I'm still hoping there's a reasonable explanation for what's happening. He doesn't seem to be angry, or violent. In fact, he's acting so polite, so unbothered. "I'm not the Eveline Grace Davis you're looking for. What does she owe you? Money? I'm not her."

He blinks at me, then his lips curve into a smile, then he's laughing. His laugh is full and pleasant. Not sinister at all, like I'd expect a kidnapper's laugh to be. In other circumstances, I would've found this guy – this Oscar guy – attractive.

"Oh, you're funny, Evie," he says as he walks the last few steps to the bed. He sits on the edge, so close to me that I can smell his cologne – something fruity, something expensive. "I knew you were the real deal. Ibuprofen?" He shakes the blister before my eyes, and I shake my head. He shrugs and leaves it on the nightstand. "You don't know me, but I know you, Evie."

Why is he repeating my name over and over? It's unsettling, and every time he does it, my heart skips a beat. I open my mouth to say something, but nothing comes out.

"I've been watching you for months. Since February 6, to be exact. Don't look at me like that. I think it's important to keep track of the dates and events that have meaning to us. Like your birthday, on March 3rd, and that time you won that writing contest in high school, on October 15. And February 6, the day your name popped up in my Facebook feed when you commented on one of my friends' posts. She was looking for book recommendations, and there you were, giving her a list of your favorite books. You're such a bookworm, Evie. I've always had a thing for bookworms."

I'm trembling now. And sweating profusely. The temperature in the room is just right, but inside me, everything is boiling. I think I have a fever.

"What do you want from me?" I say in a voice that sounds too meek, like I've given up already. But this guy... He's creepy. He's a stalker. He's been watching me since February. We're in June.

He reaches out to touch my face, and I flinch. His hand stops inches from my cheek, and to my relief, he pulls back, then clears his throat, as if he's doing his best to be gentle and take things slowly. He's not happy with my reaction, I can see it in his eyes, but he's keeping up the façade of calm and politeness. He's not a nice guy. He talks and acts like he is, but I know he's not. A nice, decent guy would never kidnap a woman whose name popped up randomly on his social media.

What was it? My profile picture? I shiver when I remember the day I took it. I needed a good photo for my socials and my profile on the freelance site I work on, so I put on makeup for the first time in months, straightened my long, blonde hair, and snapped a few selfies. I was happy with the result. I looked pretty. Okay, maybe even sexy. When I updated my profile picture on Facebook, I got more likes than on any of my other posts. Now, the memory of that day makes me sick. Oscar saw my profile picture and instantly thought I was his type. I don't feel flattered in the slightest.

"What I want, Evie–"

"Are you going to hurt me?" I blurt out.

"N-no."

"You're hurting me right now." I rattle the chain again. "Let me go, then. Just uncuff me."

"I will, but first–"

"This is kidnapping. You know that, right? You know this..." I pull at the chain as hard as I can. "This isn't normal."

"Stop that. You're hurting yourself."

"No, you're hurting me! Just let me go." My voice drops to a whine. "Please, just let me go."

He frowns. "Evie, I need you to calm down and listen to me."

That's the last thing I want to do. In fact, every time I think about the word "calm", panic grips my insides. I'm breathing fast, and I feel beads of sweat gathering at the roots of my hair. I start moving my legs, rubbing them together under the duvet. It's too hot, I have no air, and the lack of windows is driving me crazy.

"Evie." He places a hand on my knee, and I freeze. "Listen."

"Just let me go," I whine. His hand on my knee makes my stomach turn. I wonder if I should kick him. He'd fall right off the bed, and then what?

"Evie!" This time he yells. Right in my face, and spittle hits my cheeks. "Calm down! I'm trying to tell you something!"

Now I freeze for real. Completely. I can't deal with people yelling at me. Getting angry at me. It's been this way since I was a child, and my father would get mad out of nowhere and start screaming at me and my mom, and neither of us usually knew what had triggered him. This is another reason I avoid people. Friendships and relationships. Because people get angry, and people yell, and I don't know how to deal with it.

"Good," Oscar says. "Good." He takes a breath and shakes his head slightly, as if he's trying to remember what he wanted to say before I made him lose his temper. "What I want, Evie, is to take care of you."

Wait, what?

"I want to provide for you. I will give you everything you want, everything you need, everything you deserve. Because I know you, Evie, and you're worth it. You can't see it yourself. You've been isolated for so long, living in a bubble, afraid to put yourself out there, thinking that you're not enough. I want to tell you that you are enough. You're so much more than enough, and I will make sure that your life is perfect. From now on, you won't have to lift a finger. All you have to do is... exist. You're the perfect woman for me already, you don't have to change a thing." He motions at the room. "I made this for you. I decorated it myself. It's lovely, isn't it?"

He looks at me, waiting for an answer. I start crying silently. Tears run down my cheeks, in rivulets, and I can't stop them. My vision blurs, and I blink fast, but the tears won't stop. On the contrary, they multiply.

There's a box of paper tissues on the nightstand, and he pulls a few out and starts dabbing at my face. He doesn't say anything, doesn't seem to be angry, which is a good thing, because I don't want him yelling at me again, but at the same time... what the hell?

What the hell is going on? What the hell is he thinking? How sick can he be to think this is what I want? He sounds like he's doing me a favor, fulfilling my dreams.

"I don't want this," I say, just in case that's what it takes to break his delusion.

"Of course you do, Evie. I know you do."

It's not.

"I know everything about you, remember? I know your deepest secrets, your deepest desires."

I doubt that.

"Listen, this isn't everything. This room." He wipes my eyes and, to my horror, even wipes my nose. "I want to uncuff you and show you something. It's a surprise. Actually, I have two surprises for you, and you're going to love them. But you must promise that you won't do anything stupid." He looks into my eyes, but I don't react. He sighs. "Okay, look." He points at the table and the two chairs on either side of it. "The furniture is bolted to the floor." Then he points at the closet. "And to the walls. You can't pick it up and you can't push it, trust me. It won't budge. Nothing in here can be used as a weapon."

I was afraid of that. I was afraid he's the type of person who's thought of everything. And now that he's pointing out these things, I can see that the chairs are bolted to the floor. If he uncuffs me, what can I hit him with? The box of tissues? Or the blister of Ibuprofen. There are literally no other objects on the two nightstands and the table.

"Also, I am bigger and stronger than you," he adds.

I know that already. I'm not a fighter, and I know I don't stand a chance if I try to attack him.

"So, do we have an agreement?" he asks. "I will uncuff you, and you will behave."

I nod. What else am I supposed to do? He doesn't seem to want to hurt me, but underneath his polite demeanor, now I know he has a temper. I must not let myself be fooled by his gentleman act. This man kidnapped me. Of course he will hurt me. We just have different definitions of what hurting someone means. He's not right in the head. I can't trust him.

He pulls out a key from the back pocket of his slacks, and I watch him unlock the cuffs. My heart is beating in my throat. I feel like I'm about to puke, but I swallow hard and try to control my body's reactions to stress and panic. Fear is like a membrane that vibrates close to my skin. I'm wrapped in it from my toes to the top of my head. I think I will never not feel fear.

"Easy," he says when the cuffs are off.

I rub the red marks on my wrists as I gently place my feet on the floor. I'm wearing the clothes I was wearing last night, except I'm in my socks. I keep my eyes on Oscar for a moment, and then I bolt.

I can't help it. It's pure, raw instinct.

I throw myself at the metal door and bang on it with my fists, yelling at the top of my lungs, "Help me! Someone, help me!" Of course, the door doesn't budge. I turn around and see that Oscar hasn't moved from where he's sitting on the edge of the bed. He's looking at me with what seems to be disappointment. There are two more doors, and I launch myself at them, trying the knobs and pushing my body into them, but of course they're locked.

"Are you done?" he asks. He stands up slowly.

No, I'm not done. Yes, he's bigger and stronger than me, but maybe I have a chance... Maybe. I have to try. I have to...

I slam right into him, and he easily catches me, turns me around in his arms, and holds me tightly as I scream and thrash. My feet lift off the floor, and I try to kick him. He lets out a grunt, but other than that, I completely fail to even give him a hard time.

"Shh," he whispers in my ear. "Evie."

I start sobbing as I go limp.

Chapter Four

The Other One

Abbi and Finneas are blowing up her phone. Sydney has put it on silent, and she's currently sitting in a café, having a mocha latte and playing with the napkin, folding it and unfolding it in meaningless patterns. She left her mother's house in the middle of one of her stories about the offending next-door neighbor, and stopped here, a few blocks away from the apartment she shares with her fiancé.

The apartment she used to share with her ex-fiancé.

She must go back there, she knows that. But she doesn't want to do it without having some sort of plan. She avoids reading their texts. It doesn't matter what they say at this point. Their apologies fall flat, and she doesn't care about their explanations. It's done. There's no going back, neither with Finneas, nor with Abbi. She lost two people she loved in one strike.

She finishes her latte and gets up. On the walk to the apartment building, she tests various things she could say to them in her head, but as she takes the elevator to the ninth floor, she decides it's better to keep it short. The second she enters the apartment, they both start saying the same things as before.

"We both love you so much."

"We know you love us, too."

"This is so hard. An impossible situation."

"What would you have done if you were me?" Abbi asks her.

"Not slept with my best friend's boyfriend," Syd thinks to herself. She goes into the bedroom and takes out a second suitcase. At least she has one packed already, so... silver lining? She starts throwing in clothes and personal belongings.

"You don't have to do this," Finneas says.

"What do you mean?"

"You don't have to move out now. No one expects you to."

Syd laughs bitterly. "Oh, no one expects me to? Wow. Thanks."

"We can talk about it," he insists. "Let's sit down for a minute and talk about it."

"Why? So you can tell me about how it all happened in detail? Your love story, in chronological order?"

"No. Syd, of course not."

"Go away, Finn. Let me be for a second. Let me finish here."

He throws his hands up and retreats to the living room, but Syd barely has time to take a breath before Abbi takes his place.

"I never wanted this to happen," she says.

"Sure you didn't."

"Syd, please. I know you're hurting, but please slow down. Listen to Finn. You don't have to move out. This is your place as much as it's his."

They've done fifty-fifty on rent and bills since they moved in together. A year ago, they talked about buying a place, but the prices were through the roof, and now Sydney is happy the universe had seemed to be against them back then.

There are many ways in which she can reply to the preposterous thing that has just come out of Abbi's mouth. Does Abbi think Syd can sleep in the bed where she and Finneas... No. Does Abbi think Syd can breathe the same air as them for another minute? She would hold her breath right now if she could. She doesn't say anything, though. There's no point. And when Abbi keeps talking, Syd tunes her out. She sits on the suitcase to zip it up, then drags it out of the bedroom, pushing against Abbi so hard that her ex-best friend almost falls over.

"Where are you going?" Finneas asks.

Syd throws her bag on her shoulder and grips the handles of the two suitcases.

"None of your business," she says.

"Your mother's place?" he asks, then sighs and runs a hand through his blond, disheveled hair. "Syd, you really don't have to do this. It doesn't have to end like this."

She looks into his deep blue eyes, and her heart aches. He's handsome, her ex-fiancé. Before work started taking up most of her time, they used to go to the gym together every morning. Twice a month, they'd go to the climbing club, challenge each other and compete in a cute, totally healthy way. They used to have so much in common.

"You know what? Yes. I'll be at my mom's place when you have time to send me the rest of my things. The coffee maker is mine, and so is the crockpot. Pack them well, so they don't get busted."

"I can bring them myself."

"I'd rather you didn't. Anyway, take your time." She turns to Abbi. "I'm sure you can help him separate my things from his. There are a few more clothes left in the closet. You can keep the blue dress, I know you always liked it."

"Syd..."

Now she's really going to cry, which means she needs to get out of here. Her keys are in the bowl that sits on the console table in the hallway, and she wonders if she should take them or leave them. She leaves them. She can't imagine herself ever coming back here, so there's no point in having a set of keys.

It's done. It's over. For real. So done and over that if Finneas doesn't send over her crockpot, she won't fight for it.

Neither he nor Abbi follow her, but she can feel their eyes on her back as she's waiting for the elevator. The doors open, she steps in, and she gives them both one last look. She's been so wrapped up in her relationship with Finneas and her friendship with Abbi that now she has no one to help her. They were her only friends. Such a huge part of her life, that it feels like she's getting half of her body chopped off and thrown into the trash as she's leaving.

Should she fight this? They gave her no choice, took all her power, threw her into a situation she can't control. No, this is happening, it's already happened, and trying to fight it would be pointless.

Chapter Five
The One

I try to calm down, even though it's the last thing I want to do. The less I struggle, the more relaxed his grip on me is. I want to turn around and claw his eyes out, scratch his face until he's a bloody mess, but I don't have it in me. Right now, I want him to let go of me, to stop touching me.

"This is new to you," he says, "I understand, and that's why I'm going to be forgiving this time. Just this once, though. I expect you to behave properly, Evie. I don't ask for much in exchange for everything I'm going to give you. But it won't kill you to show a little gratitude."

I shiver. Finally, he lets go, and I stumble forward. I wrap my arms around myself as I slowly turn to look at him. My stupid tears keep falling and falling, and it's hard to hold in the sobs. At least now I can wipe my eyes with the back of my hands.

"You're not used to being taken care of," he continues saying, and I swear I have no idea what he's on about. "No one has ever shown you how much you're worth. I'm going to change that."

"I don't understand," I say.

"Let me show you the first surprise."

He walks towards me, and I take a step back, but before I can escape him, he grips my arm and leads me to one of the doors. My body is still in flight mode. The urge to bolt is strong, but I must fight it because I have nowhere to go, and if I start being difficult again, that will enrage him.

I feel like there's a lot of rage lurking inside Oscar. He reins it in, and he's probably done it all his life, which means it only festered and festered, and when it explodes, that will be the end of whoever happens to be in his vicinity. That person will probably be me.

He pulls out a set of keys and sticks one in the lock. The door opens, and my heart gallops as I cross the threshold. God knows what he understands by "surprise". The guy is sick.

It's a bathroom. Just a simple, harmless bathroom, with a sink, an oval mirror above it, a toilet, and a tub. It's just as pink as the bedroom. The tub is huge, and at the foot of it, there are floor-to-ceiling shelves that are filled with beauty products. Shampoo, hair masks, creams, serums – all expensive brands I can't afford to buy. Not that I need all this stuff. Pink-colored bottles, peach-colored jars, amber-colored vials. So, this is the surprise? I steal a reluctant glance at Oscar. He's kidnapped me so he can put me in here and give me a spa treatment?

"I feel like I should warn you right now," he says. "Don't try to use, say, the toothbrush as a weapon. It won't work." He places a hand on my shoulder and points at the ceiling. My blood freezes in my veins. "Cameras. Everywhere. Don't even wonder about blind spots. There aren't any. I will know what you're up to at all times."

"But I... How am I supposed to use the toilet?"

He shrugs. "I'm sure you know how to use a toilet, Evie."

"I need privacy."

"No, you don't."

"At least a shred of it."

"Unnecessary."

He sounds determined. I don't think I can change his mind, and I once again feel like I'm going to puke. Except I don't think I can puke with him watching.

"Look, Evie, I'm not one of those boys you used to date."

The last time I dated someone was in college.

"I know women don't fart rainbows that smell like roses and lavender."

The horror of his crude words! More than the words, the dismissive way in which he says them. I feel my face heat up.

"There should be no secrets between us," he goes on. "The levels of intimacy we will achieve... Trust me, I know couples who will envy us."

"Oscar." I say his name for the first time, and it almost makes me gag, but maybe he will finally listen to me. "I can't use the toilet knowing that you're watching me."

"Evie." He places a hand on my cheek, and I want to turn my head and bite it. I stand there, motionless, hoping he won't linger. "I assure you, there's nothing related to your body or your bodily functions that would ever bother me."

I nod, and he removes his hand. There's no point in arguing. He's not going to let up. Also, I want this conversation to end.

"These are all yours." He motions at the bottles and jars, but I can't focus. He picks up a few and starts talking about how they're organic and he chose them for my skin type, but his words go right past my head.

My mind goes to when I was eleven, twelve, thirteen, just dealing with the first changes in my body, which meant spending more time in the bathroom. It didn't take long for my father to become obsessed with the time I spent in the bathroom. How much toilet paper I was using, how many times I flushed the toilet – "How many times do you have to pee, Eveline?". He would literally listen to see how long the water ran, and when the water bill came in the mail, he'd stick it in my face – "See how much it costs to take three showers a day?". Never mind I showered once in the evening.

His constant pestering made me develop a UTI. Yes, apparently you can get a UTI if your levels of stress and anxiety are through the roof. And when that was under control, I developed IBS. For years, I battled both. I was rarely off medication, and I only managed to heal when

I went away to college. By that time, I was convinced there was something wrong with me. I was too weak, too sensitive. But then the symptoms went away, little by little, until I could finally have a healthy relationship with... well... the bathroom. Except for when I had an exam or had to make a presentation in front of the whole class.

It wasn't me. It had never been me. It was the fact that my dad had literally watched every move I made while living with him and my mom, especially when it came to spending time in the bathroom. What was I doing in there? What was taking so long?

And now, Oscar is going to watch me. Actually watch me. Through all these cameras. A cramp seizes my lower abdomen, and I cringe. I can't go through that again. Does he realize he's not taking care of me, but torturing me? I think he does. I think he gets a kick out of it.

What the hell am I going to do? I have to get out of here. There has to be a way. I'll let him show me all these things he wants to show me, and maybe then he'll go away and leave me alone, so I can properly inspect the place. There has to be something he's missed.

"Do you want to see your second surprise?"

Oh, right. There are two surprises. I nod.

He beams at me, then motions for me to walk in front of him. He leaves the door to the bathroom open, and I let out a breath of relief. I half expected him to lock the door again and announce I will have to use the bathroom on his schedule. My dad would've loved to do that to me. I bet he fantasizes about it even now.

We stop before the second locked door, and he shoves the key into the lock. I honestly don't know what to expect when the door opens.

Chapter Six

The Other One

First, Sydney tells her mother that she broke up with Finneas. She tells her the truth about him and Abbi, and her mom is sympathetic, but maybe not as much as Syd expected. She and Abbi have been best friends since college, and therein lies the problem. All three of them work in the same field – Syd and Finneas for the same company, and Abbi for a different company where now Syd cannot apply for a job. And if her mother is sympathetic about the time she's wasted in a relationship that led nowhere, she's less so when Syd breaks it to her that she had to quit and is now jobless.

It only takes a few days of living together for her mother to resort to the way she was before Syd went to college.

"And you're telling me you don't have any money put aside?" she asks her as she's cooking dinner and Syd is on her laptop at the kitchen table, sending in job applications.

"Not really." The truth is she has some money, but it's not a lot, and she'll need it for a new place.

"So, you can't contribute to the bills?" Syd doesn't say anything, so her mother goes on. "If you're going to live here for God knows how long, you have to help with the bills, Syd! And the food. Nothing is free, you know."

"I know," Syd says under her breath.

Her mother has always been obsessed with money. Not that she ever lacked money, but she always behaved like she did. Like there was not enough for everyone, and there was certainly not enough for a woman to raise her daughter alone.

"I'm afraid I'll have to take on more clients," she tells Syd. "I'm already working myself to the bone. But I'll do it, of course. Is there anything I won't do for you?"

"Seriously, Mom. You don't have to take on new clients. I'm only staying for a few weeks, until I find something."

"And how will you pay rent without a job?"

"I will get a job."

"So, you'll get a job first and then get a new place? We're at the very beginning of a financial crisis, Syd. No one is hiring."

"I honestly don't see or feel the financial crisis."

"Really?" Her mother turns to her, hands on her hips. "Do you listen to yourself? Do you even read the news? Or is it all fake?"

"Mom..."

"Why did you have to quit your job? So what if you're working for the same company as Finneas?"

"We were on the same project!"

"You could've asked to be moved, right? I don't know what you IT people do, but certainly there were other projects they could've put you on."

"What's done is done." Syd starts typing furiously.

Her mother sighs and turns back to the stove. "I'll take a few more clients. We'll get through this. You and I... We always manage, don't we? We're survivors."

Syd doesn't say anything. They have dinner and spend a pleasant evening watching an old movie, with popcorn and chocolate ice cream – the cheap kind, because of course they can't afford Ben & Jerry's. They can, in fact. Both of them. Her mother is sitting on a pile of cash, Syd is sure of it, and Syd herself isn't entirely broke. It's a thing in their family – always pretend you have less. Syd doesn't complain about it, because even though she knows the phenomenon is called "lack mentality" in spiritual circles, she feels it's safer this way. There are other "old beliefs" around money that are more dangerous than this, like whatever those people who spend their whole paycheck in one day have.

It doesn't last long, though, this cozy atmosphere between them. The next day, Syd's mother bemoans her prolonged showers.

"It shouldn't take you more than ten minutes to wash yourself!"

And the moment the sun sets and it starts getting dark, she yells at Syd that she needs to control her habit of leaving the lights on everywhere in the house.

"You walk out of a room, you turn the light off. Why is it so hard?"

Syd has a few interviews lined up, but she can't wait a day longer. She'll have to figure out how she can schedule some apartment viewings.

Chapter Seven

The One

Books. On the floor. Heaps of them. This room is smaller than the bedroom, and there's not a trace of furniture in it. The carpet is thick and plush, and there's a reading nook in a corner, with a beanbag, two square pillows, a thick blanket, and a basket that's filled with something I can't identify from the doorway. I feel Oscar's hand on my lower back, and I jolt and take a few steps inside the room.

"What do you think?" he asks, and I can hear the excitement in his voice.

He expects me to be excited, too. He probably expects me to do a little happy dance for him. That's not happening.

"Umm..." I try to buy myself some time.

I pick up a book and force myself to make out the title. It's hard to focus. It's called Chasing Bella, and the cover is a pair of golden handcuffs and a red high-heeled shoe. It looks familiar. I set it back down and pick another. This cover is an intricate artwork with flowers and shining knives. A chill runs up my spine. I know these titles. They're both on my ever-growing list of books that I want to read. The TBR pile – the beast every reader worth their salt is trying to tame, but not quite. Because there's satisfaction in ticking off books you've meant to read since forever, but there's also another kind of satisfaction – a pleasure of the guilty sort – when instead of reading what's waiting for you on the nightstand, you keep buying books.

"Well?" Oscar is losing his patience. "What do you think, Evie?"

"This is..." Weird. Unsettling. Sick. I turn to him and wave the book I'm holding. "I've been meaning to read this."

"I know!" He's beaming again. He makes a gesture that encompasses the entirety of the room. "These are all books you want to read but can never find the time. Now you have all the time in the world. With nothing to worry about, no job, no clients bombarding you with emails, you can read all day." He walks over to the reading nook and gives one of the pillows a pat. "Comfy, see?" Then he picks up something from the basket, and I see it's a chocolate bar. "And you have snacks right here." He drops the chocolate bar and grabs a book from atop the beanbag. "Your favorite. I figured you'd like to re-read it."

My stomach drops. Scarlet Temptation. It's not my favorite book, because any reader worth their salt knows it's impossible to pick one favorite, but it's among the best new releases this year. A five-star read.

And that's when I look more closely at the books around me. They're all the same genre. Dark romance. A genre that I've been favoring for a while. These types of books help me escape the daily routine, make me forget that I don't really have friends, don't really have a social life, and I haven't dated in ages. They help me unwind after a day of writing boring articles for boring businesses, they help me dream of things that will never happen to me. No dark, twisted Prince Charming sort of guy who looks like the god Apollo and is a billionaire under thirty will show up at my door, claim me as his own, then give me a life of luxury and adoration. No...

No.

My knees give in, and I crumble to the floor. I can't help it. I can't stand anymore, all the bones in my body seem to have turned to jelly.

No.

I hear Oscar walking around the mounds of books. He won't stop talking.

"There's another small surprise, and I thought I'd let you discover it, but to hell with that, I can't wait to tell you! You'll notice some of these paperbacks aren't even available to buy. I made them just for you, so you can have the titles that are only available as eBooks. I don't understand why so many authors just release eBooks and call it a day. Oh well. I know you like paperbacks, so I made them especially for you. Oh, and I'll keep adding to your collection. I know new stuff is published every day, so once a week, I'll bring you the new releases. I want you to be up to date. With so much time on your hands now, I know you'll go through these easily."

I'm on my knees, curled up, and I cover my face with my hands. This isn't happening. This can't be happening to me.

And I know I've spent the past two or three years fantasizing of exactly this thing happening to me, since I discovered dark romance and never looked back, but this is not how it works. I remember there were articles written about it, explaining how women who read romance and declare the A-hole male characters their book boyfriends would not actually date those men in real life. There is a huge, huge difference between what people like to read and what they want to experience. Damn it! Men who read action and adventure books don't want to be chased by gangsters through dark alleys! This isn't even about women and their reading preferences.

Now I have no doubts left that Oscar is completely mad. Someone who can't distinguish between reality and fiction is not someone I can reason with.

What do I do? What the hell do I actually do?

I realize too late that he's been silent for a few minutes. He crouches beside me now, and I flinch away, but he grabs me by the back of the neck and forces me to look at him. He's still holding Scarlet Temptation in his other hand.

"I got you the whole series. The fifth book will be released in three months, and I'll get you that one too. On release day."

Three months. He's fully convinced I'll still be here in three months.

"Aren't you happy, Evie? This is all you've ever wanted. Now, I know I'm not exactly rich, and I'm not in the mafia either. I promise you, I'm not. But I will do my best." He passes me Scarlet Temptation. "I read it, you know? So I can understand you better, understand your dreams and desires. I will make sure to fulfill each and every one of them."

I remember some of the things Damon Crux did to Fiona, the female lead in Scarlet Temptation, and I'm sure my face turns green, because Oscar immediately lets go of me and stands up. I let the book drop to the floor and cover my mouth with my hand.

"Anyway, the whole place is yours to enjoy. Sorry there are no windows, but you know how this goes. It's all in your books." He waits for me to say something, and when I don't, he sighs. "From now on, all you have to do is exist, Evie. I will feed you, clothe you, and provide for you. And if you need anything, all you have to do is ask. I am watching and listening."

He hesitates for another moment, then leaves the room. I hear the electrical sound the metal door makes when it opens and shuts, and I know I'm alone. Except I'm not. There are cameras and microphones everywhere. No blind spots, no privacy. I am trapped in what he probably believes is a gilded cage but is in fact a basement. A pink basement.

I pick myself off the floor, but I'm wobbly on my feet. I stand there, in the middle of the room that Oscar probably expects me to call the library, and I'm unsure of what I should do next. I need to lie down. Will it be the bed or the beanbag? The beanbag is closer, so I drag myself there and plop down. I stare at the snack basket, but there's no way I can hold anything down.

This is ridiculous. Of all the reasons men kidnap women, this one makes the least sense. Though, maybe I shouldn't think this way. There are no logical reasons for men to kidnap women. Ever.

I know I should do something useful, like check this entire place and find that one thing that Oscar missed which will give me an advantage. I'm sure he missed something. He isn't that smart, is he? But he's stalked me for a long time, learned everything about me. Do I regret being who I am now that it has turned out to be my undoing? Do I regret reading that first dark romance book three years ago? I don't even remember the title.

What I do remember is the name of the very first romance book I read when I was a teenager – A Dance of Destiny. My mother had quite the collection in the attic. She went up there every few days to retrieve another book. We had a proper bookshelf in the living room, like all self-respecting families did, but my father forbade her from displaying her filthy books among the classics that he'd amassed over time and never read himself. So, my mom was forced to put her books in the attic, and she'd go up and down, up and down, every time she bought a new one. The attic wasn't locked, so one day, out of curiosity, I went up there and chose a book. She didn't say anything when she saw me reading it. Well, she did, in fact – "Don't let your father see you." And since then, I was hooked.

I read her entire collection, then started adding to it, saving money just so I could buy a book every few weeks. My mother and I bonded over those books, and that made life at home easier for both of us. Then I went to college and made sure to send her new books from time to time. I hated that I was able to escape, and she was still trapped there, but there was nothing I could do for her. Even now, she is trapped. And I'm trapped, too.

My mother and I don't call each other often. We grew apart at some point, and I don't send her books anymore. Will she realize that I've vanished off the face of the earth? Will anyone?

I drop my head in my hands and cry again, silently. I will give myself this one last crying session, to get it all out of my system, and then I'm done. I'll pull myself together and focus on getting out of here. There's no way I'm going to let this happen to me.

Chapter Eight

The Other One

The apartment is not what Sydney expected, and she gives the agent a look that says so. The agent, a blonde woman in her late thirties, classy and polished, shrugs.

"It's all I can do with the budget you gave me. I can show you two other places, but they're not very different from this. At least this one is in a better neighborhood."

"It's a shoebox," Syd points out.

"Well." The agent frowns but doesn't say more than that. Her phone pings with a text, and she's suddenly busy with, probably, a client who's not on a tight budget, like Syd.

Syd takes a few steps, and she's already on the other side of the apartment. It's a loft. The "bedroom" is upstairs, and it's no more than a sleeping place that's big enough for her to put a mattress in, and maybe a lamp. The stairs are wooden, creaky, and not very sturdy. Downstairs, there's a couch and a small kitchen, and not even a closet for her to put her clothes in. She'd have to buy one, or maybe a simple rack would do. She can't splurge on furniture now.

It kind of hurts that she contributed to various things in the apartment she used to share with Finneas, and now that's all money down the drain. She could call him and ask him to meet for a serious, adult conversation. After two years of living together, she feels like this breakup is a lot like a divorce. They should talk about the financial side of it, but Syd doesn't feel like she can do it. She doesn't even want to see him, let alone sit across from him in a café and negotiate.

It's fine. She can make do with what she has, and she'll soon get a new job. At least the loft has its own bathroom. The water, heating and electricity all seem to work fine, there's a small fridge that's in good condition, and the walls aren't peeling too badly.

"I'll take it," she says.

The agent smiles. "Great! I know it's not what you wanted, Ms. Murphy, but given your situation at the moment, this is a good decision. There will be a one-month deposit, of course."

"Of course."

Two hours later, she's back at her mother's house, feeling lighter, but not in a good way. Her bank account is lighter, her soul still feels heavy. She gives her mother the good news and tries not to roll her eyes when she sees her let out an exaggeratedly long breath of relief.

Syd makes herself a cup of coffee and sits down at the kitchen table to send in more job applications. She's been to interviews, but she hasn't had any luck so far. It turns out most companies are looking for people with more experience than she has. The only reason she got a job with the company she used to work for was Finneas. Not that she isn't good at her job, or a fast learner. She just isn't that great with people, and she has a feeling that's why it's so hard for her to make a good impression at interviews. They want to see confidence and enthusiasm, and all she can give them are short answers and forced smiles.

She isn't usually like this. She can pretend, obviously, make an effort. But not now, not when she's in pain after her world just fell apart, and she found out that she doesn't mean that much to anyone, really. These people keep saying that they love her – Finneas, Abbi, her mother – but they don't.

"Syd, Finn is here," her mother shouts from the living room.

Syd closes her eyes for a moment, takes three deep breaths, then stands up. She keeps her back straight as she walks out of the kitchen. Her mom is at the front door, hands on her hips, watching Finneas unload boxes from his car.

"There isn't space in the house for all your stuff, Syd," she says.

"Don't worry, I'm moving out next week and taking everything with me."

"Finn," her mom shouts at her ex. "Leave the boxes right here, by the door. Syd found a place, so there's no need to carry them upstairs."

"Great," Syd thinks. *"Shout as loud as you can, why don't you? So the whole neighborhood hears."* She doesn't say anything. She thinks about how good it will feel to be out of here next week. She'll be on her own, with no one to lecture her about the bills and how life isn't as cheap as it used to be. She hasn't been alone in a while, but it can't be that bad, can it? She'll get used to it.

"So, you found a place," Finn says as he carries two boxes into the house, one on top of the other. He places them next to the wall and looks at her as he awkwardly wipes his hands on his jeans. "Where?"

"Why would I tell you?" It's hard to look into his blue eyes. He's as handsome as ever, and her core aches.

"I can help you move. Abbi can help you decorate."

She shakes her head. "Please stop talking."

"Syd..."

"I asked you to send over the rest of my things, not come here in person."

"I wanted to see you."

"I didn't."

"Syd, don't be like this."

"Like what?" She's making a great effort to keep her voice down. The door is open, and she's certain her mother's archnemesis is listening from her front yard. "What are you saying, Finneas? That I shouldn't be... hurt?"

"That's not what I meant."

"You want me to be nice to you, that's what you want. To you and Abbi, so you don't feel like crap."

"No, I really don't mean it like that."

"Then?"

He looks at her for a moment, then shrugs and goes to fetch the rest of the boxes. They don't talk as he finishes carrying them into the entry hall. Syd's mother is watching them without saying anything, and at least for that, Syd is grateful. She would've liked to see her mother show a little more support, maybe go off on Finneas and tell him he's a moron, and a jerk, and he doesn't know what he's missing. For someone who hates making a scene, Syd sometimes wishes the people who claim they love her made a scene for her. But it's fine. It's better this way. More dignified.

"You know you can call me anytime," Finn says. "If you need help moving, just ask, and I'll drop everything."

Sydney huffs. "Right."

She slams the door in his face and stands there until she hears his car pull out of the driveway. She finds it hard to breathe, but then there's a hand on her shoulder, and she leans into her mother's touch. It's rare... her mother touching her like that. It's not a hug, but Syd will take it.

"He's just a man," her mom says. "You know how they are."

"Yeah."

He is just a man, and it's not like she expected that much from him, anyway. He's handsome, fairly successful, and a decent person. She thought it would be enough to make an unproblematic husband and – why not? –

father one day. That's the most to be expected from men, and Syd learned that from her single mother. The bare minimum, really, and it turns out Finn wasn't even able to give her that.

That's not what hurts the most. Men are men. Abbi, though... Abbi was her best friend, and Syd can't stand to think about how much she invested in their friendship, how much she sacrificed for Abbi. She can't believe Abbi cast it all away. In college, they made promises to each other, promises so deep that they were almost vows. They meant something to Syd, and nothing at all to Abbi. Because Abbi was always so special to her, Syd never made other friends. She knows people, sure, and if she looks through the contacts in her phone, she'll find a few cool girls she can call and have lunch with. But it would be nothing serious. She wouldn't be able to talk to them for real. They wouldn't get her. Only Abbi could. Abbi knew what was in her soul, and she could listen to Sydney not only when she talked, but also when she was silent.

Losing Finn... she can get over that. Losing Abbi...

And now she has to do everything by herself. Clean the new place, move in, decorate, buy a new mattress... Okay, she actually has to buy a new mattress first, and then think about the rest. There's so much noise in her head, so much chaos in her soul. She will mess this up if she doesn't make a list of the things she has to do over the next few days.

"Are you okay?" her mother asks.

"Yes. I have things to do."

She walks past her mother without looking at her. It's because she can hear the compassion in her voice, and if she dwells on it, Syd is going to cry. She doesn't want to cry today just because she saw Finn and he once again disrupted her life with his mere presence.

"I'll make your favorite for dinner," her mother says.

"Thank you. That means a lot."

It really does.

Chapter Nine

The One

It's hard to point out when my isolation from the world began. Sometime after finishing college, rather than returning to Vermont where my family lives, I chose to rent an apartment in New York. It was gradual, and when I realized that I suddenly had no one to call, no one to hang out with, I decided it didn't bother me that much. I've always been someone who can be alone with herself. I know people who can't be alone with their own thoughts, so they leave the TV on, usually on a news channel, but I'm not like that. I can live in my own head and feel like nothing is missing.

Okay, so a few things are missing. Sometimes I'd like to call someone over, so we can watch Netflix and eat popcorn. I'd like to have a friend I can share a bottle of wine with, because drinking alone is kind of pathetic, even if it's only one glass in the evening. And some nights, I miss being intimate with someone. Having someone to hug and talk to until we fall asleep. But all that would mean putting myself out there. Reaching out to old friends, and maybe downloading one of those dating apps. I wouldn't even know what pictures of myself to use and what to write on my profile.

Dangerous. I dared to put one sexy selfie on my social media and look where that got me. Dating sites are out of the question.

On the other hand, if I ever get out of here, it's like... the worst has happened already. It can't happen twice.

How did I even end up so alone? Okay, I was obsessed with making money because I didn't want to get a roommate, and the rent was steep. Fresh out of college, with a degree in English Literature – which is basically useless in this day and age – I started doing freelance work. I can write anything. Any type of copy. Blog posts about how to take care of your indoor plants? No problem. Sales articles explaining how space heaters are safe and budget friendly? I got you. I even wrote articles about hairbrushes, cat food, and what not to do when Mercury is retrograde. Being able to write about anything and everything is a superpower when you have to pay the bills, and pay them fast. The only thing I haven't yet tried is fiction ghostwriting. I feel like I'm not ready yet.

Work occupied most of my time and mental space for a while, and when my friends called, I would tell them I couldn't go out. "Not tonight. I have to finish a project. Maybe next time." They stopped calling, and I didn't even notice, until I did, and it was too late. I've never been the kind of person to reach out first, so if my friends weren't going to reach out, I was just going to get used to enjoying my own company.

I made new friends, though. Granted I haven't seen them IRL. When I started reading dark romance, I discovered a whole new world I hadn't known before. Readers gathered online, on forums and groups, and it was easy to join and start chatting about my favorite books. I found my tribe, and it was even better than my old friends from college, because I could talk about the books I loved. People who've studied English Lit don't usually read what I read. Even after college, when reading is not a requirement, most stick with the classics and with "real" literature – the kind that is deep and says something about the human condition. Which I get. I mean, I love it too. But I like to think of myself as an eclectic reader, which means that I give a fair chance to all genres. And I'm not ashamed that I like to read dark romance, except when I'm in public. At home, I read paperbacks. On the subway, I always take my Kindle.

Anyway, it's better if people don't see what I read. It's none of their business. They tend to judge. And stalk, apparently. If I am to believe what Oscar says, he found me when I left a comment on someone's post about the books I read. Frankly, I don't remember the post. Since I started being active in the dark romance community, I've been commenting on a lot of posts that ask for book recommendations. I always make sure I do it inside the groups, where there's a certain level of privacy, but maybe

I didn't pay attention this one time, and I commented on a post on someone's profile. And that post was public, or that person is friends with Oscar.

Of all the things that could've gotten me into trouble...

It's surreal. I can't wrap my head around the fact that I'm here, in a basement, and that someone's watching my every move. At least he hasn't hurt me. Not yet.

No one's looking for me. I've been gone for only a few hours, but I know I'll be gone for days, weeks, and still, no one will be looking for me. My clients are online, and when they realize I've gone MIA, they will be pissed, they'll cancel the projects, and the freelance site will refund their money, then they'll look for another writer and not even wonder what happened to me.

My online friends won't even notice my absence. I chat with a few ladies who are older than me, and maybe they'll reach out once or twice, but if they see I'm not logging in anymore, it's not like they can do anything about it. They're not even in the same state as me.

My mom might call at some point, and she'll see my phone is turned off. Then what? She'll wait for me to call her back because she knows I'm a loner and busy with my writing, and when I won't, she'll call again in a few days, and maybe then she will realize something's wrong. But how long will that take?

No one is looking for me, and no one will be looking for me for a good while. I'm on my own. Oscar chose the perfect victim.

Enough wallowing in self-pity. Facts are facts. This is happening to me right now, and I don't deserve it. I never did anything wrong, but it doesn't matter. I repeat to myself that at least he hasn't hurt me yet. It could've been much worse. The effects of the sedative have worn off, and I can think clearly. I still have a headache, so I'm going to take an Ibuprofen and drink as much water as I can. I need to stay hydrated.

So, I pick myself up and drag myself to the bathroom. There are no bottles of water lying around, but there's a pack of plastic cups on the sink, which means the tap water is good to drink. So much for luxury. I don't think Oscar knows what luxury is. He said it himself: he's not rich. Not that it matters. Good God, it really doesn't matter one bit. Even if he were rich and locked me in a gilded tower, it would still be insane. If he locked me up in a palace and fed me caviar with expensive champagne, I would still want to claw his eyes out and escape.

I take an Ibuprofen and drink two cups of water. I look at myself in the oval mirror. My eyes are sunken and rimmed red, my face is pale, and my hair hangs in clumps on my shoulders. I notice that I'm shaking even now, and I can't help it. It's like I'm constantly cold, or have a fever, or both. The mirror. I could drop it on the pink tiled floor, and it would shatter into a thousand pieces, and I would have more than one weapon. But Oscar is watching. I'm sure he's thought about it already and has adequate measures in place. It can't be the mirror. It has to be something he hasn't thought about.

Okay, time to learn this place inside out.

I start with the bathroom, since I'm here anyway, and I inspect every single corner and every single object. There's nothing heavy enough to be used as a weapon. All the containers for the cosmetics are made of plastic and rather small. I notice the ventilation system – grilles installed where the wall meets the ceiling. The air is slightly stuffy, but breathable. At least I won't suffocate.

I move to the bedroom and start pulling at the furniture gently, trying to conceal what I'm doing in case Oscar is glued to the cameras. Nothing budges. Just like he told me. I study the bed and then crouch down and look under it. The nightstands have no drawers, and in fact, there are no drawers in the entire basement. Only shelves that I can't pull out. Time to see what's in the big closet.

Basic undergarments and socks – new, soft, and smelling fresh. When I see the clothes, my heart drops. It's all dresses, skirts, and revealing blouses. Not one pair of jeans, not one T-shirt or baggy sweater. They're all made of satin, cashmere, and... silk? I'm not sure I can recognize silk, but when I touch one pair of pajamas, I can bet this is what silk feels like. There's sexy lingerie too, and a pair of high heels with red soles.

I decide I'm not getting out of my clothes unless he makes me. He probably will. He'll make me undress, take a bath as he stands there watching, then he'll steal my clothes, probably burn them to get rid of the evidence, and make me wear something sexy for him. As I think about this scenario, I lower myself to the floor in front of the open closet and try to breathe evenly. There's no point in working myself into a panic attack thinking about things that haven't happened yet, thinking of the ways he will humiliate me but hasn't yet. The headache has subsided, and being able to think clearly was supposed to be a good thing, but it turns out it's not.

Alone in the basement, with no way out, and nothing that my captor has missed that I can use against him, all I can do is think about all the horrible things he'll do to me.

Chapter Ten
The Other One

Sydney is a hundred percent sure she's bombed this interview too. It didn't help that within ten minutes of entering the office, her phone vibrated once, twice, then a few more times, and no matter how fast she scrambled to find it in the depths of her bag, it just kept vibrating, until the lady and the guy interviewing her started giving her nasty looks. She managed to turn it off, but it was too late. Now she's walking out of the building and turning it on, reading Abbi's texts.

She stopped reading Finn's, but she can't completely ignore Abbi, even if she never responds. As she's going through the last few texts, her phone starts vibrating again, and Abbi's name is on the screen. Syd hesitates, biting the inside of her cheek. The phone stops vibrating, then starts again not a second later. Abbi isn't giving up. Not today. Syd might as well answer.

"Hey," she says into the phone.

Silence, then she can hear Abbi let out a breath of relief. She didn't expect Syd to pick up, and now she doesn't know what to say. That makes Syd feel a little better. She's tired of feeling like she's the only one affected by this mess.

"Hey, Syd! I'm so glad you answered. I mean it. I've been trying to reach you. But you know that."

"I've been busy."

"Yes, Finn told me that you got a new place. I'm happy for you. I really am."

Syd rolls her eyes. She's feeling a headache starting to bloom between her temples, and she wonders if she's made a mistake picking up Abbi's call.

"Abigail, what do you want?"

She hears a sharp intake of breath. Apparently, after what her ex-best friend has done to her, she still has the gall to behave like she's the one who's offended by Syd's cold behavior.

"Let's have lunch. I just want to see you. I want to talk to you. Please, Syd, can we talk?"

She should say no. She should tell Abbi to stop calling her and hang up.

"Okay, fine. When? Where?"

Abbi is so relieved Syd said yes that she wants to meet in half an hour. She doesn't want to miss this opportunity, take the risk of Sydney changing her mind.

They meet at a café they used to frequent when they were best friends, and Finneas was Syd's boyfriend, not Abbi's. As she sits down across from Abbi, Syd promises herself this is the last time she's coming here. She orders a latte and waits for Abbi to say whatever she needs to say, so they can both finally move on and never talk to each other again.

"Let me start by saying I'm so, so deeply sorry."

"You'll have to come up with a new text at some point," Syd says, unimpressed. She's frankly fed up with Abbi and Finn apologizing but doing nothing to fix it. Not that there's anything they can do.

"I want us to still be friends," Abbi says. "I know it won't be the same, but I want you in my life, Syd. I can't imagine my life without you."

"You'll have to try really hard then. I'm sure you'll manage eventually."

Abbi hangs her head for a moment. She sips her black coffee and recovers.

"I can't help that I love him. I tried. I fought it when I realized I had feelings for him, and for a time, I thought it would be okay and it would go away, because of course Finn loved you and had no eyes for me. I don't know when that changed. I don't know when he started seeing me as more than a friend, and we started spending more time together, texting more often, talking on the phone past midnight. You were gone a lot, business trip after business trip, and it just... happened."

Sydney drinks more of her latte. She looks at her cup and estimates there are three more sips left. When she's done, this conversation will also be done, and she'll get up and leave. She doesn't have to listen to this. Maybe Abbi thinks she's doing her a favor by telling her how it happened, but she's not. She's just hurting her more, reminding her that neither she nor her ex cared enough to keep it in their pants for Syd's sake.

"I just want you to know that even though he loves me, he loves you too," Abbi continues, and Syd thinks she's going to be sick. "I love you."

Syd takes a sip of her latte. Two more left. She can see the bottom of the cup.

"I think it's worth working this out," Abbi says. "It's worth making an effort. I will never forget what you did for me, Sydney. I'll never forget how we met that night and how it changed my life. *You* changed my life. I was so dumb, so naïve, and college was just... confusing. And I was never a good judge of character. Without you, I don't think I would've made it."

Syd can't look at Abbi, at her luscious blonde hair and perfect skin. She can't blame Finn, after all, can she? Men like feminine women, and that's something Sydney is not. She can't decide if Abbi is being genuine, or if she's just saying these things because she thinks it's what Syd wants to hear. She could be honest, or she could be manipulative. Truth be told, Syd herself is not a good judge of character right now. Not after the two most important people in her life betrayed her, and she's having difficulties wrapping her head around it.

"I am so grateful for you," Abbi pushes on. "Grateful that I have you in my life. You're special to me, and I just... I don't want to lose you."

Sydney finishes her coffee and picks up her phone, which is sitting next to her cup. She brings up Abbi's number and turns the phone slightly towards her so Abbi can see the screen.

"What are you doing?" Abbi asks, perplexed.

Syd taps on Block This Number. She watches Abbi's face crumple as her eyes fill with tears, and she thinks, *"Good, I'm finally getting through to her."* Finn's number is next, then as Abbi looks away, Syd goes into her social media apps and blocks them both on there, too.

"You don't have to do this," Abbi says.

"No, I do. I really do." She drops her phone into her bag and pulls out her wallet to pay. "Don't contact me again." She waits for Abbi to meet her eyes, then she drives it home: "This is the last time we talk, the last time we see each other." She leaves the money on the table, turns around, and leaves the café. Abbi doesn't stop her.

Sydney starts walking and doesn't stop until she's on the subway platform. The train comes to a stop, and she almost gets on. There's so much chaos in her head and in her heart, but she snaps out of it in time to take a step back and realize she's on the wrong platform and this train would take her to the apartment she used to share with Finneas.

Now it's their apartment. Finn has replaced her with Abbi, and Syd is certain they've moved in together already. Her home is now the cramped, crappy apartment that's waiting for her, empty and impersonal.

It's okay. She can do this. She's strong, and she's just proved it to herself by doing what any sane person would do: she cut off the toxic people who betrayed her. It was the right thing to do, and no one could convince her otherwise. She'll be fine, because she'll go home, to this place that's all hers, where there's no one to lie to her or lecture her about leaving the lights on, and she'll order pizza from a cheap place, and watch Netflix on her laptop.

Sydney. Is. Okay.

Chapter Eleven

The One

I hate to admit it, but I'm starting to feel hungry. I had hoped that when Oscar showed up with food, I'd have the guts to refuse to eat it. But it's been hours. He hasn't come back yet, and now all I can think about is food.

When the hunger settled in, I started drinking more water, until I realized I needed to pee. Badly. I held it in for as long as I could, but eventually, I had to go. I grabbed a towel and wrapped it around my waist, and I peed that way, trying to conceal myself as best as I could. I peed like that three times today, and I feel humiliated just thinking about it, but what can I do? Water is the only thing that distracts me from the fact that I need food.

People can survive without food for days. Weeks? But not without water.

I hear the electrical sound of the metal door, and I perk up. I'm out of tears, and the fight has gone out of me. I just want... I don't know what I want. To eat, for one – because the hunger has given me another headache – and maybe sleep.

Oscar steps in, but his hands are empty. He's holding them in his pockets as he looks at me. I don't get out of the bed. I've been vegetating like this for the past hour.

"I know you're hungry," he says. "I'll bring dinner down in a bit, but I need you to do something for me first. Not even for me. For you." When I don't say anything, he continues. "Get out of those clothes and take a shower. You saw what's in the closet. You have plenty of options to pick from. What you're wearing now needs to go. Leave everything outside the bathroom door."

I knew this was going to happen. I'm not shocked. I don't move, though, but he knows I got the message, so he turns on his heel and leaves.

I groan as I get up. It's not that I don't want to take a shower. I've been dreaming of one the whole day. After so much crying and crawling all over the floor, I feel sticky and smelly. Maybe he won't be watching now. He's busy with dinner, right? He said he'd bring it down in a bit. If I hurry, I can be done in five minutes, and maybe he won't look at the cameras in those five minutes. I'm probably just lying to myself. Either way, better get it done quick, or I fully trust he's capable of letting me starve. So much for his promises to feed me and provide for me.

I go into the bathroom and close the door behind me. The bathtub doesn't have a shower curtain. He said to leave my clothes outside the door, which means I have to strip before getting into the tub. The bath towel is my friend again. I try to wrap myself in it as I remove my

T-shirt, and I think I'm doing a decent job. It's easier to remove my jeans, and when I'm done, I look at my clothes one last time, knowing my captor will probably burn them tonight. They're not my favorite clothes by any means, but they're mine, and I feel comfortable in them. I feel like myself. From this point on, I'll have to wear the revealing clothes he got me, and I don't know why, but it feels like this simple action has a deeper meaning. I'm doing what he wants. I'm following his rules, his orders.

The water is just the right temperature, and I step into the tub without removing the bath towel. I unhook the shower head and hold it in my hand, then sit down in the tub and curl up within myself before I finally remove the towel and place it on the edge. This way, I can wash myself decently enough without putting on a show for Oscar. He can see the curve of my back, my arms, and my legs, but that's all. Nothing indecent. That's what I hope, at least. It's not easy to wash this way, but I make it work.

I shampoo my hair quickly and don't bother with a hair mask or even conditioner. The idea is to be clean, not pampered. When I'm done, I wrap myself back in the towel and step out carefully. I don't want to slip and break something. And this is when I realize that I forgot to get a set of pajamas from the closet. I curse under my breath as I pad over to the door and crack it open. The little pile of clothes is gone. I open the door another inch, and I see that Oscar is in the bedroom, setting up dinner on the table. Dinner for two.

Before I can slam the door shut, he calls to me, "Don't be shy, Evie." He looks up from what he's doing, and our eyes meet. "Do you want me to pick something for you to wear?"

"No." My voice sounds croaky. Like I've been smoking all my life. In reality, all I did was cry all day and scream a few times. "I just want a pair of pajamas." His brows furrow, and I can tell he's very much displeased with my answer. He wants me to wear something sexy, I bet. But I can't... I just can't. I'll die of embarrassment. I need to convince him to pass me a pair of pajamas. "Please. I don't feel well."

He rolls his eyes. "Fine."

He walks to the closet, grabs one of the two sets, and throws it at me. My hand juts out to catch it, and my towel nearly unravels. I grasp it with my other hand, and somehow slam my elbow into the door frame. It hurts so bad that tears gather in my eyes. It's all good, though. The towel is in its place, and I got the pajamas. When I look at Oscar, he's grinning. I slip into the bathroom and get dressed quickly.

I feel thoroughly humiliated as I step out again and approach the table. He's already sitting in one of the chairs. I can smell tomato soup, grilled chicken, and roast veggies. My stomach rumbles loudly, and I pull my abdomen in, trying to make it stop. It doesn't work. I'm starving, and there's no reason to pretend otherwise. I sit down.

The first thing I notice is that all the dishes are plastic, and the utensils, too. I have exactly one spoon, one fork, and one knife, all made from cheap plastic, the kind that breaks if you apply too much pressure. There's white wine in two plastic cups, one for me and one for him. The utensils he's using are also made of plastic. He's not taking any chances.

"Bon appétit," he says.

I wait for him to start eating, then I dig in. I briefly think of the possibility that the food might be laced with sedatives, but I'm too hungry to care. It's not, I convince myself. Why would it be? He has me right where he wants me. There's no need for more sedatives.

"I noticed you haven't read today. You truly must not be feeling well."

I chew a piece of roasted potato and swallow. My eyes are trained on him, and I think... he really likes talking. He eats slowly, pensively, and every time he looks at me, I see that the crease between his brows grows a little bit deeper. He's displeased with me. Disappointed in me. I try to slow down my pace, because he clearly doesn't like my table manners, and I don't want him to get mad and take the food away.

"You know, Evie, I'm making an exception tonight. Because you're not feeling well. But wearing pajamas at dinner is not acceptable. You don't see me wearing pajamas, do you? Starting tomorrow, you have to do better, okay? Dress appropriately for breakfast, lunch, and dinner, wash yourself, do your hair and makeup. God knows you have everything you need, and more. And all the time in the world."

He's staring at me. He won't let up, so I nod.

"Good," he says. "I'm glad we understand each other."

I'm either losing my appetite, or I've had enough, because now I'm pushing the food around my plate more than eating it. I drink the wine, though. That's liquid courage that I need, and there's not nearly enough in the cup. I don't believe he brought the bottle with him.

"We'll take things slowly," he says. "For a few days. Until you get used to things. To us."

What's he getting at? God, another glass of wine would be great!

"I know you need time," he says. "And besides, you're a woman of value, Evie. Women of value don't sleep with a man immediately, and I respect that."

The wine, and the soup, and the rest of the food I've ingested threaten to lurch back up, and I swallow hard. I place my hands on my knees and squeeze tightly, trying to get a grip. Sex. He's talking about sex. And he's saying... He's saying it won't happen tonight. Does that make me feel better? Calmer? Lighter? Yes. For now. I'll take it, but I'm also painfully aware that if he's talking about sex, that means it will happen at some point. When he decides a woman of value is supposed to finally give in.

I need to change the subject because if he keeps talking about this, I'll break down and cry again.

"I think we should get to know each other better," I blurt out. "First, I mean. Before anything of that sort happens."

"I know everything about you, Evie."

"But I don't know anything about you, Oscar." God, I want him to stop saying my name all the time!

"What do you want to know?"

Good question. "Your name." As if he's going to tell me...

"Oscar Octavius Miles."

And now I know for sure that he has no intention of letting me get out of here with my life. I want to ask him... I really want to ask him what he wants to do with me. If he wants to keep me forever, or if he'll kill me when he gets bored of me. Because he will get bored of me. Hell! Real couples – happy, fulfilled, solid couples – get bored all the time! And I want to ask him... Has he done this before? Have there been other women before me?

I look around the room with different eyes. Everything seems to be new, from the bed sheets to the carpet, and the clothes, the towels, and all the products in the bathroom. I make a mental note to check the mattress later, see if it's new or used. It's good quality – that I can tell just by sitting on it.

"Anything else?" A beat. He snaps his fingers in front of my eyes. "Evie, you spaced out. Anything else you want to know?"

"Um... Your age?"

"Twenty-five. Do you also want to know my sign?"

So young. One year younger than me. He looks older, though, so I would've never guessed. I wonder if this is his house. Can a twenty-five-year-old even afford a house like this? With so much space for the basement?

"I don't believe in astrology," I say. Conversation. I need to make conversation, and maybe he'll tell me something I can use against him. "What about your job? What do you do?"

He takes a sip of his wine and smiles. "I'm in IT. I'm a bit of a genius, as they say. I started college early, finished early, but I've been working since high school. Some of the jobs I took back then were less legal. Now I don't bother with those shenanigans. Better safe, right?"

Right. Especially when his hobby is kidnapping women and keeping them in his basement. Well, that answers my real question. He can afford this house. I can tell he's proud of his job and of the fact that he is, as he's put it, "a bit of a genius". This makes his age irrelevant. I'm not dealing with a normal twenty-five-year-old. I'm dealing with a psycho, probably a narcissist, who thinks very highly of himself, and has the money, and especially the brains to do whatever he wants.

The crease between his brows is back, and he stands up abruptly. He's done eating, and he's done answering my questions. It's like he can see the cogs turning in my head, and he hates it. He wants me focused on being the perfect girlfriend, not on escaping him.

"Time for bed." He starts cleaning up the table. "I want you to use the bathroom first."

"Why?"

"Because I need to cuff you to the bed. For the night."

My eyes widen and my hands start shaking. I grip the edges of the table to keep from falling over.

"No," I whimper.

"Yes."

"There's nowhere for me to go. Why do you have to restrain me?"

"Evie." He stops what he's doing and fixes me with his gaze. His eyes are dark blue, which would be a nice trait if he weren't a psychopath. "Go use the bathroom. Now."

His order is final. He won't argue with me any further, and I feel like if I push him, something bad is going to happen. I shuffle to the bathroom, like a beaten dog, with my tail between my legs.

God, I'm pathetic. And it's only the first day.

Chapter Twelve

The Other One

Sydney takes a step back to check if the painting is straight on the wall. It's not. She readjusts it, checks again, adjusts it some more. It's an old painting made by an anonymous artist, and she's sure it was cheap when her mother bought it in her twenties. Syd found it in the attic and asked her mom if she could take it. She doesn't have anything to decorate her apartment, and she rather likes this still life of a vase with withering flowers. It's dark and moody, perfectly representing the way she feels right now. The frame is gold and gaudy, and chipped in various places. Perfect, indeed.

Sydney feels chipped, too. Cracked on the inside. Like she's a porcelain doll someone fiddled with carelessly until they dropped her on the floor. She's not broken completely, and with a bit of glue and time for the cracks to heal, she'll be as good as new.

Two days since she's blocked Abbi and Finneas, and her phone isn't blowing up anymore. Her mom calls sometimes to check on her, and Syd tries to sound cheerful for her own sake. The more cheerful she is, the less her mother is inclined to give her one of her well-intended lectures.

The only other people who've called recently are Angela and Liv, whom Syd used to work with. They wanted to make sure that she's all right and invited her out a few times. But Syd knows they don't actually care about her. They just want to find out what happened between her and Finn, so they'd have some juicy gossip to pass around the office.

Syd takes a last look at the painting and has to admit that it looks kind of pathetic. But that's okay. It means it fits right in with the rest of the things in this apartment. She doesn't even have a TV. She and Finn bought one together last year – a super fancy, super expensive LG OLED – but it's not like Syd can tell him to split the TV in two. And she won't humiliate herself by asking him to give her half of the money. Maybe she should. Maybe she's being dumb. On the other hand, if Finn weren't a total jerk, he would've offered.

With a sigh, she plops herself on the couch and reaches for the pizza box. There are two slices left from last night, and they're about to become her lunch. She takes one between her fingers and studies it. Should she bother with the microwave, or would reheating it make it taste worse? Her phone rings, interrupting her thoughts.

It's the lady from the last interview she had. It takes her three seconds to inform Syd that she's not a good fit for the company and that she wishes her luck in the future. Syd thanks her and hangs up.

"Oh well," she says to herself as she decides against reheating the pizza. "At least they called."

She takes a bite and chews slowly, and as she's chewing, she feels pressure behind her eyes. She doesn't want to cry, but then there's pressure in her chest too, and in her throat, and she has to force herself to swallow the stale pizza that's definitely not edible anymore. She puts the slice down and curls up on the couch, on her right side. She hugs her knees to her chest and squeezes her eyes shut. The tears come, and she can't stop them. It's fine. It's okay. She can allow herself to cry for a minute. No one can see or hear her.

It will be her secret.

Chapter Thirteen
The One

On the second day, I'm still pathetic. The third day – pathetic. He uncuffs me in the morning and drinks his coffee while I eat breakfast. Then he leaves me to my own devices until lunch, when he drops in for five or ten minutes to bring me food and check up on me. We have dinner together, he makes me use the bathroom, and then he handcuffs me to the bed for the night.

This is our routine.

He controls the lights – bright during the day, dim at night, but never completely turned off. The same air circulation system that takes care of the steam and odors in the bathroom is installed in the other two rooms – which I call the bedroom and the library – keeping the air breathable. The headaches have stopped, the crying has not. I cry late at night, as I lie on my right side and my entire body hurts from sleeping in the same position. I cry during the day, every time I try to distract myself with a book. The books that once brought me joy and a form of escape are now torture devices.

I tell myself I'm done crying at least five times a day. I'm never done crying.

I can't tell for sure how many days have passed. Four? Five? I wonder if my mother has tried to call me, only to find that my phone is off. I wonder if she panicked and called the police. I wonder if they're looking for me, and if Oscar has left any clues that will give him away. I wonder how long it will take them to find me.

Maybe I shouldn't think about escaping anymore, and I should think about surviving until they find me.

Oscar is not so bad. If I do as he says and don't complain, he's affable and talkative. He's great at making small talk, something that I'm not. The only problem is that he'll talk my ear off and not actually say anything. He talks about insignificant things, never says anything relevant about himself, and goes in circles a lot. He's told me the plot of a movie he's recently watched three times already. And because I'm such a bad conversationalist, I don't know how to make him talk about himself. Beyond facts like his name and what he does for a living, I don't know how to get deep, important things out of him. Like, maybe, what his childhood was like, what his parents did, how they raised him. Not that I know anything about psychology, but it would help me understand what kind of person he is. What makes him tick, as they say.

It would help me understand why he's doing this to me. Why he thinks I'm the right woman for him. If I know that, maybe I'll have a chance of changing his mind. I doubt it, but I need to cling to some kind of hope here, or I'll go insane.

It hasn't even been a week – I don't think – and I'm still pathetic. Every day, more pathetic than the last. Because now I'm dressing up for him, brushing my hair and putting on makeup. Not because I want to, but because it's easier. Easier to please him than see the disappointment on his face, which during our second dinner together turned into disgust. I could feel this tension in the air, and I couldn't take it, so I started playing his game.

I shouldn't be doing this. I should fight him at every step, push against him, against his orders and his rules, but I can't do it. I don't have it in me. When I see his eyes fill with rage because of some little thing that I'm doing wrong, fear grips my insides and I feel sick, because I'm thinking that the more affable he is when I do things right and he's in a good mood, the worse he will explode when I cross him and he gets into a bad mood.

He still hasn't touched me. While I'm grateful and I sigh with relief every night when all he does is cuff me to the bed and walk away, I know one of these nights something will change. He will want more. He hasn't kidnapped me to keep me here like a trophy on a shelf, and not take me off the shelf to play with me. He said so himself. He's giving me time. That time will expire at some point.

This morning, he places the food on the table as always and comes over to the bed. I wait for him and don't flinch when he sits down next to me. He caresses my wrists as he uncuffs them, scolding me for pulling at my restraints during the night.

"I don't do it intentionally," I say. "It's hard to sleep on one side."

"I'll bring you another cream. This one isn't working."

The cream works just fine, and the red wounds would be healed by now if he didn't keep handcuffing me to the bed frame every night. I don't say any of that out loud.

I eat my breakfast – a soft, buttery omelet with bacon and roasted cherry tomatoes – and Oscar drinks his coffee as he scrolls on his phone. He never has breakfast. He told me that he's doing intermittent fasting, and his coffee is black with no sugar. He works out in his garage every evening. He told me that, too. When he comes down with dinner, he smells fresh after a shower, and his hair is sometimes damp.

These are, basically, the only things I've learned about him. Useless.

"Are you done?"

I nod as I use a napkin to pat my lips. My table manners have improved.

"Good. Please use the bathroom."

"What?"

My heart picks up the pace. This is new. Until today, he's always cleared the table after breakfast and gone to work.

"Now, Evie."

"Are you going to cuff me again?"

Because why else would he order me to use the bathroom? He shoots me a glance that says it all. That's exactly what he's going to do.

"Why?" I insist.

"Today is a special day. Go to the bathroom first, then I'll tell you."

My legs shake as I do as he says. I don't need to use the bathroom, but I force myself. The routine of the past few days hasn't made me forget that Oscar is, in fact, unpredictable. For all I know, he might cuff me to the bed and leave me there until dinner.

When I return, I find him changing the sheets. He hasn't done this before, and I stop in my tracks and watch him. It takes him two minutes, and then he's done, the old sheets are in a pile on the floor, and he's patting the bed, signaling for me to get in.

"What's going on?" I ask. "Why are you doing this?"

I lie down obediently, and he proceeds to snap the cuffs around my already painful wrists and lock them with the key he keeps in his pocket.

"I'm bringing a cleaning lady today," he says. "You're not supposed to lift a finger, and I can't clean this place. So, I hired a cleaning person."

"What?" My heart is beating in my throat now. And in my temples. Everywhere in my body. "How will that work?"

"Like this." He pulls the duvet over me and makes sure it hangs low over the edge of the bed and covers my cuffed hands. "You will not move from this spot. I told Rita that you are my wife, and that you're sick. Bedridden. You need peace and quiet, and this has always been your special place in the house."

"The basement?!"

"Yes. Where all your books are. You don't like the agitation upstairs, with all my friends and colleagues dropping in, me working all the time, all those Zoom meetings that give you headaches."

"And she believed you?"

"Of course she believed me." He looks into my eyes, and a shiver runs up my spine. "Because it's the truth. And if you tell her otherwise, you would be lying to her, Evie."

I open my mouth to say something, but nothing comes out. I'm at a loss for words.

There's no way.

I look at the metal door and the keypad. There's no way anyone will believe this is normal and that I'm just a bedridden wife with eccentric requests.

"I'm not your wife," is all I manage.

Oscar smiles and reaches out to tuck a strand of hair behind my ear. I'm thinking that if I had the guts to turn my head, I could bite him.

"You might be one day," he says. "Why not? I think we're perfect together."

He gets up and inspects his handy job. When he nods, I know he's satisfied because the handcuffs aren't visible.

"Remember." He points a finger at me. "Don't move. Sleep, if you can. If she's not too loud. You can ask her to be silent. You're the mistress of the house, after all. And do not try to make Rita aware of the handcuffs. She's a sweet, innocent lady who cleans people's houses for some extra cash. She has two daughters, both in school, and a husband who works two jobs. They're both doing their best to save money to send their daughters to college."

"Why are you telling me all this?" My stomach growls, and I feel like he should've warned me about his plan before I ate the entirety of my breakfast.

"Because if you do anything, Evie, there will be consequences. One wrong move on your part, one misplaced word, and there will be ugly, ugly consequences."

Chapter Fourteen

The Other One

Sydney snaps her laptop shut, then cringes and opens it to check the screen. No damage, it's fine. She ought to be more careful with the few things she has, but her mother just called saying she's feeling ill and she might need to call an ambulance, no matter how expensive it is. Syd told her to wait for her, and now she's scrambling to get out of the apartment as fast as she can. She considers taking a cab, but it's much too expensive. Not as expensive as calling the ambulance, but still... If her mother really is sick this time, they will need the money. With this traffic, a cab won't be much faster than the train, and that's what Syd tells herself as she makes the decision.

All the way there, she checks her phone every two minutes. She texts her mom twice but doesn't get a response. She's really starting to worry. Her mom is a hypochondriac, or at least that's Syd's personal diagnosis. As she sees it, the problem with these people is that it's hard to tell when it's just in their head or they're sick for real. She's not sure whether all hypochondriacs are the same, but on top of it all, her mother doesn't trust doctors. If she's thinking of calling an ambulance, then it must be serious, and Syd can only hope she's not too late. She should've sucked it up and taken a cab.

She gets there, sweaty and panting, and takes out her key. She can already imagine going in and calling for her mother, only to get no answer. She can imagine walking into the kitchen...

"What are you doing barging in here like this?" her mother shouts at her from the couch.

Syd stops in the middle of the living room, blocking the TV. It's on a news channel, and her mom immediately tries to see around her.

"A girl got kidnapped. So pretty and young... You should see her picture. You're pretty and young, Sydney. Are you being careful? Now that you're living all by yourself, you're not getting home late, are you?"

"What is the matter with you?" Syd says it in a low, measured tone. For two reasons. One, she doesn't have the energy to be angry with her mother, and two, she doesn't want to start an argument. "I came as fast as I could. How are you feeling? Do you still want to call an ambulance?"

Her mother lets out a surprised "oh" and touches her hand to her chest, gently rubbing where her heart is. As if she's forgotten she was feeling ill, and now Syd's just reminded her.

"I'm feeling a little better."

Syd lets out a breath of relief and plops down on the couch. The news seems to have moved on from the kidnapped girl.

"But I felt this sharp pain, and it scared me," her mother says, shaking her head. "It's a good thing you came. I'm better, but that's just pure luck. I could've been worse, and who knows how you might've found me."

"Mom, look at me." Syd places a hand on her mom's knee, hoping it will get her to focus. "You're not sick."

"Of course I'm sick!" Something changes in the way she looks at Syd. She gets up and starts rifling through a stack of envelopes. "I'm worried sick! You lived here for a month, and you beefed up all the bills. Are you going to contribute?"

"Worried sick is not the same as sick," Syd says. "And I didn't live here for a month. It was barely three weeks."

"Well, are you going to contribute?"

Sydney pulls out her wallet. She doesn't have much in terms of cash, but that's just because no one carries cash around anymore.

"I can transfer you some money. How much do you need?"

"I haven't made the calculations." She drops the bills and sits back on the couch, smoothing down her skirt. "Anyway, it's fine. What kind of mother would I be if I took money from my unemployed daughter? Do you think you'll make rent next month?"

Syd pinches the bridge of her nose. She doesn't know what to say. So many thoughts are going through her head, and none of them are nice.

"I'll take a few more clients to make ends meet, no big deal," her mother goes on. "And if you can't make rent next month, all you have to do is ask. It will be an effort to help you, but I'll do it."

"I don't need help." Syd stands up and looks around the living room, trying to decide if she should leave or stay for a few more minutes. She's come all this way for nothing. "Are you sure you're feeling okay? Do you want me to make you some tea? Do you need me to go to the drugstore and pick something up?"

"No, no. I'm fine."

"Okay. Okay, I'm glad you're fine. But, Mom... You can't do this anymore."

"Do what?"

"You can't call me and make me come here immediately, only so you can tell me it was a false alarm. You gave me a fright, and for what? I have things to do. I can't come running every time you think you're sick. It takes me nearly an hour and a half!"

"I don't think I'm sick. I am sick! It just so happens that by the time you get here, I feel better. What? Would you prefer it if you found me lying on the floor unconscious? Would that make you feel better? Like you're not wasting your precious time to come see me and make sure I'm okay?"

"No, it's not like that. Honestly, Mom! Of course it's not like that."

"Yes, it is. You're too busy for your own mother."

"That's not true, and you know it. Every time you call, I come. I took the redeye three weeks ago, remember?"

"You should thank me for that one. I know it was a false alarm, but thanks to me, you found out about what Finn was doing behind your back."

That's not how Syd sees it, so she keeps silent.

"Anyway, it wasn't a false alarm now. I'm still feeling a bit off."

"Are you sure you don't want me to make you some tea?"

"No."

"Okay, Mom." Syd grabs her bag off the couch. "Listen, I love you. I do. Don't take this the wrong way because I really don't want to argue. But next time, don't call me unless it's for real."

She silently curses herself the second the words tumble out of her mouth. She didn't want to say it like that.

"I mean, call me any time," she tries to fix it. "To talk, you know? But don't ask me to run here unless it's... you know."

"For real." Her mother is seething, Syd can see it. "You know what, Sydney? I love you too. You're my daughter. But I just want to know... If I call you again and tell you I'm feeling sick, what will you do? Block me? Like you did to poor Abbi?"

"Poor Abbi?! Are you kidding me?"

"She called me and told me everything. All she wanted was to apologize and explain what happened. I'm not saying she's innocent, but she's your best friend. Your best friend ever. I remember when you brought her here the first time. How happy I was to see you happy. You didn't have a best friend all through high school, and I was so worried about you away at college, all on your own. And then you brought Abbi, and I saw how much you cared about each other. She messed up with Finn, but I wouldn't blame it all on her. After all, she didn't hold a gun to his head and force him to cheat on you. He seduced her. He would do that. He's the type. It won't last between them, you'll see. It's stupid to lose Abbi over a man, Syd."

"Okay, stop. I don't need a lecture on this, and in fact, I don't want to talk about it anymore. I've moved on. Please don't mention either of them to me. They're equally to blame."

Her mother shakes her head and reaches for her phone. "You blocked Abbi, and you're going to block me the minute I inconvenience you."

"You can never inconvenience me! What are you talking about?"

"I won't give you the chance." She taps on her phone, and Syd watches her perplexed. "There. Done."

"What? What did you do?"

"What do you think?"

Syd stares at her mother for another few seconds, then pulls out her phone and dials her number.

"Are you kidding me?!" Her mother has just blocked her. "What is the matter with you? For real! How old are you? Five?" She's yelling now. "I can't believe this! What the hell, Mom?"

"Now you don't have to even think about me, let alone worry about me, or rush here when you're so busy."

"Ugh!" It's all Syd can say. She turns on her heel and heads to the front door.

All she can do is match her mother's energy. She'll come around soon enough and unblock her number, and all this will be forgotten. It's not the first time she's flipped on Syd in such a dramatic and childish way. She can have a huge fight with her right now, but it will only make things worse. If Syd leaves and doesn't make a big deal out of it, then her mother will probably unblock her in a day or two. If she doubles down now, that will only make her mother even more stubborn, and she might cut her off for a week or more.

This is the best course of action, she thinks as she stomps down the sidewalk. It's weird that she can't call her own mother, but then again, she doesn't need anyone, anyway. In fact, Sydney is going to take a break from humans and focus on herself for a while.

She'll stop at the grocery store on her way home, buy herself a bottle of cheap wine, then order her favorite cheap pizza, watch cheap reality TV, and forget everything that happened today.

Chapter Fifteen

The One

He leaves the door open when he goes to bring the cleaning woman. My heart skips a beat, and I almost jerk up and throw my legs over the edge of the bed, but then I hear voices from outside, and I stay put. I grit my teeth.

"My wife is very sensitive to noise," I hear him say. "This neighborhood is loud and crowded, children everywhere, dogs... Not that we have anything against them. One day we'll have children of our own. But right now, until she recovers, she needs peace and quiet. This has always been her special place in the house, where she comes to read and have a few moments to herself."

What a load of bullshit. But I have to admit, he sounds very convincing. When the woman appears in the doorway, I see that she's nodding, her eyes wide and filled with understanding.

There's no way, I keep telling myself. Even if he leaves the door open, retracted completely inside the wall, so the woman doesn't see it's made of metal, this is still a basement. No windows. The furniture bolted to the floor and the walls. She will know something is wrong.

They enter the room, both carrying cleaning supplies. Oscar is carrying a wireless vacuum cleaner.

"Oh, poor dear," she gasps when she sees me in bed.

The duvet covers my hands. I'm covered up to my chin, and I must be a sight with my disheveled hair and dark circles under my eyes. Oscar shoots me a stern look.

"Hi," I say. "I'm Evie."

"I'm Rita. I will be as quick and as quiet as I can. You rest, Mrs. Miles. I will take care of everything."

As if I could get up and help her. The irony. Oscar smiles and says he'll leave us to it, and if Rita needs anything, he's just upstairs.

And he leaves the door open. To torture me. Or to make Rita think there's nothing shady going on here. Or both. As Rita starts dusting, all I do is stare at that open door. It taunts me.

"I hope you get well soon, Mrs. Miles," she says when she notices I have no intention of sleeping. "You live in such a lovely neighborhood. It's a shame you can't enjoy it. My husband and I looked at the houses here a few years ago, but dear God, we couldn't afford even the tiniest one. Not back then, and not now."

I peel my eyes off the open door with great effort, and I watch her as she wipes the table with a damp cloth. It's starting to smell like cleaning products, something fresh and citrusy, and it's a smell I welcome. I welcome her presence, too. Another human being. I don't consider Oscar a human being.

"The neighborhood is busy," I say. I make it sound like a statement, but it's in fact a question. I'm looking for confirmation.

"Oh, yes. It's great for families, so it makes sense. And there are two schools close by that are very good."

I'm not locked in a house that's in the middle of nowhere. On the contrary. I'm locked in a house that's in the heart of civilization. This is a good thing, right? There are people outside, people who will notice something. Anything. If I scream loud enough... No, that won't work. It didn't work on the first day. The walls are soundproof, and no one gets through that door unless they know the code. But at the very least, I know that if I do manage to get out of here, save myself, I'm not surrounded by forest or a barren field. I can run straight to the neighbors, and they will help me.

"Do you live far from here?" I ask Rita.

"Pretty far." She shakes her head. "The prices are really something in this area."

"And do you clean for some of our neighbors, too?"

"Oh, no. This is my first job in this neighborhood. Who knows, maybe I'll get more now that I'm working for you and Mr. Miles. I'll ask him to put in a good word for me. Do you think he'll mind?"

"He won't mind at all," I say absentmindedly.

Who would've guessed? I'm not that bad at making small talk. Except this isn't small talk to me. I'm trying to get as much information as I can from this woman, but of course Oscar was strategic and hired her only after he was certain she hasn't worked for anyone else in the neighborhood. Or she would've known that Oscar Octavius Miles is not married.

"I'm sorry, I've got to vacuum now," she says.

I nod and let my head fall back on the pillow. The vacuum cleaner is not loud at all. It's one of those new ones, wireless and silent, too expensive to be worth it. Oscar pays attention to everything, to every single detail. He cares about his wife and her sensitivity to sound so much that he bought the most expensive vacuum cleaner on the market just to make her recovery easier.

Rita moves towards the bed, and a thought crosses my mind. I don't have to say anything to her. I don't have to explain. I just have to show her, and she will know. Then she can do something. The door is open. She doesn't have to do something right now, she just has to finish the cleaning, walk out of here, and go straight to the police. She's moving closer and closer to the bed, she's bending down to vacuum under the bed. This is my chance.

I shift under the duvet until the edge that's covering my cuffed hands lifts a bit. Not enough. I shift again.

Rita turns off the vacuum cleaner and looks at me.

"I'm sorry, I know it's loud. Oh, do you want me to tuck you in better?"

I break into a cold sweat. Before I can stop myself, I look up at the cameras. I mentally curse my lack of control.

Why can't I be strategic, like Oscar? I'm messing this up, I can feel it.

"No, Rita. Please continue."

I need the vacuum on, so the sound would drown out any sound Rita might make when she sees that I'm a prisoner here. Fortunately, she nods and starts vacuuming again. She's bending down low to get farther under the bed.

I use my leg to slowly lift the duvet and gather it between my knees. One inch at a time, but I have to be careful and wait until Rita is right in front of me, blocking the cameras. Finally, she's in the right position, and she mouths a "sorry" at me when she vacuums right under my head. I lift the duvet a little more, and I know she's seen the handcuffs when she goes still.

She turns off the vacuum.

"No," I whisper. "Turn it back on."

Rita straightens her back and puts a shaking hand over her mouth. She looks at me with wide, terrified eyes, and her shock matches mine, because I did not expect her to react this way. She's being too obvious!

"Rita, please. Don't do anything. Don't say anything."

I try to be as quiet as I can. I'm so quiet that I'm not even sure she can hear me. Who knows where Oscar hid the microphones?

"How can he do something like this to his own wife?" Rita asks, and even though she's whispering, I feel like her voice is so loud it bounces off the walls.

"I'm not his wife."

"You're not Evie?" Her eyes are even wider now, if that's possible.

"My name is Evie, but I'm not his wife. Listen, you have to help me. Finish the cleaning, get out of here, call the police."

It's like she can't follow instructions. Which makes sense, because she's in shock, and when people are in shock, they react in unexpected ways. More often than not, all logic flies out the window. She backs away from the bed and looks around her.

"No, not now. Pretend like everything is fine."

"What do I do?" she whispers back.

"Rita, calm down. Listen to me. There are cameras everywhere."

Her mouth forms an O, and she looks up. Of course. Damn it, she looks up at the ceiling.

"Rita, please. You have to stay calm. Look at me. Look at me."

It's too late. I hear Oscar's steps thudding down the stairs. And I realize there are stairs leading down to the basement door. Good to know? Maybe. But this tiny piece of information won't help me now.

Rita hears him too, and she drops the vacuum cleaner and turns in a circle, looking for a weapon, I assume. I can see in her eyes that she's out of her depth.

I push the duvet off me and throw my legs over the edge of the bed. What if Oscar hasn't heard or seen anything, and he's just coming down to check on us? I should get back into bed and cover my hands, and Rita should calm down. We're acting crazy right now, probably writing our own death sentence, like two idiots. But then I see Oscar in the doorway, and I see what he's holding.

I fall to my knees.

Chapter Sixteen
The Other One

Sydney is curled up on the couch with her phone, the credits of a movie she barely paid attention to rolling on her laptop on the coffee table. There are two boxes of pizza, one of them empty, an array of dirty glasses and cups – from wine and coffee – and a few empty cans of Diet Coke. She's focused on the screen of her phone, brows knitted as she scrolls and taps, scrolls and taps. She's blocking all the friends she has in common with Abbi and Finneas.

She feels better knowing they can't contact her anymore, and she will feel even better after she makes sure they have as little access to her as possible. She's set all her social media profiles to private, and now she's cleaning them up. From three hundred-something friends on Facebook, she's down to a hundred and sixty. She's been busy the past two hours and a half, and she can't even remember what the movie was about.

She's noticed that the quiet has started to bother her lately, so she puts on a movie just to hear people talking in the background. She used to judge her mother for always having the TV on a news channel, and she still judges her because the news is toxic, but she's starting to see how what she's doing is not much different. She tried listening to music, but for some reason, it only annoyed her. Fictional people running around on her screen, living their fictional dramas while she's ignoring them, watching from the corner of her eye, soothe her. There's probably a psychological explanation, but she can't dwell on it, because then she'll start dwelling on other things too, things that will make her plunge into a pit of despair and depression.

She can feel it. No, she can hear it. Depression knocking on her door.

She checks her friends list one more time, then her followers on Instagram. She deactivated her Twitter account – X, she keeps reminding herself it's X now – though it's all the same, since she retweeted exactly two things four years ago and then stopped using it. She rarely posts on social media, and now she will probably not post at all, but she likes checking it. Interesting things pop up sometimes, and it gives her a weird sort of satisfaction to see that her friends from middle school and high school haven't done anything extraordinary, either. She knows it's petty, but she can't help it, and besides, it's harmless. Another of her little secrets.

One of said friends has shared a missing person case, and Syd taps on the article. She usually scrolls over these types of news, but this one catches her eye because it's local. She scans the article, taking in the details – Eveline

Grace Davis, 26, blonde hair, brown eyes, 5'3", van-ished on June 20, around midnight, after her regular run to the convenience store one block away from her home. Her mother was the one who reported her missing after eight days of not being able to reach her on the phone.

Syd blinks a few times, thinking she must've read wrong. Eight days of not being able to reach her daughter, and finally the mother decides to report her missing? But then again, why is she surprised? Syd could vanish right now, and no one would know. Maybe Eveline Grace Davis was in a similar situation when she got taken, and that made her a perfect victim.

Was Eveline Grace Davis betrayed by everyone in her life, and that's why she lived alone, isolated and with no friends? Did Eveline Grace Davis have a fight with her mother, and that's why the woman thought nothing of it when she couldn't reach her daughter?

Sydney studies her picture for a long time. She's pretty with long, straight hair that's dyed caramel blonde, and big, brown eyes. The picture seems to have been taken somewhere outside, in a park, and Eveline is smiling, showing off her slightly crooked incisors that give her a unique charm. She isn't wearing any makeup, and there isn't a single line on her face. Naturally rosy cheeks, a button nose, and full lips. She's pretty, and she doesn't even know it. If anything, her smile is unsure, and there's a question in her eyes, as if she's looking at the person taking the picture and wishing they would tell her how to pose and what to do with her hands.

The article doesn't reveal much more about Eveline. She is a freelance writer, working from home, and her parents miss her very much and are praying for her safe return. Sydney types Eveline's full name into Google and reads everything she can find about her. Unlike her, Eveline was active on social media, mostly in reading groups. In her profile picture, her hair carefully frames her face, and her lips are cherry red and pouty. She's a few levels over pretty, and Syd might say she's downright beautiful, and still completely unaware of it.

Sydney shakes her head and puts her phone away. She's spent too many hours staring at it, and now she has a headache. Though another cause for it might be that she hasn't drunk water since morning. Or since last night. With a groan, she pushes herself to a standing position, and with another groan, to her feet.

She stretches, and various things in her body crack and pop. She feels a hundred years old. She trudges into the bathroom and thinks it's high time she took a shower, but she doesn't have the energy. She stops in front of the mirror and looks at her own reflection. Her thin lips morph into a cringe. Her short brown hair is messy, and her green eyes look dull and are rimmed with red. She's lost weight, which means she's lost all the muscle she worked so hard to build at the gym, back when she and Finn went together. She never had any fat to lose, since she was always skinny and boyish. She feels weak. She is weak.

"A perfect victim," she says to her reflection. "A victim of bad friends, cheating lovers, and narcissistic parents. Nothing new under the sun."

Because most of her generation is this way, isn't it? Sydney isn't special at all. So many women get cheated on, lose friends, and never talk to their parents. She's sure Eveline Grace Davis went through some of that, if not all of that, and now she's dead. She's been missing for too long, and all who are praying for her are actually praying for her body to be found, so her family can bury her and move on with their life.

In the end, everyone just wants to move on. Something bad happens, and people don't stop to process it, they just focus on the moving on. Syd herself is repeating it over and over, like a mantra: "I'm moving on", "I've moved on", "I'm not even thinking about it". So far, the words haven't translated to real action, much like words of affirmation one repeats in the mirror every morning, hoping they'll work one day. Words mean nothing without action, without actual movement. Moving on means... moving.

"I should hit the gym one of these days," Syd says to herself as she turns on the water and washes her face. "I should go climbing again."

Both things she used to enjoy. After the shock to her system that all this breakup mess has been, it will be like starting over. It will hurt, and she will have to eat better to rebuild her muscle mass, but maybe it will distract her.

Depression is knocking on her door, and she needs to find something to do, or she'll open the door and let it in.

Chapter Seventeen

The One

Rita sees it too, and she panics. She's walking backwards now, and Oscar is advancing towards her. She's forgotten that the chairs don't move, and she tries to grab one. The chair doesn't budge, and she stares at it confused, like she's unable to make the connection between why the furniture is bolted to the floor and the fact that I'm cuffed to the bed. She gives up on the chair and bolts towards the bathroom, turning her back on Oscar. Before she can slip inside, he comes up behind her and hooks the metal chain around her neck.

I scream. I pull at my restraints and try to crawl towards them, but all I get is a sharp, terrible pain in my wrists. I stop pulling for fear that I might end up severing my own hands.

"No! Stop! Please, stop! She doesn't know anything, I swear!"

"You're lying," he says between gritted teeth. "Like you lied to her about your situation. You're happy with me, Evie. You have everything you could ever wish for, and your life is perfect. Why couldn't you tell Rita the truth? Now look what you made me do."

"No!" Tears run down my face. "You don't have to do this. Let her go. Please."

"I can't." Rita collapses, and he falls onto one knee with a grunt, never letting up. She's sputtering, choking, clawing at the chain that's restricting her airway. "It's your mess, Evie, and I have to clean it up."

I keep saying no, I keep screaming at him, and every few seconds, I seem to forget that my hands are cuffed, and I pull again, until blood coats my wrists. Now that there's some lubrication, maybe I can free myself. No such luck. Oscar made sure the cuffs are tight. I watched so many movies where people get out of handcuffs by breaking their thumb, and I think it's a small price to pay. Except I can't do it. I don't know how, and the pain is too crippling. What happens in movies is lightyears away from real life.

Rita is thrashing and kicking, but she's lost steam. She's slower, sluggish, and Oscar isn't making much of an effort to hold her in place.

I'm on the floor, crying, but I've stopped screaming and begging him. I hoped someone would hear me, seeing how the door is still open, but the house is silent. No one is coming. I want to look away from the horrible scene playing out before me, but I think I owe it to Rita to watch until it's over. It's my fault this is happening to her. As much as I hate it, Oscar is right. He did warn me there would be ugly consequences. The moment he said it, it went right past my head, because I was too excited about the prospect that I might escape today. As usual, he didn't make any mistakes. He knew this would happen, so he was ready. It's not like when he came down here, the chain just happened to be lying on a table upstairs, somewhere.

It goes on and on. I had no idea it takes so long to choke someone to death. Another thing movies get wrong. It makes sense, though. People would stop watching if these scenes were realistic. I've calmed down completely, and I am limp, all the energy in my body consumed. I look and feel like a puppet, strung up from my hands. If not for the cuffs, I would be sprawled onto the floor, like a rag.

At some point, I notice that Rita has stopped struggling and gurgling. Oscar waits a few more beats, just to be sure, then releases her, and the body falls with a thud. He drops the chain and wipes his forehead. The whole thing seems to have been quite a workout for him. On his hands and knees, he crawls towards me. I look at him, but I don't see him. He inspects my wrists and curses under his breath.

"Are you happy, Evie? Does this make you happy? Are you that much of an attention seeker that you had to do this?"

What is he on about? If there's one thing that I am not and have never been, it's an attention seeker.

"Look at your wrists. Why would you hurt yourself like this? And why would you hurt that poor woman?"

"I didn't hurt her," I whisper. "You did."

"No, Evie. You did. I told you what would happen, and still, you chose to be selfish. You chose to think about yourself and your lies, instead of thinking about this innocent woman who was only trying to pay the bills and save for her kids' college."

I shake my head, but I don't have the energy to keep arguing with him. Does he really believe what he's saying? He can't be so out of touch with reality. I think he's saying these things not because he believes them, but because he knows they're hurting me and messing with my head. It's not working.

Is it?

This is not my fault. I didn't strangle Rita with a chain.

No, he's right. It is my fault. I disregarded his warning, and I made him do it. Had I kept my stupid mouth shut and my hands hidden, Rita would be finishing with the bathroom right now, then getting out of here with some cash in her pocket.

"Come on, let's get you back into bed."

I feel like he's touching me everywhere as he's hauling me up, but I don't fight him. Once I'm back in bed, he pulls the duvet over me and just looks at me for a minute. He's on his knees, and he's stroking my hair lightly, pushing it out of my eyes. I feel empty. This man just killed a woman in front of me, and now he's acting all caring.

"You're being ungrateful," he says, but he doesn't sound angry. More like disappointed and resigned. "I do everything for you, and it's not enough. Relationships are hard, Evie. No one said otherwise. But it takes two to make it work. Think about that, okay? And read your books. They will help. Don't think I haven't noticed that you haven't read at all these past few days. I have a box of books upstairs, and I want to bring it down to you, but how can I do that when you don't appreciate the efforts I make? Didn't you always say that all you wanted was a total break from work so you could read day in and day out? Here I am, fulfilling your wish, and what do you do? You ignore the library completely. You don't have to work anymore. You don't have to work ever again. Your time is all yours, free of any obligation. Do you see what I mean when I say you're being ungrateful?"

I look past his shoulder. He stops stroking my hair, but his presence is still too much. He's suffocating me. I feel like I don't have air. A single tear makes its way down my temple.

Oscar sighs. "I want to make you my wife one day, but not like this. Didn't you like it when she called you Mrs. Miles? Eveline Grace Miles. It rolls off the tongue."

"I don't want to be your wife," I manage. Not that I think it will make any difference that I'm expressing my disagreement with his plans.

"Nonsense. Relationship goals, remember?" He raises his dark eyebrows and grins. "No? Well, I do." He readjusts the duvet over my shoulders. "I have work to do now. Work that you've created for me. And to make matters worse, Rita only cleaned the bedroom."

He gets up, assesses the situation, and starts by gathering up the cleaning supplies. He takes those out, then comes for the body. I close my eyes. I don't need to witness this, too. It's enough that I can hear the sound it makes as Oscar pulls it by the arms. Finally, the door closes, and I am alone.

Alone with my demons. If I didn't have them before, I have them now. They're loud in my head, yelling at me that I did this, I did this, it's all my fault.

What's Oscar going to do with the body up there? Wait for night to come and bury it in his backyard? That seems unlikely. It's a busy neighborhood, and I bet there are cameras everywhere. It's better if I don't think about it. He's left me handcuffed, which tells me the concern he showed for my bleeding wrists was fake.

It's all fake. He doesn't care about me. He doesn't want to provide for me. He doesn't even like me. It's been only a few days, but sometimes I feel like he resents me. Then why is he doing all this? Why is he insisting on playing this game? It makes no sense. It doesn't seem to bring him joy. It's an idea he got into his head, and he's acting on it blindly.

I close my eyes, because if I keep them open, I can't help staring at the spot where that woman died. It must be noon, and I'm not tired, but what else am I supposed to do? It's the first time I'm cuffed to the bed during the day. The only thing that will alleviate the throbbing pain in my wrists is sleep.

Chapter Eighteen
The Other One

Sydney keeps telling herself that nothing lasts forever. Her relationship with Finneas didn't last forever, and neither did the dream of getting married to him and building a family together. Her friendship with Abbi didn't last forever, and that had a much better chance than her relationship. Lovers break up more often than friendships end. Or maybe it's the other way around? It could be that the chances of these two things happening are equal.

Misery has made a philosopher out of Syd. With no one to talk to, she talks to herself, mostly in her head because she feels weird talking out loud. She does it sometimes, and after a few minutes, she stops. She's never been more in touch with her inner voice than she is now, but it's frustrating that it doesn't seem to be smarter than she is. After weeks of introspection, she would've expected at least one or two out-of-the-box ideas that would get her out of this rut.

She keeps applying to jobs and running around the city to get to interviews, which at least forces her to shower, brush her hair, and dress nicely. It takes two or three days without interviews for her to regress to looking like a homeless person.

Today, she almost walks out of her apartment in her pajamas. She catches herself in time, curses under her breath, and goes back in to throw on a pair of jeans and an old T-shirt that smells. She needs bread, eggs, and some sort of fruit, so she's going to the grocery store even if she doesn't feel like it. She feels invisible as she walks down the street, and in the store, as she's browsing the aisles, an old man bumps into her and apologizes, eyes wide, as if he has no idea where she popped up from. Syd rolls her eyes and makes her way to the cash register.

Outside, she catches her reflection in the grocery store window. Her hair is sticking out at odd angles, which reminds her she needs a haircut. She notices a brown stain on her T-shirt, which could be coffee or Diet Coke. A young woman meets her eye from behind the window, and Syd pulls out her phone awkwardly and pretends she's busy checking her messages. In fact, what she's checking is the news. Nothing on the Eveline Grace Davis case. The police are still looking, and her parents are still praying. She can't say why, but Syd has become quite attached to Eveline. She knows the girl is dead, and her case, like so many others, will probably never be solved, but she can't help herself. She scours the Internet for new articles every day.

Behind the store window, the young woman has moved on, and Syd gazes at her own reflection once more.

She looks like a victim and feels like a victim. Unlike Eveline, though, at least she's not that pretty. She doesn't know why she's thinking about this, but that should keep her safe, right? No one wants her. She doesn't even want herself right now. She's worth so little that no one would ever think to kidnap her.

Chapter Nineteen
The One

I wake up with a start. Before I remember that my hands are cuffed, I try to get up and instantly regret it. My head is pounding, my heart too, and my wrists are two open wounds. I fall back onto the pillow with a groan. The lights are bright and they're probably the cause of the headache. That and the crying, and all that has happened today. Oscar isn't back yet. Everything is as he left it. I can't tell what time it is.

It's past lunch, for sure, because I'm feeling hungry. My body has gotten used to the imposed schedule, and that's how I know I should've eaten my second meal of the day already. He's busy. It must not be easy getting rid of a body when you live in a busy neighborhood and your neighbors are families with children and dogs.

I use my legs to pull the duvet off me. I'm sweaty underneath, and I'm worried I might have a fever. The position I'm lying in is really uncomfortable, though I've sort of gotten used to sleeping on my right side.

I wait, and I wait, and I stare at the cameras, wondering if Oscar is watching. I need to use the bathroom but it's not too urgent, and I try not to think about it. Because if I think about it too much, I will definitely need to use the bathroom. Oscar is coming, for sure. He's just late because he has to do all that work that I created for him.

I need to distract myself somehow. Would I read right now if I could? No. I tried on the second day of my imprisonment, but I couldn't get into it. These stories about women who are kidnapped, traded, or forced into marriages... I used to like them. Now they make me sick. They always fall in love with their captor. Stockholm Syndrome. But guess what, real life is not like in the dark romance books. In real life, the villain really is a psycho, and he's definitely not a teddy bear with his victim. In real life, even the idea of being touched by him makes me gag. And I hate with every fiber of my being that I have to eat with him and make conversation, that I have to dress up for him and pretend we're a happy couple.

With nothing else to do, and unable to read, I've spent the first week of my imprisonment pacing the floor. At least I got my steps in. I stretched a few times, but not too much – I didn't want to put on a show for him. I sniffed all the jars and bottles in the bathroom and eventually indulged in a few hair and facial treatments. I don't feel like they helped. The circles under my eyes are darker and deeper than ever, and my skin doesn't appreciate the lack of sun. I'm as pale as a ghost.

The rest of the time I spent lying down and staring at the walls, running various scenarios in my head, imagining what I would do when I escaped.

What would I do? My mind goes there again, and I let it. It's something to think about, something to look forward to, though after what happened today, I feel like I'm very close to losing all hope. But as they say, delulu is the solulu. I recently saw a video where some psychologist explained how it was proven that being delusional helps avoid depression. Like, being delusional about celebrities and making up scenarios in your head about meeting them and becoming friends. This psychologist person said that as long as they're not pushed too far, these daydreams can help people escape reality just a little bit, just enough to help them sidestep depression and navigate life during tough periods.

I've never been into celebrities, I've always been delulu about book boyfriends. When they love a book or a series, some readers write fan fiction, so they can live in that universe for a while longer. I sort of do the same thing, but in my head. I imagine new scenes, sometimes with a whole different vibe than in the book, and I'm the main character the hero – or villain, in this case – fawns over. Now I can't even do that. I need to distract myself badly, or I will cry, but Oscar has taken that from me, too. Not just my physical freedom, but also the freedom of my thoughts and daydreams. I'm sure that if I were into a celebrity, he'd find a way to ruin it for me in two seconds.

I doze off at some point, and later on, I start awake again. The lights are as bright as ever, and it doesn't make sense, because it's probably night by now. My stomach rumbles loudly, and I really, really need to use the bathroom. It's almost non-negotiable. I've slept for so long, but the headache has not abated. I sit up, trying to protect my wrists as much as I can. If the handcuffs were tight before, now they feel even tighter. One close look clears up that mystery: my hands and wrists are swollen.

I choose one of the cameras to stare at and do so for at least five minutes. Like a staring contest – that is if Oscar is on the other side, looking at me on a screen. It might not be enough. I wait another few minutes. Okay, it's not enough.

What is he doing? Has he forgotten about me? Is he doing it on purpose, punishing me for Rita?

I don't want to do what I'm going to do next, but I'm hungry, thirsty, and I need to pee. I stare at the camera and start begging. I say everything and anything that goes through my mind. I apologize for Rita. I say I'm sorry that she didn't finish the cleaning. I'm sorry that I was ungrateful, and it won't happen again. I've been thinking, like he asked, and I want to show him that I am grateful, and I appreciate everything he's doing for me. I tell him he is a great provider, and that no one has ever taken care of me like this before.

I go all out. I trample all over my pride and any decency I have left and say all the things I believe he wants to hear.

After a few minutes of that, I wait again with bated breath. He has to come. He can't leave me like this, cuffed to the bed frame, or I'll wet the bed soon. Nothing happens. A choked sound leaves my lips.

"You can't," I say. "You can't do this to me. You said you're going to take care of me. And I believe you. Because I have no choice." I rattle the chain and wince. I really can't make a statement this way, the pain is too bad. "Oscar! Please, you have to release me. I need to use the toilet. Right now. I mean it."

Nope. Nothing happens.

I'm sweating. This is exactly what he wants: to make me sweat. It's part of the torture, of the punishment he thinks I deserve. Maybe I do, but it's been hours. A whole day.

"Okay, I get it. I've learned my lesson. Oscar! I've learned my lesson, I promise. How long are you going to leave me like this? Another few hours? Days?"

I choke on the last word, because I know he would totally be capable of starving me to death. I won't die of starvation, I will die of thirst, in my own filth, and it will be hell. Tears run down my face. I can't stop them, and I'm frankly surprised I can still produce them, seeing how dehydrated I am. Crying will only dehydrate me more.

"Oscar, please. Don't leave me here like this. Not like this."

I don't know how long I cry. I fall in and out of sleep, and I'm sure I have a fever because I feel delirious. I dream I'm in my apartment, drinking tea and trying to finish a project, and I need to pee, but I want to finish the paragraph first. It feels real. And when I wake up and I feel the wet sheets under me, I'm certain it's a dream. I can't make the distinction anymore.

Oscar doesn't come. He doesn't come during the night, and he doesn't come in the morning. I spend the day like the day before – crying, begging, and napping – and all that's different is that now I'm also disgusted with myself. Disgusted that I couldn't hold my bladder, even if I know it isn't humanly possible to do so for two days in a row, and disgusted that I'm still hoping, with all my being, that he will come.

I want to live. But more than that, I don't want to die like this.

Chapter Twenty
The Other One

The only reason Sydney dares to go to the climbing club today is because she knows Finn's schedule and she's certain she won't bump into him. They always went together. It was her club first, discovered via a simple Internet search when she felt like picking up a new hobby. Then Finn started going with her and eventually became friends with the club owner. Sydney wasn't interested in making friends; she just wanted to climb. Not a lot of girls frequented the club, and she was grateful for Finn's company, even though Finn spent most of his time chatting with the other guys. "Talk less, climb more," she used to tell him as she rolled her eyes, and then rolled them extra hard when Finn laughed.

Good times.

No, not good times. He cheated on her with her best friend.

Still, this was her club first, and she likes it here. She hasn't been in ages, but it doesn't matter. Even if her body is weak, she can take it slow, no pressure, no goals, and just enjoy the physical activity. Use it as meditation.

She exchanges a few words with the guy at the front desk, then gears up and gets ready. She stretches as she looks up at the wall, calculating her moves. She prepares herself mentally and hopes her body will remember what to do. It feels odd to be here all by herself, but it's fine. It's a familiar place, and she can spot some familiar faces around her. She nods at a guy she recognizes, and he nods back. She's the only girl here today. Not that she's worried about it. In her whole life, she's been approached by men, maybe, twice. With her short hair and boyish physique, she'd be surprised to hear anyone think of her as feminine. Even with Finneas, she had to make the first move.

"Hey, Sydney! Long time!"

She startles at the sound of Jim's voice. He's the owner of the club, and he's currently crossing the room to her. She gives him a smile.

"Hey! Yeah, you know what it's like. Life."

"Life does have a unique talent of getting in the way, doesn't it?"

"Yeah."

He's standing very close to her now, and she wants to take a step back, but she doesn't. Jim is a big guy, intimidating for those who don't know him. Syd knows he's a teddy bear, though. He has a beautiful wife who's a mildly successful fashion designer, and two kids at home.

"Listen, Syd," he says in a low, kind tone. "I heard about you and Finn."

"Oh."

"He told me."

Of course he did. They're friends. At first, they only saw each other at the club, then they started going out for drinks. They didn't make a habit of it, and Syd never cared. If Finn was friends with Jim, it didn't mean she had to be too.

"It's no big deal," she says quickly. She doesn't know if Finn also told him why they broke up, but just in case he did, or Jim found out from someone else, she doesn't want him to think she's still hurt over it. "We don't have to talk about it."

"No, I know. I would never..." He doesn't finish the sentence. "Anyway, I just wanted to give you a message from him."

She bristles at his words but does her best to hide it. She should stop him. She doesn't want to hear any messages from Finn. It starts to dawn on her that coming here was a mistake. The place was hers first, but it no longer is. Because Finn is good with people, and she isn't. He makes friends everywhere he goes, while she is a loner even in a room full of people she's forced to interact with. She's thinking about her former job, in particular.

"He won't come here anymore. He got a membership at another club. I'm friends with the guy who runs it, so it's all good. He wants you to have this place to yourself and not worry about accidentally bumping into him. Okay, that's the message." He releases a breath, a little too sharply, and smiles awkwardly. "I'll leave you to it now. Sorry to interrupt. But, Syd, it's good to have you back."

"Wait." Her hand stops inches from his impressive biceps. "I have a message for Finn."

"Oh?"

She starts removing her climbing gear as she speaks. "It's not fair to him to be forced to find another club. You're friends, and he loves it here. So, I'll be the one to step away."

"Oh, no. That was not the point at all! I swear to you, Syd."

"No, it's okay. I get it, Jim. No hard feelings, really. I just think it's the right thing. Okay?"

He scratches at the back of his neck, then shrugs. "Okay. I mean, I don't know what happened between you, and it's none of my business. Whatever you decide is good with me."

Syd nods. "Tell him I hope he's doing well, and not to worry about me. I moved to a different place, so it's a little harder for me to get here, anyway."

"If you want, I can recommend a club."

"It's okay, thanks. I'll do a quick search for something around my area."

"Well, let me know if I can help you with anything."

"Will do. Bye, Jim!"

"Bye!"

She can't get out of there fast enough.

Finn wants her to have the place to herself. Oh, how nice of him. What a lovely, thoughtful gentleman. It makes her sick to her stomach. She's surprised she didn't throw up all over Jim's bulky chest when he gave her Finn's very important, very sensible message.

She can't go to the gym she used to go to, and now the climbing club is out of the picture. Because it wasn't enough for Finneas to rob her of her best friend and the future she had envisioned, he had to take everything from her. Every little thing. Her job, all the places she used to frequent and like... What's next?

It was a bad idea to get out of the house today. It was naïve of her to think that she could go back to the activities she used to enjoy. It's official: she needs a new hobby. Maybe swimming or horseback riding. But she's afraid of the water, and the second one is expensive.

Maybe she should take up knitting.

Sydney is pissed off as she walks briskly to the subway station. Anger is a good sign, though, if only for the simple fact that it's not depression.

Chapter Twenty-One
The One

I don't look at him as he walks through the door, and he doesn't talk to me as he uncuffs me and lifts me off the bed. I don't fight him. I'm too weak, both physically and mentally. I don't ask him what he's doing, but it's obvious. He's taking me into the bathroom. He deposits me on the edge of the tub and reaches over to turn the water on. He smells great – a citrusy cologne – and I smell like sweat and piss. I turn my head, not wanting to risk our eyes meeting. I am so ashamed that I could die. Which is conflicting because I also want to live.

He starts peeling off my clothes. I cringe and curl into myself, and he frowns and pulls at my shirt harder.

"If you want me to be gentle, you'll have to cooperate," he says.

His voice is low and sounds tired. It sounds like there's rage right beneath the surface, and it's my decision if I want to pour gasoline over the embers and start a fire. I stare at his chest, knowing that he's looking at me, waiting for me to meet his gaze. I won't. What I do, though, is give in.

I relax, and he pulls off my shirt gingerly, being careful with my wrists. Now I'm half naked before him, and I cross my arms over my chest. I'm shivering, but he ignores it. He ignores me even as he makes me stand up so he can roll the pajama bottoms and my underwear down my legs.

Skin on skin as he helps me into the tub. I start crying, I feel so humiliated. The tears run down my cheeks, and my shoulders tremble slightly. He doesn't touch me more than necessary, and once I'm in the tub, with the hot water rising, he leaves me there and picks my clothes off the floor.

"Wash yourself if you can," he says. "If you can't, I'll help you."

I shake my head.

"I'll come bandage your wrists later."

I don't know what later means. My sense of time is skewed at this point. I can hear him in the bedroom struggling with something, then I hear the bed creak. He must be changing the sheets. I lean my head against the edge of the tub and take a few deep breaths. I am so hungry that I could bite into Oscar the next time he comes close to me. He hasn't mentioned anything about food, but I have to trust that he'll feed me once I wash myself. So, I open my eyes and gather all the strength I have left in my body to shampoo my hair and scrub my skin raw. It's not easy with my wrists so swollen and painful. I pick at the dried blood carefully, cleaning the wounds as best as I can. The water turns slightly brown.

"Better?"

I startle at the sound of his voice. He's standing in the doorway, looking at me. I nod. He comes in and sits on the edge of the tub. I bring my knees to my chest to cover myself, but he doesn't look at my body. It should make me feel better. When he undressed me earlier, it was almost clinical. Since he kidnapped me and locked me up in his basement, he hasn't looked at me that way once, even if he always wants me to dress nicely and put on makeup. I don't get him. Maybe I should've studied psychology instead of English Literature.

He has a first aid kit, and I let him dab Betadine on my wrists and bandage them up. He works fast and clean, and his hands are steady, like he's used to doing stuff like this. Once again, I wonder if I'm his first victim, or his second, or his dozenth. He's young, though. Twenty-five. Too young to be a serial killer, right? I should've watched true crime shows in my teens instead of romantic comedies.

Today, more than ever, I feel like I don't have what it takes to be one of those victims who escape.

"Can you get out on your own?" he asks. "Without getting your bandages wet."

"Yes."

"I'll go bring dinner, then."

Cold and efficient. I can tell he's not happy about the situation, about the state I'm in, and that he had to change the sheets, and possibly the mattress. I hear the metal door opening and closing, and I get out of the tub quickly. I want to be dry and dressed before he returns.

The bedroom smells nice. He changed the mattress, like I thought, and he sprayed some lemon-scented air freshener. I go to the closet and choose a simple long, black dress. It's soft, made of satin, with thin straps. It shows too much skin for my taste, but I console myself with the idea that no matter what I'm wearing, there's no way for me to look sexy. I've lost weight and my bones are jutting out. No man would ever find that sexy. I don't even have breasts anymore. The metal door opens, and I stand in the middle of the room, waiting. It closes behind Oscar, who is carrying a tray. At the smell of food, my stomach rumbles loudly. Yep. Definitely not sexy.

Why is he even keeping me here if he won't use me in that way? I mean, God forbid, that's not what I want! He doesn't really talk to me either, so he's not using me for mental or emotional support. He doesn't seem to be a loner. He doesn't give off that vibe. What is Oscar Octavius Miles' deal?

We sit down to eat. He's brought me painkillers but doesn't let me have them until after I'm done eating. No wine tonight, just water.

"I heard what you said, and I've thought about it," he says.

I perk up. Heard what I said? What did I say? Then my mind clears, and I realize he's talking about all the begging I did while staring at the camera closest to the bed.

"It broke my heart that I had to punish you like this, Evie. Don't make me do it again."

Broke his heart. What heart? He's just saying words with no real emotion attached to them.

"I know you've learned your lesson now, and it makes me feel at peace with what happened. I think it was necessary to push our relationship forward, to push us towards each other. Finally, you see that I'm important to you."

He is important to me. Because he's the one who feeds me, and he has the key to the handcuffs.

"You've always been important to me," he continues, "And I'm glad what I feel for you is finally reciprocated. We will do better from now on. Be better."

A chill runs through my body. What's he getting at?

He looks up from his plate, which he's barely touched, and I notice a sort of gentleness in his gaze. Earlier, when I was in the tub, and I was filthy, smelly, and pathetic, he showed indifference at best, disgust at worst. Now all that is gone, replaced by... tenderness?

Oh God, this can't be good!

"Say something, Evie. Am I important to you?"

I swallow heavily and try to control the chemical reactions in my body. Maybe I ate too fast, maybe I ate too much. I should've paced myself. The food and water, combined with his words, are threatening to give me a bad case of indigestion.

"Yes."

"Yes, what?"

"You're important to me." And then I add, "Oscar."

Oscar Octavius. What kind of people would call their child that? Such a pompous name. But making fun of his name in my head isn't enough of a distraction. I feel like I'm going to puke. I take a sip of water and force it down, where I will it to stay.

He gives me a smile. "Good. I'm glad to hear it."

You made me say it, asshole.

"Well, now that we're on the same page, it's time for bed, right?"

My face falls. He's just released me, and now he wants to cuff me again. I place my hands on the table to draw his attention to my wrists.

"Please don't cuff me tonight. I don't think I can take it."

"Evie, I must."

"Oscar, please. Just this once. I've been cuffed to the bed for two days straight. I can't..."

He stands up and starts placing the empty and half empty plates back on the tray.

"You can use the bathroom while I take this upstairs. I'll give you ten minutes."

"Oscar..." I get up and wonder if I should throw myself at him. On my knees. Would it impress him if I crawled on my knees?

"Don't forget to brush your teeth."

"You know I have nowhere to go and nothing to do," I say. "Why do you insist on cuffing me?"

He looks into my eyes, and at least some of the tenderness from before is still there. I hope this means I can keep pushing and he will give in.

"Because we're sleeping together tonight."

And my hope is chased away by his words. He can't risk my pushing a pillow down on his face and sitting on it until he stops breathing. My shoulders slump.

"Ten minutes," he says.

I watch him as he approaches the metal door and punches in the code. He's always careful to block my view with his body. I've tried to see the code many times with no luck. He's gone, and I decide to make good use of those ten minutes. After being cuffed to the bed for two days, I'm panicked that he will do that to me again.

When I sit on the toilet, I don't care about wrapping a towel around my waist anymore. He's seen me already, all of me, and he knows my body more intimately than he should, even if he hasn't touched me. Yet. What will happen tonight? I brush my teeth and try not to think about it. This is what will save me: not thinking about it. It won't save my body, but it will save my soul.

Briefly, I wonder if I'm strong enough to fight him. I flex my arms but the pain in my wrists reminds me that I'm in no condition to fight. Plus, I can barely stand on my own two feet. Two days lying in bed did a number on my muscles. Who would've known it takes so little to lose all muscle mass in your limbs and back?

I hear the metal door, and I curse under my breath. That sound alone will be the death of me one day. Sometimes it triggers panic, and other times it triggers relief. Panic that he's back and he wants something from me, something I don't want to give him, and relief that he hasn't forgotten about me and won't let me starve.

I walk into the bedroom like a zombie. He looks at me appreciatively and taps on his phone. The lights go dim.

"Don't change. I like this dress on you."

My heart is beating wildly. He motions for me to lie down, and I do it. I hate how obedient I am, but after seeing what he did to Rita, and after he's proven to me that he will resort to torture if necessary, I follow his instructions. He cuffs my wrists over the bandages. When I wince, he sighs and loosens the handcuffs. I almost can't believe that he's showing me this tiny bit of indulgence. Then he takes off his pants and climbs into bed with me, in just his T-shirt and underwear.

I can't breathe.

He cuddles to my side, pulling me to him. My back is pressed to his chest, and his arm is draped over my body. I can feel his breath on my nape. I am so still, I might as well be dead already.

"Relax," he says. "We're just sleeping together. It feels nice, doesn't it?"

I don't understand what he's saying. I don't understand what he's doing.

"I told you I've read some of your favorite books. I know how this goes. I won't do anything until you ask me to. I will wait. My patience is infinite. Like Damon Crux, right? What did he say to Fiona? That she'll have to beg him for it."

My eyes are wide and my breathing is shallow. Behind me, Oscar yawns.

"You're so good at begging, Evie. I can't wait for you to beg me for it."

For the rest of the night, I rack my brain trying to figure out if this is a good thing or a bad thing. I will, obviously, never beg him for... that. But I never thought I'd be apologizing for things I didn't do and begging him to forgive me and let me use the bathroom like a decent person, until he left me handcuffed to the bed.

He makes it sound like I have a choice. Like I have some control left. I don't think that I do.

Chapter Twenty-Two
The Other One

The fact that she can't go to any of the places she used to paralyzes Sydney. These days, she only gets out of the house if she has an interview, or to get groceries, or go to the drugstore when the headaches become unbearable. She's sleeping badly, her eyes hurt if she spends too much time in front of a screen, and she's lost her appetite, which might be good for her wallet, but not great for her health.

What health? What does it even mean to be a healthy, functioning adult? Some days, she feels like she's going crazy. Like she's becoming wild. When she gets outside and interacts with people, she feels like an alien. And they can see it. They can see it in her eyes, and they instinctively step away from her.

It might be all in her head, though.

After too many failed interviews, she decides to apply to a few start-ups. Syd is in IT and has some experience, but not a lot. She's a fast learner, but that doesn't seem to impress anyone in an interview. Not anymore. Maybe she's out of touch with what employers expect to hear from her during an interview, and she should go on YouTube, or even better, on TikTok, and take some advice from the younger generation. Except... she was under the impression she was the younger generation... Confusing. This world. It doesn't take her long to conclude it's getting more and more confusing each day.

Working for a start-up will mean a lower salary, but at this point, anything is better than nothing. She can make it work if she budgets.

Syd spends the day applying to jobs, and when that's done, she isn't sure what to do with herself. Okay, so she can't go to her old gym, and she doesn't have the energy to look for a new one. But she needs to move, because her body has gotten into the habit of popping in various places every time she sits down or stands up. Sometimes it hurts. She opens YouTube and looks through a few Pilates videos before choosing one. Luckily, when Finneas delivered her things to her mother's house, he brought her yoga mat, and then Syd was inspired enough to take it with her.

After only ten minutes of Pilates, she's sweaty and uncomfortable. She opens a window and pushes on until she finishes the routine. As she takes a shower, she feels a sense of achievement that she hasn't felt in a long, long time. How could she be so stupid as to not realize that what she needed was to move her body? That's it. She doesn't need a gym or a new climbing club. The space in her apartment is limited, but that's no excuse to not exercise every day from now on. Pilates it is, and when she gets bored of that, yoga or aerobics. She can make this work. She can make anything work, she only needs to remember who she is.

For the first time since she walked in on Finneas and Abbi in bed together, Sydney has a good day. She even cooks a healthy dinner for herself – two cups of mixed veggies and one cup of protein in the form of grilled chicken. The veggies were frozen, and she threw them in the oven, and the chicken is pre-cooked. Good enough. Better than cheap pizza.

It doesn't last, though. After dinner, she has a glass of wine. She doesn't feel like watching Netflix, so she ends up scrolling on her phone. There's nothing new on her social media since she's blocked so many people, and somehow, she makes her way into her photo gallery. Selfies of her and Finn. Selfies of her and Abbi. She considers deleting the pictures, but it hurts too much. It hurts to see them, but for some reason, the thought of not seeing them ever again hurts even worse. Her whole photo gallery encompasses her past. Vacations, birthdays, anniversaries, business trips, silly moments at the gym or in the office... Dinner dates with Finn, coffee dates with Abbi. That time when she and Abbi treated themselves to a full spa day. She can't erase all of it.

And now she's thinking about them. She's curled up on the couch, a pillow under her head and an old blanket over her legs, and she's thinking about Finn. Her chest fills with dread when she realizes what this is. She misses him. She misses his kisses and his hugs. The way he smells when he's fresh out of the shower, the way he used to wrap her in his arms possessively, so she couldn't move even if she wanted to.

Sydney shivers and pulls the blanket up to her chin. It doesn't do much to soothe her. She drops the phone on the edge of the coffee table and hugs herself as hard as she can. It's not enough. Her own arms around her body are not enough. She misses the feel of Finn's strong arms, the way he used to pin her under him and tickle her neck with his nose.

This is bad. She had a good day, but now it's over. It's late in the evening, and it's like she's coming down from a high. She misses Finn so badly, and in such a raw, physical way that she could die right now. It pisses her off. She shouldn't miss him at all, but more than that, if he were here, ready to hug her and give her everything she wanted, she should feel disgusted by him. She should feel sick just at the thought that he might touch her. He betrayed her in the worst possible way, and Syd needs to remember that, especially in moments like this, when she feels so utterly alone and unloved.

After she calms down a little, a thought pops into her mind. Maybe she should start dating again. Put herself out there. Plenty of dating apps to choose from. It would make the transition easier, right? For sure, it would distract her.

It might not be the perfect solution, but it's something, at least. She reaches for her phone and downloads the first dating app she comes across in the app store.

Chapter Twenty-Three

The One

I fall asleep towards the early hours of the morning. With him pressed against my back, it's too hot, but that's not why I've fought sleep the entire night. He's here, and no matter what he says he'll do or won't do, I don't want him catching me off guard. I don't trust him.

I startle awake when I feel him shift. I snap my eyes open, but I don't move. He turns on his side, stretches, then he's up on his feet, rounding the bed to me. He smiles down at me and pulls the key out of the pants he discarded the night before.

"How did you sleep, Evie? Good?"

I nod.

"I'll be down with breakfast in a bit, then I have to run. I'm afraid I've slept in. Hasn't happened to me in a while."

He yawns, then puts his pants on, and he's out of the basement before I have time to react. Not that I have any reactions left in me. I hug myself, grateful that I'm in one piece. I know I should go to the bathroom, wash up, brush my teeth, but I'm so tired that even the idea of doing all that makes me want to collapse back into bed. I run my fingers through my tangled hair and force myself to walk to the table and plop into my chair. I should be grateful he's feeding me breakfast.

Great. New fear unlocked. That I'll starve to death.

When he returns with fried eggs and bacon, toast and a glass of orange juice, I almost ask him to promise me that he will always bring me food at least once a day. I form the sentence in my head as he unloads the tray before me. He hasn't brought coffee for himself, and I can see he's in a hurry. Okay, all I have to do is ask him to promise me. But I can't. I can't bring myself to do it. It would be so sad and pathetic. And besides, even if he promises me, it's not like it will mean anything. As I said: I don't trust him.

"Have a good day, okay? And for the love of God, read your books, Evie! I went through so much trouble getting them for you. And there's a box waiting upstairs. Don't make me regret building you a library."

"Okay," I say as I stuff a piece of bacon into my mouth.

He shakes his head and sighs. It's like he's a patient, responsible adult dealing with a stubborn child. Never mind that I'm one year older than him.

"It will be good for your mental health," he says. "You can't stare at the walls all day, or you'll drive yourself crazy. Today is a new day. Do something different than you did these past two days. Napping, crying, and staring at the ceiling is not healthy, Evie."

My mouth would drop if it weren't stuffed with eggs and toast. I look at him, and he looks at me, and he gives me a grin that totally means he knows he's talking bullshit and he's doing it just to see my reaction. I focus on chewing and swallowing, then I drink half of the orange juice. I don't say anything. His grin widens. It's like he's winning at a game I didn't even know we were playing.

"Work awaits," he says. "I'll drop by to bring you lunch."

And then he does something that almost makes me jump out of my skin. And out of my chair. He leans in and places a kiss on my head. I squeeze my hands into fists and force myself to stay put. He doesn't linger, at least, and before I can recover, he's out the door.

I'm breathing heavily. I look at my breakfast. There's half of it left, but I can't manage another bite. At least he hasn't cleared the table, like he always has before. This means he left the plastic utensils, which are useless as weapons. And he'll probably make sure they're all there when he brings me lunch.

At least I'll get lunch.

The first thing I do is to change into pajamas. Then I pace the room for half an hour, my thoughts going in circles. I can't focus on any one thought in particular but I know that I need to move. My muscles need the exercise, or I'll be crippled before I am dead. I stretch for a bit, then try to do push-ups on my knees and fail dramatically. All this time, I've been stupid. I should've exercised every day.

But that's okay, because it's one thing I can change. It's one thing I have control over. I spend another half hour doing squats and lunges. My body is sore at the end, but I feel better. I feel just a tiny bit more powerful.

This is good. I will do this every day, maybe twice a day after I build some endurance.

With nothing else to do until lunch, I go into the library and pick up a book. It's ridiculous that my days are structured around Oscar's visits. I'm not growing dependent on him, am I? Not in that way. I will never want to see him just because he's another human being I can exchange a few words with. He's not a human being at all, I've established that already.

I read the first page of Her Fierce Protector and have to close the book when I realize it's a kidnapping story. I can't stomach it. I sit down on the thick carpet and go through a whole pile of books before I think I've found something that I can read.

It's about a woman whose husband owes money to the mafia, and when they come to collect it and he doesn't have it, he offers them her as payment. The big, scary mafia boss takes one look at the woman and decides she's the one he's been looking for – the woman of his dreams. A week or so ago, I would've read this book and sniggered to myself at how unrealistic it is. What man would offer his wife as payment to the mafia? Now, having seen what Oscar is capable of, I feel like this scenario is just as realistic as him strangling the cleaning lady to teach me a lesson. I shudder and force myself to read. If this book can distract me for a few hours and make me forget where I am and what I have to endure, then it's a good book. Five stars.

I feel like it will be very hard for me to rate any dark romance five stars ever again.

The book does grab me, and before I know it, it must be lunchtime, because I hear the metal door whirring open and closed. I get up, my knees cracking in protest, and stalk into the bedroom. Oscar is frowning at the breakfast I left unfinished.

"I don't think you really appreciate what I'm doing for you, Evie. I've made this with my own two hands. For you." He looks up at me, and I can see that he is upset. "For two days straight, you whined that you were hungry and about to die of starvation, and now I come home to this."

I have to say something. He's waiting for me to say something, and it must be the right thing. For a moment, I wonder what it would feel like to tell him exactly what I'm thinking, to act defensive and stubborn, to act true to myself. It would feel good, but at what price? It's better to not find out. One day, I will stand up for myself, but it can't be today. The memory of Rita's body thrashing on the carpet, and of the hunger gnawing at my insides is too fresh in my mind.

"I've been reading," I say, holding up the book. "I lost track of time. I thought I'd finish eating later, but then I found this book, and it completely drew me in. It's such a good story. I can still eat the leftovers."

I just said the right thing because his eyes mellow down.

"It's cold now. Just eat your lunch."

I sit down, placing the book on the table, next to the plate. He's brought a plate for himself, but instead of sitting down to eat with me, he loads it back onto the tray, along with the remnants of my breakfast.

"We're not eating together?" I ask.

He sometimes has lunch with me. If not, dinner, and coffee at breakfast. Except for today, because he was in a hurry. Except for yesterday and the day before yesterday, because he was punishing me.

"I just remembered I have something to do. I can't always eat with you, Evie. I have a job and a social life. You have to start being more grateful and less controlling. Isn't it enough that I cook for you and take care of you when you hurt yourself?"

I feel my wrists throb under the bandages. They probably need changing. The skin must breathe to heal properly. I don't say anything, because it seems that I've pissed him off, though all I did was ask a simple question: "We're not eating together?" That's all I said. He could've interpreted it as, "I got used to eating with you, and I like it", but no. What he chose to hear is that I am controlling. So, this guy is in IT, but two plus two equals five in his head?

What I really meant by that question is: "What's happening? Why's the routine changing again? Am I in trouble?"

That would be the wrong thing to say, so instead I look at my plate and whisper, "Sorry."

"Yes, you should be." He grabs the tray and looks at me critically. "I'm glad you're reading again. Consider washing yourself, too. Don't think I haven't noticed that you didn't brush your teeth today. Your hair looks like a bird's nest. A man likes to come home to a clean, beautiful, nice-smelling woman. Sleeping in your arms should bring me joy, not make me wonder if you have a vendetta against soap and water. Especially if you're going to work out."

I cringe. This is not the tongue-lashing I expected. I never know what will set him off.

"It's not a suggestion, Evie."

"Yes, I know. I will do better."

"Good. And it's good that you're working out, so I'll make sure you have plenty of protein. You must put some meat on those bones. From now on, you will eat everything on your plate."

"Okay."

"Okay. I have no desire to hug a skeleton at night."

He turns on his heel, and once again, I try to peer over his shoulder when he punches in the code. No luck. Once he's gone, I focus on my meal. I know he's watching. Always watching, taking stock of when I brush my teeth and when I don't, how much water I drink, how many times I go to the bathroom, and God knows what else. He's probably paying attention to things I'm not even aware I'm doing. Or not doing.

I eat my lunch carefully, one bite at a time, and make sure to clean the plate. Then I take my book and go sit on the beanbag in the library. I pull the snack basket close and choose a bar of milk chocolate. I will lose myself in the book until dinner and not think about the next thing that will make Oscar angry. But then I get to the part where the main characters have sex, and I have to close my eyes and take a few deep breaths. I can't keep reading. I can't finish this book. I can't even bring myself to skip to the end.

I wonder if Oscar will notice if I just stare at the pages without reading. I wonder if he'll be able to tell that, instead, I'm making scenarios in my head about him meeting his end in all sorts of gruesome ways.

Chapter Twenty-Four

The Other One

Sydney steps out of the office building where she's just had an interview. The building is old, recently remodeled, but the company on the second floor is new. She feels like the interview went well, she might be getting a call in a few days, and the day is lovely and sunny, so she decides to treat herself to a cup of coffee. She finds a small, cozy café one block away, goes in, and as she puts in her order, she spontaneously decides to add a butter croissant to it. Everything is a little overpriced here, but she figures she deserves it.

She sits at a table in a corner, pulls out her phone and brings up the dating app. She made a profile a few days ago and swiped a little, got about a dozen matches, but then felt weird about it, closed the app, and refused to look at it until today. Is she ready to chat with the men she matched with? She can try...

She has four unopened message boxes. Two of them are boring, just a generic "hey" and "what are you up to?", as if the guys didn't even read her profile. The third one is some guy who freaked out immediately when she didn't read his messages and respond and went on a rant about women always leaving men hanging, thinking that's mysterious or something. Syd blocks him and deletes the messages.

"Ew," is her reaction.

The fourth is nothing special either, but at least he read her profile, because he asked about the ending of the movie Parasite, which she mentioned as her favorite. Syd starts typing a reply, wondering if the guy, Travis, is still around. Maybe he, too, is upset with her for swiping on him then leaving him hanging. She didn't know there were unwritten rules for being on dating apps.

He writes back instantly, and Syd smiles despite herself. She sips her coffee and takes a bite of her croissant. For the next twenty minutes, she chats with Travis, mostly about movies and his hobbies. Why his and not hers? Because she doesn't have hobbies anymore. She won't say she likes climbing, because she's done with that, isn't she? She doesn't think she'll take it back up again. Plus, she doesn't feel like talking about herself. She doesn't feel like she has much to say, and she certainly doesn't want to tell him about the most recent events in her life.

Travis is into fast cars and F1. He rides a motorcycle, and he proudly tells her about that one time when he almost died in an accident. Syd doesn't know how to feel about it. He's interesting up to a point, so she keeps the conversation going. She orders another coffee. She tells him she doesn't think she'll ever want to ride with him; she's too scared.

"Okay, I get it," he writes back. *"But if you don't want to ride with me, maybe you'll want to ride me."*

Sydney stares at her phone in temporary shock. She doesn't know what to reply to that, so she doesn't.

"Or are you scared of that, too?"

She starts typing something, then changes her mind and simply exits the app. For a minute, she looks out the window at the people passing by and wonders if she's being ridiculous. Travis was probably making a joke. Sort of unnecessary and rude, but a joke nonetheless. Maybe she's overreacting, but at the same time, his words gave her the ick. She can't help feeling the way she feels. She taps on the dating app once more and sees that he wrote her a few more messages.

"Come on, don't be like this!"
"We're both adults here."
"I know what I want, you know what you want..."
"Come on, for real?"

"For real," she whispers to herself as she deactivates her profile and deletes the app from her phone.

In fact, she doesn't know what she wants. She knows what she doesn't want. Travis and guys like Travis, who don't seem to be very different from guys like Finneas. The dating app was a mistake. The idea of dating and getting herself out there again was, in itself, a mistake. She's not ready.

She's feeling bitter now, and she wants to go home but forces herself to finish her croissant and second coffee – since she spent so much on them – and wait for her mood to shift. She walked into this café feeling good about herself and the world, and she doesn't want to leave it feeling the opposite.

To distract herself and forget about Travis, she scrolls through her almost bare social media. An article about the missing young woman, Eveline Grace Davis, pops up, shared by one of Syd's old high school friends. It's Eveline's mom talking about her daughter in the gentlest, kindest, most heartbreaking way.

Eveline was a loner, it seems. She never hurt anyone, was never mean to anyone, she was an introvert and a genuinely good person who always minded her own business. Her family cannot come to terms with the fact that something so horrible happened to her and that she's gone. They're praying, still praying, for Eveline to be returned to them safely, but her mother says towards the end of the article that her greatest pain is that Eveline had such a bright future ahead of her, so many years to explore this world and what it has to offer, and she will never get to enjoy any of it. Which is to say... Eveline's mother believes that Eveline is dead.

That makes something inside Sydney's chest hurt, and it soon transfers to her stomach. She can't finish the croissant. It's too sweet all of a sudden, and she really wants to go home. Her mood has shifted all right, just not in the way she thought it would. She wipes her hands on a napkin, grabs her bag, and walks out into the sun. She takes a few deep breaths then starts walking towards the subway station. She's feeling better already.

But it's sad, so sad that Eveline's family has given up on her. She doesn't understand why she feels such a strong connection to this young woman she's never met. She thinks that if she were Eveline's friend, she would never give up on her. She would pester the police until they did their job. She would investigate the case herself, if that was what it took.

It's weird that Syd is having these thoughts. By the time she gets on the train, she's fantasizing about stumbling onto the place where Eveline is being held and saving her. She's done it before – caught herself fantasizing about being someone's hero. In the past, it was with people she knew. Like Abbi. This is the first time she's thinking this way about someone she doesn't know.

Except she feels like she knows Eveline. From the articles she's read, she sounds a lot like Sydney. Not like Sydney in general – strong, and capable, and passionate about so many things – but like Sydney now – betrayed and broken, isolated and unemployed.

If she sees herself in Eveline, maybe that means Sydney is ready to save herself.

Or maybe, it's not that deep, and Sydney truly wants to save Eveline because the young woman seems to be the epitome of innocence. She's always had a soft spot for these types of characters, so feminine and ethereal, too good for this world. Once again, her thoughts return to Abbi.

No. She stops herself from going there. She was wrong about Abbi.

Is she wrong about Eveline? It could be that all these articles she reads online are deceiving. Still, Syd would save Eveline if she could, and maybe, just maybe, Eveline would prove her right.

The fantasy makes her feel better, so she plays with it in her head for the rest of the day. For once, she doesn't need a pill to sleep soundly.

Chapter Twenty-Five

The One

A few more nights of sleeping with Oscar pressed to my back, and I'm almost used to it. He sleeps peacefully, I sleep in spurts. I spend half the night listening to his steady breath, and close to morning, I fall asleep despite myself. But I sleep lightly, like a small animal knowing she's prey, knowing that the largest, scariest night predator is onto her scent.

When he wakes up at around six, or seven, or it could be eight – I have no sense of time in here, and it's intentional on his part – he uncuffs me and brings me breakfast, then disappears until lunch. He only has dinner with me, and even then, he doesn't seem to be very involved. I ask him about his day – since that's what a good woman does, right? – but he replies in few words, then focuses on his food. I stop bothering.

I keep reading my dark romance books. Oscar brings me the box he's told me about for what feels like a dozen times now, and I pretend to be excited about the new releases. I have paperbacks that don't exist because the authors haven't yet released them, and some authors will never release their books in paperback format. I should be over the moon. I'm not, but that's what Oscar expects, so I play my part as well as I can. Lately, he's been giving me this half-grin half-frown, and I think it means I'm not a great actress.

The only way I can stomach the stories is if I tell myself that I'm reading them for research. Not for the characters, not for the plot, and God forbid, not for the sex. I'm looking for ideas about how to escape. The main female characters are kidnapped, traded, sold, or they have to offer themselves willingly when they can't pay a debt or make rent. These books come up with the most ridiculous scenarios imaginable, and I used to love the diversity. The same love story between the innocent victim and the terrible villain, always told slightly differently, each author adding their own spin, their own unique flavor. With no exceptions, the villain turns into a cinnamon roll for the heroine before the end. He saves her many times over, from guys that are worse than him, from himself, and sometimes from herself, if that makes sense. It doesn't. Not to me, not anymore.

These books that used to be my favorite... They have all kinds of things in them. But if there's one thing that's missing, it's exactly the thing I'm looking for – ideas on how to escape. Because the heroine never wants to escape. Why would she, when she's equally tortured and worshipped? And then more worshipped than tortured. In many cases, the forms of torture are, in fact, forms of worship in disguise.

It's definitely not what's happening to me. All these heroines fall in love with their captors, sometimes within the first ten pages. These books aren't about escaping, they're about surrendering. They're useless to me, but I keep reading them, and when I can't read anymore, I stare at the pages and make sure I turn them regularly, because I don't want Oscar to think I'm ungrateful. He's watching.

Of course, I know he can't be watching all the time, but when I think he missed something, some small, insignificant thing that I did without realizing, he points it out specifically when he brings my meals. He's probably recording me, then. It's nerve-racking, and I have days when it's the only thing I can think about.

I have days when I finish my breakfast and don't move from the chair for an hour, and just stare at the opposite wall and imagine that I'm invisible. If I don't move, I'm invisible, I don't exist in this space, and he can't see me. I play this game in my head and freeze when the pressure of being observed is too much. I close my eyes and imagine myself somewhere else – a beach, a forest, a busy marketplace. I don't know if I want to be somewhere else and alone, or somewhere else and surrounded by people – as many people as possible. I don't know what I want anymore, and when I look in the mirror, I don't recognize myself.

Another night of fitful sleep. I feel him stir beside me. He stretches, yawns, and murmurs a drawn-out "good morning". I respond because he expects me to be well-behaved. He lingers for a moment, then throws himself out of the bed with a sigh, uncuffs me, and goes to fetch breakfast.

This time, when he comes back, he has a cup of black coffee for himself and sits down with me. My heart starts beating faster because he's once again changing something in our routine. At first, it was breakfast for me and coffee for him, light conversation, or him tapping away on his phone. Then it was breakfast alone, and him in a hurry to get to work. Now it's breakfast and coffee again, and I can't help but wonder, "What now? What am I bracing myself for?".

I'm so stressed that the food feels heavy in my stomach. The orange juice only manages to bloat me.

"Done?" he asks, and I know something's up.

I nod.

"Go use the bathroom."

I freeze, like when I'm playing the game where I'm invisible. He frowns, and I spring to my feet. If he says I have to use the bathroom, then I have to use the bathroom. I feel like crying.

It's his MO. He creates a routine for a few days, enough for me to start feeling a little more comfortable, then changes one thing, and my stress levels spike so high that I feel nauseated. In the bathroom, I pee, then flush the toilet and let the water run in the sink for two full minutes while I stare at my reflection and try to calm myself down. When I return to the bedroom, I find him waiting for me on the edge of the bed. He's playing with the key to the handcuffs, rolling it between his fingers.

I know I have to walk to him, but I can't convince my legs to move.

"I'll be working from home today," he says. "Come on, Evie. I have a meeting in half an hour, and I have to make sure you're tucked in before I bring in the new cleaning lady."

I bite the inside of my cheek. Hard.

"This place is slowly turning into a pigsty," he says as he pats the spot next to him. "Come on. It's just for a few hours. I'll ask her to work quickly."

He's bringing someone again. Putting someone in danger again. And he's enjoying it, I can see it. He loves how he can instill fear in me with just a few words.

I have no choice, so I walk over to the bed and lie down, trying not to touch Oscar. When I feel his hands on mine as he secures the cuffs around my wrists, I shudder. He removed the bandages the day before, and the skin is healing well enough. It's rougher, too.

"You remember what happened last time," he says."

"I do."

"It can't happen again, okay? You made a mess, and I had to deal with it. I can't keep sorting out your messes, Evie."

"Of course."

"You know the story." He covers my hands with the duvet, then looks into my eyes as he brushes a few strands of hair from my face. "Don't make a scene. Make small talk, instead. Make a friend. Rita was nice, wasn't she? She could've been your friend."

I try not to think about Rita's family. For sure, they're looking for her, and it's just a matter of time before the police figure out she came to this address to clean.

"Okay," I say.

"Okay what? You will behave?"

"I will behave."

"Good girl." He beams at me, and I must say that his smile – his real smile – is not unpleasant. He has perfect white teeth. "I'll be upstairs, working, but I'll keep an eye on things." He leans in to kiss me on the forehead.

Then he rushes to the door and punches in the code. My heart is in my throat, and my stomach feels like it's moved up into my chest, and I feel like throwing up and crying at the same time. My hands shake, and I cling to the edge of the duvet to make sure that it stays in place and covers the cuffs effectively.

This woman, no matter who she is... I will protect her. I must. What happened to Rita will not happen to her, even if that means I will spend the rest of my life in this basement.

I hear them as they descend the stairs. Oscar left the door open, so the newcomer wouldn't find it suspicious. After all, the fact that I'm down here, in a place with no windows, is odd enough. She can't see the metal door that retracts into the wall. She walks in first, then he follows, carrying the vacuum cleaner, like the gentleman that he is.

"Evie, this is Nora," he says, a relaxed smile on his face. "Nora, this is my wife, Evie."

"Hello, Mrs. Miles!"

"Hi, Nora!" I try to smile as wide as I can. I hope it doesn't look creepy, or it will defeat the purpose of putting this woman at ease. "I'm sorry you have to see me this way. I haven't been feeling well lately."

She gives me a sympathetic look. "Don't you worry about it, Mrs. Miles. I'm here to help."

"Evie. Please call me Evie."

Oscar seems pleased. I hate that he's reduced me to a puppet whose sole purpose is to please him by playing a role, but if that's what it takes to keep this woman alive...

No one else will die because of me.

Chapter Twenty-Six
The Other One

Sydney has a good feeling when she picks up the phone and hears the cheerful voice at the other end. Her feeling is confirmed when the news comes that she's been hired. She shoots to her feet and starts pacing her cramped living room but keeps her voice steady and professional.

"Yes, I can start next week. Sounds great, yes."

It's a start-up, the pay isn't great, but none of that matters. At least it will give her a reason to make herself look presentable and get out of the house every day. She'll meet new people, maybe make new friends. Once the call is over, she attacks her closet with fervor, taking out all her clothes and putting together possible outfits. She wants to start on the right foot and make a good impression.

In terms of wardrobe, Syd is doing fine. All those business trips forced her to buy quality items, and she has plenty of shirts and dress pants. However, this company is not as stuck-up as the one she worked for before, so she'll need to think in more casual terms. She combines a classic white shirt with a pair of dark straight-leg jeans, but then finds it impossible to decide between white sneakers and black boots. The best way is to try everything on, so she does. And then realizes she doesn't have a full-length mirror and has to struggle with the bathroom mirror while standing atop a stool. It's not ideal, but it does the job. She just needs to be careful not to slip and break something.

For the next hour, she tries on various outfits, messes with her hair – which is in dire need of a cut – and goes through her makeup collection. She throws away a foundation that expired a month ago, and a mascara that is completely dried. Syd is not a fan of makeup, but she'll make an effort when it counts, like on her first day at a new job. All this work builds up an appetite, and before she knows it, her stomach rumbles, and she's craving a burger with fries.

So much for eating healthy. But she decides to not judge herself today. Getting this job is a win, and she deserves to celebrate it. She picks up her phone and orders from one of her favorite places. As she waits, she scrolls through her social media, then taps on her contacts. She feels like calling someone and telling them about the interview, the company, the good news. She feels like sharing. With whom, though? Normally, the first person to know the fresh, exciting things happening in Syd's life would be Abbi. She blocked her number, and she won't unblock it. How pathetic would that be? Besides, she's not sure Abbi would be happy for her after the last discussion they had.

Her mother. Syd taps on her number but surprise, surprise! She's still blocked.

"I can't believe this."

It's been days! A week or more; Syd hasn't kept count. It's ridiculous that her mother hasn't unblocked her number yet. On the one hand, it means she's fine and she hasn't had any health scares. On the other hand, it hurts. They had an argument, and Sydney thinks it wasn't even the worst argument they've ever had. Her mother got mad when Syd refused to forgive Abbi just because she is – was! – her best friend. And then she got mad when Syd told her to only call her when she had a real problem.

She was too harsh to her mother. Now that some time has passed and she's gained some perspective on things, Sydney can admit she said some things to her mom that she shouldn't have said. Even though her mother exaggerates sometimes, it's important that she trusts Syd. In case something bad really does happen.

Syd drops her phone and leans back on the couch. She rubs at her eyes and temples and lets out a sigh. She'll have to go there and hope her mother opens the door. Not today, though. Tomorrow. It's already late, and she's waiting for her food. She also needs to put her clothes back in the closet.

She spends a nice evening all by herself, enjoying her food and a glass of wine. She stays away from her phone. Lately, she's developed a toxic relationship with it. Every time she picks it up, she's either tempted to unblock Finn's number, or she starts looking for new articles about that girl who disappeared. When she doesn't find any, she re-reads the old ones.

The next day, she wakes up early and does Pilates first thing. She feels better. So much better, in fact, that she's almost a different person. And she changes her mind about paying her mother an impromptu visit. Yes, she said some things she regrets, and one day she will apologize, but her mother is behaving like a legit child. What sort of parent blocks her own daughter? Syd's life is finally taking a turn for the better, and she won't ruin her mood by going there and risking another immature argument with her mom.

"It's fine," she tells herself. "It can wait. Besides, she'll probably hate it if I make the first move. She'll say I'm not respecting her boundaries."

This is her last weekend as an unemployed person, and Syd is determined to use this time to hype herself up, so she can make a good impression on Monday. That means some self-care and another burger with fries because she's noticed all her pants are a little loose on her hips.

Chapter Twenty-Seven
The One

Nora is a sturdy woman with strong arms, gray hair chopped short, light blue eyes, and kindness permanently etched on her face. She carries a few extra pounds but moves swiftly and silently. She starts in the bathroom, and I hear her humming to herself as she cleans, then moves into the library, where she rearranges the books in neat piles, so she can thoroughly vacuum the carpet. It's been an hour and a half, and only the bedroom is left to clean. She seems to be more focused and meticulous than Rita, and less chatty too. I wonder where Oscar found her. I wonder if she has a family – a husband and children waiting for her at home.

She's dusting the furniture, throwing me occasional glances. I smile, and she smiles back. I can't help staring at the open door. Right there, so close, yet completely out of reach. Oscar has his eyes glued to the cameras, I'm sure. If I managed to somehow get out of the handcuffs, I wouldn't even make it to the door. He would be down here in seconds, like he was when Rita freaked out.

I should make small talk with Nora. Befriend her. Not only because Oscar suggested it – his suggestions are all orders – but because it's the simplest way to prevent her from becoming suspicious. Does she think I'm odd when she looks at me? Eccentric? That would be the least of my worries. But what if she thinks I'm hiding something?

"I'm sorry I can't help," I say. "I'm feeling very weak today."

"Nonsense," she says cheerfully. "This is my job, and you need your rest."

"I didn't expect to be confined to bed for so long," I say. I don't know what I'm doing. I just want to keep the conversation going, I think. "The peace and quiet down here helps, though."

"I get it. It's a busy neighborhood."

"It is."

"Cars always going up and down, up and down... I saw one of your neighbors has a particularly noisy one. It must drive everyone around here nuts." She shakes her head. "I don't understand these young people and their obsession with noisy cars."

"Me neither."

"You have so many books, Mrs. Evie. I can't remember the last time I had time to sit down and read a book. I always tell myself I will read a few pages before bed, but every night, I just crash, then it's morning and I have to start all over again. No time to read. I have two books on my bedside table, gathering dust. I wipe them clean and leave them there. I should put them back on the shelf, honestly, but I can't bring myself to do it. If nothing else, at least it looks like I'm reading before bed." She laughs. "I'm being silly, I know."

"No, you're not silly. You work too much. I hope you can take a break soon."

"I hope so, too. Oh well. But don't worry, Mrs. Evie–"

"Just Evie, please."

"Evie. I like working. I like being of service, you know, helping people, making their life easier. I cook too. I like it more than cleaning, but I'm not fussy. I'll take any work that comes my way and helps someone have a better, easier day."

Wow. I don't know what to say to that. Do I like working? I'm a freelance writer, and even though I like the activity itself, I can't say that I feel like I'm of service when I compare two types of hairbrushes in a 400-word article.

"Thank you." I decide that's the safest thing to say. "You can imagine I would do the cleaning myself... It's just that I'm not in the best shape now."

She waves me off. "You have other things to do. You and your husband. He told me that he works in IT and you're a writer. Working with your brain is much harder than working with your hands."

I blush. I don't know why I'm suddenly feeling uncomfortable, but I am. I never had a cleaning lady. But then again, it only takes one hour to clean my cramped apartment, so even if I could afford one, what would be the point?

Oh God, my apartment. This month's rent is already paid, and I'm sure the police are looking for me already. Right? Right. My mom has surely figured out that I'm missing, and until they find me, she'll make sure I don't lose the apartment. It's not the most amazing place, but it's mine. Though... it's where Oscar drugged and kidnapped me. Now that I think about it... Can I go back there without having a panic attack every time I enter my building?

Nora is humming again. I spaced out and instead of interrupting my thoughts, she returned to the task at hand – dusting the surfaces. She leaves the two nightstands last, but eventually, she ends up hovering over me as she picks up the plastic cup on my nightstand and wipes under it. I make myself as small as I can. Very, very small under the duvet, which I'm holding in place with my trembling fingers.

"Do you want me to change the sheets?" she asks. "I can help you stand, and then you can sit for a minute in that chair," she points over her shoulder, "And then I'll help you back into bed. I'm strong, so you don't have to worry one bit. You look like you're as light as a feather."

I can imagine Oscar upstairs, his face so close to the screen that his breath fogs it up. If I say the wrong thing now, or if I act suspicious, this will be the first and last time I see Nora.

"Oh no," I say, my voice trembling. I realize that's not a good thing, and I clear my throat and force a smile. "Oscar has recently changed the sheets. He likes doing it. Um..."

He likes doing it?! No man likes changing the sheets! What the hell is wrong with me?

"I mean he likes doing it for me," I add quickly. It doesn't sound much better. Doesn't make much more sense. "Because... because I have a specific way in which I make the bed. I mean when I can. I can't now, and he does it. He does it perfectly. Just the way I like it."

Dear God, shut my mouth before I say any more stupid things.

Nora's face softens. She places one hand on her heart and nods.

"You are so lucky, Evie. Your husband loves you so much. I can tell. He would do anything for you, wouldn't he? Very lucky, indeed. Listen to an old woman who's seen plenty in her lifetime. Men like Mr. Miles are rare. And you're both so young and beautiful! You have a bright future ahead of you. I can already see your children, perfect little cherubs." She catches herself and adds quickly, "That is, if you want children. I don't want to assume."

What the hell am I supposed to say? I only wanted to make small talk, and it seems to have turned against me. The idea of having Oscar's babies... No. I can't think about that. I can't.

"Do you have children?" I ask, hoping she won't notice I'm desperately trying to change the subject.

"Yes, one." She's done dusting, and she picks up the vacuum cleaner. "It's hard, I won't lie to you, but a child can save your life sometimes. Not a lot of women will say that, but I will. Mine saved my life."

I want to ask her if it's a son or a daughter, but she starts vacuuming the carpet. It's a great excuse to leave the conversation up in the air. I try to relax, knowing that she will come close to the bed again, and I have to look like everything is fine and I'm not handcuffed to the bed frame. I figure the best way is to clear my mind and not think about anything. Not dwell on the fact that everyone who meets Oscar seems to believe he's God's gift to me – his poor, bedridden wife.

Nora bends down with a grunt, pushing the vacuum cleaner under the bed, and I hold my breath. It goes smoothly, and then she's vacuuming the other side of the room. I look up at the ceiling and keep my mouth tightly shut, so Oscar sees that I haven't and I won't say a word.

"All done," Nora says.

She starts gathering her cleaning supplies, and within a minute, we both hear Oscar thudding down the stairs. He appears in the doorway, handsome and affable. He looks satisfied. His right hand is in the pocket of his slacks, and I hold my breath. But then he pulls it out, and he's holding his wallet. I exhale.

"I'll help you with that, Nora," Oscar says as he takes the vacuum cleaner from her. "All good?"

"Yes. You can check if you want," Nora says.

"No need. Let's go upstairs. My wife needs to rest."

"Of course."

Nora waves at me, a big smile on her face. I don't wave back, but I tell her it was nice meeting her.

Oscar lingers behind. He waits for her to be out of sight, and then he says to me, "I'm proud of you." He follows her upstairs.

The door is still open.

Chapter Twenty-Eight
The Other One

Sydney sits at her desk, which is small and square, wedged between Layla's desk – Layla is one of her new colleagues – and the window. The view isn't great – a parking lot that's always full – but it's better than staring at a wall. The office is wide, airy, and modern. Everyone is working at their little table, focused on the screen of their laptop, headphones or earphones blocking out what's happening outside their bubble. When they talk amongst themselves, they whisper, and if they need to have a longer conversation, they retreat to one of the two conference rooms. The rules seem to be simple and easy to follow. Compared to her previous job, everyone here is laid back, and Syd feels like she's going to fit in just fine.

She met her team, then spent half an hour talking to her manager, who is a woman in her late thirties. There are two other managers, but they're both working from home today. One of them has been sick for a while – long Covid – and the other is some sort of a genius that no one questions, so he comes to the office when it suits him. When Layla tells her that, Syd uses the opportunity to ask if she could work from home at some point. Not that she is considering it. Getting out of that cramped apartment is, at this point, more important to her mental health than money.

"Working from home is fine," Layla says, "But maybe wait a month before you put in your first request?"

"Sounds good."

Layla shrugs. "Personally, I don't like it. With one toddler and a husband constantly building something in the garage, I'd rather pay the nanny and come here every day." She chuckles, as if to let Sydney know it's not so bad, and she's exaggerating for the sake of making a joke.

Syd smiles and says, "Oh, I feel your pain," even though she doesn't. She's been feeling all kinds of pain lately, but her situation is not permanent, and for that she is lucky. Layla may be trying to be funny, but Syd can hear the regret in her voice.

Family. Family is a permanent thing. So you better like the one you're building.

Syd was this close to building something with the wrong man, and now that she thinks about it, she's grateful things happened the way they did. She steals another glance at Layla's profile, then turns to her laptop and starts on the first task of the day. Sure, going through a breakup sucks, moving out is not easy, and being unemployed almost broke her spirit, but other people have bigger problems than her.

Later, she attends two meetings, both short and to the point, and she has lunch with Layla and the rest of the team in one of the conference rooms. The kitchen is too small to fit them all, and usually, people here prefer to either eat at their desks, or go out for lunch. There are plenty of cafés and restaurants in the area. However, since Sydney is new, the manager suggests they have lunch together on her first day of work, to give her a chance to get to know all of them better.

They don't talk about work at all, which is surprising and refreshing. At Syd's previous company, they always ended up talking about work, no matter the environment. It was the only thing they had in common. The people here are friendlier and much more relaxed. Some of them have families, like Layla, but most are young and not even thinking about marriage or children. Their manager, Helen, is divorced.

They attack her with the usual questions, and Syd tries to keep things light. She doesn't want to give too much away, but she doesn't want to lie either. She casually tells them she's ended a relationship recently and she's going through some changes, but things are looking good. Helen changes the subject, and Syd is grateful. She knows her new colleagues mean no harm, but they seem to be quite chatty and nosy. For the rest of the lunch hour, they talk about movies and books. Layla says every time a movie or TV show that's made after a book comes out, she stays away from social media to avoid spoilers, and makes it her mission to read the book first. Syd doesn't see the logic in it, but she's never been an avid reader, so she's happy to listen to the back-and-forth between Layla and the others while poking at her salad.

By the end of the day, she falls into a strange mood, low and heavy, as if her batteries are drained. She thinks it's because she hasn't interacted with so many people in a while, and now she's feeling overwhelmed. She thought she would fit right in with this cheerful team, but it only takes her a few hours to realize that they're vibing at a frequency she's not attuned to. They seem happy. Even Layla, who groans when the workday is over, but then shows Syd pictures of her son.

It's her. She needs to do better. Be friendlier, get more involved. Throughout the day, she spaced out too many times, and she's sure Helen noticed at least once. She has to start acting like she wants to be here, because she does want to be here.

She misses the past. But the past was fake. An illusion and a scam. Syd needs to stay grounded in the present and appreciate the things that are good and healthy for her right now. Like living on her own, being part of a young and easy-going team, taking up exercise again – even if it's just her with her yoga mat, in her living room – and rediscovering herself.

She should do more of that – rediscovery of the self. At lunch, Layla talked a lot about books and the difference between fiction and non-fiction. She said that most people read fiction to escape, and when they want to learn something or better themselves, they turn to non-fiction.

She said that while she reads both, she feels like fiction books have helped her grow the most. There's something about the way fiction challenges the reader with various scenarios and ways in which the characters react. Syd didn't understand much of her colleague's reasoning, but as she gets on the subway to go home, she thinks about the passion behind her words. Maybe it wouldn't be such a bad idea to stop by the bookstore and treat herself to a book.

She hasn't read in years. She doesn't even know which genre is her favorite. She'll just pick something that sounds good and has a pretty cover, and if nothing else, at least it will replace the screen time before bed and help her fall asleep faster.

Sydney's first day at her new job. Not particularly great, not too bad either. Decent. She can live with decent.

Chapter Twenty-Nine
The One

The door slides shut later. The handcuffs come off. And Oscar is on cloud nine, doing a little dance as he's changing the sheets. I watch him from across the room, horrified. I've never seen him like this. As usual, I have no idea if it's a good thing or a bad thing.

"I am so happy you're getting along with Nora," he says.

"I can see that," I murmur.

"What's that?" He raises an eyebrow. "Oh, right. She's nice, isn't she? She liked you, too. She asked me if there's anything else she can do to help, aside from cleaning. It got me thinking. I can bring her around more, so she can keep you company when I'm busy."

"How would that work?" With the handcuffs, the keypad, and the door... open? Not open?

He shrugs. "We'll figure something out. You and I." He beams at me as he fluffs up the pillows. "We can do anything if we put our heads together."

He starts humming a tune that sounds familiar. I pale when I realize it's the same thing Nora was humming half an hour ago. He was paying attention. So much attention. Watching and listening.

"Bed's ready," he says. He gathers the dirty sheets off the floor. "I'll bring you lunch, then I have a meeting. I thought working from home today would give us more time together, but something exploded at work, and I have to take care of it. I have, like, twenty emails I have to reply to. Sorry."

"It's okay."

"You have your books, though."

"Yes."

"So, you're fine."

"I am."

He nods and sprints out of the basement. I sigh and run my hand over my face, but I try to do it subtly. I am fine, in fact. For now. All things considered, today is a decent day. Oscar is in a good mood, and the new cleaning lady is alive and well. I'm just glad nothing happened to her. I don't even care I had to spend another two hours cuffed to the bed frame on top of the endless hours of the night. I behaved today and no one died. Oscar is happy. I am happy.

He comes back with lunch and drops it on the table, in front of me. He gives me a wink and disappears upstairs. I'm grateful something exploded at work and he's busy with that. I don't really understand what he does, but that's probably because he hasn't given me specifics. Or because these IT jobs are always confusing.

Lunch is different today. I mean, it's soup and beef lasagna, which I've had before, but it's... tastier. The roasted tomato soup is spiced just right, with two basil leaves floating on the surface, and the lasagna is juicy, with plenty of parmesan on top. When did Oscar have time to up his cooking game? Most likely, he made all this while Nora was down here, and because things were going so well between me and her, he cooked with extra love and joy.

No, scratch love. I don't think he's capable of it.

I take my time to savor the food because I know there's nothing else to do after. Except for reading. I wonder if I should ask Oscar to bring me something different. I could tell him that I feel a little burned out on romance and I need a palate cleanser. Or two, or a dozen. What genre would be a good choice? Nothing dark, and nothing that has a love story at the forefront. Adventure? Something like the Indiana Jones movies.

Or I could ask Oscar for something else. When I was in college, I kept telling myself that once I graduated, I would get a new hobby. Something other than reading every book under the sun. But then I had rent and bills to pay, plus college debt, so ideas like painting and learning how to play the piano went on the back burner. Would Oscar buy me canvases and acrylics? Hm. He will probably say all I want is to get my hands on some paintbrushes so I can stab him in the eye.

What am I doing? I push the empty plate away and stand up. My hands turn into fists at my sides. I can't think like this! Taking up new hobbies when I'm locked up in a madman's basement... What is wrong with me? It's like accepting that I will never get out of here. That I will spend the rest of my life here. It's giving up.

I can't give up. Even if I can't see a way out now, that doesn't mean things won't change. It's barely been... two weeks? Three? Seriously, what is wrong with me? I can't succumb to this fate so soon. I can't be this weak.

They're looking for me. They are. By now, my face must be plastered all over social media, and who knows? Maybe the police are actually getting close. So close. It's just a matter of time before that door opens and someone in uniform walks in instead of Oscar.

I'm not taking up any new hobbies. I won't learn how to paint in this basement. I won't read adventure books in this basement. I refuse to let Oscar ruin anything else for me.

To change my dreadful mood, I start stretching and warming up for a light session of calisthenics. My mind won't be strong if my body isn't. I must take care of myself. For instance, because I'm cuffed to the bed every night and my wrists are a mess, I have no strength in my hands. I need to fix that.

For an hour and a half, I stretch, work out, pace the room, stretch some more. I take a shower and wash my hair. I'm not shy anymore, and I don't try to cover myself as I use the bathroom in all the ways a bathroom is supposed to be used. It's not the lack of shyness, in fact. I just don't care. Oscar doesn't, so why would I? I don't think about it. When I'm in the bathroom, my mind is blank. I've made this pact with myself that the bathroom is going to be the place where I think about my situation the least, specifically because it's the place that dehumanizes me the most. I do my worst thinking in bed, and considering how much time I'm forced to spend there, it's enough to drive anyone crazy. I must protect the little sanity I have left at all cost, and if that means dividing the basement into sections where only some things are allowed and others are not, so be it. It only works if I don't tell Oscar about it. I must keep these little mental tricks to myself and hold onto the power that they give me. Control. I can control this space in this way. This space that was built to control me.

I spend the day in my head, keeping my hands busy and my mind full of soothing thoughts. I apply more skincare products than is necessary, and I brush my hair like the court ladies did in medieval times – a hundred times for extra shine. I peruse the snack basket and pretend to read. Instinctively, I know when it's dinner time, and I get up and walk into the bedroom minutes before Oscar shows up.

We sit down to eat. The food is again on a different level than what he's been feeding me until now, and Oscar doesn't hesitate to elucidate that mystery for me.

"I asked Nora to cook. She's happy to do it, and I don't mind paying if that means more free time for me. To tell you the truth, Evie, it's been challenging to juggle everything. It's not easy to be the provider."

As if anyone ever asked him. I swallow my thoughts and chase them down with a sip of red.

"But don't worry about it." He gives me a pleasant smile. "Everything has a learning curve, and I think I have this one figured out. I'm nothing if not a problem solver. That's what a true provider is. A fixer."

I must agree with him. He's much more bearable when he's in a good mood.

"You probably got used to my cooking," he continues to make conversation. "But this is okay, right? You like Nora's food."

"I do."

For a moment, I am certain he will ask me if I like it more than his cooking, and a knot forms in my stomach. A tiny one. Everything is going so well, and I just pray, "Please don't ask me. Please don't ask me." Because if I say yes, he'll get mad and call me ungrateful. But if I say no, and that his cooking is better than Nora's, he'll know I'm lying, and that's not acceptable. Of course Nora's cooking is better than his. "Please don't ask me. Please don't ask me."

"Great! I'll have her cook all our meals, then."

Oh, thank God! I can finish my meal in peace. I can't believe the trivialities that can give me a panic attack these days...

We're done, and I'm ready to be handcuffed to the bed. I go to the bathroom without him asking, I wash up and change into pajamas. I lie down in bed, on my right side, and hold my hands in position. He comes over, leans in, and places a kiss on my forehead. Well, this is new.

"Good night, Evie."

What now?

He doesn't reach into his pocket for the key. He stares at me for a long moment, and I realize he's waiting for me to say it back.

"Good night, Oscar."

He smiles, dims the lights with a tap on his phone, then leaves.

I lie there, dumbstruck. The first night when I don't have to sleep with my hands cuffed. I should feel relief. I should feel gratitude. I have the bed all to myself, and I can sleep right in the middle of it if I want to. I can actually sleep, not spend the night staring at the wall as he breathes steadily in my ear, his arm draped over me.

All I can think is: he's changed the routine again.

Chapter Thirty

Oscar

Evie was exciting in the beginning, but now the novelty is wearing off. He's bored of working from home, and he's started to hate that he needs to constantly be on his phone to keep an eye on the cameras. It doesn't help that she never does anything interesting, never talks about anything stimulating. He expected more from someone who reads all day, especially since her genre of choice is dark romance.

She's difficult, too. Always complaining, never showing any gratitude for what he does for her. She's hard to be with. Hard to love.

Evie is a challenge, for sure. Some days, he thinks she is the challenge he needs to get to the next level, to evolve as a person, become the man he's supposed to be. Other days, she's a burden and he wants out. He never thought he'd crave freedom so soon after getting what he wanted – her, body and soul, all his.

He dutifully brings her breakfast, then he's out of the house, driving to his favorite café in the city, where he sits in the farthest corner, next to the window, from where he can see people passing up and down the street, up and down, going to work, taking their lunch break, going to the gym, shopping, chatting, drinking too much coffee, always on the go, go, go. Most of these people are utterly unaware of their surroundings. In a sea of humans rubbing elbows and bumping into each other, never taking their eyes off their phones, everyone thinks they are alone. The center of the world. If they don't pay attention, they think no one else does.

Oscar does, though. He pays attention. He observes.

The woman in the blue dress and shiny black sandals flips her blonde hair over her shoulder and presses her phone to her ear, all the while smiling sympathetically at another woman with a stroller and a toddler in tow.

Red looks good on the brunette who's crossing the street. Too bad that neckline doesn't compliment her body shape and she can barely walk in those heels. If someone set about to following her home later tonight, she wouldn't be able to run.

A petite redhead with thick-framed glasses and a splatter of freckles on her cheeks enters the café and orders two americanos, one flat white, and two lattes with various specifications and toppings. Her eyes are glued to her phone as she waits. Every five seconds, she nervously pushes her glasses up her nose.

One hobby, and one hobby only has stuck with Oscar through the years. He loves observing women. Fascinating creatures, wrapped up in their inner worlds, gliding about, happy one second, sad the very next, doing too much, giving their all, receiving little, faking smiles, proving themselves, acting like they're in on it, never being enough. At some point, he concluded they're all sort of similar, essentially the same if you strip them down to their core, and so his quest for the ones who stand out began.

He watches them all. On the street, on social media, in his office, in the cafés around the city. Until he sets his eyes on one, and then he only watches her. From watching casually, he graduates to watching obsessively. He learns where she works, where she lives and with whom, where she does her grocery shopping, how often she visits her family, and how many close friends she has. He makes new social media accounts, with VPN and all the security measures in place, and follows her on all the platforms she's on. Within a week, he knows what her favorite food is, which song she's listening to on repeat, and the last time she had intimate relations with someone. Also, who that someone is. He enters her life from afar, gets closer and closer, until he's right behind her. If she weren't so absorbed by her phone, she would feel his breath on the back of her neck. He doesn't reach out, though. He watches her, follows her home, his steps too light for her to notice, and it helps that he looks so harmless, with his preppy glasses and clean-shaved jaw. He does it once, twice, for a week, for an entire month... Then he usually moves on. He rarely stalks the same woman for more than four or five weeks. He loses interest quickly, or another woman gets his attention.

This is what he calls type one. In Oscar's head, women come in three different types. Type one is the one you stalk but don't touch. She's interesting, but not that interesting. She falls short in one area or another. Usually, she's too independent. If you were to reach out, she'd make a scene.

Type two is the one you stalk, assess, and eventually approach. You stage a meet-cute and start something that lasts a while. She's easy, and that's why it works. But you don't want to keep one that's easy. What you want to keep is... a type three woman. You stalk, assess, approach, snatch.

She lives alone, but she's not independent. Not in a way that matters. She's isolated, invisible, beautiful without knowing it. She lives in her head, talks to herself when she thinks no one's watching, and has the most fascinating conversations. She laughs at her own jokes and dances around her kitchen as she makes herself pancakes. When she gets out of the house, she hides it all under a loose hoodie, because she was not made for this world, and she knows it.

That was Evie for Oscar. Type threes are hard to come by, probably because Oscar has standards, and those standards are high. Evie was the first to meet them, so she was the first he took and brought into his home.

Now he's not so sure anymore. Evie doesn't talk to herself, doesn't laugh at her own jokes, and doesn't dance around the basement. Probably because she knows he's always watching, but still. She doesn't even read, though that's her favorite thing in the world. It's like she changed the day she woke up handcuffed to the bed, and Oscar has been waiting for her to change back, but it's like she's punishing him. All the things he liked about her – she refuses to let them shine through.

He must be patient, he reminds himself as he watches the freckled girl balance the five cups of coffee as she makes her way out of the café. She has tiny ears and a button nose. Her hair is slightly fried towards the ends, which makes him think that dark red shade is not her natural color. She's focused on the task at hand, oblivious to her surroundings. She hasn't noticed him at all, and he's been staring at her for the past ten minutes. He looks away, so he doesn't see where she's going, but he knows it must be one of the office buildings in the area. He must be patient with Evie, he reminds himself, so this urge to replace her with someone more malleable and less challenging goes away.

Evie is the first. The first time he's taking this hobby of his to the next level. He wishes her to be the last too, because he feels the need to settle down. He chose her carefully, watched her for five months to make sure she was the one. He gave himself plenty of time to tire of her and move on, but it didn't happen, and he took that as a sign.

Now he feels like it's happening. He's here, pretending to work, when in fact, he's looking for a distraction. He's moving on. Evie isn't interesting anymore, if she ever was. Maybe he was wrong about her, wrong about what could be between them. On the other hand, relationships are not easy. And he was looking for a challenge, someone to make him into a better man, otherwise he would've taken and kept one of the type twos.

He must be patient. What's he doing here, fantasizing about his old ways, when Evie is waiting for him at home? He taps on his phone to bring up the camera feed. Evie is in the library, reading.

Oscar smiles.

Chapter Thirty-One

Oscar

A few more days of the same routine with Evie, and Oscar is ready to throw in the towel. Maybe he wasn't made to settle down, after all. The same woman, day in and day out. Sharing a bed with her, feeding her three times a day, making sure she has everything she needs and more. And for all that effort, to only get tepid conversation and a few fake smiles in return.

No relationship is perfect, and Oscar is pragmatic enough to not expect his one to be. But he's been giving so much, sacrificing his time, putting all else on hold just to be available for Evie twenty-four seven. She is more than his girlfriend. She is his fiancée, and when the circumstances require it, he calls her his wife. And it sounds nice. "This is my wife, Evie." It sounds right. One day, it will be true.

He's tired. And bored. He's been trying to hype himself up by thinking about the future. Evie will get used to her new life, eventually. How could she not? It's an easy life, and she doesn't have to do anything. She will look forward to seeing him in the morning, chatter excitedly all through breakfast, read her books until lunch, tell him all about it when he drops in with her food. For dinner, she will slip into a nice dress, and in bed, she will climb on top of him. Before their one-year anniversary, she will proudly walk around and do her yoga with a growing belly. He will watch it all happen on the cameras, and he'll love every minute of it.

That's the future he envisions when he feels himself slipping away from Evie. It warms his chest, reminds him of why he's doing this in the first place, and encourages him to stay resilient and try harder. For her. For them. For their future children.

Today is not a great day, though. His usual daydreams don't work. They've lost their flavor and left him restless and irritable. He has no patience with Evie as she pokes at her food and makes zero effort to keep the conversation going. He wonders if she might be depressed. She isn't grooming herself, despite his insistent pleas and explanations about how it's a woman's duty to herself and to her partner to take care of herself and make sure she looks, at the very least, presentable. It could be that she's depressed, he thinks, and in need of medication. If that's what she's struggling with, then it's not her fault, and he will have to be understanding and find a solution for her. He'd have to fix it. Fix her.

But Evie has no history of depression. He dug deep into her past before making the decision that she was the one for him, and he found nothing of the sort. A strange, melancholic child, an introverted teen, and then an avoidant, self-sufficient adult. Because of all those things, Evie needs him. Now that she has him, and the weight of the world has been lifted off her shoulders, she should be happy and full of life. She's the exact opposite, though, and it baffles him.

If it is, indeed, depression, he'll find a way to get her the right medication. Not today, though. Today, he is beyond exhausted, and so over the way she treats him, like he's her enemy, not her ally. It's like she doesn't want to be helped. Oscar is drained, and as the saying goes, you first need to help yourself to be able to help someone else, especially when that someone shows resistance. He must fill his own tank, or there will be consequences.

Once he's out of the house, he can breathe more easily. He gets into his car, pulls out of the garage, and as he's idling in the driveway, considering his options, pulls out his phone and scrolls through his contacts. It's the middle of the day, and everyone he knows is at work. He should be at work too, but one of the perks of being a genius IT manager at a start-up company is that he's always ahead of the game and can take a free hour or two whenever he wants. His thumb hovers over a name. Miranda. One beat, two beats... What the hell. He taps on her phone number, and she answers after the second ring.

Miranda is a type two. One of the easy ones. So easy that Oscar only calls her when he's completely depleted and can't be bothered with convincing the other type twos on his roster that he's been busy but he's back and oh-so-enamored with them. Even the low-effort ones require some effort, especially when he's been ignoring them for a while. Miranda is minus a hundred effort. He calls her now, and she doesn't ask him why he vanished on her for a month.

"My shift ends in an hour," she says. "My place?"

She lives close to the restaurant where she works. It suits him, and he has plenty of time to get there.

"Can't wait to see you, Pookie. I've missed you." He can hear the excitement in her voice, but oh how he hates that name! "See you in a bit."

Pookie. Makes him gag. Maybe he will gag her before they even reach the bed, and then he won't have to kiss her, either. It will feel less like he's cheating on Evie. If it's mechanical and perfunctory, then it will be like it's nothing at all. All he needs is release and a bit of attention from a woman who's enthusiastic about it, and that will be enough to recharge his batteries. He told Evie he would wait, and he meant it. With her, it will be different. Meaningful. But until then, he has needs, especially if Evie is going to make him work even harder for it.

One day, he will get his reward.

He checks the cameras and sees that Evie is in the bathroom. He has no interest in watching her do... that, so he closes the app and decides he will not look at it while he's got another woman on his mind. He puts on music and starts driving to Miranda's place.

He stalked Miranda for two weeks before staging a meet-cute. He rushed it a bit, and it was risky, but she gave him the perfect opportunity when she signed up for a cooking class, so he threw caution to the wind, signed up too, and hoped for the best even if he hadn't had time to dig deep into her past. Miranda turned out to be easy-going and scatterbrained. Older than him, a college dropout, stuck in a waitress job, with dreams of becoming a chef. She had no talent in that direction, and every failure was the end of the world, so she gave up the cooking class, but not before Oscar got her number and took her out on a few dates that ended at her apartment.

Oscar finished the cooking class. When he starts something, he always finishes it. It is one of his core values.

He finds a parking spot a block away from Miranda's place. On his way there, he walks by a flower shop, and on impulse, goes in and buys her carnations. Basic, yet effective. Miranda will appreciate the gesture. As he resumes the walk to her apartment, his thoughts wander back to Evie. When was the last time he bought her flowers? Did he ever buy her flowers? He can't remember. He bought so many things for her – beautiful dresses, sexy lingerie, luxury cosmetics, and books! Flowers would mean a vase. A vase can be broken. No, he can't let Evie have something made of glass or porcelain. Maybe a plastic vase. Yes, that could work.

Miranda buzzes him in, and as he takes the elevator to her floor, he once again tries to shift his thoughts from

Evie. He must not think about her now. She's taking too much of his mental space already, and not giving a lot in return. He doesn't understand why people say women are usually givers, while men are takers. With Evie, it's been the other way around since day one. It's either his karma, or he got the wrong girl.

No. He can't think like that. Because if he got the wrong girl, that means the right girl is still out there, waiting for him, while he's wasting his time on a lost cause.

No, no, no. Evie is the right girl. She must be. She's the one. She's his future wife. You don't just call it quits and replace your future wife because you hit a rough patch. Plus, Oscar started this thing with Evie, and when he starts something, he always finishes it.

"Pookie! Oh, you brought me flowers!"

Miranda's wrapped around his neck instantly, and he's wondering if she might want to taste the flowers, since he's feeling like shoving them into her mouth right about now. If she calls him Pookie again...

"You're so sweet."

She goes in for a kiss. He turns his head and presses his face to her neck. She giggles, oblivious to the fact that she's just been rejected. She takes the flowers from him but doesn't have time to find a vase before Oscar takes a hold of her wrists and starts pulling her towards the bedroom. He has a thing for women's wrists. As far as he's concerned, it's not the worst kink to have. With

Miranda, he'll just bruise her a little. He can't afford to leave deeper marks, or she might complain. Though she hasn't complained about him ghosting her... Who knows what else she would forgive? From the outside, she certainly looks like a better choice than Evie, who will not give him an inch unless he kills someone in front of her.

Oscar knows she's not a better choice than Evie. Miranda has friends, tons of them, and she talks to her mother on the phone every night. But that's not what disqualifies her. He could overlook all that and take the necessary precautions. The issue is her personality. Easy-going and scatterbrained means she can't be counted on. One minute, she's perfectly fine and content, the next, she throws a tantrum because she broke a nail. Oscar has seen her switch moods, and it isn't pretty. When Miranda is mad, usually because of some first-world problem, she is not above throwing things at the walls. And if one happens to be standing between the thing in her hand and the wall...

Miranda would play along for a while, especially since she knows him. They've been on and off for a year now, with Oscar sometimes disappearing for six weeks straight. It would be fun for her to have him all to herself, but then she'd get bored of playing house. Unlike Evie, she doesn't read, nor does she have any other hobbies that are home-bound. She'd quickly come to miss her superficial friends and endless conversations with her mother, enough to find a way to gouge his eyes out.

And Oscar doesn't think she'd be impressed if he killed someone in front of her.

When they're done and Miranda reaches for the pack of cigarettes on her nightstand, Oscar feels disgusted with himself. And her. Smoking is such an ugly habit. He doesn't linger. He picks up his clothes and goes to wash up and get dressed in Miranda's tiny bathroom.

"You're going to ghost me again," she says from the bed as he's getting ready to head out.

He adjusts his glasses and gives her a sheepish smile. "I should be at work now. I'll call you later."

She laughs and takes a long drag from her cigarette. "It's okay. I don't mind. I'm not in the right headspace for a relationship anyway."

She's not lying. Oscar knows she's been dating, but the second a guy tries to lock her down, she flees. What would she do if he locked her down? Literally, not figuratively.

"Thanks for the flowers," she says. "They're lovely."

He nods, and then just stands there for another minute. It feels weird to leave like this. For lack of a better idea, he walks over to the bed, leans in, and plants a kiss on her lips. She grins at him, and he has to pull away because the cigarette smoke is too heavy. He regrets the kiss, but between that and the flowers, maybe Miranda won't block his number before he's out of her building.

She did say she doesn't mind. But she minds. She's not lying about not wanting a relationship, but she's lying about not minding being treated this way.

If he locked her down, she'd make his life hell. She'd make him pay for every instance when she was disrespected. By him, by other men, and by her own insecure self. And then she'd kill him. She'd find a way.

That's why Evie is the right girl. Evie will never find a way. She doesn't want to.

Chapter Thirty-Two

Oscar

Evie has become so dull that Oscar has stopped spending his nights with her. She's cold, just lying there, in his arms, unmoving, barely breathing, wide awake until the early hours of the morning, while he struggles to ignore her and sleep. It doesn't feel like he's holding a woman, more like he's clinging to a husk. No matter what he feeds her, she doesn't put on weight, as if her body is refusing to assimilate the nutrients in the food. Maybe she's sick. Maybe he doesn't care anymore. It's not like she's trying, so why would he? He has his limits.

He's stopped cuffing her to the bed frame at night. They have dinner, she uses the bathroom, then he tucks her in and dims the lights. He thought she would be happy and grateful, but a few nights have passed, and she hasn't said a word about it. Not that she misses having him next to her, or that she's sleeping better now that she can occupy the whole bed.

Evie never thanks him for anything. And he does so many nice things for her.

Lately, he's stopped, though. He has no motivation. If there's no positive reinforcement, then there's no enthusiasm on his part. Once, he slept in, rushed to take a shower and leave the house, and forgot to bring her breakfast. He didn't look at the cameras until his own lunch break, and that was when he remembered. He cursed under his breath and ran home to make her lunch. Evie didn't say anything. They ate together, and she pretended like nothing had happened. He was relieved. Oscar didn't like feeling guilty, and when he'd realized he'd forgotten to feed her the most important meal of the day, that was exactly how he'd felt. Her lack of a reaction put him at ease.

It didn't last. Because why wouldn't she say anything? Did she care so little about what they were doing here, about what they had together, that it was the same to her if he came to see her in the morning or not?

This wasn't like that time when he left her without food for two days. That was to teach her a lesson, and it was different.

The next time he forgot to bring her breakfast, he felt less guilty. Another time, he forgot to bring her lunch and didn't check on her for a whole day.

"She's very thin," Nora says to him, snapping him out of his thoughts. She's cleaned the basement and now she's making lunch for both of them. "She looks weak and sickly." She shakes her head. "I hope she's okay."

He doesn't say anything. Nora is right, and it's all his fault that Evie is doing even worse than a week ago.

Skipping meals is causing her to lose the last of the muscle and fat deposits she has.

"Is she okay, Oscar?" Nora asks, stopping what she's doing to look into his eyes. She seems genuinely concerned.

He nods. "She's fine. We've hit a rough patch, that's all."

He can see that Nora wants to say something else but stops herself. She shakes her head and resumes peeling potatoes.

"It happens to the best of us," he says, feeling like he must reassure her that everything is fine and he's got it under control. "No relationship is perfect."

"Oh, don't I know it!"

"She's dealing with her own stuff, and I've decided to give her some space for a while."

Nora purses her lips. Oscar wonders what she's thinking, and if she's going to say it.

"Why don't you let me bring her food when you're busy?" There. She said it.

"Absolutely not." He takes his cup of coffee and moves away from the kitchen counter. It's Saturday, and he doesn't have work. "Evie is my responsibility. Don't worry about her. And don't worry about us. We'll figure it out."

"All right."

"Thank you for everything you're doing. It's more than enough." With that, he goes upstairs and locks himself in his home office.

This room used to be a bedroom, which he turned into a home office when he bought the house. It went through a few more changes when Oscar decided that Evie was the one, and now, one wall is completely covered in screens. On each screen – a different angle of the basement. In the beginning, he spent a lot of time in here, just staring at the screens, taking in every little detail – how Evie brushed her teeth, how she drank water in small, dainty sips, how her hips swayed as she paced the room, the way she sat on the floor of the library and looked through her books. Everything about her, no matter how regular or insignificant, he found fascinating.

Now he's sitting in front of the screens but isn't looking at them. He's on his laptop, working ahead on a project he started with his team a week ago. Thank God he loves his job, otherwise he doesn't know what he'd be doing while Nora is downstairs, cooking. Such a boring Saturday. He could go down to the basement and spend it with Evie, but he doesn't feel like it. He loses himself in his work for a while, then when Nora lets him know lunch is ready, he goes downstairs, thanks her, and brings it to Evie.

Her hair is like a bird's nest, and she's wearing the same clothes as yesterday. He sighs as he sets the table. He doesn't say anything. There's no point.

"This looks delicious," she says.

"Nora made it."

"I really like her cooking." A pause. "And yours."

"I took a cooking class a year ago."

"Wow. That's... unexpected."

She looks at him with wide eyes, but that's all she says. Of course she's not going to praise him further. She never does. Oscar knew she lacks people skills, but this is ridiculous. He's not in the mood to give her a lecture, though, so they have lunch in relative silence.

Sunday isn't any better, and by Monday morning, he's desperate to return to the office. Since Evie's been living with him, he's worked from home a lot, and from one or two cafés he likes. The office has been an afterthought, and he's glad to notice that he's missed it. Plus, this new project is giving his team headaches, though to him, it's very straightforward. Maybe he can help them better in person than over email and Zoom.

As per usual, when he gets to the office, everyone is happy to see him. He feels appreciated here, and as he's chatting with Kyle, one of the programmers in his team, and waving at Helen, the other manager, he wonders why he doesn't come here more often. This Evie business has disrupted his life completely. It's almost unhealthy. What's it called? Codependency? When one partner can't seem to breathe without the other? He can breathe without her just fine, as long as there's some distance between them and he doesn't check the cameras on his phone. She never does anything interesting, anyway.

"Who is that?" Oscar stops Kyle mid-sentence when he sees the new person at the window desk, next to Layla.

"Oh, the new hire."

That desk has been empty for months since Madison, one of Helen's girls, heavily pregnant with her second baby, decided to become a stay-at-home mom. For a while, they didn't try to hire anyone to replace her, thinking they were doing just fine, but then Helen decided to look for someone when Layla complained the workload was killing her, and slowly killing her marriage, too. Office drama. Not something Oscar is into.

"Sydney," Kyle adds.

Oscar nods, and his gaze travels from Sydney back to Kyle. "Sorry, you were saying?"

Kyle needs a moment to remember what he was talking about, and Oscar waits patiently, giving him all his attention. That's one thing he does with acute awareness when he interacts with people. What they don't know is that he can seem fully focused on them and get the gist of what they're saying enough to repeat keywords back to them, when in fact, he's thinking about something else. More often than not, someone else. Now he's listening to Kyle and nodding while his mind is stuck on Sydney. The new hire. There's something about her.

She's petite, with pixie hair and big eyes. Normally, he's not into short-haired women, but on Sydney, it looks good. Her smile is reserved when Layla addresses her, and her shoulders are slightly hunched as she's typing away on her laptop, like she's trying to make herself small. She's wearing an oversized shirt and straight jeans, with a classy leather belt to elevate the look. Nothing too flashy, but clearly thought-out. When she thinks no one is looking, the corners of her lips curl downward, and a crease appears between her brows. Someone less experienced than him will probably say she's focused. He knows that's not it.

"Anyway, Sydney is cool. A great addition to Helen's team," Kyle says.

That snaps Oscar out of his trance. He's been staring past Kyle's shoulder at Sydney, and Kyle eventually noticed. Not good. He used to be able to control himself. He used to be careful. What happened?

No need to dwell on it. He knows what happened. Evie.

"Not very social," Kyle continues. "Sometimes she has lunch alone in one of the conference rooms, and when she returns to her desk, her eyes are red. Weird, right? But other than that, she's cool."

"So, what you're telling me is that you have nothing better to do than follow the new hire around?" Oscar keeps his tone light, as if he's joking.

Kyle straightens his back. "I have plenty to do. It was just an observation."

Oscar shakes his head, and that makes Kyle feel inadequate enough that he clears his throat and announces he'll go back to work. Oscar slips into his closed office, not before glancing at Sydney one more time. She hasn't noticed him.

Chapter Thirty-Three

Oscar

Oscar doesn't approach Sydney the first time he sees her. The next day, he greets her when they cross paths, her coming out of the kitchen, him going in, and then he locks himself in his closed office and only gets out on lunch break, when he has to drive home to Evie. When he comes back, he has a team meeting in one of the conference rooms, then he's back in his office, pretending like he's already forgotten about the new hire. She's on Helen's team, anyway, so it's not like they have anything to talk about.

Two more days go by, and he observes her from a distance, but he does it so subtly that no one figures out he has an interest in her. It takes him all of five minutes to learn that she's almost completely wiped out her social media accounts after she broke up with a certain Finneas, who is now dating a certain Abigail. Both their accounts are filled with selfies of the two of them doing cool-looking stuff together – picnics in the park, a weekend in the mountains, a fancy night at the opera. Finneas has no photos of Sydney on his accounts, while Abigail has a few, which are no older than the beginning of this year. He digs deeper, and it's easy enough to conclude that Sydney and Abigail used to be friends. Best friends, maybe.

No wonder Sydney prefers to have lunch alone. With such a heavy past, it makes sense she'd want to avoid Layla and her clique. Helen's team has made gossiping into an art. Oscar doesn't allow it as much on his team, though he knows they all indulge when he's not around. He also understands the red-rimmed eyes when Sydney emerges from the bathroom, though some days are better than others.

She doesn't use her social media at all, it seems, never shares anything or likes anyone's posts. On Instagram, he can't follow her because her account is set to private, and even though he makes a new account that is a perfect copy of one of her friends' accounts, he still can't get through. He could hack his way into her account, but he doesn't think he'll find anything interesting in there, so he doesn't bother. She's more interesting in real life than on social media. He has a feeling she's blocked Finneas and Abigail everywhere, or they blocked her, because there seems to be no connection between them anymore. Aside from those old pictures on Abigail's Facebook.

On Friday, as he brings Evie her breakfast and then rushes out of the house, he decides it's time to approach Sydney. He feels like he knows enough about her, even though, normally, he would spend much more time watching her. The fact that they work in the same office makes things easy. The day before, he took the time to follow her home, and it saddened him to see where she lives. Not the best neighborhood, and the façade of her apartment building is... patchy, to say the least. He doubts it looks better on the inside.

He doesn't know much about this Finneas guy she used to date, but there's one thing he knows for sure: he wasn't, and most likely still isn't, a provider. Abigail made a mistake. She should've chosen her friend. Then again, Sydney wouldn't have gotten a job at Oscar's company, and Oscar wouldn't have met her. He'll have to remind himself that even if Sydney's past sucks, it was for the best. It delivered her to him.

He pays attention to when she's going to the kitchen for another cup of coffee. She had one when she came to the office, but he didn't follow her then. He casually follows her now, and they meet by the coffee maker.

"Sydney, right?"

"Um, yes. Hi. You must be Oscar."

They don't shake hands, just nod at each other. If she didn't offer, he's not going to, even though he wonders what her tiny hand would feel like in his. He's been assessing her every gesture and reaction. From the way she sits at her desk, huddled close to the window, he knows that she likes her personal space to be personal. They stand a few feet from each other. The coffee maker whirrs and sputters. It's an old one, but it does the job. The coffee isn't great, but it's free and within reach. Oscar has come to appreciate it.

"Nice to finally meet you," he says.

"Yeah. I've seen you around, I mean."

"Yes. Sorry about that. I should've introduced myself sooner, but I haven't been in the office in a while, and I had a lot of catching up to do."

She nods.

He's lying. He's ahead, like he's always been. But he wants her to know that he's been absorbed by other things.

"So, do you like it here?" he asks.

"Oh, yes. Everyone is so welcoming and lovely."

He doesn't ask her where she worked before because he knows. A much bigger company, and for a better salary. Considering her experience, she shouldn't be here, but the fact that her ex works there forced her to quit at a very bad time. The job market is a disaster, and he knows Sydney is here only because she couldn't find anything else.

Considering his experience, he shouldn't be here either. It's different in his case. As a manager, he's paid better, but that's not why he stays. His salary isn't enough to cover his expenses, especially not now that he has Evie. What he loves about this job is that he can work from anywhere, and no one asks him why he only drops by the office once or twice a week, as long as he's on top of his tasks and meetings. This week, he's been in every single day.

The coffee is done, and he pours two cups. He gives her one.

"Well, have a great day!"

"You too," she says. "See you around."

"For sure."

Simple. Subtle. She has no idea he basically knows everything about her. It helps that he can see her desk from his office. Later, when everyone takes their lunch break, Layla leans in and asks Sydney something. Oscar guesses she's inviting her to have lunch with her and a few other people. Sydney smiles and shakes her head.

Oscar waits until he sees Sydney walk to the kitchen, and then out, with a cardboard box in her hand. She goes into one of the conference rooms, and Oscar loses sight of her. He waits patiently for another ten minutes.

Today, Evie will have to go without lunch.

He brought his with him and put it in the fridge, and now he gets up and goes to retrieve it. Seemingly unintentionally, he walks by the conference room. The door is ajar, and Oscar can't see Sydney, but he can hear her. She's sobbing silently.

He knocks on the door, and she stops. She doesn't say anything, and he peeks his head in from behind the door, as if he's not sure he's allowed to come in. He catches her dabbing at her eyes with a paper tissue. When she sees him, she flashes him a feeble smile.

"I'm sorry. This is so embarrassing. I don't know what came over me. I'm having a hard day, I guess."

"Helen?" he asks, furrowing his brows. He walks in but remains by the door, lunch box in hand.

"God, no. She's great!"

"Layla?"

"No, never."

She crumples up the tissue, and he wonders if he'll have to go through all the people in the office before she gives him information on her own.

"It's not about work or the people at work," she says. "Sorry, silly me. Please sit down."

"I don't want to intrude–"

"You're not."

He sits down in front of her and unpacks his lunch – a generous ham sandwich, cut in two. Sydney is having a salad. Or trying to. She's barely eaten half of it. One glance is enough for Oscar to assess that even if she ate all of it, it wouldn't be enough calories.

"Do you want to talk about it?" he asks gently.

"No. Yes? I don't know."

He smiles. "What I can promise is that it'll stay between us. I'm not a fan of the gossiping that happens around here."

"I know, right? Me neither."

She feels better already. He can tell by the way her eyes light up when she looks at him.

"There isn't much to tell." She starts poking at her salad, her eyes downcast and brows knit together. "I was engaged to this guy up until recently, he cheated on me with my best friend, and now it's over. Not just the relationship, but my life as I knew it. I'm not crying because of him, really. Please don't think that. It would be pathetic. I guess I'm crying because... so many things have changed, and not for the better."

"What has changed?"

"Well, for one, I had to move into this tiny apartment, and last night, my oven stopped working. It didn't work great before. It took ages to heat up. And now it's dead."

"I'm thinking the landlord should take care of that?"

"Yeah. He said it's new, so it's my fault. I must be using it wrong."

Oscar chuckles. "How can you use an oven wrong?"

"Beats me. But that's what he said, and I don't have the energy to argue with him. Anyway, it's ridiculous." She chuckles, albeit forcefully. "First-world problems, right? Who cries because of a stupid oven?"

"I don't think you're crying because of the oven. You said it yourself. It's all the sudden changes, and they're overwhelming."

She catches her lower lip between her teeth and stares at him. Her chin trembles slightly, but she takes a deep breath and fights the tears. She's not going to cry in front of him. It would be great if she did, but she's not going to.

"Yeah. I got used to Finneas fixing everything around the house when we lived together. Now I'm on my own, and I'm at a bit of a loss. But I'll be fine."

"Finneas?" He laughs, then shakes his head and tries to look serious. He fails. "I'm sorry. But... Finneas?"

"An unusual name, I know." She's smiling now, which means she's not bothered by him making fun of her ex's name.

"Unusual?" He laughs a bit louder.

"I'm sure it means something fancy in some ancient language."

"Well, that saves it."

They laugh together. Oscar notices how Sydney relaxes. She occupies more space now, with both her elbows on the table as she covers her face with her hands, then looks at him through her fingers. Her cheeks are flushed, and her bright eyes are dry.

"And you will be fine," he says. "You're right about that."

She puts on a serious face. "How do you know that?"

"You look like the kind of person who finds her way, no matter what."

"I hope you're right."

"I can take a look at your oven, if you want. I'm no expert, like Finneas, but it's worth a shot."

Sydney laughs. "I'll think about it. Thank you for offering."

Oscar shrugs and takes a bite of his sandwich. The fact that she hasn't immediately invited him over to fix her oven tells him she's not a type two. She's not easy, and he likes that. He likes it a little too much.

She resumes eating her salad, and they make small talk for the rest of the lunch break. She tells him about other inconveniences she's had to deal with since the breakup, but she downplays each and every one of them. The second she realizes she's complaining about something, she downplays it and changes the subject. Oscar says the right things at the right moments, and by the time the others are returning to work, Sydney is censoring herself less. They're making progress. She trusts him. In a few days, he's certain she'll ask him to fix her oven.

Later, he sits at his desk and brings up the cameras in the basement. Evie is in the library, sunk into the beanbag, reading and eating the last snacks in her snack basket. He'll have to stop by the supermarket and buy her more. She's so thin, and he's made her skip lunch. He feels bad now. He'll make sure she gets a hefty dinner.

He looks over at Sydney. She looks up from her laptop, and their eyes meet for a second. It's as if they're communicating telepathically. Oscar knows there's no such thing, and he interprets her stolen glances as a sign that she's into him. Why wouldn't she be? He's friendly, likable, a great listener, and helpful, if she'll let him.

What does this mean for Evie? If Oscar likes Sydney, and Sydney likes Oscar...

His gaze returns to the cameras. He can't give up on Evie so soon. He'll give her another chance.

Chapter Thirty-Four

The One

This past week, Oscar has changed our routine so many times that we don't have one anymore. I live in a constant state of anxiety. I don't know if he'll cuff me to the bed at night and wrap himself around me, or if he'll let me sleep alone, my hands free, the bed all to myself.

I don't know if he'll bring me breakfast in the morning or let me fast until lunch. I don't know if I'll have a full home-cooked meal made by Nora for lunch – soup, second course and dessert – with him chattering away as we eat together, or if I'll have stale Chinese takeaway dropped in haste. I don't know if I'll have dinner.

Two evenings in a row, I don't, and I resort to putting on his favorite silk dress with the dipping cleavage and the thin straps that hang off my bony shoulders like I'm a coat hanger and not a living, breathing human. That earns me dinner, words of praise, and a night with him glued to my back, his breath on my nape as I stare at the wall and imagine I'm outside, alone in an open field, under the night sky, counting stars.

I miss breathing fresh air. I miss the sun, the moon, the clouds. I miss the world. I miss feeling the rain on my skin. When Oscar is gone for hours and I'm tired of staring at pages filled with twisted romance games that I refuse to read, I close my eyes, lean back in the beanbag, and imagine I'm outside. Sometimes I'm in the city, surrounded by traffic and frantic people trying to get to places. They bump into me, their arms brush mine, and I welcome it. A siren wails in the distance, my lungs drag in the smell of car exhaust fumes mixed with people's expensive perfumes and the scent of vanilla and burned sugar from a bakery nearby.

Other times, I'm in the park. The sun warms my face, a mellow breeze plays in my hair. It smells of cut grass and hotdogs from the cart I always pass by, my nose scrunched up. I don't like hotdogs. I used to love them when I was little, after I discovered them at a local fair, then kept asking my mom to make them at home. She refused, saying they were processed, cheap food that had no place in a healthy diet. One day, after I'd been pestering her for a week, she went to visit a friend. My dad took me to the grocery store, where he filled the shopping basket with two packs of uncooked hotdogs, bread, ketchup, mustard, and mayonnaise, and that was the first and only time I allowed myself to believe that he loved me. We returned home, where he boiled them, dumped them on a plate, squirted equal parts of the three sauces all over, and cut thick slices of bread on the side. He watched me as I dug in, arms crossed over his chest and a grin on his lips as I wolfed down one hotdog, two, three, four, five, until I declared I was stuffed.

"You better finish them before your mother gets home," he said.

"I can't. If I take one more bite–"

"What?"

"You know what." I rubbed my bulging belly.

He pursed his lips, and as he fixed me with his gaze, pushed the plate towards me. There were three more hotdogs left. He squirted dollops of mayonnaise on them.

"Finish your food, Eveline."

I was about to protest, but his gaze hardened. I stared at the hotdogs, already feeling sick.

"I went through all this trouble for you," he said. "Are you going to be ungrateful?"

"N-no," I stammered.

I ate the remaining hotdogs, struggling to keep them down. My father poured soda pop into a glass, which I also felt like I couldn't refuse. I drank half of it before running to the bathroom. I didn't make it in time. The living room carpet took the brunt of it. My father laughed thunderously, grabbed a beer from the fridge and went out on the porch to read his paper. When my mother came home, she found me on all fours, crying, trying to clean the carpet, making it all worse. I was only seven. She started yelling, then crying, then throwing things at my father. The whole thing amused him to no end.

"She won't be asking for hotdogs anytime soon, will she?" he said.

He was right. I didn't touch them ever again.

Now, lying in the library, surrounded by books about innocent women falling in love with villains who share too many traits with my father, I imagine myself walking through the park, stopping in front of the hotdog cart and ordering one. My stomach growls painfully. Oscar fed me breakfast before taking off in the morning, but lunchtime came and went, dinnertime too, and he hasn't returned. I'm hungry and sleepy. If I put on his favorite dress and the red-soled shoes, will he bring me food? Maybe.

Three meals a day aren't guaranteed anymore. He promised to take care of me, provide for me, keep me fed and comfortable. Because I'm worth it.

I'm worth lies and gaslighting. My father knew it. Oscar knows it. My choice of books finally makes sense. This is what happens when you don't go to therapy and wait for life to smack you in the face with the breakthrough that everyone eventually has – it's you, you are the problem.

It's me, and what I'm living now is a consequence of my unresolved, unhealed issues.

I drag myself to the bathroom, brush my teeth and my hair, then walk like a zombie to the bed. I plop down, face in the pillow, so I can cry into it silently. Oscar doesn't like it when I cry. He prefers me happy and pleasant, though he knows it's fake. He never tells me I'm trying too hard because I'm not.

I wake up blinded by the overhead lights. I rolled onto my back during the night, and now I'm covering my eyes with my arm, cringing at the sharp pain under my eyelids. Oscar dims the lights when night falls and turns them on to the max in the morning, like he's God, ordering the sun to rise and set, and the moon to wax and wane. This tells me he's paying attention, watching, controlling my environment from behind the cameras. I get up and run to the bathroom. When he comes in with breakfast, he needs to find me clean and dressed, or he'll punish me further.

As I'm fixing my brows and applying mascara, a thought strikes me. What if he doesn't come? He's forgotten about me before. It was intentional, as punishment for Rita, and for some reason, now that I think back to it, what happened then scares me less than the idea that one of these days he'll forget me unintentionally. I'll slip his mind, and before he remembers he has a girl locked up in his basement, I'll be dead.

No, I can't think like this. I just saw him yesterday morning. It's been a day, not a week. But time flows differently here. Slowly. It stretches and drags, irrelevant since I have nowhere to be and nothing to do. The days feel longer than they are, especially when I'm so hungry that I can't think straight. I finished the snacks in the snack basket. Another promise Oscar made and then proceeded to ignore more than fulfill – that he'd keep my snack basket full.

I hear the metal door groaning and whirring, and my heart slams against my rib cage. I slip out of my pajamas and jump into a clean dress. The skirt is pleated, and the bodice would've been tight on someone with more meat on her bones. I slip back into the bedroom, but my fake smile falters when I see Oscar bringing in a box of books.

"Good morning, sleepy head!" He sounds cheerful.

He gives my outfit an approving nod, and I force myself to look curious, not disappointed. I press a hand to my rumbling, aching stomach.

"Come see what I got you. Fresh new releases. And as usual, just for you, books that aren't even in print yet."

He places the box on the table, and I go check it out. There's still a chance I may get breakfast. If I don't upset him, that is.

"Thank you." I start taking the books out, touching their covers gingerly and reading the blurbs on the back. "This is the last book in the Impossible Redemption trilogy. I've been looking forward to it." I open it and read the first paragraph.

He beams at me. "Tell me I'm not the best husband in the world."

I swallow hard. There's a bitter taste in my mouth, and it's not just because I'm starving.

"Well, future husband," he amends, adjusting his black-framed glasses.

"You are." I sit down and continue reading the first page. One, I'm too tired to stand, and two, I know it pleases him when I read the books he goes to such great lengths to get me. If I do everything right, every little gesture, if I say the right thing at the right time...

"Nora is making eggs and bacon," he says. "I'll go bring them."

Relief floods my body. The metal door whirrs open, closed, then open and closed again when Oscar returns with the food. It smells so divine that my mouth waters. He pushes the box of books to the side and places the tray in front of me. As usual, he only has a cup of black coffee. I dig in while holding the book in the other hand.

"Evie, put the book down," he says. "Eat like a lady."

"Of course," I say, mouth full. "Sorry."

He frowns. He doesn't approve of my talking with my mouth full either. His rules are endless and random.

"So, Nora is here," he says. "She'll come in and clean."

I nod. Thank God for her! I think Oscar has grown tired of cooking for me. I have nothing against takeaway, but he seems bored of getting that for me, too.

"I've been thinking," he goes on. "You've behaved very well lately. I'm proud of you, Evie. How about this time you don't stay in bed while Nora is here?"

I choke on a piece of bacon, cough, and chase it down with a gulp of orange juice.

"I don't understand," I say. "That would mean–"

He shrugs. "I trust you."

It means he won't cuff me to the bed frame. Will he leave the door open, like last time? He has to. My heart is beating so chaotically that I'm afraid I'll be sick from too much excitement. He has to leave the door open, otherwise what will Nora think? A keypad is a keypad. But a metal door that slides into and out of the wall? There's no way in hell anyone would think that's normal.

He reaches over and places his hand on mine. He squeezes my fingers to get my attention and make it a point that this is very, very serious.

"I trust you, Evie. You know what to say. You know how to behave. You won't put her in danger, will you? You like her, and she likes you. I think she considers you a friend. She's been cooking for us, coming over to clean the house, since you can't."

I can't because the basement is the only part of the house I've ever seen. It makes sense that Oscar also needs the rest of it cleaned. I realize that Nora might be here all the time. Well, not all the time, but often. Does Oscar bring other people, too? Friends? Family? Does he have a family? I'm here, in this pink and gold prison, and who knows who's upstairs at any given time?

"Are you ready for this?" he asks. The gravity in his voice makes this feel momentous. "I think you are. But I need to hear it from you."

"I am."

He smiles. "Finish your breakfast." Then gets up and carries the box into the library, leaving the last book in the Impossible Redemption trilogy where it is, by my elbow.

I shovel food into my mouth as fast as I can, barely chewing. Contradictory feelings churn within my body – hope in my chest, anxiety in my belly, dread in the back of my throat, choking me. Oscar trusts me, or so he says, but I can't trust him. He will be upstairs, as usual, his eyes glued to the cameras, his ears trained on the speakers. Nonetheless, this feels like an opportunity. To what? Whisper something to Nora as I help her clean? Get a sense of what's beyond the metal door? Maybe I can get close enough to look. He will never let me slip out, but maybe I can take a peek.

I don't know. I don't know. I finish the glass of orange juice and notice that my hands are shaking. I shove them between my knees and smile up at Oscar as he clears the table.

"Pace yourself," he says, and I don't know what he means, but then he tips his chin towards the book.

"Oh, I will."

He leaves, and I nervously await his return. With Nora. The door whirrs open, and he steps in first, carrying the vacuum cleaner. I grab the book quickly and pretend like I'm reading. It takes Nora one minute to appear. Her arms are loaded with cleaning supplies.

"Mrs. Miles, so good to see you!"

I lift my eyes from the page. "Please, it's Evie. Good to see you too, Nora."

"How are you feeling?" Concern flashes over her features as her eyes scan me from head to toe. "You've lost weight." She glances at Oscar, but he's focused on his phone.

"I've always been small," I say. "I mean, yes, I've lost a few pounds, but it's nothing serious. I'm feeling better, actually."

"Much better," Oscar says, shoving his phone into his pocket. "She's back on her feet." He looks at me, gives me a nod, then turns to Nora. "Right. I'll leave you to it. You know where to find me if you need anything." He walks to the door but stops before slipping out. "I'll close the door if you don't mind. I have a friend crashing upstairs. Nora, you've seen him. It's not even noon, and he's had a few." He chuckles awkwardly as he studies my face. "Ben, you know him, Evie. His girlfriend kicked him out again, and I told him he can crash on the couch until they get things sorted."

What is he talking about? Who's Ben? He's never mentioned him before. I look at Nora. She's shaking her head, as if to say that, yes, she's seen the state this Ben guy is in, and it's such a sad business that his girlfriend kicked him out.

"I don't want him barging in here, bothering you," he says. "He's a good guy, but he's unpredictable when he's like this." He looks at Nora. "The last thing my wife needs is to listen to Ben's drama. When he starts, I swear, he can go on forever." He laughs.

"You don't have to explain anything to me, Mr. Miles," Nora says. She's started sorting her cleaning supplies, putting aside the ones for the bathroom.

"Okay, then. If you need anything..." He winks at me and steps out. He punches in the code, and the door starts closing.

Nora swirls around at the strange sound the door makes. Her eyes grow round and wide at the sight of it.

I jump to my feet and go to her side. Before I reach out to touch her arm, she turns to me and takes a step back, searching my face for answers. For something that makes sense.

I can't believe Oscar just did that. We're trapped in here together, and I can tell her everything now. I can...

I won't.

Oscar made it clear. So clear. I didn't see it earlier, but I see it now. I understand.

He said to me: "You know what to say. You know how to behave. You won't put her in danger, will you?"

This is a test.

Chapter Thirty-Five

The One

"Safe room," I blurt out. "We were supposed to turn the basement into a safe room but changed our mind."

Nora blinks, her eyebrows still raised, but her shoulders relax somewhat. I know I must convince her.

"It was my idea. I... I saw that movie with Jodie Foster. Do you know it? Panic Room. For days, I couldn't stop thinking about it. It's a safe neighborhood, but you never know."

"I know the movie," she says.

"Right. Well, I pestered Oscar until he relented. He said a panic room is too hard to build and unnecessary, but we can do a safe room. There was plumbing already, but no bathroom, so we started with that. The library was supposed to be a storage room. But the impression the movie made on me wore off after a while, and I fell in love with the space. I loved coming down here, where it's so quiet. Oscar was relieved when I changed my mind." I laugh, hoping it sounds genuine. "The door and the keypad were installed already, so we kept them."

Nora lets out a long breath and nods. This is a good sign. She eyes the door and rubs her palms on her apron.

"But you know the code, right?"

Her question makes me feel lightheaded. I take a step back, then another, feeling my knees turn to jelly. I reach the bed and lower myself on the edge.

Nora notices and hurries to my side. "Are you okay, Evie? You've turned pale all of a sudden."

I touch my forehead with trembling fingers. "I'm always pale. I'm okay. A little thirsty."

She looks around, grabs the plastic cup that's on my nightstand, frowns at it when she sees it's empty, then goes to the bathroom to fill it from the tap. She's back in seconds.

"Here."

"Thank you." I take two sips and feel a little more grounded. "Of course I know the code," I say.

She looks at me like she doesn't know what I'm talking about, then remembers she asked me and smiles.

"Oh, good," she says. "I mean, of course you do. I don't know why I asked. Don't mind me. What do I know about safe rooms?" She laughs, and I laugh with her. The atmosphere is relaxed. "Well, better get to work."

For a moment, I thought she was going to ask me to punch in the code, prove to her that I know it. She's a kind, understanding lady. She probably thinks I'm completely insane. Scared of my own shadow, riddled with phobias. I don't blame her if that's what she believes. If I must act crazy to keep her safe from Oscar, I'll gladly do it.

Nora starts with the bathroom. I wonder if I should leave her to it and lie down or read my book. I'm sick of lying down, and I don't want to read that despicable book. What I want is to make conversation – small talk, even if I'm bad at it. I want to be around her – another human being – and feel normal for a change. I get up and join her in the bathroom, where she's scrubbing the sink. I sit on the edge of the tub.

"Can I help?" I ask.

"Oh, no. Out of the question." She shakes her head emphatically. "One, this is my job that I'm being paid to do, and two, you're too weak. Seriously, Evie. Are you sure you're okay? Maybe we should call your husband, see what he thinks."

"No!" It comes out loud and shrill. "No," I say again, willing my voice to drop down, calm and even. "He's busy. Working. And then there's Ben. Plus, I'm feeling better."

Nora shakes her head and sprays the mirror with a solution that smells like oranges. "You're so lucky to have him," she says.

"Yes."

"He's patient," she continues, "And kind."

My jaw clenches imperceptibly. "Yes. He's very understanding of my peculiarities."

"A true provider. They're hard to come by, I must tell you. Take it from an old woman."

"You're not that old." I badly want to steer the conversation in a different direction, but I don't know how.

"Really? The gray hair doesn't give it away?"

"I have plenty of gray hair." I touch my roots. They're starting to show a little. I dye my hair caramel blonde. That's what's written on the box. I do it myself, at home, to save money.

"Eh. I stopped dyeing my hair so long ago. I don't regret it. An old woman like me... Who do I have to impress?"

"It's not about doing it for someone else."

"If I had a husband, maybe. But he left when our baby was barely six months old. Can you imagine? This is why I'm saying it's so hard to come by a true provider, and you're lucky you and Oscar found each other. You're both lucky."

"I'm sorry. What happened?"

She waves her hand, and I think she doesn't want to tell me, that it's too hard for her to talk about it, but it turns out she just needs me out of the way so she can scrub the bathtub.

"I should've known," she continues. "Should've never married him, and when things started going bad between us, should've never thought that a baby was going to save us. But I was young. Stupid. Now I know that a baby can't save a broken relationship. It can only strengthen a relationship that's already strong."

She falls silent, then uses the shower head to rinse the tub. The forceful water spray against acrylic fills the silence, and I wrap my arms around myself. I'm grateful she's shared this bit of her life with me, and I hate it that she thinks Oscar and me are perfect together. I want her to know that my life is not a fairy tale. Or maybe it is, seeing how the original fairy tales were dark and gruesome, with evil mothers – yes, mothers, not stepmothers – ogres, devils, and chopped off toes.

"I guess my mom thought the same when she had me," I say. Honestly, I don't know what my mom thought. Most likely, I was an accident. "When she gave my father the news that she was pregnant, they had a fight. He packed up his things and left. He was gone for days."

Nora straightens her back and looks at me with deep interest. Her blue eyes darken slightly, and it seems a shadow has fallen over her face. I blink. Surely, the overhead lights are playing tricks on me.

"When he returned, they mended things and decided to stay together. From what I heard, my grandpa – Mom's dad – found him and talked to him, convinced him to not get a divorce. Thinking about this now, at twenty-six, maybe he shouldn't have interfered. My dad resented my mom for having me, basically shoving me down his throat so he would stay with her, and resented me from the day I was born. Anyway, it doesn't matter. When I left for college, I made sure to put distance between us."

Nora swallows heavily, looks at her rubber-gloved hands, then around the bathroom to see if she's missed anything.

"Those were different times," she says. "Divorce was something shameful. I know because I never heard the end of it from both my parents and my in-laws. I put distance between us too, but much later. When my ex left, I had nothing. No job, no help from family because they thought it was all my fault, and a baby to raise on top of everything. I didn't think I'd pull through."

She fills a bucket with water, preparing to mop the floor, and I take the hint and step out of the bathroom. I lean against the doorframe, feeling silly for loitering like this when I'm a perfectly healthy woman, capable of cleaning after myself.

"I'm ashamed to say that I had a moment, only a moment," she goes on, her voice strained, "When I thought my baby would be better off without me."

A knot forms in my chest. She's silent again as she cleans the floor tiles, the cotton mop gliding over, leaving them damp and shiny. All the cleaning solutions she's using smell of oranges and lemon zest.

"I couldn't do it," she says as she rinses the mop, wrings it, and straightens her back. There's a sharp crack. "And I never thought about it again, no matter how hard things got." She looks at me and smiles. "I'm sorry about your father. You and your mother deserved better, just like me." She moves towards the library. "I'll organize these books while the floor dries."

I follow her into the room, spotting the new books Oscar has randomly dumped on the floor. I pick two up and carry them to the piles I've pushed against one of the walls. The room is claustrophobic with all these paperbacks, and in an attempt to make it more breathable, I've stacked the books as high as I could without them toppling and tried to occupy a single wall with them. The library is small, maybe thirty square feet, and the more books Oscar brings, the more it seems to shrink.

"Do you have a system?" Nora asks.

"Um... I tried to organize them alphabetically, but it got too complicated. So, no?"

Her gaze falls to the empty snack basket. "Uh-oh. I need to revisit the grocery list. Can't believe Mr. Miles forgot to tell me to get snacks for you. Which are your favorite?"

I shrug. "Milk chocolate, pretzels, Oreo cookies, kettle chips... Whatever you can get, I'm happy."

She nods and removes her rubber gloves. "Better start dusting these books."

"I can do it."

"Are you sure? You're still looking quite pale. I don't mind if you want to lie down for a bit."

I grit my teeth. I look pale because I haven't seen the sun in weeks. I motion for her to pass me a clean, dry cloth.

"I'm sure. A little activity will make me feel better."

She smiles. "Or you're possessive of your books, which I totally get and respect."

I blush slightly. If only she knew the one thing I dream of doing with these books is build a bonfire and burn them.

"I'll get the vacuum cleaner," she says.

She returns to the bedroom as I start running the cloth over the paperbacks at the top of the piles. I'm not going to dust them all, and the new ones are new, so I'm not going to wipe them at all. Even for someone who has all the time in the world, it would be a waste of time.

Two minutes pass, and Nora isn't back with the vacuum cleaner. A jolt of fear zaps through my body. I drop the paperback I'm holding and run into the bedroom. Nora has her back to me; she's facing the bed. My heart hammers in my chest and my throat feels dry.

The chain and the handcuffs are tucked underneath the mattress. Oscar didn't say anything about the sheets, and I haven't either.

"I will change them," I choke out.

"Sorry?" She turns around, and I see she was only typing on her phone.

"The sheets."

"Oh, of course. I remember. You like the bed made a certain way." She chuckles and shakes her head. "Oh, Evie! You're the quirkiest person I know."

I grimace.

"I mean it in a good way," she adds quickly. "Don't think that I'm judging. I have my own quirks. Like, let's see... Oh! I collect snow globes. I love them. I got my first one as a gift when I was a teen, and I was hooked. You should see my collection. I'm proud of it, but people have told me it's a weird hobby."

Nora tucks the phone in the pocket of her apron, which is so large that I didn't notice there was anything in it. And then it strikes me. She has a phone.

"I was just adding snacks to the grocery list," she says as she grabs the vacuum cleaner. "Sad to say, but at my age, I forget things."

She has a phone.

She walks past me into the library.

She has a phone, and I can't ask her to use it because Oscar is glued to the cameras and the speakers. The door wasn't the only test.

Chapter Thirty-Six

The One

Oscar is pleased with my performance. He brings me lunch made by Nora, dinner made by Nora, and fills the basket in the library with snacks bought by Nora. It seems all is well again. At dinner, he's cheerful and talkative, and I'm certain he will want to sleep next to me tonight. Usually, when he's in a good mood, that's the consequence I need to suffer.

However, as he tucks me in bed, he kisses me on the forehead and boops my nose playfully. The cuffs remain tucked under the mattress.

"Sleep well. I mean it. You had a full day today, and tomorrow won't be any different."

My heart flutters in my chest, a caged animal screeching, *"Enough! I've had enough! Stop torturing me!"*

At my perplexed expression, he laughs. "I have a surprise for you. A reward for being such a good, well-behaved wife. But I won't say another word. Sleep now."

He runs the tips of his fingers down my forehead and my eyelids, and I close my eyes to humor him. He dims the lights and leaves the basement, the door whirring ominously behind him.

Him telling me he has a surprise for me is the perfect way to ensure I will not be able to sleep. I toss and turn until the early hours of the morning, worrying and wondering, the word "reward" taking dark connotations in my mind. Oscar can take a positive thing and turn it into an instrument of torture. What will it be this time?

The sharp lights wake me, and for a few seconds, I don't know where I am. I groan and turn on my side, bury my head in the pillow. It smells unfamiliar. Not like the detergent I use. My eyes snap open, and it all comes back to me.

I spring up and out of the bed, like a coil that's been wound up too tight. I'm in my kidnapper's basement, and today is a special day. I know he wants me clean and nicely dressed to receive my surprise, and as much as I hate prettying myself up for him, I have to do it, or whatever terrible thing he's prepared for me today will be dialed up to horrible if he feels he must punish me.

He shows up with breakfast just as I step out of the bathroom in a baby blue dress, sheer tights, and black ballet flats.

"Good morning, sunshine!"

What sunshine? "Good morning," I say, smiling.

He places the food on the table, and it doesn't escape me that he hasn't brought his usual cup of coffee.

He looks at my dress, eyebrows raised. "Great choice! Do a twirl for me?"

I bite my tongue – not too hard, the idea is to stop myself from saying something I'll regret, not draw blood – and do as he asks. The skirt lifts slightly as I twirl a few times.

He beams at me. "You're beautiful, Evie."

"Thank you."

I stop, feeling dizzy. I'm aware of his gaze on me, and I keep my eyes downcast. Whatever I do, I must be sure none of it can be interpreted as an invitation.

"Okay, eat up. I'll go grab my coffee and your surprise. Are you excited?"

"I am." And I bite my tongue a little harder. The pain keeps me grounded.

He rushes out of the room, his steps bouncy and energetic, and I sit down at the table and grab onto the edges because I feel like I'm about to take off. I feel flighty; like I'm about to float off the ground if I don't hold on to the furniture that's bolted to the floor.

When I regain some of my composure, I take the plastic knife and fork and cut a bit of egg. It tastes and feels like cardboard on my tongue, but I force myself to chew and swallow. I do it again and again, until I've eaten half of what's on my plate.

The metal door whirrs open, and I freeze. *"Please, God, let it be an actual surprise,"* I think. *"A good surprise. Harmless, and wholesome, and nice. Let it be a nice surprise, please."* I feel like crying. I'm so exhausted by

Oscar's tricks and tests that I'm about to burst into tears at the most inopportune moment.

He's talking to someone. "Yes, this is a special door. Wait until you see the special place it hides. Do you like pink? Is pink your favorite color?" He's cooing.

What?

I'm on high alert.

I hear a gurgle. A child's laugh.

I think I'm going to be sick.

The door opens fully, and Oscar steps in. In his left hand, he's holding a thermos, and in his right arm... a toddler. A little girl. She has dark hair that curls around her tiny ears, big brown eyes, and she's wearing a pink dress with rainbows on the collar and the hem of her sleeves and skirt. She can't be older than one. Her mouth forms an "o" as she takes in the pink bedroom and the gold sheets that cover the bed. When she sees me, she turns into Oscar's arms and hides her face in his neck.

He laughs. "Don't be shy. This is my wife, Evie."

He leaves the door open, which doesn't escape me. It doesn't matter. I can't move. My body has merged with the chair.

Oscar brings the girl closer, places his thermos on the table, and tries to make her look at me.

"Say hi to Evie. She'll play with you today, while I work." Then he looks at me. "This is Bobbi. Say hi to Bobbi."

He's talking to me like I'm a toddler, too.

"Hi, Bobbi. Nice to meet you." I do my absolute best to give her a genuine smile. There's no reason for her to be as terrified as I am.

"Will you take her?" he asks. "Bobbi, will you go to Evie for a minute? I forgot my laptop upstairs."

I reach out. After a moment of studying my face, Bobbi reaches out to me, and I take her into my arms. I hold her in my lap, feeling her warm, little body against my hollow chest. She's plump and soft, and I'm like a skeleton – all sharp bones that poke through my skin and clothes. She fusses and grabs the edges of the table with her tiny hands.

"Okay," I say. "You're okay."

She reaches for the last pieces of bacon on my plate, and I have no clue if bacon is good for babies her age. My mind draws a blank. She grabs the bacon and stuffs it in her mouth, then spits it out, looking at it like she's not sure whether she likes it or not.

I don't know what to do.

I'm in a state of panic. Frozen. My breathing is shallow. I inhale and exhale in spurts. I'm close to hyperventilating. Where is Oscar? Where is–

He left the door open.

On instinct, I get up, the movement so abrupt that poor Bobbi's knees get knocked against the underside of the table. She wails, looking up at me like she doesn't understand what just happened and why she's in pain, and I stare at her round face, greasy with bacon, and it dawns on me... I'm responsible for this child.

Oscar stole her. Oh my God, he kidnapped her and brought her to me.

I start pacing the room, cooing to her and bouncing her in my arms, trying to calm her down.

"Shh... it's okay. I'm sorry, baby. I'm so sorry."

She sniffles and calms down somewhat. I grab two napkins from the box on my nightstand and clean the grease, the tears, and the snot.

"It's okay... It's okay..." It's more for myself than for her.

She still has bacon clasped in her hand. The second I manage to get her relatively clean, she starts munching on it again. She's back to being happy, at least. I keep bouncing her as my gaze returns to the open door.

On the other side, the lights are dim. I can see a set of wooden stairs that lead to the ground floor. The banister is made of wood, and it shines, like it's just been polished. A door creaks open at the end of the stairs. I can't see it, but I hear it. And then I hear Oscar's footsteps as he descends.

It's too late.

Did I really have a chance? Could I have held Bobbi tightly and run with her? No. I know the answer is no. Oscar would've caught us upstairs, and who knows what sort of punishment he would've deemed appropriate? At this point, I don't care about my own life anymore. I don't have a life. And I think he knows it because he always threatens someone else's life to control me. Nora, and now this child.

I knew he was sick. Now I know he's incurable. There will be no redemption for him; not here, and not in the afterlife. If he believes in such a thing.

"Sorry it took so long," he says as he walks in and punches in the code, making sure to block my view with his frame.

The door slides closed, and I let out a breath. How is it possible that I'm feeling better with the door closed than with it open? Because there's no temptation anymore, which means that I'll stay put for sure, since I have no other choice, and I won't inadvertently put Bobbi's life in danger. The choice has been taken away from me, and for that, everyone is safe.

"Got my laptop and Bobbi's block set."

He sets the laptop on the table and waves the block set in front of Bobbi. She drops the bacon, which lands on the carpet, and reaches for the box, which she can't quite fit in her arms. I help her.

Oscar frowns. "What happened here? Did she cry?"

He crouches down and cleans the bacon with a napkin.

"A little," I say. "I'm a stranger to her."

"No, you're not. You're my wife."

Is he aware he's not making sense half the time? I keep my thoughts to myself.

"Here we go!" He takes Bobbi from me and sets her on the plush carpet. "See? It's pink. Like your dress." Bobbi giggles at him. Her tiny hands are pulling at the box, trying to open it. "Let me help you with that." Then he shoots me a glance and changes his mind. "Actually, you play with her, Evie. I have work to do."

I sit down next to Bobbi, and we open the box together. The blocks are made of smooth, polished wood, they're colored red, green, yellow, and blue, and they have numbers on them. Bobbi starts stacking them randomly, and I help her.

I can't focus, though. Oscar is absorbed by his laptop, typing away, pushing his glasses up the bridge of his nose from time to time. He's acting like this is the most normal day, and we're a normal family spending precious moments together. Bobbi is cooing and talking to the wooden blocks in a language only she understands. On autopilot, I respond with "yes", and "I know", so she doesn't feel like she's being ignored. But I'm checked out. My body is here, in the room, in this pink and gold basement, but my soul is floating outside of my body, and outside of this house and neighborhood, outside of this world.

"Is her mother upstairs?" I hear myself say.

"Why would she be upstairs?"

"I... I don't know."

"Don't be silly, Evie."

He smiles, and I know he knows what he's doing. Then he proceeds to ignore me.

I play with Bobbi, because what else am I supposed to do? He's not going to answer my questions. What questions? Do I even have the guts to ask him if he kidnapped Bobbi? If he's going to make me raise her down here, in his basement? If today was the last day she saw the sun and felt the wind on her cheeks? I don't. Because I don't want to know.

An hour passes, and Bobbi starts being fussy. She crawls all over the carpet, is bored with the blocks, and plays with my stockings, pinching them, pulling at them and letting them snap back against my leg. This keeps her entertained for a while, and I just sit there, shell-shocked still, waiting for the other shoe to drop.

Oscar closes his laptop, taps on his phone for a minute, then joins us on the floor and starts gathering the wooden blocks. I help him, so he hopefully doesn't notice how absent I am.

"You're going to make a wonderful mother," he says.

"Oh."

"One day."

Which I translate to meaning "not yet". Maybe today's test – or experiment, or whatever this is – won't end up in tragedy.

The blocks are back in the box, and I realize Oscar has counted them. Not that I've had the presence of mind to tuck one away.

"Come on. Time for your nap." He takes Bobbi in his arms, along with the box, and makes to leave.

I eye the laptop.

"Oops!" He grins at me as he grabs it and tucks it under his arm. "See you at lunch?"

As if I have a choice. Maybe I have plans today and we can't have lunch together. Maybe I'm seeing a friend.

"Sure."

"You did well, Evie. I mean it. I'm so proud of you."

The door opens, closes, and I'm alone. I burst into tears.

Chapter Thirty-Seven

The One

"Change of plans," Oscar says as he comes in.

I peek my head out from the library and see Nora behind him, carrying a food tray.

"We'll have lunch together tomorrow," he says.

"Okay. Hi, Nora!"

"Hello, Evie darling!" She sets the tray on the table and proceeds to clear out the remains of my breakfast. "I'll keep you company for an hour. Is that okay?"

My curiosity is piqued. "Sure."

I like Nora, but I'm also painfully aware that Oscar is changing things up again. Why? One look at his face, and I have my answer.

He seems to be disgusted by me. He takes in the dress that has exactly two grease stains from Bobbi, and my panda eyes from crying with makeup on. I press my fingers to the corners of my eyes and feel the caked mascara gathered in my fine lines. He doesn't say anything. He doesn't have to.

"You two have fun." He makes his exit, and the door closes behind him.

Nora steals a glance at it but doesn't seem concerned. She's accepted my explanation about the safe room.

"Is Ben upstairs?" I ask.

She blinks at me, looking lost for a moment, then recovers quickly and shakes her head.

"Yes, poor boy. His girlfriend isn't talking to him, and he's started looking for a place to rent. They're not going to mend it this time."

I nod as if I know what she's talking about. All I can think about is that if this guy named Ben has been upstairs all this time, then he saw Bobbi. Oscar didn't steal Bobbi, only borrowed her. She's probably back with her parents. Maybe he was just babysitting, but then I have to wonder... What mother in her right mind would ask Oscar, a man – and a young one at that – to babysit her daughter?

"Come on and eat," Nora says. "You need to start putting on some weight."

"I'll wash up first."

In the bathroom, I cringe at my reflection. The harsh lights make sure the mirror doesn't lie. I wash my face with cold water until my skin is raw and sensitive, and I feel like I can behave like a normal human being around Nora. I'm grateful for her, but I know that when she's with me, she's in danger, and I need to put on a show to keep her safe. Oscar was pleased with me earlier, but then I went and cried for an hour after he and Bobbi left, and now he can't stand to look at me.

His shifting moods only impress me to the extent that I know they can result in cruelty. I must redeem myself.

Back in the bedroom, I give Nora the brightest smile I can muster.

She smiles back. "Quick, before the soup gets cold. I need your feedback. I think minestrone soup is too basic, but your husband asked me to make it today."

I taste the soup. "It's delicious."

"Oh, good. I wanted to make you lentil soup. Maybe next time."

"I like lentil soup, too."

She nods and gestures for me to hurry up and eat, as if eating faster will make fat magically grow on my frail bones and weak muscles.

"You do get out of the house, though," she says, half a question, half a statement.

That makes me freeze for a second.

"Take some fresh air, go for a walk," she continues. "Rest and quiet help so much, but I just think you'll heal faster if you go out in the sun once in a while."

I nod. "Mhm. No, I definitely go out, usually in the evening."

She smiles. "I can imagine you and your husband, hand in hand, taking a stroll around the neighborhood."

I nod again and make sure my mouth is full, so I don't have to lie to her over and over. I'm afraid my composure will slip and that will be the death of her. Literally. I know Oscar is watching and listening intently. I move from the soup to the salad bowl. Even if it's a salad, it seems the main ingredient is grilled chicken.

"So, tell me about your day," she says.

I shrug but I can't bring myself to say something. Bobbi comes to my mind. And Oscar's words – "You'll make a wonderful mother one day." I swallow heavily.

"What book are you reading?" Nora continues as if she can't sense my unease. I hope she can't. "I used to read when I was like you. Young, unworried about the future. Though my taste in books is a bit different. My favorite book of all time is The Picture of Dorian Gray. Do you know it?"

"I haven't read it."

"How about I lend you an old copy I have lying around the house? And you lend me one of your books."

"Wait, no. I did read it. In college."

Her eyebrows shoot up, creating deep wrinkles across her forehead. "And what did you think?"

"I loved it back then. We studied it in a Gothic Lit course."

"Oh, did you study Literature in college?"

"Yes."

She narrows her eyes slightly and bites the inside of her lip. It's as if she wants to tell me something but doesn't quite know how to phrase it.

I give her an encouraging smile. "Okay, just say it."

"What?"

"Whatever you want to say."

"What do you think I want to say, Evie?" She's smiling too.

I roll my eyes. "How does an English Lit graduate end up reading dark romance books?"

She covers her face with her hands and peeks at me from behind her splayed fingers.

"Sorry. You must think I'm a snob now. That I'm judging you."

I laugh. "Not at all. To be honest, I don't know the answer to that question." I shrug. "It just happened. Back when I was a teen living with my parents, my mother read romance books. I read her entire collection, and that got me into reading. I read the classics next, but I guess after I finished college and there was no reason for me to read heavy literature anymore, I went back to my love of romance. With an edge, this time."

She ponders my explanation for a second. "That makes sense. So, like, how are the stories? What are they about?"

I tense up. My spine pulls up on its own, and my shoulders square, as if I'm readying myself to receive a blow, or two, or three. I don't want to talk about this. How did we get to dark romance?

"Like, do the women get stalked or kidnapped, and then fall in love with their aggressor? They get married and have kids?"

I feel my chin starting to tremble. There are a few leaves and bits of grilled chicken left at the bottom of the bowl, and I just push them around. A slice of carrot cake is waiting for me, but I don't think I can eat it.

"And they live normal lives?" Nora goes on with her very spot-on assumptions. "What do they tell their kids when they ask, 'Hey, Mommy, how did you meet Daddy?' Or the stories don't go that far?"

"They don't," I say, my voice a whisper.

I feel choked up. I take a sip of water and clear my throat. It's not helping. Tears sting my eyes. I blink rapidly but can't stop one from tumbling down my cheek. I wipe it quickly, turning my head away.

Nora doesn't miss it, though. She reaches over to squeeze my arm.

"Evie, what's wrong? Did I say something inappropriate? Ignore a silly, old woman. What do I know? The last book I read was twenty years ago."

"No, no," I wave her off as more tears roll down my face. "I'm sorry. I'm fine."

"You're not fine. What's going on? Tell me, Evie."

She squeezes my arm harder. I should pull away, go to the bathroom to fix myself, but I need the physical connection. I need someone to hold me as I break down.

I don't know how to explain what's happening to me. How I'm feeling.

"I'm not ready to have children." Of all the things, that's what comes out of my mouth. I look at her, my vision blurry. "Nora, I'm not ready. I can't."

She frowns. "Well, if you're not ready, no one says you should have them. Did your husband say something? Did you two talk about this?"

I bite my lip. We're looking into each other's eyes, into each other's souls... And I want to tell her everything. I want to beg her to save me. Behind her, the stupid metal door is closed. Earlier today, when Oscar made me hold Bobbi, the door was open. I should've dropped the girl and run for my life. She wasn't mine. What did I care what happened to her? If the door were open now, I would bolt out and not care what happened to Nora.

But of course, it's selfish to think this way. I'm responsible for every person Oscar forces into my space. If I saved myself and they had to suffer the consequences, I would never forgive myself. The guilt would gnaw at my insides until... until I'd take drastic measures to make it stop. To make all of it stop.

I take a deep breath and release it slowly. Then another. And another. I imagine roots growing from my soles and plunging deep into the ground, penetrating the pink carpet and the cement underneath. I force a smile to my lips.

"No, I... I don't know what got into me." I pull away from her and wipe my face with my hands. "Ugh. I'm not feeling well. I think I need to lie down."

"Of course."

She helps me to bed. I toe off my ballet flats, and Nora tucks me in. The handcuffs and the chain are safely hidden under the mattress, invisible if you don't know to look for them.

"I'm sorry if I upset you," she says.

"You haven't. I'm not having a great day, that's all."

I'm not lying. Oscar's games are killing me little by little. The stress he's constantly putting me under has become too much.

Speaking of the devil…

The door whirrs open, and he's standing there, too disappointed and disgusted to step inside and take a good look at me.

"If you two are done, I have some errands to run," he says.

Nora whips around and rushes to clear the table.

"Anything I can help with, Mr. Miles?"

"No, thank you. You can go home for the day."

He digs into his pocket, and my heart lurches into my throat, but he's only taking out his wallet to pay Nora.

"Until next time, Evie," she says. "Get some rest."

"I will, Nora. Thank you for the delicious lunch."

"I'll leave the carrot cake," she says.

I half expect Oscar to protest, but he's silent. They leave, and he doesn't spare me another glance.

I pull the duvet over my head and sink into the blessed darkness. I'm going to pay for crying and being a killjoy the entire day. I know I am.

Chapter Thirty-Eight
The One

I don't get dinner. I don't get breakfast the next day. By lunch, I've eaten half of the snacks in the snack basket. I tell myself I need to ration them, just in case I don't get dinner again. I try to distract myself with my mountains of books, arranging and rearranging them, first by size, then by color.

Oscar pops in eventually, drops two Styrofoam containers with Indian food on the table, and shoots me a displeased look.

"Feeling better?"

"Much better. Thank you for asking."

I've showered and put on a little black dress. I look stupid in black, shiny heels in the middle of the pink room, but I'm trying to focus on the simple fact that I want to eat. Regularly, if possible. Despite tooting his own horn, and Nora telling me how lucky I am, Oscar Octavious Miles is very far from being a provider. He's a big, stubborn, cruel baby with a toy in his basement. A toy he forgets about more and more often. One day, he'll forget about me completely.

Or worse. He'll decide he's over playing with toys, and he'll rip my limbs and throw me in the trash.

"Good." He turns his back to me.

He doesn't want to stick around, and I take that as a bad sign. He hasn't slept next to me in a while, and the handcuffs haven't come out from under the mattress in I don't know how long. It's ridiculous that I almost want him to cuff me to the bed and stay the night, but I fear that his growing more and more distant will eventually result in my demise.

I must stop him from leaving. Keep him here a moment longer.

"In fact, I'm feeling so much better that I was thinking..."

He turns around, blue eyes curious behind thick-framed glasses.

I hesitate. I haven't been thinking about anything. I don't have a plan. The easiest way to make sure he doesn't leave me to starve is to do what the women in the dark romance books do. But I can't.

I just can't.

"What?" His harsh tone jolts me out of my trance.

"That I miss writing. I was wondering, can you, maybe, bring me a pen and paper? A notebook?"

His features darken. How fitting. In all the books I've read, the Alpha male's eyes darken at least once every ten pages. It doesn't matter if he's a mafia boss, a cold-hearted killer, or a shapeshifter with a deadly curse on his head.

His eyes darken with rage, or lust, or both. And his stare does all kinds of things to the woman's core.

What Oscar's dark stare does to me is that it makes me want to curl within myself, crawl under the bed and throw up the liters of water I've been drinking all day to stave off the hunger.

This is not a romance.

"Do you think I'm stupid?" A rhetorical question in a low, threatening voice. "Is that what you think of me, Evie? Are you taking me for a fool right now?"

"N-no. Of course not. Why would you think–"

"Pen and paper? So you can write a note to Nora next time she's here?"

I take a step towards him, putting my hands up. "Never in a million years–"

"I know everything about you." He's raising his voice. "I know you don't write longhand. The last time you needed a pen, you turned your apartment upside down and didn't find one. You had to go to the convenience store to buy a pen, so you could sign a contract one of your tech-impaired clients wanted physically signed and scanned."

All the blood drains from my face. If I've been as pale as a ghost until now, well, now I am translucent. To what lengths did Oscar go to stalk me before grabbing me?

He gives me a sinister grin. "That's right. I know all your little quirks, all your secrets."

I doubt that, but I'm not going to argue with him.

"I'm not an idiot, Evie. There will be no pen and paper, so you can write tiny, squiggly notes and pass them to poor, unsuspecting Nora when you randomly hug her or cry on her shoulder. And by the way, stop with the crying. I've had enough of it. Every time I check the cameras to see what my lovely wife is doing, I see you ugly crying all over this place. It's like you're trying to mark every inch of it with tears and snot. Enough!"

I jump back when he screams at me.

"I'm not your wife," I say in a tiny voice, so tiny that he shouldn't even hear it.

He takes off his glasses and pinches the bridge of his nose.

"I can't." He sighs. "I can't do this anymore."

An invisible claw grips my stomach. What does that mean?

"Please," I say, though I don't know what I'm begging for. "Please."

"Please what, Evie? Please be more understanding than I already am? More patient? You should listen to Nora, you know. She's wise. She's seen things, suffered, pulled through all on her own. She's had a hard life compared to you. You have everything you could wish for," he motions at the room, "And all you do is moan, and groan, and mope, and complain. And cry! You cry so much that I don't even want to see you anymore. You make me not want to be in the same room as you. You repel me, Evie!"

I cringe, pulling away, making myself small.

"What do I do with you?" He turns away, shaking his head, puts his glasses back on and runs a hand through his hair. "You tell me, Evie. Where do we go from here? I've given you so many chances."

"I know," I say.

"You know." He gives me a cold appraisal, not impressed with my effort of prettying myself up for him. "You don't know anything. You don't know me, Evie. You don't know what I'm thinking, what I need, what I want."

"Tell me, then." I take a small step towards him. "I'm here to listen."

He huffs. For a second, I think he will give in, mellow down, open up to me. His emotions have shifted from anger to disappointment to confusion, as if I'm not the only one who's betrayed him by behaving erratically, but the whole world has betrayed him by not being what he wants it to be.

Then he shakes his head and rolls his eyes, and the anger is back. Better contained, still dangerous.

"I'll bring you an old laptop. I'll wipe it clean, and you can use it to write. When Nora's here, I'll safekeep it for you. No funny business."

"I never intended–"

"Stop it. You're embarrassing yourself, and you're embarrassing me. How could I pick someone so dumb?"

I bite my tongue.

"Anything else?" he asks. "Any other requests?"

"No."

"No?" He raises his eyebrows at me.

"I just miss writing, that's all. Thank you for bringing me a laptop."

"You're welcome."

He waits one beat longer, then turns around and punches in the code. I don't even try to see it. I wait for the door to close, then tear into the Styrofoam containers. Butter chicken, simple rice, naan, and two dipping sauces. No cutlery. I'm so hungry that eating with my hands doesn't bother me. If anything, it feels more satisfying.

Chapter Thirty-Nine
The One

My fingers hover over the keyboard. I type a sentence, hit backspace before finishing it. My mind is blank – as blank as the page – though my body is vibrating with overwhelming feelings. There's a sharp pain in my lower left side, right above my hip bone. My stomach is a ball of churning acid, my chest feels too narrow for my lungs, and my throat is parched no matter how much water I drink.

Oscar has brought me an 11-inch notebook that only has a word processor on it, Minesweeper and Solitaire. No other programs installed, and no connection to the Internet. He's kept his promise.

"Go ahead and write," he said, "If you missed it so much."

I can't.

I keep writing the same sentence and deleting it before I get to the end of it. Over and over. Because the sentence is true, and what would come after it would also be true, and I can't put it all down for Oscar to read.

"I don't know if I can take this anymore, and some nights I pray that..." Backspace, backspace, backspace.

I close the word processor and open Solitaire. Since he hasn't deleted it, it means I'm allowed to play.

I didn't lie to him; I do miss writing. I miss watching cringey K-dramas, scrolling social media and listening to music, though I didn't listen to music that much. I'm the kind of writer who needs complete silence to think. If there's background music or the neighbors are being too loud, the ideas shy away from me, my sentences run on and don't make sense, and I have to get up and do something else until the quiet is restored and my thoughts settle.

I can't write a single thing knowing that Oscar will read it. I don't know what I was thinking, asking him to bring me something to write. Like I could express myself freely, type how I feel. It would only give him ammunition.

I play Solitaire for hours. I don't notice that I haven't gotten lunch or dinner today. I play Solitaire for most of the night, and when I can't keep my eyes open, I allow myself to eat a peanut butter bar from the snack basket. I fall into a restless sleep and dream of playing cards falling from the ceiling, slowly drowning me. They keep falling until the room is filled with them, and I can't breathe, can't move.

I wake up with a start and realize I've tangled myself in the duvet. I drink a glass of water, then stare at the wall until the lights brighten and I hear the dull whirr of the metal door. My stomach growls impatiently, and I press my fist into it. I don't want Oscar to see how easy it is to torture me. I don't want to beg for food like a beaten animal that doesn't understand what it did wrong but hopes its master will forgive it and not let it starve.

Oscar unloads the tray onto the table – scrambled eggs, three big slices of fried bacon, two small sausages, toast and butter. It means Nora is here. Oscar used to cook for me, but not anymore. I'm not as worthy as when he thought he got the right girl.

"Good morning," he says. "Sleep well?"

"Yes."

He grins. He knows I'm lying. I wonder exactly how much of his time he spends checking the cameras, watching me do practically nothing all day and all night.

"Go wash," he says.

I execute his order without protest. When I return to the bedroom, he's just turning off the laptop after having checked it.

"No inspiration?" he asks.

I shrug as I dig into my breakfast. The toast is still hot and the butter melts on it.

"Do you think the muse might be more willing today?"

"I don't believe in muses," I say.

"What do you believe in?"

Freedom. To think, to create, to exist. Freedom for the sake of it.

"It's been a while, that's all," I say instead. "I don't know what to write about."

"You could write something for me."

Why would I do that?

"Like what?"

"A letter? A poem? A poem in a letter?"

I focus on eating, afraid that he'll soon say something that will curb my appetite. I need this food in my stomach. I know I'm not chewing it properly, and that I'll feel sick and bloated, but better that than hungry.

"Evie, are you listening to me?"

I raise my gaze to meet his. "Yes, of course."

"Write something for me today, or I'll take away the laptop."

"Okay."

He sighs and leaves me alone. He hasn't brought his coffee with him, and on the one hand, I'm glad I don't have to suffer his presence all through breakfast, but on the other hand, I know it's bad – very bad – that he's losing interest in me.

As the door slides closed behind him, I slow down and focus on chewing my food. I can take my time now. I drag the laptop closer, turn it on and immerse myself in Solitaire. In the background, my mind is thinking about his request – to write something for him. I tell myself I'll try. I'll make an effort, just so I don't have to suffer unexpected consequences he's failed to mention.

I'll write him a haiku.

Shackled to the bed,
Hope dwindles with each heartbeat,

Freedom just a dream.

Not great. Not half bad. I'll write it down as soon as I finish this Solitaire round. Will he find it hilarious?

The sound of the door opening snaps me out of a deep trance I didn't notice I'd fallen in. It feels like my brain is swimming through molasses as I blink at the screen and see I'm still playing Solitaire. I look at the plate before me. Empty. At least I ate everything, cleaned out all the crumbs.

Oscar and Nora are chatting about the weather as they come in. She's carrying a tray filled with goodies. Is it lunchtime already?

The haiku. I don't remember how it went. I exit Solitaire and open the word processor quickly, but what good will it do me when Oscar sees the blank page?

"I'll take this," he says, closing the laptop and tucking it under his arm. "I'll get it fixed in no time, don't worry." He winks at me.

Nora watches the exchange. "What happened?"

"My wife managed to get a virus onto her laptop."

"Oh, my! That's bad," Nora says. "It's bad, right? You can lose everything."

"We have backups," Oscar says.

The absurdity of this exchange makes me want to laugh. I smile, and Oscar smiles too, thinking I'm going along with his game, when in truth, I'm this close to losing all my marbles and exploding into hysterical laughter. I must remember that Nora is here, and if I misbehave, I'll be putting her life in danger.

"I'll be upstairs, scanning this thing."

He leaves us, and I'm grateful. Nora starts talking about the food she's made for me, saying it's a special recipe she learned from her mother. I stop her and ask her to tell me what she was telling Oscar earlier. About the weather.

"Finally, we're having a few warm days. It's been so cold this week, unnaturally cold for September, if you ask me. It hasn't rained much, so at least there's that. I'm just not ready for fall. It's beautiful, but I'm a summer soul. And for me, having to rake the leaves every week is a deal breaker. I'd rather mow the lawn. It's faster and easier on my back."

I listen to her and feel tears stinging the back of my eyes. I blink rapidly to chase them away and imagine what she's describing. It's fall outside. Chilly, though blessedly sunny today, and the streets are covered in rusty fallen leaves. I inhale deeply, and I swear I can smell the damp earth.

"Evie, are you all right?" Her voice has dropped a notch, and she reaches for my hand. She studies the dark circles under my eyes, and her chin trembles slightly, as if she wants to say more but is holding back. "You can tell me anything. You can trust me." She squeezes my hand.

I drop my gaze, looking at her hand on mine, letting myself absorb her warmth. Her kindness. I can trust her... I know I can. That's not the problem. The problem is that if I tell her the truth, Oscar will kill her like he killed

Rita. I can't watch her struggle and kick on the floor as he's strangling her with a chain.

I force a smile to my lips. "I'm just tired."

She shakes her head. "You've lost weight. You're not eating enough."

I bite my lip. *"Because he's not feeding me,"* I want to say.

"I'll make you a good, healthy dinner. Three courses! And dessert," she says, patting my hand. "Promise me you'll eat all of it."

"I promise."

I wonder if Oscar intentionally doesn't bring me food even when there's plenty of it, cooked by Nora. I wonder if he'll bring me the dinner she's already planning in her head. When he doesn't feed me, he's probably punishing me for random, little things. Like, I didn't read that book he went through so much trouble to print for me, or I forgot to brush my hair, or I went to bed without showering.

I must do better. I must respect his rules that he never wrote down for me but expects me to know by reading his mind. I can do better if I try, but I'm just so exhausted. These past few days have felt like limbo. If someone asked me what I've been doing, I wouldn't know what to tell them.

Rotting. I've been rotting away.

"I don't want you to think that I'm nosy," Nora says. "I'm just worried about you. I have to ask, is everything okay with your husband?"

I chuckle bitterly.

"Are you two spending time together? Talking?"

"Well, not as much as we used to," I say. Which isn't a lie.

She shakes her head. "That's not good."

I cock an eyebrow. "What do you mean?"

She lets go of my hand and leans back in her chair. "Communication is so important. I was young and didn't know something was wrong when my ex-husband started pulling away. He was silent. Absent. He was never a great talker; more of an introvert. He kept to himself, didn't share his thoughts with me unless I pestered him. When the baby came, it got worse, to the point where he was coming home late, avoiding me. I was busy and constantly tired, and I couldn't pay attention to him, couldn't sit him down and ask what was wrong. We ended up getting a divorce. He made up his mind without me. When I tried talking to him, it was too late. In his head, he'd rationalized leaving us, and nothing I said could change his mind."

"This is not the same situation," I say.

She nods but doesn't look convinced. "What I learned is that when a man loses interest in a woman, it's up to the woman to work a little harder, keep things going in the relationship."

It sounds so wrong that I bristle. I straighten my back and place my hands in my lap before she can see I'm squeezing them into fists, fingernails biting into my palms.

"Men are not like us. They don't love like we do. Which doesn't mean they don't love us. They don't know how to express it. They're not good at introspection like we are, and we just have to help them a little bit in that department."

"We have to do the work for them," I say, feeling myself getting angrier by the second.

"No. We're doing the work for us. For the relationship. To save our marriage."

"You regret not saving your marriage," I say.

"I do."

"Was he a good man?"

She smiles. "He was a man. How great can we expect them to be?" She pauses, waiting to see if I have more to ask. When I swallow my words, she continues, "It was hard when he left me, and for a long time after."

I get up, feeling like I can't stay put anymore. "I'm sorry you had to go through that, Nora. I'm sorry. But what Oscar and I have is different."

"So, you're saying he's not pulling away?"

I shrug. "What if he is? What if all this narrative about 'forever' and finding 'the one' is a lie? I mean, not a lie, but something that's unattainable. We've been trained since we were children to think that romantic relationships are the pinnacle of our existence. What if that's not true, and we have to learn to let go when things don't work anymore? It's fine, it doesn't mean we've failed."

She is silent for a moment, then says in a lower, gentler voice, "People get hurt when relationships fail."

I open my mouth to say that while that's true, people also heal after a time, then stop myself because I realize none of this applies to me. She's talking about people getting heartbroken, but if my "relationship" with Oscar fails, which part of me will get broken? An arm? My ribs? My neck?

My hands fly to my throat in an instinctive gesture of self-defense. When Nora regards me oddly, I rub my hands over my face, acting like I'm tired.

She jumps to her feet and starts clearing the table.

"You know what? Don't mind me." She chuckles awkwardly, like she feels she's crossed a line. "You and your husband know better. I'm an old, bitter woman who's stuck in the past, and I'm probably giving you really bad, outdated advice. I have to remind myself often that the younger generations know what they're doing and don't need our old-fashioned opinions."

"No," I protest quickly. I don't want her to think she's upset me. Even if she has. "I value your advice. Thank you for cooking for me, and for spending time with me. I don't see... um... a lot of people."

She's got everything loaded on the tray and is shaking her head at me. Behind her, the door opens, which means

Oscar is right on time. I bet he's been watching us like a hawk, listened to every word we said.

"You need to get out more," she says. "It's lovely outside. Maybe we can go for a walk together. When you feel better."

"Yes," I murmur, exchanging a glance with Oscar. "When I feel better."

"Get some rest," she says. "I'll get a start on the most delicious dinner you've ever had. Five stars, I promise. I'll be in the kitchen for a while if you want to join me."

"Maybe I will."

She leaves, and Oscar waits for her to go up the stairs before giving me the laptop.

"Write something, or I'm taking it back," he says.

I chew on the inside of my lower lip, thinking about what Nora said – "People get hurt when relationships fail." Her experience with her ex-husband, while terrible, doesn't compare with the torture Oscar has been putting me through. How much worse can it get? Is there any way I might walk out of here alive?

And why haven't they found me yet? Surely, the police are looking for me. I haven't been forgotten. Someone cares. Someone will come.

"Can we talk?" I ask.

"Now?" He studies me for a second. "Now's not a good time. I have work."

"Later. At dinner?"

He nods. "Write something."

He leaves, and before I turn on the laptop, I make a vow to myself to not open Solitaire. Not a promise; a vow. Who would've thought I'd get obsessed with the most boring card game in the world? But it makes the time pass faster. It makes it roll off my awareness, allowing me to shut my mind off and not worry about anything for an hour, two, five, ten.

He wants me to write. I will write.

Chapter Forty

The One

hey mom

sorry I didn't text you earlier, I needed to get away for a while

hope I didn't scare you or anything

I just needed some time off

I've been going through some things lately and had to take a step back

anyway, I just wanted to let you know

talk to you later, I'll call you in a few days

Hey guys! I decided to take a break from social media, but now I'm back. I've been dealing with some personal issues and realized I needed a real detox. No technology. Let me tell you, it wasn't that bad. LOL I finally got to read all the paperbacks I've collected through the years. I need new book recs! What are you reading now? I'm just finishing the Impossible Redemption trilogy. Sooo gooood!

"What's this?"

Oscar has been staring at the screen for five minutes. He must've re-read what I've written a dozen times.

I make myself small and poke at my food. Nora has outdone herself. Three courses, as she promised – bruschetta with freshly chopped basil and cherry tomatoes that go with sweet onion soup, and grilled chicken breast with mashed potatoes and gravy. For dessert – the biggest chocolate chip cookie I've ever seen. I'm nibbling at a piece of bruschetta, my eyes fixed on Oscar's face. I'm not hungry. I should be, but I ate well at lunch, and I think my stomach has shrunk. I got used to having one meal a day, and sometimes not even that. I feel bad that Nora worked so hard and I can barely look at the food, let alone consume it. The smell is incredible, and somehow, too much.

"You asked me to write," I say.

His gaze moves from the screen to my face. He hasn't brought anything to eat for himself, which means he only came because I told him I wanted to talk to him. He has no intention of staying the night. Not that I want him to, but him not wanting me anymore is worse than him wanting me to be his girlfriend, fiancée, his future wife.

"This is our way out," I say.

"Out of what?"

"A relationship that clearly isn't working. You're unhappy, Oscar. I can see it. Why stay unhappy when you could be free? Free to find someone you truly click with."

What I'm actually saying is, "free to kidnap someone else", but I won't dwell on it. That won't happen. Because this plan of mine is terrible; not a plan at all, really, and it's already failed. But I had to try something. Anything. I came up with this.

"The text is for my mother. All you have to do is charge my phone, turn it on, and send it. It sounds like me. It is me. This is how I talk to her, I promise."

He pushes the laptop away, places his elbows on the table, and rests his chin on his joined fingers. It almost looks like he's praying. His gaze is curious, surprised, but there's a hint of something else in it, too.

"The other thing is for the biggest dark romance group I'm in. I'm sure you already know my Facebook password. Just go in, post that, and everything will be fine. People do social media detoxes all the time."

"I'm sorry, why would I do all this?" His tone is calm and gentle. I don't know what it means.

I put down the bruschetta and let out a sharp breath. I have to repeat myself. He isn't listening.

"Oscar, you can let me go. I will never tell anyone. Just let me go. I will walk out of here, back to my life, tell everyone I needed some time off, and that's that. Over. Done. I will never mention your name, never mention this place. After all, it's no one's business our relationship failed. It happens all the time. We're both adults. We can admit this isn't going anywhere. We'll go our separate ways. No hard feelings."

"No. Hard. Feelings." He pauses after every word.

His gaze is intense, locked onto mine. Dread boils and bubbles in my stomach, and I can't look away. I must seem confident even though I'm not. Maybe I have a chance here. The tiniest chance. And if I don't, maybe his reaction will give me some information about what's happening out there. I want to know if they're looking for me, at least.

Lately, I've been thinking... If they are looking for me, then I should be all over the news. That's how it goes. Then... Nora would know, right? The idea that no one's noticed my absence makes me feel sick. It's not impossible that this is exactly what happened. My mom doesn't check up on me often. If she called once and my phone was off, it doesn't guarantee she remembered to call a second time. My dad doesn't care. He never calls me, not even on my birthday. I have no siblings, I'm estranged from all my other family – I barely even know them – and I have no IRL friends. Did the guy from the convenience store notice I stopped coming for my usual midnight snacks? Who am I kidding? I am the perfect victim, and that's why Oscar chose me.

He won't just let me go.

Even though he could. If I'm right and no one even noticed I've been gone – again, Nora would've seen my face somewhere – then he could let me walk out of here.

"You know," he says in the same cool tone, "Reading is a sign of intelligence. What do all smart people have in common? They read. But I'm starting to wonder if your choice of literature isn't, in fact, making you dumb." He waits for me to say something. When I don't, he sighs. "Do you think I'm an idiot, Evie?"

"No. I'm only saying that if the relationship isn't working – and it's not – we can choose to move on."

It's his delusion, not mine. He's the one who calls me his girlfriend. Or wife. I don't even know which one it is anymore. From day one, he's behaved like this is normal, like he's the perfect man who only wants to provide for his woman, and not once did he utter the words "kidnapping" and "prisoner". I don't know if his delusion is real and he truly believes we're together, a young couple that's hit a rough patch, or if he knows exactly what he's doing, who he is and who I am to him – kidnapper and victim – and the sole purpose of the story is to mess with my head.

He grins. "So, you're not only taking me for a fool, you also believe the relationship isn't working." His grin stretches until it becomes creepy. Unsettling. "Tell me, Evie, who's fault might that be?"

I shrug. "It's no one's fault. As I said, these things happen."

"Out of the blue. They just happen."

"We're not a match."

He jumps to his feet, so suddenly that if the table weren't bolted to the floor, it would've rattled. He slams his fists on it and leans over, close to my face.

I shrink in my chair but don't look away. My heart hammers in my chest. I squeeze my hands into fists, ready to defend myself if I have to.

"We're not a match. You dare say that to me." His tone has changed. Anger pours out of him. "After everything I've done, everything I've sacrificed. I swear, Evie, no one has ever made me work so hard for something in my life. Up to a point, it's a welcome challenge, but you've gone past that point some time ago. I built this place for you, I bring you your favorite books, keep you dressed and fed. You haven't given me anything in exchange. Not even a kiss, Evie. Not even a genuine hug. You're cold, rigid, and unpleasant. If this relationship isn't working, it's your fault. You've intentionally ruined everything."

Tears should be running down my cheeks, but I realize my eyes are dry. His little speech doesn't impress me. Because it's all fake. I'm tired of this stupid, false narrative. We're not having a serious conversation right now because he insists on clinging to the delusion.

"Why can't you just let me go?" I ask, voice even.

At that, he goes back to grinning at me, then bursts into laughter. He emanates a mix of rage and amusement tinged with sarcasm.

"Do you really think I can let you go? That I'll let you pack your things and walk out the front door?"

"Why not?"

He moves away from the table. Starts pacing. "Oh, Evie." He takes off his glasses, runs a hand over his face.

"Why not?" I stand too, determined to get something real out of him. "Is it too late to do that? Are the police looking for me? Is my face all over the news? Is that why we can't just backtrack on this stupid situation you got us in?"

He closes the distance between us in a heartbeat. I don't have time to move out of the way, and before I can get another word out, his hand is wrapped around my throat. My eyes bulge in my head, and I stare at him as I try to pry his fingers off me. He squeezes harder, until I sputter and cough.

"No one's looking for you," he says. "No one cares. I'm the only one who cares, Evie, and if you lose me, you have nothing. You want this to end? Are you sure? If you are, I can make it end, but it will be on my terms."

"Let go," I say through gritted teeth. I can barely talk.

"I will. In a second." He pulls me close and bares his teeth at me. He looks unhinged, and for a beat, I'm convinced he's going to bite my face. It doesn't make sense. But he doesn't make sense. He's crazy. "I want to make sure you understand something first. I will say this once. I won't repeat myself. Are you ready?" He pulls me even closer. I can feel his breath on my lips. "Are you listening? Okay. Rest assured, Evie, you will never walk out of here alive."

He lets go and pushes me away at the same time. I stumble and fall onto the bed.

Oscar surveys the table and frowns. "Such a waste. And Nora has worked so hard. Ungrateful. Why am I not surprised?"

"Leave it," I say. "I'll finish later."

Frankly, I don't know where all this courage is coming from. Normally, I wouldn't talk back to him. His words – "you will never walk out of here alive" – have shifted something in me. What does it matter if I talk back? The worst that can happen is that he'll kill me. He's made up his mind.

"Fine," he says. He throws me a disgusted look as he tucks the laptop under his arm. No more Solitaire for me. "I heard you and Nora talk. She gave you good advice. Instead of talking nonsense about how we're not a match, how about you listen to her? She's wise. You're not. I should bring you some classics, or you'll become dumber every day."

I close my eyes and let out a sigh, waiting for him to leave. I need to be alone, so I can lick my wounds and dissect every word he said. The fact that he's going to kill me eventually is clear to me. But when I asked him if the police are looking for me, he said no. He went all emotional and said no one cares about me.

Finally, he turns his back and punches in the code. I'm feeling so pumped right now that maybe I could jump him. I'm weak and a few pounds lighter than when he brought me here, but maybe I stand a chance. If I get to my feet now and launch myself at him like I mean it.

My brain urges me to do it. My limbs don't move.

"Good night, Evie. Do better."

He walks out and punches in the code from the other side of the door.

I release a long, heavy breath. I should've done it. What's wrong with me? He's going to kill me! I should've bypassed my crippling fear and jumped on his back. He's trained me too well.

But the police are looking for me. If they weren't, Oscar wouldn't have exploded like that.

Chapter Forty-One
The One

The water's gone cold, but I don't have the energy to get out of the bath. I want to stay here forever. If I don't hold onto the edges of the tub, I start to float – I'm that light. I have panties and a bra on. Oscar is not getting a show from me.

He's punishing me again by withholding food. I haven't gotten breakfast or lunch, and he hasn't come in to get the leftovers from last night's dinner. There are a few soggy pieces of bruschetta left, and I might just eat them if I get hungry enough.

I slide underwater, holding my breath, closing my eyes. The world fades away, all sounds muffled by the water rushing into my ears. All I can hear is my heartbeat. My thoughts slow down, and I almost feel safe. Protected. I wait until I feel pain in my chest, then emerge, gasping for air. I wipe the water from my eyes and blink at the bright lights.

I'm about to add more hot water to the tub when I hear the metal door open. My heart picks up the pace, and I feel all the muscles in my body become tense. I fix my gaze on the bathroom door, waiting for Oscar to open it.

There's no privacy to be had in this place, not even when I want to soak in a relaxing bath.

Nothing happens. He doesn't come, even though I can hear noises from the other side of the door. I give myself another minute to calm down and prepare to face him after the fight we had the night before. I dry myself and use the towel to cover my body as I slip out of the wet underwear and put on a new pair. Today I'm wearing a pink, frilly dress. I look like a stupid Barbie doll in it, but I don't have much of a choice. Oscar keeps taking my dresses to wash them and forgets to bring them back.

I take a deep breath, nod to myself, and walk out of the bathroom. I stop in my tracks, mouth agape.

Nora is cleaning the table, stacking the plastic plates one on top of the other, while telling a young girl – a child, no more than seven years old – that she has to do her homework first, and then she can color in her coloring book.

"The sooner you get to it, the quicker you will get it done," Nora says, her tone kind and motherly.

"But it's math! I hate math," the girl pouts.

"I know. I never fancied it either." She looks up and sees me. "Oh, Evie is here. Hi, Evie!" Then, to the girl, "Evie will help you. I bet she's good at math."

"I'm... not," I say on autopilot.

The door is open. Nora is wiping the table with a paper napkin, the girl is digging into her Wonder Woman backpack and getting out books and notebooks, and the door... is open.

"Evie, this is Celeste."

"Hi." The child smiles and waves at me. She has red hair, pretty freckles all over her face, and big blue eyes. She's wearing a school uniform.

"Hi," I murmur.

I don't know how to react. I don't know what's happening, so I'm frozen in place. I haven't moved a muscle since I stepped out of the bathroom. Thank God my body knows how to breathe on its own. I look at Nora for an explanation. I'd start asking questions, but I'm not sure how to phrase them so as not to raise suspicions.

"Celeste's parents have a little emergency they need to sort out, so they asked your husband to watch her for an hour," Nora says.

"My..." I blink and shake my head to put my thoughts in order. I touch my temple with trembling fingers. "Where's Oscar? Upstairs?"

"Yes. He let us in. Busy working, as usual. He said helping Celeste with homework will be a welcome distraction for you. But if you're tired–"

"I'm not."

Celeste has climbed onto one of the chairs, and she's confused as to why she can't drag it closer to the table. She's pulling at it, frowning. I watch her, and I can tell she's smart. Sharp. She gives up and leans forward to reach for her books. The crease between her brows doesn't let up as she looks around and studies the pink room. Her eyes fall back on me – the pink doll in the pink dollhouse.

"I didn't know Oscar was married," she says.

Nora laughs, which startles both me and Celeste.

"How could you not know?" she says. "You come over all the time."

"Over to the house," Celeste says. "But not here." She looks up at the ceiling, and I wonder if she can spot the cameras. She shields her eyes from the bright lights and looks back at me. "I've never seen you before," she says.

"But you heard about her," Nora says.

Celeste thinks for a moment. "Mm... no."

Nora seems to be at a loss, and I don't know how to handle this. What's Oscar thinking? To let Nora bring this girl here – this girl who's obviously his neighbors' daughter! What am I supposed to do now? How do I keep lying to them? If I fail to convince Celeste that I'm Oscar's wife, what will happen to her? What's he capable of?

It was one thing to bring a toddler, another thing entirely to bring a seven-year-old.

The door. Is. Open.

I walk to the table, stop next to Celeste, and look at her schoolbooks – math, science activities, reading, writing. She has two coloring books she's put aside, one with forest animals, the other with dinosaurs. She's taken out two pencil cases, and she's sharpening a pencil in preparation for the dreaded math homework.

My fingers start itching. My heart is in my throat, and my stomach is one big, heavy knot.

"I don't go out much," I say. "I'm not feeling well, so I spend a lot of time down here, with my books."

Celeste studies my profile as she opens the math workbook. "You must've gotten married recently," she says. "My parents have been living here since before I was born, and we've known Oscar since he moved to the neighborhood."

"Enough chit-chat," Nora says. "Let's see those additions." She taps the page in front of Celeste.

"Additions are easy," the girl says. "It's subtractions I hate."

She focuses on the exercise, and I feel relieved that I don't seem to have to convince her about anything, after all. I shift from one foot to the other as I watch her go through the first exercise. I sneak glances at Nora, who's stacked the empty plates and leftovers in a corner of the table. She smiles at me when she catches me looking, then goes to wash her hands in the bathroom sink. My eyes shift to the open door. There's a tingling in my toes, and I flex them inside the ballet flats. It feels like my soles are on fire. I can't stay still.

Celeste murmurs something to herself and moves to the next exercise. She doesn't need my help; she's doing fine. I move away from her, slip around the table, my gaze traveling upwards to the cameras. Is he there? Is he watching me? What does he think will happen? Right now, I myself don't know what I'll do. Does he? I reach the other side of the table and grab the back of the chair to steady myself.

"Mm... I don't think I got this right," Celeste says, looking up at me. "Will you check, Evie?"

"Sure."

My heart is hammering in my temples as I stretch over the table to look at Celeste's workbook. She pushes it closer to me and hands me her pencil. For a moment, I stare at the pencil as if I've never seen such an object in my life.

"I need to pee," Celeste says as she hops down and runs to the bathroom just as Nora is coming out. She slams the door behind her.

Nora shakes her head. "Kids these days. Why do they always have to bang the doors?"

I blink at her. I can see her lips moving, and I know what each word that comes out of her mouth means, but the message of her full sentence is lost on me. I don't know what she's talking about. I don't know why she's here. There's a little girl in the bathroom who doesn't know she's being watched by a creep through cameras. Unless... he's not watching.

Something feels off.

I have a pencil in my hand and a math workbook to write in.

"I'm helping Celeste," I say. "But I don't know what I'm doing. Will you have a look?"

Nora laughs. "It's first grade math! How hard can it be?" She pulls out a pair of reading glasses from the pocket of her apron and joins me at the table, nonetheless.

My hand is shaking so hard that I can barely guide the tip of the pencil. My writing is scraggly and barely intelligible.

He kidnapped me. I'm a prisoner. Help me.

She takes a step back and stares at me, her blue eyes searching my face carefully. Her lips part but no words come out.

What am I doing? I've just doomed her.

I hear the toilet flush, then the water running.

The pencil moves quickly as I write, my hand even less steady than before.

Don't react. Where is he?

How will that help me? Knowing where he is... It's not like I know the house. In the bathroom, the water stops running. I can imagine Celeste drying her hands, lifting herself on her tiptoes to check her hair in the mirror. She's not in a hurry to get back to her homework. She hates math.

Nora is frozen. At least she's listening to me, not reacting.

I bite the inside of my cheek. Hard. I taste blood. The door is open, and it would be stupid of me not to run. I've missed so many opportunities already. If I do this, I'm signing Nora's death sentence. Celeste's too, possibly. Will Oscar truly do something bad to them? Celeste is his neighbors' daughter. He can't just make her disappear when her parents have sent her over to his house themselves. And Nora... She's been cleaning and cooking for him for weeks now. Surely, her family knows where she works.

I must do this. Now. I must run.

I squeeze the pencil in my hand and take off. I'm not John Wick, but this is the only thing that I have resembling a weapon. I bolt out the door and stop in front of the stairs. My head is spinning. I look up, and it seems to me like they're never-ending, even though there are probably less than a dozen steps. It's dark. After the bright lights in my room, my eyes refuse to adjust. There is a wooden door at the end of the stairs. I grip the handrail and propel myself towards it, praying my legs don't give in halfway. I'm so stressed, so afraid, that I feel a tightness in my chest.

The door is within reach. I grasp the knob, but it lunges open, pulling me with it. I stumble on the last two steps and feel a strong hand on my arm. I look up into Oscar's eyes.

His jaw is tight. His fingers press so hard into my flesh that I let out a cry. He pushes me back, and I almost slip down the stairs. I grab the rail with the other hand and find my footing. He moves closer to me, not letting go of my arm, and closes the door behind him. We're climbing down the stairs, one step at a time, him pushing me, me going backwards. Tears run down my cheeks, and I can't stop them.

"Where do you think you're going?" he asks in a tight, barely contained voice.

"Let go. You're hurting me. Please let go."

To my shock, he does. I trip over my own feet and land on my back at the foot of the stairs.

"What's going on?" I hear Celeste ask from the room in the basement.

"Nothing," Nora says quickly. "Everything is fine."

"Evie fell!" Celeste sounds agitated.

"Just an accident," Nora says.

Oscar hovers over me. He leans down to grab me and pull me to my feet, and I remember I still have the pencil. I take a swing at him, letting out a pathetic battle cry, and catch him in the jaw. He grunts and leans away. I turn onto my hands and knees so I can push myself up, feeling weaker than ever. I see Celeste is trying to get to me, but Nora is holding her back, positioning herself between her and the door.

"Are you okay?" Celeste yells.

"She's okay, honey," Nora says. "Oscar is helping her."

Using the wall for support, I get up and face Oscar again. He's between me and my only escape route, holding his jaw. I don't see any blood, though. I barely managed to scratch him. Crying out, I lunge at him with the pencil, but he catches me and holds me at arm's length.

"Calm down," he says. "You're only hurting yourself. And them."

I sob as I try to get him off me. To get past him. I can see the stairs and the door, and I can't believe I was so close.

"Stop it," he hisses before pushing me into the room.

I open my mouth to scream, but he gives me a look and shakes his head. He's standing in the doorway, still covering his jaw with one hand. He looks past my head, at Nora and Celeste.

"It's time to go home," he says. "I saw your dad's car pull in the driveway."

Celeste hesitates for a moment. I turn to look at her and notice her eyes are wide and her chin is trembling, like she's about to cry. Nora starts packing up her things, avoiding my gaze. The girl shoulders her backpack and rushes out of the room and up the stairs without a word.

I collapse on the edge of the bed, breathing heavily. Oscar didn't do anything to her. He let her go home, and she will tell her parents. She's running home now, probably yelling at her father from across the front lawn that Oscar is hurting Evie. They will call the police. It's the normal thing to do. And if they don't do it right away, they will see what I wrote in her math workbook. This will be over soon.

"What did you think you were doing?" Oscar asks Nora.

She shrugs and stumbles over her words. "I-I'm sorry."

He advances towards her, and the relief I felt seconds ago vanishes. He has a murderous look in his eyes.

"Run," I yell at Nora.

She turns to look at me, shock marring her features, and that's when Oscar grabs her by the arm and pulls her out of the room. She follows him instead of fighting him. I jump to my feet.

"He will hurt you! You must run!"

I rush to catch up. Oscar has already punched in the code, and the door is closing. I am determined to slip through, but then I see that he has his hands around Nora's throat. He's strangling her, and she's clawing at his hands, eyes wide, mouth agape and soundless.

I stop in my tracks, not knowing what to do. The pencil in my hand has proved to be useless. I'm still squeezing it, my fingernails digging into my palm.

The door slides closed before me.

Chapter Forty-Two
The One

Hours pass. I'm curled up on the floor, knees to my chest, back against the cold metal door. I rock back and forth, back and forth. My eyes are dry. There are no more tears, and I'm horribly dehydrated, but I can't bring myself to get up. I contemplate crawling to the bathroom for a glass of tap water, but while my brain sends all the right signals to my body, my limbs refuse to move.

"He killed her," I whisper to myself. My own voice sounds weird to my ears. Like it's alien, like it doesn't come from this plane of existence. "He killed her."

What about the girl? Did Celeste make it back home? Did she tell her parents about what happened here? If yes, this should be ending soon. All they have to do is check her math homework. Parents do that, right? They check to see if their kids did their homework. What I wrote on the upper edge of the page in pencil is all the proof they need to call the police.

This will be over soon. Yes. I rub my eyes, let out a groan, and take a few deep breaths. I need to be ready. I need to get up, drink some water, and prepare to be rescued. They will ask me questions. I have to make sure my answers are as clear as possible, so there will be no doubt about what Oscar did to me. To Rita and to Nora. I can do this. I just need to... get off the floor.

It takes me another hour to pull myself together enough that I'm not shaking anymore. I pace the room, stare into the cameras, keep myself moving and alert, afraid that if I sit down, I'll get stuck again. Nothing happens. No one comes. Oscar doesn't bring me any food, which doesn't surprise me. One, he's mad at me. Two, he's busy dealing with Nora's body. The lights dim at some point, which means the sun has set and it's time to go to bed. I won't be able to sleep tonight, so I don't even attempt it. I will stay up until I get rescued.

It doesn't happen during the night. The silence is maddening. I don't hear policemen breaking into the house, I don't hear their heavy boots thudding down the stairs to get to me. I fight sleep with all my might, listening, waiting, hoping.

It doesn't happen in the morning. The lights brighten up, hurting my tired eyes. My stomach rumbles, and I eat an energy bar from the snack basket. I must ration the snacks because I know Oscar is punishing me again.

It doesn't happen by lunch, and it doesn't happen by dinner. No one comes. The silence is so deep, so intentional, that I start wondering if Oscar is upstairs at all. If he's still watching me. The lights dim, it's night again, and I'm sure it's an automated system. My stomach is unhappy, growling and gurgling. I eat half a bag of chips and drink a lot of water. Despite myself, I fall asleep and wake up when the bright lights announce it's morning.

No sign of Oscar. No sign of anyone. If the police don't come, then he has to. He must, or I'll starve here. Then at some point during the day, a thought hits me: what if he ran away? It makes me jump to my feet and pace the basement like a wild animal trapped in a cage. Bathroom, library, bedroom. Bathroom, library, bedroom. I feel like I'm going crazy. What if Oscar realized he wouldn't get away with Nora's murder like he did with Rita's? What if he got into his car and drove away, leaving me behind? He could be in another state by now.

I feel like I'm suffocating. I press my hands to my chest and stare into the nearest camera purposefully.

"Hey! I know this is my punishment. I understand. I'm sorry for what I did. And I'm not asking you to bring me food, okay? But... just let me know you're there. Okay? Come talk to me. Or give me a sign."

Nothing. Not that I expect him to come running. I pace for a few more minutes, then choose another camera and try again.

"Hey! Hey, come on! Let me know you're there." I beg like this until my voice becomes choked up. "Please. Please don't leave me here. I've learned my lesson this time, I promise. Please."

He doesn't come. He doesn't have to come if he doesn't want to see me, but he could... make the lights flicker. Anything to let me know he hasn't abandoned me. It takes all the inner strength I have left to not freak out. Hour after hour passes, and I try to distract myself. I nibble on the few snacks I have left, page through books, unable to read a single word, pace, curl up in a corner, pace some more, curl up in another corner.

What can I do? What can I do to draw his attention, force him to give me a sign – any sign – that he's there?

I know. It won't be pretty. It will come with consequences whether it works or not, but at least I'll have my answer.

I go into the bathroom, plug the sink, and turn on the water to the max. I stuff toilet paper into the overflow hole, and the sink fills up quickly. I step away when the water hits the pink floor tiles. I watch it flow in all directions, getting closer and closer to the threshold. The door to the bedroom is wide open, and the water starts seeping into the thick carpet. I stand to the side, arms wrapped around myself, waiting to see what happens.

If something happens at all.

The first thing I hear is hasty footsteps on the other side of the metal door, then Oscar cursing loudly, and the door finally slides open. I hold my chin up as he enters the room and rushes into the bathroom, his shoes making sloshing sounds on the soggy carpet.

"What were you thinking?" he yells at me as he turns the water off and unplugs the sink. "Are you crazy?"

I stand just out of his reach. He wants to grab me but gets distracted by the ruined carpet. A string of curses leaves his mouth. In his haste, I expected him to forget to punch in the code to close the door, but he's more calculated than that.

"Where's Nora?" I ask. "Did you kill her?"

He sighs and runs a hand through his dark hair. "Now I have to clean this, because you won't."

I would if he gave me a mop. I'd also try to stab him with the mop handle.

"Why don't you bring Nora to clean it? Is it because you killed her?"

He looks up at me, stunned for a second. Like he can't believe I just flooded the bathroom to get a reaction out of him.

"You're insane," he says. "I try to help you, I'm doing my best, taking care of you, giving you everything, and what do you do? You choose to rot in here and become paranoid."

My chin starts trembling. I swallow hard and blink a few times to make sure I don't start crying. I am so angry at him that a gruesome image flashes before my eyes. What if I push him into the bathroom, so hard that he slips on the wet floor and hits his head on the sink? Can I do it? Do I have it in me?

"You need help," he says.

"You're right, I do." My voice is shaking.

"In the form of medication!" he yells. "I thought about it, I hesitated... But now I know it's the only way you will get better."

My stomach sinks. "No. What do you mean by that? What sort of medication?"

"Antidepressants."

"You can't make me take anything."

He laughs.

I realize he's not concerned about my taking it or not because he intends to put it in my food. This is going from bad to worse.

"I'm not depressed." I try to keep my voice calm and even. "I'm sorry I flooded the bathroom, but you weren't answering me. I needed to know that you haven't left me."

"Leave you? No. I should leave you, but I'm an idiot, aren't I? I can't give up on you so easily, though I'm close, Evie. I'm this close." He looks at the soggy carpet, curses again, then walks around the damp spot to get to me. "In the library with you. Now. I have to clean the mess you've made."

I try to avoid him, but he's quicker than me. He grabs me by the arm and pushes me into the other room.

"Don't lock me in here," I scream as he slams the door in my face. "Oscar, please! Let's talk about it." I hear the key turn in the lock.

"About what, Evie?"

"I'm not depressed. I don't need medication. Please, just tell me Nora is okay. Tell me you didn't kill her."

"Oh, so you miss your friend. That's why you decided to act up." He tries the door to make sure it's locked. "Is that the problem? That you're feeling lonely? Well, guess what. I'm feeling lonely, too. Maybe I'll fix it for both of us."

I wait for him to explain, but he falls silent. A minute later, I hear the whirring of the metal door.

"Oscar?"

He left.

"Oh God." I rattle the door futilely. There's no way I can break it. "Oscar?"

A few minutes pass, and I hear him come back. From the sound of it, he's struggling with something. A bucket and a mop, probably. Cleaning supplies. He curses under his breath. I press myself to the door.

"Oscar?"

"What?"

"What do you mean when you say you'll fix it for both of us?"

"What?!"

I sigh, trying to keep my emotions in check. With everything that's happened, I'm bordering on hysterical, and that's the last thing he needs to sense coming from me. Maybe he wanted to scare me when he said he'd put me on medication. Maybe he's serious about it.

"Loneliness. You'll fix it for both of us. How?"

I can hear the water slosh and drip into the bucket when he wrings the mop.

"How do you think?" he says. "I'll bring you someone to keep you company. See? I care about you, Evie. Even after the disaster you caused today."

I feel like I've been punched in the gut. My mind instantly goes to Bobbi and Celeste. I know their parents live around here, and Oscar would never kidnap them. But what if he kidnaps a baby from somewhere else? He tested me with Bobbi and Celeste, and now that he knows I do well with kids, what if he intends to bring me one and leave it here?

"Someone?" I ask. "What do you mean by someone?"

He doesn't answer.

"Oscar? Who will you bring?"

Again, no answer. I can hear him cleaning the bathroom, so I know he's still here and he can hear me.

"Oscar, it better not be a child," I say, my voice sounding desperate.

"Will you be quiet and let me focus? I'm trying to figure out how I can salvage the carpet."

I let out a sob. "Oscar, don't bring anyone, okay? I don't need company. I have you. I'm not lonely, I promise."

He slams his fist into the door, making me jump away.

"Evie, if you don't shut up..."

He doesn't finish the sentence, and he doesn't have to. Knowing how his mind works, the threat of him getting some novel idea about how he can punish me better is enough.

I trudge to the beanbag, plop down, and stare at the door. I keep quiet.

Chapter Forty-Three

The One

I'm shocked Oscar lets me out of the library later. I even get food.

"Will you behave?" he asks, pointing a finger at me. He's on his way out.

"Yes," I say, dutifully sitting at the table.

He eyes the damp spot on the carpet, then squints at me and nods. As always, he makes sure I can't see the code when he punches it in.

I dig into my meal, relieved he hasn't left me to starve. My plan worked. But I can tell the food isn't cooked by Nora, and I feel a lump in my throat even as I chew and swallow. I try not to think about it, but how can I not? I will never see her again. After what happened to Rita, I promised myself I would protect Nora at all costs. I failed. I lost my mind, thinking I could escape, and now my only friend in this dreadful place is no more.

I am convinced Oscar killed her. He strangled Rita right in front of my eyes, and that's all the proof I need that he did the same to Nora. He dragged her out of the room first, but not because he didn't want me to see him do it. He loves torturing me, loves showing me exactly what the ugly consequences of my actions are. When he killed Rita, I was handcuffed to the bed frame, so I couldn't do anything, even though I tried. I wasn't restrained now, and he didn't want to risk my jumping on his back. Together, Nora and I could've had a good chance at overpowering him.

It frightens me how calculated he remains in the most critical situations. I am starting to doubt Oscar can ever be taken by surprise or thrown off even for a second.

I enjoy my little victory for now. With food in my belly, I can think again. Not as clearly as I'd like, but the desperation I felt earlier, when I was worried Oscar might've taken off and left me here to die, has tapered off. I will allow myself to feel good about the fact that I got his attention, and he brought me food, and think about what comes next later.

What comes next...

I shudder as I try to bat the thought away. I can't. The terror that he's going to kidnap a child and bring it to me to raise in this basement comes back full force. I'm happy that I've eaten for sixty seconds straight, and now I must push the plate away and run to the bathroom to splash cold water on my face. I feel sick but determined to keep the food down. I need the nutrients.

I stare at my reflection in the mirror. My cheeks are hollow, the dark circles under my eyes look like black holes. My hair has lost all its shine. It's thin and matted to my skull, and my mousy brown roots are showing. For years, I've been dyeing it at home. I can't afford to go to the salon, and box dye works for me. I haven't seen my roots grown so much in a long time, and it strikes me how old they make me look.

I can't stop the tears from falling. I drop my head and sob, my bony shoulders shaking. This is what I've become. A shadow of a woman. This is what Oscar has done to me.

At least I am alive. It doesn't warm me much, but even after so much pain and mental torture, I'm afraid of dying. I'm afraid of him physically hurting me, snuffing the life out of me. Maybe that's why I haven't tried harder to escape. He's taunted me with the open door. Each time, I wanted to run, and each time, it felt like a trap. Self-preservation made me stay put. When I finally didn't stay put, Nora paid with her life.

I wash my face and tell myself I can get through today. What else can I do? One minute at a time, one breath at a time. My mind keeps wandering to Nora. It doesn't matter if my eyes are shut or wide open; all I can see is Oscar's hands wrapped around her throat, and the shocked expression on her face as she stares right into his eyes.

I take a shower and wash my hair to distract myself. I nibble at the leftovers, and when the lights dim, I slide into bed, wrapping the duvet tightly around me. I'm exhausted and sleep comes easily.

I startle awake when I hear the all too familiar whirr of the metal door. This is unusual. My heart is hammering in my chest as I sit up, safely wrapped in the duvet. I watch the door slide into the wall, my sleep-addled brain coming up with worst-case scenarios. Oscar has never come down here in the middle of the night. He either spends the night or leaves me to sleep in peace.

Every time he changes something, every time he does something he's never done before, I think he's done with me. Bored. He'll kill me and get rid of my body, find himself another toy.

He stumbles into the room, and I can see he's got someone with him.

Not a child, thank God! Not a baby.

He lets out a frustrated grunt as he struggles to hold the woman upright and punch in the code. She's petite, with short brown hair, dressed in straight-cut jeans and a white T-shirt, and she's heavily drugged.

"No, don't bother to help," he says sarcastically.

He hauls her up into his arms and carries her to the bed. He's swaying a little, and I realize he's drunk. I've never seen him drunk before. Not even tipsy.

I disentangle myself from the duvet and hurry to put distance between me and him. And the mysterious woman. I realize I'm acting like an idiot. I should check to see if she's okay.

"What did you do to her?"

"She's just very tired, needs to rest." He's slurring his words.

He drops her on the bed and digs for the handcuffs that are hidden under the mattress. Swiftly, he secures both her wrists.

"Did you drug her? Did you kidnap her?" I wrap my arms around myself. I'm shaking, even though the temperature in the room is perfect. I don't know how he does it, but it's never too cold and never too warm. He controls the temperature like he controls the lights. With ease. Like he's the god of this place.

He grins at me. "Evie, you get the strangest ideas into that pretty head of yours." He closes the space between us and pokes me playfully between the eyes. "Must be all those dark books you're reading."

I step away from him.

"You're so dark, aren't you?" he continues, chuckling. "You look so innocent. Who would ever think?"

"What did you do to her?" I avoid him again and glance at the woman on the bed. She's completely out of it. "Why did you bring her here?"

"I promised to bring you someone to keep you company. A friend. I always keep my promises, Evie. Come on. You know me. Do I ever disappoint you?"

"You're sick," I say through gritted teeth. It's a bad idea to talk to him like this, but I can't help it. I'm boiling with anger. "You're the worst person I've ever met. You lie, you manipulate, you gaslight. You kidnap people. You kill people. You're a psycho."

His eyes widen behind his glasses. They're slightly askew on his nose, and he straightens them gently.

"Psycho," he says. He sounds calm. "You don't know what you're talking about."

I open my mouth to express my bafflement with him, but nothing comes out.

He straightens his posture and fixes me with his gaze. A chill runs down my spine. Because I realize he's not as drunk as I thought he was.

"You don't know, Evie." He sounds serious. Intentional. "Because you haven't seen psycho." The grin is back on his lips. It makes his face look crooked in an unhinged way. "You haven't seen psycho yet."

He points a finger at me, shakes his head, then moves towards the door.

I step closer to the bed, put myself between him and the unconscious woman, but it's too little, too late. There's a weakness inside me. I feel like it's ingrained. The few times when I'm brave are the wrong times.

"When she wakes up, tell her how things work around here," he says. He punches in the code, the door opens, and before it closes again behind him, he waves dismissively.

How things work around here.

I stand next to the bed and look down at Oscar's newest victim. In the dim lights, I can see that she's pale.

Thin, small, helpless. Like me. She's breathing softly. She doesn't seem to be hurt, except for the red prick on her neck, where Oscar injected her with the same thing he injected me with. When she wakes up, she'll have one hell of a headache.

I sit down next to her and run my hand over her cheek. She doesn't stir. I don't know what to do. Should I try to wake her up now? What good would it do? Better to let her sleep. For once, it makes sense to delay the inevitable. I'm not looking forward to the moment when she realizes she's been kidnapped and put in a basement that looks like a pink dollhouse.

At least I'm here. When she opens her eyes, she'll see me, and hopefully, she won't be as scared as I was when I woke up in this place with my hands cuffed to the bed frame. I slide to the floor and hug my legs to my chest, my chin on top of my knees. I watch over her like a sentinel.

"What's your name?" I whisper. "I can't wait to meet you."

I bite the inside of my cheek because I know how bad it sounds. As messed up as this is, she'll be the first person I can truly talk to. I couldn't talk to Rita or Nora, or Celeste. But this woman, whoever she is, is going through the same horrible fate as me. I can be real with her, tell her everything without having to worry about censoring myself. We won't talk about the weather and how nice the neighborhood is. We will talk about what's happening to us, and maybe we'll figure it out together. Maybe she'll help me understand what I did to deserve this.

Maybe she'll be able to answer my questions.

Is anyone looking for me? Is there a missing person case? Am I all over the news? Is anyone aware – anyone at all – that I've been gone without a trace for nearly three months?

"Wake up," I whisper as I start rocking back and forth. It's hard to sit still. I'll wait – of course I'll wait – but I wish for her to wake up already, so I can begin this new chapter of my imprisonment. So we can begin this new chapter of whatever Oscar has in store for us.

He never does things randomly. He said he's brought me a friend, but I know there's more to this move. I'm scared to learn what it is, but I'm also anxious to meet this girl and see why he chose her. How alike are we? Is she weak too, and brave at all the wrong times?

Wrong times or right times, maybe we can be brave together.

Chapter Forty-Four

The One

A groan comes from the woman on the bed, followed by a whimper.

My eyes snap open. I didn't mean to, but I lay down on the floor at some point during the night and fell asleep. I sit up now, on my hands and knees, and look at her. I can see her lips moving, as if she's trying to say something. Her eyebrows furrow. She stretches one leg and tries to bring her arms down to her sides.

My heart picks up the pace. I scurry closer to the edge of the bed.

"Hey," I whisper.

She opens her eyes. Blinks a few times. I can tell her vision is blurry. Mine was too at first.

"Hey," I say again, giving her a smile.

She has big green eyes framed by long, dark lashes. I'm close enough to count the freckles on her nose.

She doesn't say anything, just stares at me for a moment, then her gaze shifts from my face to the room. The walls, the ceiling, the table and the wardrobe, the metal door. She tries to move her hands again, but all she manages is a few inches. The chain rattles, the cuffs dig into her wrists. She winces.

"Hey." It's like "hey" is the only word in my vocabulary.

"No," she says in a small, choked whisper. "No. No, no, no."

She's starting to freak out, pulling harder at the restraints. I reach out and take her hands into mine. She freezes at my touch. I realize my hands are as cold as ice.

"You're only hurting yourself," I say.

"Uncuff me," she says. "Uncuff me right now."

"What?" I don't understand what she's saying. Why would she believe–

"Why are you doing this to me? Where am I?"

Our eyes lock, and I realize she's angry. At me. I pull away, scrambling to my feet. She thinks I did this to her, and she's not scared like I was when I first woke up in the basement; she's furious. Studying her again, I can see that, yes, she's thin, but she's fit. Real muscles cover her delicate frame, and even with her hands secured to the bed frame, she can kick me and seriously hurt me if she wants to.

"No, it's not me," I say, raising my hands in defense, making sure I'm a safe distance away from the bed. "I didn't do anything. I don't know you. He brought you in a few hours ago and handcuffed you to the bed. Like he did to me... um... three months ago. Or at least I think that's how long I've been here."

She purses her lips and looks me up and down, eyes slightly squinted. I'm sure she has a killer headache.

"I know you," she says after a full minute. "My God, I know you!"

"What?"

"You're Eveline Grace Davis. You disappeared back in June. Your photo was all over the news for a while."

My knees give in. I crumble to the floor, and for once I'm grateful for the thick carpet. I don't care how pink and ugly it is; it cushions my fall. I shake my head as I stare at her in shock. She's just said the words I've been so desperate to hear.

Then it dawns on me. "What do you mean 'for a while'?"

She gives me a sad, sympathetic look. "You know how it is. The world moves on fast."

"You mean they stopped looking?"

"No," she hurries to reassure me. "I'm sure it's not like that. They just..."

"They're looking for a body."

She winces and nods. We're both silent for a few minutes. She's stopped struggling, and she's inspecting the handcuffs instead. I feel like she's avoiding my gaze on purpose. A tear rolls down from the corner of my eye, and I wipe it quickly. I need a moment to compose myself, to wrap my head around what it means that the police are looking for a body. My body. Is there still a chance that they'll find me?

Us. That they'll find us.

"What's your name?" I ask.

She sits up in bed, a resigned expression on her face. "Sydney. Sydney Murphy."

I give her a smile. "I'm Evie. I would shake your hand..." I bite the inside of my lip. "Sorry. That's stupid."

She regards me with curiosity. "You can call me Syd."

"Syd," I whisper, nodding. I push myself to my feet and stand there awkwardly. "How's your head?"

She scrunches up her nose. "Hurts."

"Yeah, mine hurt too when I first..." I trail off. "He gave me Ibuprofen. I... I finished the blister a while ago."

"Oscar."

My heart jolts when she says his name. "You know who kidnapped you."

She lets out a sigh. "Yes."

"You sound like you know Oscar."

"We work together. I mean, we work for the same company. I'm just an employee and recently got the job. He's one of the managers."

I cover my mouth with my hand, then reconsider and wrap both arms around myself. I move from one foot to the other. I don't know what to do with myself, how to react. She has so much information that my mind is blown.

"Tell me everything," I say.

She shifts in bed, obviously uncomfortable. "He's not going to uncuff me anytime soon, is he?"

"I don't think so. He kept me cuffed to the bed... um..." I remember when he left me restrained for two days to punish me for Rita. And then he had to change the mattress. I don't feel like telling Syd about it. "I had to gain his trust."

"Right."

"Let me fix the pillows for you," I offer.

"Okay."

I approach the bed and lean over to stack the two pillows behind her back. "Better."

"Yeah, thanks." She looks up at me, and I feel like she's still studying me, like she has yet to make an opinion about my character. "You can sit down, you know."

"Okay. Thanks." I sit on the edge of the bed but immediately shoot back to my feet. "Are you thirsty? You're probably thirsty." I don't wait for her to answer, I rush to the bathroom and return with a plastic cup filled with tap water. "Here."

She attempts to take it from me with her bound hands, but I realize it will be hard for her to bring it to her lips. The chain is too short.

"May I?"

"I think you'll have to," she says, frustrated.

I hold the glass for her, and she finishes it in two gulps. "More?"

"No, I'm okay. Thanks, Evie."

"You're welcome." I climb on the bed, tucking my legs under me. "I didn't know Oscar before this. The first time

I saw him was when he jabbed me with a needle the night he kidnapped me. He told me he'd been stalking me for months. I can't believe he kidnapped someone he works with."

"You know what that means, right?"

I avert my gaze, but only for a second. I like looking at her. I like being so close to someone, finally. Close to someone I can relate to, and who can relate to me.

"I'm not getting out of here alive," she says.

"Me neither. He never covered his face. Didn't hide his identity. I don't know what he intends to do with us, but yeah..."

"Did he ever..." She hesitates.

I wait for her to finish the sentence because I genuinely don't know what she means.

She takes a deep breath. "Did he touch you?"

"Oh, no! He didn't do anything. He... Okay, so this is strange. He brought me here to be his girlfriend. His future wife. Actually, he's been calling me his wife lately. He says he wants to provide for me and give me everything I need, so I can just... exist. But he never touched me. He said he would wait until I... Well, until I ask him to."

Syd winces hard. She looks so disgusted that I think she's about to be sick.

"How about you?" I ask. "Why do you think he took you?"

She shrugs. "I don't know. I've practically just met him. We're not on the same team at work. At first, we didn't really interact, and then we sort of became friends. Or so I thought." She looks up at the ceiling and shakes her head. "I'm so stupid. I thought he cared, and I told him my whole story."

"What story?"

"Are those cameras?"

"Yes." I look at the camera she's looking at. I know Oscar is watching us. I wonder if he's enjoying the show – the drama he's caused. I wonder if it's everything he wished for. "There are cameras everywhere, including in the bathroom. And microphones."

"Wait. So, he's watching and listening to us?"

"Yes."

"That bastard!" She stares into the camera more intently, her eyes squinting. "What's your angle here, you sicko? You put us in here together. Now what?"

I'm unfazed. I know by now that Oscar doesn't respond when prompted. He only does what he likes.

"Before he brought you last night, we had a fight," I say. "I haven't been doing well lately."

"I wonder why."

That takes me aback. I stare at her, mouth agape, and she gives me a smirk. It's a joke. She just made a joke. I let out a breath, then a laugh. She laughs with me. The tension between us dissipates.

"Go on," she says.

"He told me he was going to bring me someone to keep me company. Because I've been lonely, and that makes me depressed. And paranoid."

Her eyes widen. "That's some textbook gaslighting if I ever heard one."

"I know that, obviously, but there's no arguing with him."

"So, I'm here to be... your friend?"

"I'm sorry," I say quickly. "This is all my fault. I've been acting up, trying to get a reaction from him. I flooded the bathroom, he got mad, and now here you are. This should've never happened to you. You don't deserve it."

"And you do, Evie?"

I curl up, making myself small. "I'm the perfect victim. No friends, I barely talk to my family, zero social life, and I work from the kitchen table in my cramped apartment. I never made any effort to get out there, have a life, meet people, do better."

"That's not the correct answer," she says, her voice firm but gentle. "The correct answer is no. You don't deserve this."

From behind my lashes, I steal a glance at her. "You don't know me. You don't know what I did."

"What did you do?"

I want to tell her about Rita. How Oscar brought her the first week to clean the basement, and how I got her killed. I want to tell her about Nora. I find that I can't. The words are stuck in my throat, and I can't push them out. What will Sydney think of me? That I'm irresponsible, playing with people's lives. That Oscar warned me there would be consequences to my behaving badly, and I didn't listen.

Syd waits for me to say something, and when I don't, she sighs. "You didn't do anything, Evie."

Better to change the subject. "What did you see in the news? About my disappearance."

"Your mother reported you missing."

"When?"

"June 28."

It's like a punch to the gut. That is one week and a day after Oscar took me. I was right to think no one would notice my absence. Now I regret not calling my mother more often. She rarely calls me, but I should've done better, not wait for her to reach out all the time. It happened once or twice that she'd call me, I wouldn't be near my phone, and I'd forget to call her back for a few hours. One time, I called her back the next day, feeling guilty about it, but she acted like it was fine, and I took it for granted. Okay, maybe it happened more than once or twice.

Since my father retired and he's at home all the time, she can't talk freely anymore. Our conversations on the phone are lackluster, almost robotic, and neither of us is looking forward to them. So, I don't blame her that she reported me missing eight days after I was kidnapped, but it still hurts.

"I'm sorry," Syd says.

"Why?"

"The police questioned your neighbors. They didn't know anything. When they questioned the owner of the convenience store one block from where you live, his son told them he saw you last on the night of June 20. He said you shop there all the time and he wondered why you stopped coming all of a sudden. He thought you must've moved."

I smile. It's nice to know someone did take stock of my existence. And to think the reason I went for my snacks around midnight was because I wanted to avoid the owner, who likes to draw his clients into meaningless small talk. His son is young – maybe eighteen? – and barely looks up from his phone when he rings up people's groceries.

"You really followed my case," I say.

"I'm not usually into this sort of thing. I don't even watch the news. I don't have a TV, and I'm totally disconnected from what's going on in the world. Some of my friends shared articles about it. About you."

"What did they say about me?"

"That you're a writer and a book lover, that you keep to yourself and don't have enemies because you wouldn't hurt a fly. That you're young, bright, and beautiful, and whoever took your life is a monster."

"I'm still alive," I murmur.

"Yes." Sydney leans towards me, as much as the chain allows it. "As horrible as this is... As much as I don't want to be here... I'm glad I found you and that you're alive and in one piece."

I chew on my lower lip. "I'm alive, but I'm not sure about the one piece part."

She cocks an eyebrow. "That's metaphorical."

I chuckle. "Yes, it is."

She gives me a warm smile. "Good. Because I'm getting you out of here."

I want to hug her. I want to ask her how she's going to do that. I delay it, because if I ask her, then I must tell her everything I know about Oscar. Everything he did to me.

Not yet. For now, I just want to be with her. I want to look at her, talk to her, cuddle next to her.

I don't.

Sydney has only woken up an hour ago, and I'm already doing what Oscar wants me to do – treat her like a friend. I'm not thinking about escaping. Not really. My attempts have not only been futile, but they've caused death. I don't want to think about how Oscar will punish us – me – if we try something and fail. So, I'm not thinking about escaping. I'm just selfishly happy she's here.

Chapter Forty-Five

The One

Five minutes after the lights turn up, Oscar comes in with breakfast. The tray is loaded for two.

I jump off the bed and stand in front of Sydney. She's trying to look past me.

"Evie, I don't need to remind you of the rules, do I?" The door closes behind him, but he doesn't move. He first wants to make sure that Syd and I are calm and will not give him trouble. "You do anything stupid, someone else suffers. In this case, that someone will be her."

"I know," I say.

"You sick bastard," Sydney says from behind me.

He ignores her and advances towards the table, not taking his eyes off us. I realize he's feeling uncomfortable. He made the choice to bring Sydney here, but it seems like he's having second thoughts. She's shackled to the bed, though. The only way we could pose a real threat to him is if we're both free to move. Then, yes, if we jump him at the same time, we might win in a fight. As I'm thinking about this, it seems to me he's already taken this scenario into consideration. He's moving at a careful, calculated pace, and he looks tense.

He places the tray on the table, unloads it, then reaches one hand behind his back. He unhooks something from his belt, and when he shows it to me, I freeze.

Oscar is holding a gun.

"This is so you know that I mean it," he says. "I don't like carrying a gun around you, Evie, because I don't want to scare you. Besides, I trust you. We've known each other for a while, we've become close, and I know you've learned your lessons."

I nod. My hands are shaking, and I join them in front of my chest, almost in a prayer. He nods too, and I know he has me where he wants me. It's serious this time, and Sydney is not Rita or Nora. The cleaning women were dispensable. He wants to keep Sydney.

He wants to keep us both in his basement, and he needs us to play nice.

"Move aside," he tells me.

I glance back at Sydney, and she gives me a nod. It surprises me how collected she is. On my first day, I acted stupid. If she's afraid, she doesn't show it. There's a look of confidence – almost defiance – on her face, and I'm worried she'll do or say something that will put us both in danger.

"How are you, Syd?" Oscar asks. He holds the gun leisurely, at his side. "Did you sleep well?"

"How am I?" There's sarcasm in her voice. "Kidnapped, that's how I am." She rattles the chain for emphasis. "Why don't you uncuff me and tell me what's going on? Why are you doing this to me? Why am I here? We work together, Oscar! For a minute, I thought we were friends."

"And we are," he says. "Such good friends, that I wanted you to meet Evie. I think you two will get along well. I think you'll become best friends."

"You're not making sense," Syd says.

"Evie has been feeling lonely. She needs a friend, someone her age that she can talk to." He tucks the gun back into his belt, which means he's more relaxed. "I looked into your past, Syd, and I know you need a friend, too. I'm looking out for both of you here. Abigail betrayed you. She stole your man, and then they both threw you away like yesterday's trash. They're horrible people and don't deserve you. They never did. If you ask me, they did you a favor by sleeping together. Now you can have a true best friend."

I look at Syd, and it dawns on me. She's the perfect victim. That's why Oscar chose her. He met her at work, stalked her, and found out she's completely alone. Like me, no one will miss her. I don't know who Abigail is, but it sounds like she and Syd were friends, and then Abigail stole her boyfriend. If Syd and this guy broke up, then it means she must've lost a lot of mutual friends. That's how breakups usually work.

My mother realized that I was missing after one week and a day. How long will it take for anyone in Sydney's life to figure out she's disappeared?

Coworkers. She has coworkers. But Oscar is a manager at the company. For sure, he took care of that loose end already.

Syd shakes her head. "There's no limit to your madness." She seems to be at a loss for words, which I understand. Oscar says ridiculous, infuriating things intentionally, and then makes it impossible to argue with him.

"You will get used to this arrangement," he says, motioning at the room. "At first, it was hard for Evie, but then she couldn't deny she truly has everything she needs, so there's nothing to be upset about. I saw your apartment, Syd." He cringes. "This is so much better."

I glance at Syd, wondering when Oscar saw her apartment and in what circumstances. Did he break into her place? I need him to go away, so she can tell me everything. I also want to know about Abigail and her ex. But maybe she doesn't want to talk about them. I'm boiling with impatience. I want to know everything about her.

"There's a bathroom with a tub," he says, motioning at the door behind me that is always cracked open. "And there's a library in the other room. Evie reads dark romance, but if you're not into that, just make me a list of books. I'll get them for you." He walks to the closet and opens it. "These are Evie's things." He hesitates for a moment, a baffled look on his face. "I guess I forgot to do the laundry. Okay, I'll take care of it today." He turns to us, giving an awkward chuckle. "So many things to do in this house. It's not easy to be a provider. Now that our cleaning lady left us, I must do all the cleaning, grocery shopping and cooking. She was of great help, but I guess she had too many clients. Oh well. I miss her, but what can I do?"

I let out a sob and quickly cover my mouth with my hand. I haven't yet told Sydney about Nora. I just didn't want to spend our first day together talking about the gruesome things Oscar has done to torture me.

"It looks like you and Evie are the same size." He's still talking to Syd. "You'll share, and I'll buy some new clothes for the both of you this weekend. Okay, what else?" He looks at me, as if to ask if he's forgetting anything.

I shrug. "Will you uncuff her?"

Oscar lets out a laugh. "You're sweet. No. It's too soon for that. And you should know. Like you, Syd will have to earn my trust."

"How will she eat, then?"

"Oh, you'll have to help her." He takes a plate of food and walks over to me. "Here. Feed her."

I blink at him. "What?"

"Feed her, and then you can eat."

I exchange a glance with Sydney.

"I'm not hungry," she says.

I look at Oscar. I can feel his mood shifting. He doesn't like it when his orders are not immediately carried out.

"You will stop moping, and you will eat," he says to her.

"What if I don't want to eat?" she challenges him.

He lets out a dramatic sigh, and for a second, I think he'll give up and leave her alone. No such luck. He closes the space between them and leans over her, his hands going to her jaw. She tries to pull away, but the chain is too short, and the handcuffs dig into her wrists. She kicks her legs, and Oscar climbs on top of them, easily holding her down.

"No," I whisper, taking half a step towards the bed.

Oscar gives me a look that's filled with danger. I can see the gun sticking out from his belt, and my hands shake so hard that I spill some of the food on me. Toast, butter side down. It will leave a grease stain. He sees me eyeing the gun, and grins at me as he reaches for it with his free hand. I freeze in place. Syd is frozen, too. He pushes the gun under her chin.

"I will only say this once," he says to her. "If I tell you to eat, you eat. If I tell you to use the bathroom, you use the bathroom. If I tell you to sleep, you sleep. I control you, Sydney. Just like I control Evie. She didn't want to comply at first, and there were consequences, but then she learned, and her life got a hundred times easier than when she was on her own, with no friends, no one to take care of her, struggling to make rent. Look at her now."

He forcefully turns Syd's head towards me. We lock eyes, and while there are tears in mine, hers are dry. I don't understand how she can be so calm when Oscar is pushing the barrel of a gun to her throat. She's probably in such deep shock that she can't react.

"Evie is thriving, and you will too," he says.

Thriving is... an overstatement.

"If you listen to me," he continues. "Now, do you understand? I want to hear you say yes."

"Yes," Syd chokes out.

"Good." Oscar places the gun back where it belongs, gets off Sydney, and motions for me to take his place. "Feed her," he orders me. "I'll let her use the bathroom after, then I must get to the office. Smart of me to bring you breakfast earlier than usual, right? I knew this was going to take a while."

I'm shaking so hard that I don't know how I haven't collapsed yet. I fully believe that he is capable of shooting Syd right in front of me if she doesn't comply. I fully believe he will shoot her if I don't comply. Tears stream down my face, and I can't stop them. It's not the sort of crying that's ugly, and sobby, and snotty. It's just tears – clear and silent.

"Can I use the tray?" I ask. "I need a fork and knife..."

Oscar waves dismissively as he sits in a chair and pulls out his phone. "Sure, whatever."

As I feed Sydney her breakfast, he is engrossed by his phone. He's probably answering emails, and sometimes I think that's what his job consists of. He ignores us, but I know he's on high alert, even as he pretends he's got everything under control.

The truth is, he doesn't. Not yet. He's broken me, but he has yet to break Sydney. I have to warn her that he will. The sooner she understands she can't piss him off, or he'll torture us both, the better. I hate that I have to tell her about Rita and about how Oscar punished me by leaving me cuffed to the bed with no food and no way to use the bathroom for two days. But I must tell her, so she'll understand. She needs to know who we're really dealing with.

When I feed her the last morsel, Oscar gets up and takes out the key to the handcuffs.

"Evie, go eat your breakfast."

I hesitate, and he gives me a look that seems to be patient. For now.

"I can lock you in the library while I do this, or you can sit down and eat," he says.

"I'll eat," I say quickly and hurry to the table.

"Good girl." He's beyond satisfied. He takes hold of Sydney's hands and looks her in the eye. "Are you going to behave, Syd?"

"Sure," she says.

It sounds non-committal to me, and I hope to God she doesn't try anything when Oscar releases her. My heart is beating so hard that it's difficult to breathe. I can't take a single bite of food until I see how this plays out.

Fortunately, Syd decides to let him win. He unlocks the cuffs, and she slides out of the bed and goes to the bathroom. Oscar locks her inside and tells her to knock when she's ready.

He turns to me. "See? Things go smoothly when everyone is on the same page."

"Yes, of course." Now I can eat.

When Syd knocks, Oscar lets her out and takes her back to the bed, where he cuffs her again. She doesn't protest, doesn't try to fight him. I feel bad for her. I know how uncomfortable it is to spend hours in that position. Then Oscar clears the table and leaves, and I rush to Sydney's side.

"Are you okay?"

She nods. "You?"

"Yes."

She lets out a long sigh as she lets her head fall onto the pillow. "Don't tell me we're going to go through this two more times today."

"Lunch and dinner, yeah. But look at the bright side. At least he's feeding us."

Her eyes widen. "What do you mean? Has he ever not fed you?"

I shrug and give her a sad smile. "Do you think I'm naturally this thin?"

"Evie..." She reaches for me, though the chain only allows her a few inches. I sit on the edge of the bed and take her hands in mine. "Tell me everything I need to know about him."

"I... I want to do that, but I don't know if I'm ready." Shame grips my insides. I'm responsible for two women's deaths.

To my surprise, she nods in understanding. "Take your time."

"I mean, what's the rush?" I laugh. "For the time being, you're cuffed to the bed. You can't do anything. We can't do anything."

Also, Oscar can hear us. I don't know where the microphones are, but if we ever plot and plan to escape, he'll know all about it.

"Hey," Sydney says. "I'll figure something out."

"Okay." I don't know if I want her to do that or not. "Mm... do you want to tell me about Abigail and..."

"Finneas," she says with a groan.

"You don't have to."

She rolls her eyes. "It's fine, I'm over it."

I climb in bed next to her, settling in comfortably. For the first time in weeks, I'm excited about something. And even though Oscar has introduced a gun into the equation, as long as I'm with Syd and he's not around, I actually feel... safe.

Chapter Forty-Six
The One

I know why Oscar chose Sydney. He saw her vulnerable after being betrayed by her best friend and breaking up with her fiancé, and thought... what a great opportunity thrown right into his lap!

He didn't even have to do anything. It was too easy. Syd's life had just been turned upside down, she'd had to find a new place to live, a new job, and she had no friends to support her. Add to that her strained relationship with her mother, and Oscar instantly knew he'd hit the jackpot. Minimal effort on his part.

"If I get out of here alive," Syd says, "I will do the opposite of what I did. I will get out more, be social, make friends. Real, close friends. I'll call them every day, and I don't care if they don't like it, they'll get used to it."

I laugh, and she laughs with me. An hour ago, Oscar interrupted us with lunch. It went the same as with breakfast, then he let Syd use the bathroom and cuffed her again. We're alone, huddled together in bed, under the duvet. We're whispering to hopefully make it harder for Oscar to listen in.

"So, when I don't check in and they can't reach me for, say, two days in a row, they'll call the police," she continues. "Better yet, I'll get a roommate."

"Ever had a roommate before?" I ask.

"Aside from Finn, no. I had roommates in college. Does that count?"

"That's different. Not exactly a choice," I say. "I couldn't wait to graduate and live on my own."

"You like your space then."

I shrug. "And it proved to be my undoing."

Sydney shifts, trying to make herself more comfortable. I hate that there's nothing I can do for her.

"We live in a world where living alone as a woman is dangerous," she says. "I mean, I knew that. I know the statistics. But for some reason, it's just sinking in now."

I chuckle. "What might this reason be?"

She rolls her eyes. "Oscar Octavius Miles. What a stupid name. And he was making fun of my ex's name."

"To be fair, it seems you have a way of finding the guys with the weirdest, most pretentious names."

"I know. I think it's a curse. Or karma. If his name is plucked from the history books and he's a psycho, sign me up."

We giggle. It's hot under the duvet, but I wouldn't have it any other way. Actually, I would. If Sydney wasn't cuffed to the bed frame, and we weren't locked in a madman's basement, if neither of us had ever met Oscar, but somehow found each other, then my life would be perfect.

"What about you?" she asks. "When you get out of here, what will you do differently?"

"If," I correct her. "I'd call my mom more often. Talk to my dad, too. Maybe he's changed, who knows? I never gave him a chance after I moved out. Or..."

"Or?"

"I wouldn't do any of that, because it wouldn't matter."

She raises her eyebrows at me. "Oh?"

"Think about it. The worst has already happened to me. It won't happen again. Who gets kidnapped twice?"

"I'm pretty sure there were cases," she says.

I give her a pout. "Way to squash my hopes."

She laughs. "Are you that much of a hermit?"

I take a moment to think about it. "No. I don't know. I just think it would be hard. If I get out of here, I'll still be the girl who was kidnapped. That will never go away. If I start calling my mom every day, what would we talk about? What we had for breakfast? If I didn't have friends before, what friends would I make now? Friends who pity me? Friends who see me as a curiosity?"

"Evie..."

"You know I'm right. No one will understand what I went through."

"I will." She pulls at the chain and curses under her breath when the metal digs into her skin. She wants to turn towards me but can't. "When we get out of here, we can be roommates. What do you think?"

I move closer to her and press my forehead against her shoulder. "Us living together?"

"Yeah."

"That sounds nice."

Tears gather in my eyes. Because I know this is just a silly dream. Oscar will never let us get out of this place alive. We know who he is. It's his life, or ours. And I know for a fact that I don't have it in me to do what needs to be done to escape. Every time I tried, someone else paid for it. If I try anything now, Syd will be the one to pay.

There are stories about kidnapping victims who were kept by their kidnappers for years. I always wondered how days turned into weeks, weeks into months, and months into years, and these women survived in captivity. Until they didn't. Or until they escaped. I've only been here for three months. How long will I survive? Will I blink and it will be six months, then a year, then two years? Will I blink and stare into the barrel of Oscar's gun because he got bored of me?

"Hey," Syd pokes me with her elbow. "What are you thinking about?"

"Nothing."

"You went quiet."

"I didn't know what else to say."

She huffs. "There's nothing else to say. It's decided. I'll get you out of here–"

"You'll save me," I chuckle.

"Yes. I'll save you, and then we're moving in together. My place is tiny, so it might have to be yours."

"I don't think I can live in that building anymore."

"We'll find a new place then. Bigger. We'll split the rent and bills. It'll be easy."

I smile and allow myself to believe Sydney. Why not? Just for a few minutes, or hours. There's no harm in it.

Oscar ruins it all when he comes in with dinner. We must eat, I guess. I sort of got used to eating only once a day, or every two to three days, but I don't want Sydney to starve like I did. I'm grateful Oscar is back to caring about our basic needs, even though that means seeing his odious face more often.

He also brings in clean laundry, and when he uncuffs Sydney and lets her use the bathroom, he gives her a set of pajamas. While she's locked in the bathroom, he takes her dinner into the library. I watch him warily. It seems he's changing the rules again. I should've figured out that with her here, there would be new rules. He isn't just going to leave us alone to chat all day and all night.

"I'd love for the three of us to have a lovely dinner together, but we're not there yet," he says in a cheerful tone.

He sets the table, and as he's moving around the room, I can see he has the gun tucked into his belt. I glance at the bathroom door, then back at him. If I weren't such a scared little weakling, I'd try to tackle him and get his gun. I go as far as to imagine it in my head. Then I'd be the one to save Syd and myself, and Syd wouldn't have to risk her own life, as I'm sure she plans to do. She hasn't told me how she intends to get us out of here, but I can see the cogs turning in her head when we take a break from chatting each other's ears off and she goes quiet. Quieter than me.

"I'll have to bring another chair," Oscar says.

Syd knocks on the door. That brings me out of my trance. Oscar goes to unlock it, but before he does, he shoots me a suspicious look.

"Go sit at the table," he tells me.

He wants to keep us separated when he's in the room and we're both free. That's fine because I wasn't intending to do anything. I take a seat at the table and inspect the food – carbonara, but the bacon is burnt. This confirms two things: one, Nora isn't around anymore, and two, Oscar is distracted. He took a cooking lesson and he's an okay if erratic cook, but tonight, he was watching the cameras more than the food on the stove.

Syd steps out of the bathroom in her brand-new pajamas that are actually mine.

"No funny business," Oscar warns her.

She looks him up and down, and I become tense. He's tense too, and his right hand goes around his back.

"Of course not," Syd says.

"In there." Oscar motions for her to go into the library. "You have everything you need for a decent night's sleep."

"Beats being cuffed to the bed."

She's snarky. I never dared to be snarky with Oscar. Telling by the scowl on his face, he doesn't appreciate it. Tomorrow I'll have to instruct Sydney on how a lady should and should not behave, according to Oscar Octavius Miles.

He locks the door and takes the other seat at the table. We eat in silence for a few minutes, then he asks me about my day. I'm monosyllabic and ask him about his day, but he's more interested in how Syd and I are getting along. I don't want to reveal how much she means to me. He'll use it against me. He'll turn Sydney into a weapon to gain even more control over me, as if he doesn't control my every waking moment already.

I'm making the conversation difficult by barely engaging. When his patience runs out, he tells me I have ten minutes to use the bathroom while he takes the leftovers upstairs. I wait for him to leave first, but he motions for me to go in, and I have no choice but to listen. I hear him lock the door behind me, and I freeze. Now Syd and I are locked in different rooms, so Oscar can move freely for a few minutes, without having to watch his back.

I brush my teeth and try to make sense of what's happening, try to guess what he's thinking. He was cautious when he first brought me here, and now he must be double cautious. When I look at him looking at Syd, sometimes I think he doesn't believe he will break her like he did me. Does he regret picking her?

No. She's the perfect victim. The only thing he probably regrets is that he had to pick her for me – the other perfect victim who was lonely and needed company. Or antidepressants. I hope he's moved on from that idea.

The lock clicks, and I know my time is up. Oscar is waiting for me in the bedroom. He's wearing a white T-shirt and no pants. I avert my gaze. On the bed, the handcuffs are waiting for me. He hasn't slept with me in weeks. Why now? Because Syd is in the other room? It's as if he wants to prove something to her, or to himself.

"It's late," he says, yawning.

I rub my wrists as I walk to the bed. I haven't been cuffed to it in a while. Can he blame me for getting used to the little freedom I have? I lie down on my right side, and Oscar secures the cuffs. At least he leaves them loose enough. If I don't struggle, I won't get hurt.

He climbs in next to me, fluffing the duvet and the pillows.

"Should've changed the sheets," he grumbles.

He shuffles closer, until his chest presses to my back. His arm comes over me and across my chest, and I am still, barely breathing.

"You haven't thanked me for bringing you a best friend," he says in my hair.

"Thank you."

He kisses the top of my head. "You're welcome."

This is going to be a long night.

Chapter Forty-Seven
The One

I pull the duvet over our heads and snuggle close to Syd. The position is awkward. Because Oscar cuffed her before going to work this morning, she's stuck lying on her right side. I'm the big spoon. I whisper right into her ear, and when she whispers back, I strain to hear her. We've resorted to talking like this in hopes it will be difficult – better yet, impossible – for Oscar to listen in.

It's her second day in captivity, and Sydney has shown strength so far, as if Oscar barely fazes her, but I feel like today she's sad about something. She's not eager to talk to me like yesterday, and she's been silent and lost in thought all morning. I figure it's because of the cuffs. Her wrists are red and bruised.

"I'm sorry," I say.

I know her mood has nothing to do with me, but I can't help it. When I lived with my parents, my mother and I walked on eggshells around my father. If he was upset, it was our fault even if it wasn't. If he and my mother had an argument, I was the one to apologize because I knew that taking the blame calmed him down quicker.

I'm twenty-six, and I haven't quite shaken off the habit of immediately feeling responsible when someone I care about is mad, upset, or in pain.

"What for?" Syd asks.

"I don't know," I whisper. "I feel like there's something on your mind. You don't have to tell me if you don't want to, but I'd like to help. If I can."

She sighs deeply. "You can't help me. Not with this."

"Is it Oscar?"

A ridiculous question to ask. Of course it's Oscar. And this pink, ugly basement, the lack of windows and fresh air. The lack of freedom and dignity. We can't even use the toilet without him watching.

"It's my mother," she says. "I'm worried about her."

Syd told me about the massive argument they had after she and Finn broke up. Apparently, her mother blocked her phone number, and they weren't in touch for weeks. I can't imagine how a mother could do something like that to her own daughter. Sure, my relationship with mine isn't perfect, but at least we both act like adults. Most of the time.

"Finally, she unblocked me," Syd continues, "And we talked. She didn't apologize, but that's fine. I wasn't expecting her to. I told her about the new job, she asked me about the apartment... Anyway, she seemed like she cared, and she didn't mention Finn or Abbi for once, so I took that as a good sign. Two days later, when I called, she didn't answer. I called again after a few hours, and her phone was off. I was planning on going over to her house to check if she's okay but got distracted with work, and then... Oscar happened."

A chill spreads through my body, and I shudder.

"I'm worried," Syd says. "She's had health scares before. Most of them exaggerated or downright imagined, but once, she fainted and ended up in the ER. Turned out she was dehydrated, running errands like a mad person in the middle of July."

"I'm so sorry. How old is she?"

"Fifty-three. Not old at all. But it doesn't matter. She doesn't take care of herself, and she has this obsession that she never has enough money for the bills, so she works herself to the bone. I mean, I get it. I shouldn't judge her. It was hard growing up. My dad took off, and it was just her, raising a kid all by herself. My dad didn't pay child support, and she was too proud to go after him in court."

"That is terrible." It sounds worse than what I went through with my family. At least my parents stayed together and we had a two-income household.

"Well, men," Syd says, her tone sarcastic. "You can't expect too much from them."

"I..." I start, but I don't know how to continue.

"What?"

"I wanted to say that..." My voice chokes up.

"What?" She pokes me with her elbow and turns her head to look at me over her shoulder. "Evie, what?"

I break down in tears. "I wanted to say that I'm sure there are good men out there, but I just... After what Oscar did, I can't. I don't think I believe it."

"Not all of them are stalkers and kidnappers," she says softly, though I feel she somewhat agrees with me.

"Not just that." I'm sobbing.

"What, then? What did he do?"

"He killed... someone. Two people. One, for sure. The other one, I didn't see him do it, but I think he killed her, too."

"Who did he kill?"

"The cleaning ladies." I'm bawling my eyes out because I don't want to tell her, but I must. I'll never be ready to talk about Rita and Nora, so I just need to do it, force it out of me. Syd must know what Oscar is capable of. "He killed the first woman he brought to clean the basement right before my eyes. He strangled her with a chain." When I want to say her name, I can't. Rita. It gets stuck in my throat, and I can't push the sounds out through my mouth. It hurts too much. "He brought another woman after, and it was fine for a while. I protected her the best I could. I didn't say anything to her, never let on that I'm a prisoner here. But then... Then I was stupid. I don't know what got into me. Now I know I couldn't have escaped."

"You tried to escape?"

"I shouldn't have. It all went wrong. So wrong. And there was a kid here, and I put her in danger too."

"A kid? What kid?" Sydney tries to turn her body towards me, but of course the short chain prevents her from turning more than a few inches. She groans in frustration.

"He brings children here. At first it was Bobbi, and it was scary. I thought he'd kidnapped her and brought her to me to raise. Then it was Celeste, the neighbors' daughter. Bobbi is too young to know this is all wrong, but Celeste is seven or eight, and I think she could tell I don't live in the basement because I'm sick or eccentric." I lower my voice even more, getting so close to Syd that my breath is on her face, and hers on mine. "I wrote in her math workbook that Oscar is keeping me here against my will. I hoped someone would see it, but I guess no one did."

"In her math notebook," Syd repeats.

"Yes. I thought her parents would find it, or her teacher. It makes no sense." I'm crying so hard that I start hiccupping.

Syd shoulders off the duvet, and we both take a few deep breaths. I didn't realize how hot it had gotten inside our little tent.

"It's okay," she says. "Shh... It's okay, Evie."

"No, it's not. What if Oscar did something to that girl after he... after he..." It's weird that I can say Celeste's name out loud, but not Nora's.

"You said she's the neighbors' daughter. He'd never. It's too dangerous."

"I don't think he cares. I think he's smart enough to get away with anything."

"Evie, no... He's just a man. And men fail. I'll get you out of here, I promise."

"No." I grab onto her arm and squeeze. "Don't do anything, please. Don't try anything. He has a gun now. He never carried a gun before, and he still killed two people like it was nothing."

"Okay, okay... Calm down. Deep breaths."

I realize how pathetic I am. Sydney was talking about her mother and how she is worried about her. She was opening up to me, and I made it all about myself, and then spiraled into a weeping mess. It's hard to settle down now that all these emotions have started pouring out of me. I've been keeping them bottled up since Oscar brought Syd because I didn't want to scare her.

"Deep breaths," she keeps whispering soothingly.

She's so strong. Instead of freaking out – as anyone would – she's focused on my wellbeing.

The metal door whirrs open and startles us both. I sit up and wipe my eyes with my sleeves. Oscar marches in, and it instantly hits me that he's angry. Seething.

"Evie, go wash your face," he orders.

"I'm fine," I say.

"No, you're not. Go wash your face. Now."

I scramble out of the bed and run to the bathroom. I don't close the door, and I see how he uncuffs Syd and pulls her to her feet harshly. He pushes her forward so hard that she stumbles, then grabs her by the arm and leads her out of the basement.

"What are you doing?" I ask.

Sydney yelps and swears at him. He tells her to shut up as he punches in the code and the door starts closing.

"Where are you taking her?" I run to the door, but it's too late. It shuts before me. I bang on it with my fists. "Oscar, no! Please don't hurt her! Please!"

His answer to me is a bang on the other side – his fist against metal. I jump a few feet away and stare at the door in shock.

As with Nora, I may never see Sydney again.

Chapter Forty-Eight

The One

For the next half hour, I pace the room, bang on the door, and plead with Oscar to bring Sydney back. I don't know why he grabbed her like that, what she or I did wrong. I shouldn't be surprised, given how volatile he is. Did he hear what I told her about writing in Celeste's workbook? Unlikely. But if he did, then why is he punishing her? I'm the one who screwed up. Again.

The door slides open, and my instinct is to run to it. I'm met with a gun pointed at my face.

"Behave, Evie," Oscar says as he drags Sydney in.

I raise my hands in surrender and take a few steps back. I gasp when I see what he did to her face. There's a bleeding cut on Syd's brow, and her eye is slowly becoming swollen. Still, I'm relieved that she's alive. Oscar pushes her towards me, and I catch her.

"Are you okay?"

She nods.

I hug her, and she clings to me.

Oscar isn't putting the gun away. The door is open behind him, but neither of us is going to risk getting shot. We both watch him warily as he walks further into the room, takes something out of his pocket, and puts it on the table. It's a small, square box, smaller than the palm of my hand.

"This was meant for you, Evie," he says. "Now I don't know anymore." He walks backwards until he's standing in the doorway. He looks haggard, I notice. Like he's losing his grip. "What I do know is that I don't need two of you. Being a provider for one woman is hard enough. Sorry, Evie, I tried. I thought Sydney would be good company, but instead of making you happy, she's making you cry. I'm trying to help you, but I seem to fall short at every step, and I don't know what to do anymore. Maybe there's no way to make you happy, and at some point, I'll have to accept that, maybe, that's not on me. It's on you."

"What are you talking about? Sydney didn't do anything. I'm... I'm fine."

"No, you're not. And if she isn't helping, there's no point in any of this. There's no point in keeping you both. I'll keep the one who wants to be here." He points at the box on the table. "You have one hour to decide. Who stays, and who goes." He steps out and closes the door.

Sydney and I are left in silence, too stunned to react. She pulls away from me and gingerly taps her brow.

"Don't touch it," I say. "We need to clean it."

I pull her into the bathroom and turn on the water. I use a cotton pad to wipe off the blood. The wound isn't deep, and she doesn't need stitches. A band aid would've been nice, but I don't have one. The bathroom is stocked with only what Oscar deems necessary.

"Hold it in place," I tell her as I give her a fresh cotton pad. "How did he give you this? Did he hit you?"

"Doesn't matter," she says, wincing.

"Yes, it does. It's because of me. He doesn't like it when I cry, and with you here, he finally has someone to blame."

"It doesn't mean it's your fault. It just means he's sick," she says.

I know that, of course, but I can't properly internalize it. My brain doesn't want to fully believe it. It punishes me with guilt like Oscar punished Sydney for something she didn't do.

"Let's see what's in the box," she says, getting up and going into the bedroom.

The box. My heartbeat quickens and my knees feel wobbly as I follow Syd. It must be some new, crazy game Oscar invented to torture us. Syd takes a seat, and I take the chair opposite her. Between us lies the box. It's small and covered in velvet. It looks like...

But that's stupid. It can't be.

"Do you want to open it?" she asks.

"No."

"He said it was meant for you."

"All the more reason to not open it," I say.

"Okay."

She takes the box, studies it for a second, then carefully pops the lid. Her eyes widen at the sight of what's inside, and that reaction alone makes me feel like I'm on the edge of a cliff. Her eyes meet mine, and she turns the box around and slides it over to me.

A pink stone framed by sparkling diamonds, mounted on a gold band.

An engagement ring.

"This is–"

"Insane," she finishes for me.

I mean, it's a beautiful ring, but that's not what I was going to say.

"He wants us to decide…" My voice fades. I'm afraid to touch the ring, lest he thinks I'm choosing it for myself. It stays in the box, in the middle of the table. I don't even want to know if it's my size.

"One hour," Sydney says.

"What if we don't choose? What do you think he'll do?"

Syd looks me in the eye. "What do *you* think he'll do? You know him better than me."

"He'll choose for us."

"Is there any way to tell the time in here?" she asks.

I shake my head. How long ago did Oscar leave? How much time did we spend in the bathroom, cleaning Syd's wound? Five minutes. Ten. Fifteen? My sense of time is skewed. I shrink within myself and wrap my arms around my body. I start rocking back and forth, looking down at the table, studying the wood fibers with blurry eyes.

"Hey." Syd comes to kneel beside me. She rubs my arm. "Hey, it's going to be okay."

"No. One of us will die today, and we have to decide who."

She opens her mouth to say something, then changes her mind. That confirms we're on the same page.

Oscar will kill one of us within the hour.

Chapter Forty-Nine

The One

Sydney insists that it's not even a debate. There's no point in talking about it, and I agree, but I can't stop thinking about the consequences. Oscar said we must decide who stays and becomes his... girlfriend? Fiancée? Wife? And who goes.

The one who stays might not have a great time in his basement, starving when he can't be bothered to bring her food, cuffed to the bed when he feels like sleeping next to her – or do more. He's never done more before, but I feel like the engagement ring on my or Syd's finger will give him the right. He'll interpret it that way. Choosing to stay will be all the consent he needs.

I can't breathe. I need air, and there's no air in here. I need to feel the sun on my face and the wind in my hair. I need to feel soft earth under my soles.

Sydney is in the bathroom, inspecting her wound in the mirror. I can't sit still. I pace the bedroom, then move to the library, where I read book spines to try and distract myself. Oscar hasn't brought new books in a while, and I'm glad. The room is full, and it's started to get this smell of paper and ink, which is not pleasant at all, more like chemicals, it feels intoxicating. If there was a window, I'd open it wide, let the fresh air in. And then I'd start throwing all the books out the window.

I imagine myself ripping their pages and letting them float away, wherever the air currents might take them. I will never read dark romance again. After all that's happened to me, I don't understand the appeal of these books anymore. Why did I like them? Why did I enjoy the twisted stories and fall in love with the psycho villains posing as boyfriends? I remember the articles I read about this, explaining how women who read dark romance don't actually fantasize about those things happening to them in real life, but now I don't understand the logic of the articles either.

I feel lost. I feel like the Evie before all this was dumb, and naïve, and ridiculous, and I'm almost ashamed of the books she read. I'm not the woman I was before meeting Oscar. The problem is... I'm not sure what kind of woman I am now, after Oscar.

When I look in the mirror, I don't recognize myself. I'm not dressed as Evie, I don't talk like Evie, I don't think like Evie... I'm not Evie.

And that's why it must be me. The one that goes.

I will convince Sydney to take the engagement ring for herself and let me walk out of here with Oscar. Will he use the gun? Will he use the chain he used on Rita? Will he use his bare hands? I won't fight him. I want this to be over because I'm a shell of a person, and I don't think I'll ever get myself back.

Maybe Sydney has a chance to escape after I'm out of the picture and Oscar is more relaxed. She's braver than me, I can tell. Smarter, too. There's something in her eyes, like she knows a secret, like she has an ace up her sleeve, and that ace is probably her inner strength and bright mind.

I've never been bright. An average student at best, doing what I could to get by and come home with decent enough grades that I wouldn't enrage my father. My mere existence was not worth it. It was too expensive to raise me, feed me, and send me to school – a lecture I heard many times. All I wanted was some peace and quiet to read. Out of the way, in my room. I just wanted to be left alone.

All my life, that's all I've wanted. To be left alone.

Sydney has a mother she cares about and who cares about her, despite their differences. I hope Syd's mother is okay, and Syd's worried for nothing. It's so painful and unnecessary to lose family over an ex-best friend and ex-boyfriend who lied and cheated. If Syd finds a way to escape, she can still get her happily-ever-after. She has a job, a parent she's close with. She still has a chance at finding a decent guy and starting over. I'm too broken for any of that.

"Are you okay?"

Her voice startles me. I'm holding a random book, and I wave it at her as if she caught me reading.

"Yes," I say.

"What's that?"

"Um..." I check the title. "Where is Savannah?"

"Who is Savannah?"

"No, that's the... I mean, that's the title."

"Oh. Any good?"

"I don't know. I haven't read it."

"Well, let me know if it's any good," she says.

I laugh because I think she's trying to be ironic, but she doesn't join me. I clear my throat. "Listen, I think you should take the ring."

"I'm not doing that."

"One of us has to, and it should be you."

Syd crosses her arms over her chest. "I'd ask what the reasoning behind it is, but I won't. Because neither of us is taking that ring. We're done listening to him, Evie. He doesn't control us."

"Except he does. If we don't choose, he will."

"Let him choose." She's firm. Nothing can dissuade her. "I have other plans for us."

Plans? Plural? As much as I love the sound of that, I know it's not in the stars for me. If I can't convince her to take the ring, then what can I do? I don't want Oscar to hurt her, but I don't know how to protect her. The last time I tried to protect someone, I got them killed anyway.

She closes the distance between us and rubs my arms. "It's going to be okay. Do you trust me?"

"It's not that I don't trust you–"

I don't finish my sentence. The sound of the metal door makes us both jump.

Chapter Fifty

The One

I'm hiding behind Sydney, both my hands wrapped around her arm. For comfort, or to stop her from doing something rash – I don't know.

"Stay where you are," Oscar warns.

He's got a plastic bottle with a warm brown liquid in it, and two plastic cups. He sets the cups on the table and pours into them.

"Tequila," he says. "A little liquid courage. You have ten more minutes to decide, and seeing how you've gotten nowhere, I thought this would help."

He leaves the bottle and backs away, towards the door. Of course the bottle is plastic. He wouldn't risk leaving a glass bottle lying around.

"I'll be back," he says and punches in the code.

I can feel Syd shaking. She stays put, but I can tell it's only because of me. If I weren't here, she would jump him and get herself shot.

The door opens and closes. Sydney jerks her arm free. She shoots me a glance, and I know she's upset.

"Please," I say.

She walks to the table, and for a second, I think she's going to take the engagement ring from the box and slip it on her finger. Instead, she downs one of the tequila shots, scrunching up her nose.

"Cheap," she says. She slams the plastic cup and marches to the metal door.

"What are you doing?"

"Keeping my promise." She taps on the keypad.

"That's not going to work," I say. "You have to know the code."

"I do know the code."

I don't have time to express disbelief or shock, because the door actually whirrs open. Before I can blink and decide how to react, Sydney slips out and...

I'm left alone.

The door retracts into the wall fully. Sydney disappears up the stairs, then I hear Oscar's voice.

"What are you doing?"

They're far up, probably on the first floor. A door bangs against a wall. Syd says something I can't make out. There are sounds of a struggle.

I can't stay here, paralyzed, while she's in danger. I must move. My brain gives the signal to my legs once, twice, and on the third try, it's like I'm a puppet, pulled towards the door by strings. The last time I tried to get out...

I can't think about it. I can't think about anything, I just have to act.

There's a gunshot. Only one, and then someone tumbles down the stairs. Sydney or Oscar? I'm afraid to find out.

I don't want to get out of the room. I feel like something bad is going to happen. But I must, because Sydney needs me. Not that I can help her. How could I ever help her? If she's the one who was shot...

It's darker here. The door at the top of the stairs is open, and some light pours through. Footsteps thud down the stairs, but I can't bring myself to look up. At my feet, there's a body. Unmoving.

"Come on." Sydney grabs my arm. "Evie, come on."

The black-framed glasses sit askew on his face. His eyes are wide open, staring at the ceiling. His right leg is at an odd angle, and blood starts pooling around his torso. I can see the entry wound, right in the middle of his chest.

Oscar Octavius Miles is dead.

"Evie!" Sydney cups my face with her hands, forcing me to look at her. "Hey, it's over. Let's go."

"How did you..." My thoughts are a jumbled mess, and there's a heavy knot in my stomach. "How..."

Syd takes my hand. "You need air."

"How did you know the code?"

She pulls me up the stairs.

Chapter Fifty-One

Oscar

It's a misconception that when someone is shot in the heart, they die instantly. One of the many propagated by Hollywood. Oscar is lying on his back, eyes wide with shock. Pain thrums through all the nerves in his body; agony like he's never felt before. He can't move, can barely breathe, and is distantly aware of someone moving close to him, staring at him from above.

Evie.

He tries to blink, move his hand and grab her ankle to let her know it's not over yet, but no muscle will listen to him. He keeps lying there, sprawled and motionless, and his last resort is to will her to bend over and check his pulse. She doesn't. Then Sydney drags her upstairs, and he's alone in the semi-darkness.

He was wrong. It is over. He has a few more minutes before he loses consciousness. What will he do with these minutes? If only he could move his hand... His phone is in the front pocket of his jeans. Part of his brain focuses on the task of moving the hand, while the rest of his brain starts flashing between memories, questions, imaginings, regrets.

Evie on that first day. The excitement of showing her all the things he'd made and bought for her.

He should never have set his sights on Sydney. The idea that she could replace Evie was idiotic, and now look at him. Syd is no victim. A venomous snake in disguise, she tricked him and took everything from him. She is upstairs now. He can hear her footsteps, heavy and determined, followed by Evie's shuffling ones.

This should never have happened. It's the wrong time-line. In the right timeline, envisioned with care before Oscar stumbled and lost his way, he and Evie are in her room now, wrapped up in each other. The cuffs have no use anymore because Evie loves him for all the things he does for her and will never leave him.

His hand moves along his side, his fingers dig into his pocket, and he grasps the phone. He can blink, finally, and a tear slides down his temple. He fumbles with his phone. It's out. He can't bring it up to his face, but he doesn't have to. He can call 911 and...

And what?

The ambulance won't come fast enough. He's slipping in and out already. He's exhausted. Or maybe it will come right on time, and when the paramedics wake him up, he'll have some explaining to do.

No. He won't explain himself. He's always known he was different. It's not his fault he was born this way, and he won't explain or apologize for it.

The phone slips out of his hand.

He's bleeding out.

What a mess.

He closes his eyes and hangs onto the last thread of consciousness. Evie. Tiny, weak, stupid. An unfortunate choice, he can see that now. Sydney. The real enemy.

Type One, Type Two, Type Three. Utter nonsense.

Who will find him here, like this? Will she? She's far away now. Will she come back and weep over his body?

What a mess.

Chapter Fifty-Two
The One

The house is aglow. Mesmerizing shades of orange, yellow, and red dance on the walls as the sun sets outside. I blink, stunned, as if I've forgotten what the sunset looks like. Like this is my first day on earth.

"I saw it," Sydney says. "I saw the code when Oscar put it in."

"How? When?"

"On the first night. He thought I was unconscious, but I wasn't. I was weak, confused, and only half awake. I made him believe I was out, and I saw the code. Then I passed out. I'm not sure when... Before or after he cuffed me to the bed."

We're in the kitchen. It's fairly large, with a rectangular island in the middle, clean and organized. I notice the dishwasher is open, and clean plates and pots are waiting to be returned to the cupboards. The door to the basement is placed between the kitchen counter and the hallway that leads into the living room.

"Why didn't you say anything?" I ask Sydney.

She's looking around, trying to decide what to do. She eyes the block of knives on the kitchen island, then touches her temple with shaking hands, as if she's uncertain about something. I know what we have to do, so I don't understand why she's hesitating.

"We have to call the police," I say.

"I wanted to tell you about the code," she says, ignoring me. "But he was listening."

That's right, he was. Oscar.

Oscar has a phone. I turn back to the door to the basement, but I see Sydney marching into the living room. I hesitate between following her and going back down for the phone. In my confusion, I start pacing the kitchen and spot a cardboard box on the counter. It's filled with books. I peek in and see Scarlet Devotion on top. Anxiety grips my heart, and I let out a pathetic whimper. I decide to go after Sydney. We can't be separated.

I find her at the foot of the stairs that lead to the second floor.

"We need to get Oscar's phone," I say. "Call the police."

"It's over, Evie. He's dead, and we're safe." She starts climbing the stairs.

"Wait. Where are you going? We must get out of here." I go after her even as I'm protesting. "Sydney," I whisper-yell. It dawns on me that even if we're alone in the house, we're whispering. I don't know why. It feels strange. The house, the moment of the day, the fact that Oscar is lying dead in a pool of blood. "Syd, wait for me."

I catch up with her in the corridor. There are closed doors on both sides, except for one, which is open. Sydney goes straight for it.

"Don't you want to know why he chose you?" she says. "We have time to look around, find out who he really was and why he was so sick. Why he was so obsessed with you."

"I don't think that's a good idea," I say. "We shouldn't touch anything."

Plus, I know why he chose me. My passion for dark romance novels convinced him I was an easy victim, simply because he assumed I'd love to live a similar life as my favorite characters. However, if I think about it, that doesn't reveal much about him. About who Oscar was at his core.

"Ten minutes," Sydney says, disappearing into the room. "And then we find a phone and call 911."

I can't argue with her. She's determined to look through Oscar's stuff, and she's going to do it with or without me. I can't deny that I'm curious. She's right. It's over. He can't hurt us anymore, and ten minutes isn't going to change anything. I follow her into the room...

And I stop in my tracks.

Screens everywhere. An entire wall is filled with them. Sydney is frozen in the middle of the room, staring at the chilling display. In front of the wall, there's a long desk and a leather desk chair. The surface is littered with soda cans, dirty coffee mugs, and a few dishes with dried leftovers in them. This is where Oscar must've spent most of his time. I recognize the laptop he gave me when I told him I missed writing, and his work laptop, which is open. The screens show all the cameras in the basement. There are no other cameras in the house or around the property. Interesting.

"Wow," I say. I imagined he might've had a surveillance room, but this puts my imagination to shame. "This is a lot."

Sydney snaps out of her trance and sits at the desk, pulling Oscar's laptop in front of her.

"Let's take a look," she says.

"Isn't everything protected by passwords?"

"I work in IT, remember? I know a thing or two."

She starts typing, and I wonder what she hopes to discover. I wrap my arms around myself, thoroughly convinced we shouldn't be touching anything. Especially Oscar's things. Especially the system he had in place to monitor us in the basement. I look around the room to distract myself. The curtains are drawn, but the window is open, letting in a musty fall breeze. It's warm in here, probably because of all the technology that's on twenty-four-seven. There's an AC unit, but the open window is the best ventilation solution. I walk over to it, eager to feel the air on my face.

I part the curtains and stick my head outside, my hands gripping the windowsill. I breathe in deeply, and tears gather in my eyes. I can't believe I'm free. I can't believe I'm alive, in one piece, untouched and mostly healthy, and free. It's over. Over, over, over. A smile spreads on my lips, and my chest fills with joy and possibility.

My gaze sweeps over the front yard, the driveaway, the street, and the houses around. It's a nice neighborhood, like both Rita and Nora said. At this hour, it's quiet, and people seem to have gone inside. Dinner, homework, a game show on TV. Slow, normal lives, away from the bustle of the city.

"What day is it?" I ask Sydney.

"Sunday."

It's a school day tomorrow. After Sydney is done poking through Oscar's folders and files, we'll call 911 and all this peace and quiet will end. I almost feel bad for the families whose evening will be ruined by a slew of police cars. The thought of what's coming makes me feel uneasy. I'll be interrogated and interviewed, and I'll have to talk about what happened to me in detail. It's all been recorded, though. I look over at Syd, who's still typing, and I realize I don't know how to feel about the fact that my three months in Oscar's basement have been recorded and the police will go over every minute of it. Maybe they'll have less questions for me.

I push away from the window. "Are you done?" I ask Syd. "Please, let's find a phone."

"Almost there."

"What are you doing, anyway?"

I make to join her so I can look over her shoulder, but she waves me away.

"Go look through the other rooms," she says.

"No. I don't want to leave you here alone." More like, I don't want to be alone, even though I know I'm perfectly safe.

"Please, Evie. You might find something."

I chew at the inside of my cheek, looking between Sydney and the door, Sydney and the door. She's focused on Oscar's laptop. I notice the back of her neck is sweaty, and she touches her forehead often.

"Okay," I concede. "But I'll be back in five minutes."

She doesn't say anything, and I slip out of the room, on my tiptoes. Even though I lived here for the past three months, this isn't my house, and I feel like an intruder. I'm definitely doing something that I'm not supposed to do.

Gingerly, I open the door next to the surveillance room and peek inside. Immediately, I can tell this is Oscar's bedroom. A king-sized bed, a closet with an embedded TV, an empty glass on one nightstand next to a rectangular case for his glasses, and a dust-covered paperback on the other. Basic and functional.

I peer inside the closet and pull open some drawers. Clothes, socks, nothing special. The room smells like Oscar, and I find it makes me feel uncomfortable and slightly ill. I don't think I'll find anything relevant in here, so I get out, close the door to hopefully trap in the pervasive scent that is so uniquely his, and open the next door.

It's a bathroom. The cabinet is filled with manly things – an electric shaver, aftershave, hair gel, and his electric toothbrush is blue. There are no pill bottles to tell me he was suffering from some mental illness that had turned him into a stalker, a kidnapper, and a murderer. The bathroom smells just like his bedroom, and for a moment, I worry that I'll never get his scent out of my nostrils.

I will always smell Oscar, feel Oscar, and hear his voice as if he were inches from me. I'll always feel watched by him.

I move to the two rooms whose windows face the backyard. The first one is opposite Oscar's bedroom, and not surprisingly, it's another bedroom. I step inside and find myself in a space that's completely different from the rest of the house.

The pink, rose-patterned wallpaper is old and fading in places. The curtains are dusty red and heavy, but transparent enough to let the sunset paint the room warm and eerie. The bed is covered with a dark pink blanket with blooming roses on the edges. The TV is old-fashioned and small, pushed into a corner, like an afterthought.

As I advance into the room and look around, my heart picks up the pace and my breathing turns shallow. Instead of a big closet, there are dressers, and every available surface is covered in snow globes and framed pictures. I run my fingers over the snow globes. There are many things trapped in them – spindly trees, cozy cabins, fairy-tale castles, the Eiffel Tower. Santa Claus, a snowman, a vintage train, a dragon, a cat riding a pony.

Oscar is in every photo. A happy toddler playing with his little sand bucket and plastic shovel on a beach. A first grader in uniform, proudly smiling at the camera, oblivious to the fact that his two front teeth are missing. Oscar dressed as a carrot in what looks like his first school play. Oscar holding a chess trophy. Oscar graduating, then graduating again.

Oscar, Oscar, Oscar. Until I see a photo in which he's not alone.

My hand shakes as I reach for it. The vintage metal frame is cold to the touch. The shiver it sends through my fingers travels up my arm and grips my heart. The woman in the picture is young, but I recognize her. Her dark hair is barely streaked with gray, her cheekbones are high, her face slim, and her large smile creases her eyes at the corners. Her arm is thrown around a teenaged Oscar who's kissing her cheek.

"No..."

I feel like I have no air. I try to breathe deeply, but I can't. My chest spasms and my stomach cramps. I don't know what's happening to me; I think I'm about to pass out. I hold on to the photo tightly and use the furniture, the wall, and the doorframe to feel my way out of the room.

"Sydney! Sydney, you need to see this."

Chapter Fifty-Three

The One

I stumble into the surveillance room. Sydney has closed Oscar's laptop and pushed it away, and I find her holding her head, massaging her temples with her fingers.

"Sydney, I found something."

She groans as she glances at me from behind her arm. I show her the photo, but she seems confused. I get closer and point at the woman in the photo.

"This is Nora."

"Who's Nora?"

A fair question. I told her about Nora, but at the time, I couldn't say her name out loud. Even now, it physically hurts to say it.

"The cleaning lady."

"The one Oscar killed in front of you?"

"No, the other one. The first one was Rita. Nora was the second cleaning lady."

Syd pushes the chair away from the desk and looks at me like I've lost my mind. I know I'm making little sense. I can't find my words. I feel jittery and untethered. She furrows her brows and takes the photo from me.

"You're saying this is Nora, the cleaning lady Oscar strangled," she says. "It looks like she was more than the cleaning lady."

"She was his mother!" As soon as the words leave my mouth, my vision goes blurry. It all sinks in now. "He killed his own mother!" I'm not whispering anymore, I'm yelling.

"Wait, but..." Syd looks at me, then back at the photo. "If she was his mother, why did they lie to you? What was the point in making you think she was just a cleaning lady?"

"I... I don't know." Syd's reasoning takes me aback. I wipe my eyes and try to remember the day I first met Nora.

Sydney gets up. Or tries to, because she falls right back in the chair. The framed photo slips out of her hand as she scrambles to hold onto the armrests.

I rush to catch her. "Are you okay?"

"No. I don't know."

"You seem a little–"

"Dizzy. I'm feeling dizzy."

"All of a sudden?" I eye the laptop. "What did you find?" My first thought is that she saw something disturbing.

"Nothing." She groans and presses her forehead to my arm. "I don't know what's wrong with me. I felt fine a few minutes ago."

I run a hand through her hair. She's sweaty and a little flushed. Sydney shot Oscar not ten minutes ago, so in my book, it's normal for her to feel a little out of it, if not downright sick. Had I done what she did, I would've currently been bent over one of the toilets in the house, puking my guts out.

"It's okay," I say.

Though it's not okay, and we both know it. We have to get out of here. My initial plan to get Oscar's phone is idiotic. I realize now that I won't be able to go down the stairs to the basement and get his phone from his pants pocket. I can't even think about touching his dead body. I don't have it in me to do it. And Sydney doesn't seem to have it in her, either. In the state she's in, I wouldn't dream of asking her. We must get out of the house and start knocking on doors.

"You need some water," I say.

Syd nods. "Mhm, okay."

I try to help her up, but she's heavy, leaning half of her weight on me. Or I'm too weak. I hook one of her arms around my shoulders and hold her up by the waist. It feels like she's about to faint, that's how clumsy she is.

We take a few steps towards the door when I hear a car pulling in the driveway outside. The wheels screech to a halt, then a car door slams shut. The sharp noise makes my heart jump. I feel like it's beating in my throat now.

"Who is that?" Syd asks, voicing my thoughts.

"Neighbor?" I say, though I don't believe it myself.

"It sounded too close." She pulls herself free of me and loses her balance. "I'm okay," she says quickly. "I'm okay." She regains her balance, and using the edge of the desk for support, walks to the open window.

I follow her, and we peer outside together. We're just in time to see a woman cross the driveway to the front door. A set of keys jiggles in her hand.

"She's alive," I whisper.

Short gray hair and heavyset body, she is dressed in an elegant dusty pink suit and sensible heels. I've never seen her dressed like this. In the photo, she was ten years younger, thinner, and her hair was a few inches longer, the straight tips brushing her shoulders.

"Nora." My voice is barely a whisper. I feel choked. I want to call out to her, but I miss my chance as she slips into the house. I turn to Sydney, wide-eyed and grinning. "Nora is alive! She escaped somehow."

I make to walk past Syd and rush to the door, but she grabs onto my arm firmly. She's squeezing me so hard it hurts.

"Evie, think! Stop for a second and use your brain!"

"What do you mean?"

She pinches the bridge of her nose. "I can barely think, and even I can see it."

"See what?"

"That it doesn't make any sense. Oscar and Nora lied to you about who she was. All this time, you thought she was someone he was paying to clean and cook. Did you see him kill her?"

"He dragged her out of the room, and I saw his hands around her throat," I say.

"But you didn't see him actually kill her."

No, I didn't. I hoped Nora would come back, or if she didn't – because Oscar wouldn't bring her back, would he? – I hoped she was okay. How silly of me. Yes, I'm silly, and naïve, and I don't understand how a mind like Oscar's works. Given that Nora knew I was being held in the basement against my will, there was no way Oscar would've let her walk out of here with her life. Unless...

"She's in on it," Syd says.

"Nora would never..."

"We're not safe here." She pushes me towards the door. "We have to get out."

In the hall, Syd uses the wall for support as she urges me forward.

"Think, Evie," she insists.

I'm thinking, I'm thinking. If Nora is Oscar's mother and she was in on it all along, then this was just a game to them. They tortured me and manipulated me. But why? What did I ever do to them? I can believe that Oscar – a man – was a stalker and a kidnapper, but how could a woman be involved in such despicable acts against another woman?

Syd lets go of my arm, and I stop when I notice she's struggling to keep up.

"Are you okay? What's wrong?"

"I think there was something in that tequila," she says. "I feel drunk. Like plastered-can-barely-string-two-thoughts-together drunk. But I only had that one shot."

"I'll help you." Even as I say the words, I feel like I'm spiraling.

First, it turns out that Nora – someone I trusted and thought I was supposed to protect – is the bad guy, and now Sydney was drugged and it's on me to get us out of this mess. I can't. I can't do it. Sydney is strong. Meanwhile, I'm a fool who was so easy to manipulate that it's almost laughable. Yes, I'd laugh if I didn't have the strong urge to just curl into a ball and cry.

There's noise coming from downstairs – something clattering on the kitchen floor. Syd and I freeze, staring at each other. Silence for a moment, then the creak of the wooden stairs as someone starts climbing them.

Syd reacts faster than me. I probably wasn't going to react at all. She opens the nearest door and pushes me inside, pressing a finger to her lips. She doesn't follow me in, just closes the door, and I find myself alone in a second bathroom.

It's smaller than Oscar's bathroom, and the tiles are pink with a delicate white pattern. I catch a glimpse of myself in the oval mirror. My hair is like a bird's nest, the hollows under my eyes and the paleness of my skin make me look like I have one foot in the grave, but what's most striking is the terror etched on my face. I peel my gaze away, feeling like I might go mad if I keep staring at myself. I don't recognize the woman in the mirror.

The shower curtain is pulled back, revealing a simple bathtub. There's a square window above it, and I notice the strangest object on the windowsill - a snow globe. A beach scene is trapped inside it, a sandcastle as big as the palm tree it sits next to. Nora likes snow globes. She told me once that she collects them. At the time, I thought it was an interesting quirk, but after seeing her bedroom and this bathroom – which is obviously hers – I'm starting to lean away from interesting and more into weird territory.

"You!"

Her voice comes from the other side of the door. I've never heard Nora sound so angry.

"You ruined everything!"

I expect her to barge in, but it doesn't happen. There's a thud, like someone has just taken a fall, and I hear Sydney cry out and curse. I reach for the door handle. What stops me is what Syd says next.

"Put down the knife. You don't want to do this."

Nora has a knife. If I storm out of the bathroom now, what will I accomplish? I know Syd is in danger, but I don't understand why. It sounds like Nora knows her. She's accusing her of ruining everything. Does she know Syd shot Oscar? There are no cameras outside the basement. No feed in the surveillance room shows Oscar lying at the foot of the stairs, his limbs at weird angles. If he and his mother planned my kidnapping and imprisonment together, then it means she has access to the cameras too, but all she saw was Syd and I escape.

"Don't you tell me what I want to do," Nora rages at Syd. "It's too late now. I told Oscar you were bad news. That he shouldn't have brought you in, let you talk to Evie, get crazy ideas into her head. They were fine! Evie wasn't doing great, but she was getting there. Their relationship was on the right track. And then you showed up. You're a distraction that should've never happened. Oscar was focused on Evie. What did you tell him? What did you do to seduce him?"

"I didn't do anything. I'm a victim, just like Evie. Can't you see? How sick and delusional are you?"

"Victim? Evie was never a victim. My son took care of her. He provided for her, gave her everything she could've wished for, and more. She was perfect for him."

Nora's voice sounds choked on those last words, and I realize she's holding in sobs. She was in the kitchen first, before coming upstairs. That's where she grabbed the knife. This means she must've gone down the stairs to the basement and found Oscar's body. She knows. Otherwise, she wouldn't be talking about me and him in the past tense.

"You took him from Evie, and you took him from me," she says.

"I didn't... I didn't do anything... I just wanted to..." Syd sounds like she's close to passing out. She's breathing heavily, mumbling, and groaning in frustration when she can't express herself clearly. "Put the knife... down... Please... See reason. Just see reason." I can imagine her crawling away from Nora.

"You did it," Nora says. "It was you. Because I know Evie doesn't have what it takes. She can't hurt a fly. That's why I chose her for Oscar."

What? I take a step away from the door. She chose me... for him?

"You killed my son! You killed my only baby!"

She's going to stab Sydney, and I can't let her. I look around for something that I can use as a weapon. My eyes fall on the snow globe.

Chapter Fifty-Four

The One

The snow globe is twice as big as my hand, and heavier than I imagined. I don't have time to think. Second guessing myself would mean losing Syd. I open the door and step out into the corridor.

Syd is on her back, struggling to find purchase while her hands and legs refuse to listen to her. Nora is standing over her, knife in hand, blade ready to descend as she bends down and grabs hold of Sydney's knee. Syd tries to fight her off with no luck. Her movements are slow and uncoordinated.

I don't want to do this.

But I do it.

I shut my mind off and lunge at Nora.

She doesn't see me coming. She has her back to me, and I hit her with the snow globe right in the head. The glass shatters, and Nora lets out a startled cry before she crumbles to the floor. She drops the knife and rolls over, dazed, her hand going to her head.

Sydney blinks up at me, mouth agape.

"Come on." I help her up, and it's the hardest thing I've ever done. I'm in no physical shape to carry someone, but

I give it my all and set Sydney on her feet. "Come on, you have to help me."

She's wobbly but holds on to me, and together, we make it to the stairs. This part is dangerous. She grabs the railing, and we take one step at a time. I don't want to rush her, but I also know we must hurry, or Nora will catch up. I can hear the woman whimper and thrash around, probably trying to get up and come after us.

"Easy," I say. "We're almost there."

Sydney sucks in a breath and does her best to focus. Her knuckles are white from how hard she's squeezing the handrail. We make it to the first floor, and from there we just have to cross the hall to the front door. Syd is moving a little faster now, and I'm grateful. She's making huge efforts to stay conscious and moving.

I hear Nora thudding behind us. I turn around for a quick glance and see her descending the stairs. She's clumsy and looks confused but determined to stop us. There's blood on the top of her shirt and on her hands.

We're close to the door, so close that I can smell and taste freedom. Just as I press the door handle, I hear a cry and a thump, then the sound of a heavy body rolling down the stairs. Syd and I freeze in place. Nora has slipped and fallen down the stairs. She's lying on the floor now, and I can't tell if she's still breathing or not. I hesitate between going back to check on her and finally walking out of this house from hell.

"What are you doing?" Syd asks me, forcing the words out.

"I just..."

"Leave her." She fumbles for the door handle.

"But I..."

She manages to get the door open. "You didn't kill her." She looks me in the eye, as if begging me to get on the same page as her.

I must make up my mind. I can't forget that Nora was nice to me, but now I know it was all fake. She chose me. Not Oscar. How involved was she in my kidnapping? No wonder Oscar was indifferent to me most of the time, and was never interested in touching me, in actually taking possession of me, like the anti-heroes in my dark romance books. Maybe he didn't want me in the first place. She did. Nora wanted me for him.

I have so many questions, but the woman that's sprawled at the foot of the stairs isn't going to answer them.

"Let's go." I wrap my arm around Sydney's waist, and together, we step into the chilly evening.

Outside, it's drizzling softly. The fine rain creates blurry halos around the lights that line the street and bathe the neighborhood in a seemingly protective glow. The sky isn't completely dark, but it's getting there. Syd and I cross the driveway. When we reach Nora's car, Syd uses it for support.

"I need a minute," she says. "My mind is... It's just mush."

A car pulls up next door. This is our chance. I wave, but the driver doesn't see me as he gets out of the car.

"Hey!"

"Go," Sydney says.

"No. Not without you."

"It's just a couple of yards."

"Not without you," I insist.

She nods and clings to me once more. All we have to do is cross the patch of grass separating the two houses.

"Hey! Help! Help us!"

The man opens the rear door, and out climbs a little girl. It's Celeste. I call her name, and finally, that gets the man's attention. For a second, I wonder if he was just going to ignore me and Syd, two women running towards him, screaming for help. No, that's probably just my imagination. Celeste runs to us, and the man – supposedly her father – follows her.

"Evie?" Celeste asks, stunned. "What happened?"

Syd stumbles and falls, almost pulling me down with her. I try to get her up, but I can't. She's exhausted, and it doesn't matter anyway. This will be over in a few minutes.

"Who is this?" Celeste's father asks, catching her and holding her back when she's about to jump into my arms.

"It's Evie," Celeste says. "I told you about her! She's Oscar's wife!"

"Oscar doesn't have a wife," he says.

"Please, sir," I say. "Help us. Call 911. Right now. Please."

The door to their house swings open, and a woman rushes out. She's holding a baby, and she doesn't have any shoes on. She's oblivious to her own discomfort as she hurries to see what the commotion is about.

"What's going on?"

I turn to her. "We were kidnapped," I say. "We need you to call 911. Please."

She exchanges a look with her husband. He shrugs, and I can't believe his reaction. She's not impressed by that and shifts the baby into her other arm as she reaches for his phone, which is sticking out of the back pocket of his jeans.

"Hey," he protests. "We don't know who they are."

"That's why we're calling the police," she says as she dials.

"Thank you," I say. "Thank you."

It feels like the earth is shifting from under my feet. My weak knees can't carry me anymore, and when the tension of the last few hours – or days, or weeks, or months – leaves my body, I crumble like a rag doll that has been played with and thrown around too harshly and needs to be retired. I sit on the grass, next to Sydney, and take her hand in mine.

"We made it," I say.

She smiles at me, then her eyes flutter shut. It's okay. She can sleep now. I got her.

Chapter Fifty-Five

Unbroken Bonds: A Memoir, by Nora Miles

Excerpts

The year was 1997. I was twenty-seven, watching life pass me by as I worked tables at the only decent diner in Shelburne, Vermont. It didn't look like I was going to leave my hometown anytime soon. College might have been my only shot, but that hadn't been in the stars for me. I'd let go of that dream a long time ago, making minimum wage and still living with my parents, every ambition I'd ever had squashed by the dull reality.

No one to blame, really. I just didn't have it in me to make my dreams come true. To be fair, I couldn't say I had those kinds of dreams – fixed and fully formed in my head – that I could chase to the end of the world. My dreams were simpler. Move out, find a solid guy, get married, have his kids... Play the circle of life game like everyone around me. On easy mode, if possible. There was nothing wrong with that. People like me made the world go round. Or so I told myself every time someone I knew from high school popped back up into town boasting accomplishments.

I met Bill Davis at work. He was in his early forties, handsome, not a streak of gray in his dark hair – the only officer in our small town who looked good in uniform. He took his coffee black. He also had a wife.

He would chat me up, nothing serious. For months, we only exchanged pleasantries. One night, I was closing up late, and Bill was on the graveyard shift, in search of coffee. We sat down in one of the booths and talked for hours. That's how I found out that he and his wife, Jessica, were going through a rough patch. They'd been trying for a baby for ages, and it just wasn't happening. The process was stressful rather than pleasant, and Bill was disenchanted, to say the least. They'd been married for fifteen years. No one could stay in love for that long.

That was how it started. Bill and I were perfect together. He told me that meeting me had opened his eyes. He'd never been in love with Jessica. They got married too young. I told him I wanted to give him a baby. He told me he was going to leave her.

It wasn't an affair. I didn't see it that way. It was love, and each time I saw him, I felt like my feet lifted off the ground and I was floating. My life had meaning, finally. A solid guy – a police officer! I couldn't have asked for more. Older than me, mature. He'd gone through so much, knew what life was about. He was going to provide for me and our baby and keep us safe. His wife was too old – thirty-five – and she couldn't give him what he wanted most. For me, this was going to be easy-peasy.

It didn't happen. Three months into our relationship, and I still wasn't pregnant. I was pushing Bill to tell Jessica about us. The stress of hiding from her and the whole town was taking a toll on me. I was convinced that was why I couldn't get pregnant, though I'd been to the doctor and knew everything was fine. Bill was hesitating. As if he first wanted to make sure I could keep my promise.

Then the unexpected happened. It was bad luck or bad karma. His wife got pregnant before me, and Bill ditched me. He was bitter, I could see it. He didn't want to go back to his wife, but he didn't have a choice. He loved me, though he stopped saying it and stopped coming to the diner. He went to the competition, down the street, even though their coffee was disgusting.

Later, I found out it was a girl. Bill and I had talked about names when we were together, planning our future. If our baby was a girl, he wanted to call her Eveline, like his grandmother. I stubbornly trusted that he wasn't going to call his and Jessica's daughter that. I wanted to believe Eveline was supposed to be ours.

I was wrong. And so, my downfall began.

***

My parents found out about me and Bill. I could lie and say I didn't know how, but I was living under their roof, and crying for hours on end. My mother's heart was broken when she figured out the man who had left me was Bill Davis. She wasn't hurting for me, though. She was hurting for Jessica Davis.

My mother loved Bill's wife. Jessica was a nurse in Burlington, the nearest city, and my mom had a heart condition. She'd been suffering from it all her life. Jessica had always been kind to her, even answering my dad's calls in the middle of the night, when he couldn't get a hold of the doctor.

Everyone loved Jessica. She was a saint who could do no wrong. Everyone except Bill, but he'd gone back to her either way.

They kicked me out of the house. They gave me two weeks to find a place. I was nearly thirty, with a stable but shitty job, and I'd disappointed them by having an affair with a married man. I thought they were mad and would come around, but it turned out they would never forgive me for trying to steal another woman's husband. They had principles, my parents. Principles that weighed heavier than their love for their own daughter.

I found myself in an impossible situation. My salary was enough to cover rent and bills, but I wouldn't be left with anything after. So, when my ex-boyfriend, Kirk, called after a year of being away, working in New York for a construction company, I agreed to give him a second chance. He was rough and ill-mannered, didn't like to be talked back to, but he had a house, and I needed a place to live. I knew him, and while he wasn't exactly safe thanks to his anger management issues, he was convenient. Better the devil I knew than trying to date someone random to fill the empty space Bill had left in my heart.

One year later, Kirk and I were married. Not that it had been my dream to be married to him, but we had a baby on the way.

Bill and Jessica had had theirs already. Eveline, like his grandmother. Grace, like Jessica's mother. Eveline Grace Davis.

Evie.

***

Bill never looked at me again. He never set foot at the diner, and if he saw me in town, he would cross the street to the other side. He knew the places I frequented and avoided them religiously. He blocked my number and treated me like I didn't even exist. His wife did the same. While before, Jessica and I were friendly given that she often took care of my mother, now she acted like I was the plague itself. I wondered if Bill had told her, but I couldn't ask him. Then I wondered if my mom had told her but didn't have the courage to bring it up. After Kirk and I got married, my parents had softened towards me somewhat.

Bill and Jessica avoided me, and I should've done the same, but I couldn't. The first time I found myself skulking around the park where Jessica took her daughter, I watched them for a few minutes, then snapped out of it and turned around. I promised myself I wasn't going to seek them out again. It hurt to see them, knowing that they had the life I'd wanted for myself.

The second time it happened, I watched them for half an hour, doing my best to stay out of Jessica's sight, which wasn't easy, seeing how I was becoming huge, my belly growing with my own baby. Kirk's baby, not Bill's. I'd recently found out it was a boy, and I didn't know if I was disappointed or relieved. Had it been a girl, I would've been dangerously compelled to call her Eveline.

It became a habit. I knew Jessica's schedule – when she ran errands, when she took her daughter to the park, when she was at home, cleaning or cooking while Evie played with her toys. I was a few steps behind her, always careful, always unseen. The little girl was growing beautifully and had her father's eyes. Then my baby came, and I had to stop.

Oscar Octavius. Kirk chose his name, and I couldn't say no to Kirk when something got into his head. Arguing with him over the tiniest, silliest things usually ended up in a black eye. Now that I was stuck with the baby at home, he figured I didn't have to look good anyway. He resented the fact that he had to support me and the baby, as if I weren't his wife and Oscar weren't his son.

Our marriage went downhill. It hadn't been great to begin with, the peace in our home hanging by a thread, fully dependent on Kirk's moods. The baby's arrival didn't mend what was broken. It made it worse. Oscar slept like an angel during the day and screamed like a banshee at night. I would spend hours pacing the nursery, rocking him in my arms, and it wasn't enough. One early morning – too early – I couldn't calm him down, and Kirk rolled out of the bed to find us both – Oscar and me – bawling our eyes out, huddled in a corner. He started yelling and smashing things. He broke my favorite snow globe, the one I'd gotten for my fifteenth birthday from my grandmother. At least he didn't hit me. I was holding the baby, after all. He kicked us out, instead.

I went to my parents but was only allowed to stay one night. I'd hoped they'd understand, but they hadn't gotten over the fact that two years before, I'd tried to steal another woman's man. My mother sagely told me I'd made my own bed. Kirk was my husband, and I had to make it work for everyone's sake. The next morning, after breakfast, my father drove me and Oscar back home.

Kirk kicked us out again a week later. This time, he made it clear he wanted a divorce. I didn't bother calling my parents. I called my friend, Charlotte, who worked at the diner and was the only person I could talk to without her judging me, and she took me in. She had a spare room and refused to let me pay rent. She told me I could stay for as long as I needed.

Charlotte saved me, but more importantly, she saved Oscar. She never knew it, because while I told her everything, there was one thing I kept to myself.

***

I'd been living with Charlotte for a week. Oscar still wasn't sleeping through the night, waking up at three in the morning, wailing like the world was about to end. I felt bad for torturing Charlotte like that, though she never complained. Pacing the room with him in my arms wasn't working anymore. The only thing that calmed him down was a car ride. Charlotte let me borrow her car whenever I needed it, so one night, exhausted and in tears, I loaded Oscar into my friend's car and drove to Burlington.

I hadn't intended to drive into the city. Usually, I drove to the first supermarket and turned around, yet here I was, parked in front of the Catholic church, my hands as cold as ice on the steering wheel, Oscar mercifully sleeping in the back. The street was deserted.

All I had to do was get out of the car, carefully remove Oscar's baby seat, cross the street, and deposit him in front of the tall, wooden door. Then quickly get back into the car, drive to Charlotte's place, pick up my things, and...

And what?

Run. Where?

Start a new life. I'd failed at this one, so who was to say I wouldn't mess up again?

I turned to look at Oscar as he was sleeping, his tiny hands curled into fists. I ran my finger over his plump cheeks and pushed his soft, dark hair away from his fore-head. He was barely six months old, and here I was, so wrapped up in my own misery that I couldn't even give him a chance. I had to do better. It wasn't his fault I'd chosen the wrong daddy for him.

I cried silently for what felt like forever, and when the sun came up, I drove back to Shelburne. I only stopped once to fill the tank for Charlotte. I made two promises that day: that I was going to do everything it took to raise my son, and that I was never going to tell anyone I'd thought of abandoning him.

I kept my first promise, but not the second. The first person I told, a lifetime later, was Evie.

And now I'm telling you. And by you, I mean the whole world.

But I'm done keeping secrets. I might've not been an exemplary mother at first, but I did my best after, and I believe I succeeded. My Oscar was perfect. Smart, handsome, well-mannered, and kind. A true provider. Everything his father had never been. I worked hard to raise him on my own, sacrificed all that was required.

I need the world to know the whole story and know the real Oscar. What I write in this book is the truth, and I hope that young mothers will learn from what I did wrong, and what I did right.

***

The first years were hard. With Charlotte's help, I enrolled Oscar in daycare and went back to work at the diner. I started setting money aside, knowing I'd have to come up with a better plan. My job as a waitress wasn't going to give my son the life he deserved.

There was only one daycare center in Shelburne, and of course Jessica's and Bill's daughter went there. Until they realized Oscar was my son, and pulled Evie and enrolled her at the private school that had programs starting with preschool through high school. It wasn't something I could afford. It cost a fortune.

I later heard Jessica had insisted and Bill had had to comply. In such a small town, people gossiped. It took such a financial toll on them that their marriage was ruined. Bill resented her for making him spend so much money on their daughter, but Jessica stood her ground, and they stayed together for Evie. The atmosphere in their house wasn't pleasant, though.

I was glad he was suffering at least a little bit after breaking my heart and pushing me into my ex-husband's arms.

Between work and raising my son, it was a miracle I still had energy left to keep tabs on Jessica and Evie. Bill didn't matter to me anymore. It wasn't like I could follow a police officer around without being caught. It was dangerous enough that I was stalking his wife and daughter. I couldn't help it. I felt entangled with this family.

Oscar didn't make any friends at daycare. He was the odd kid playing in a corner. I thought Evie was perfect for him. She was sweet in her frilly dresses, adorable with her little pigtails, and when she laughed, her voice chimed like glass bells in the wind. I wanted them to meet, that was all. There was no nefarious agenda behind my wish to see them together.

One Saturday evening, I gathered my courage and took Oscar to the same park Jessica took Evie. I knew Bill was at work, and I knew Jessica liked to read while her daughter played. Evie was a child that never caused any trouble. Same as my son. They were going to get along great. I found a bench that wasn't directly in Jessica's line of sight, then sent Oscar with his little robot to befriend Evie. I told him to share his toy with her, and my boy always did as I said.

It turned out that Evie didn't want to play with his robot. She refused him twice, he insisted, and the third time, she pushed him, and Oscar landed on his butt. He quickly got up, dusted off his pants, and pulled at her pigtail. Evie started crying, and Jessica dropped her book and ran to her rescue. When she got to Evie, I'd already pulled Oscar away. His eyes were dry, and he was unimpressed by Evie's dramatics. Jessica, however, was furious.

She yelled at me, threatened to call the police if I didn't stay away from her and her daughter. She didn't say she'd call Bill. Maybe she didn't trust him to put me in my place. There was no calming her down. I spoke to her politely, but she only got more hysterical. And finally, she clarified to me why she was avoiding me like I had a contagious disease. It wasn't just the fact that I'd slept with her husband. She thought Oscar was Bill's son.

He wasn't, and I told her as much. I could tell she didn't believe me. From that day on, I had to be even more careful, and I had to take my mind off the idea that Oscar and Evie could be friends. Jessica could get me into a lot of trouble, and my life was hard enough as it was.

She thought she was better. Better than me because Bill had gone back to her. Because she was a nurse at the hospital, and everyone respected her. Because her daughter had both parents, and they were a normal family, or at least they displayed an image of normalcy. To her, my son and I were trash.

I was going to show her how wrong she was.

***

Charlotte was the only reason I was able to set enough money aside to go to nursing school. She never asked me to pay rent, and she rarely let me contribute to the bills. The only thing I bought was food, and that was because I insisted. She only wanted me to focus on Oscar, and I did. I decided to take my ADN for him, so I could get a better job and be loved and respected, like Jessica was. She wasn't better than me. I could do what she did.

With Oscar in daycare and Charlotte watching him when she could, I did my shifts at the diner, and went to school. Three grueling years of sleep deprivation, feeling like I was the worst mother because I barely spent time with my son, losing so much weight that a more serious gust of wind could've swept me away... But it was all worth it.

I had never worked so hard in my life. I'd never been so dedicated to something, so persistent in reaching a goal. I was starting to become one of those people with real dreams. Getting my nursing degree was the first true achievement of my life. Even my parents were mildly proud of me, though it was too late. I wasn't speaking to them anymore.

There were a few clinics in the city where I could get a job, but when I found out there was an open position at the hospital where Jessica worked, I went for it. I couldn't help myself. I considered it my right to be there if I wanted to be there. I wanted her to see that I'd set my mind to it, and I'd succeeded. She might've had more experience than me, and a husband who provided for her and her kid, but as far as I was concerned, we were equal.

She wasn't happy when she found out we worked in the same building. The first time she saw me in the corridor, she stopped in her tracks, her face went livid and her eyes so wide that she looked at if she'd seen a ghost. I gave her a smile. She turned on her heel and walked away. Two months later, she was handing in her resignation. I heard from the other nurses she'd found a job at a private clinic.

That was Jessica's MO. Every time I walked into her life, she went private. Her daughter was still in private school, while my son went to public school, one year earlier, because he turned out to be a genius – writing, reading, and doing simple math when kids his age were still struggling to spell their own names, which were objectively easier than Oscar's. Maybe it was her way of telling me she would always be better than me. Or maybe I was reading too much into it, and Jessica was only trying to keep herself and her daughter away from me and my son. As if I was going to do anything to them. She was exaggerating. I understood why Bill had cheated on her with me. She was a drama queen, while I was a normal, down-to-earth person.

On her last day at the hospital, Jessica found me alone at the nurses' station and threatened me again. She called me a stalker. She was going to call the police if she ever saw me again in the same places as her. If she saw me at her workplace, on her street, at the supermarket where she did her shopping, or around her daughter's school. I called her crazy and paranoid. The size of her ego! To think that my world revolved around her and her spoiled daughter.

This is what I said to her: "My world is my son. I will do whatever it takes to make sure he gets the best there is."

Once again, Jessica and I didn't part on good terms. That interaction soured me on her and Evie, and for a while, I lost interest in them. The tables had turned. The nurses gossiped about her marriage all the time, and about how she and Bill barely talked to each other. Meanwhile, I was doing great, and my son was legit brilliant.

I found a small house I could afford to rent and moved out of Charlotte's place. She remained my best friend through the years, until the horrible car accident that took her away from me. Oscar was in high school when it happened. In the face of this tragedy, we stayed strong and relied on each other.

Word got around that Jessica and Evie had a cold, distant relationship. Jessica had gone through so much trouble to protect her daughter from an imaginary threat that she'd pushed her away and turned Bill against both of them.

Poor Evie. From a safe distance, I watched her grow into this beautiful, gentle young woman whose parents gave her grief for nothing. She deserved better. A family that truly cared about her. A family like mine.

***

As the years passed and Oscar and Evie grew up, Jessica made sure they never crossed paths, and I didn't push it. From the shadows, I watched the Davis family. Bill was miserable, and so was his wife. Did I enjoy seeing that?

Maybe a little bit. He'd given me false hopes, only to ditch me and break my heart. And Jessica had shunned me as if it was my fault her husband had cheated on her. She should've looked in the mirror from time to time. She wasn't a delight to be around, that much was obvious. A man better than Bill would've cheated on her. But their daughter didn't deserve any of it. I watched her become more and more isolated, barely connecting with people, barely making friends. Her parents kept her on a very short leash, like a puppy they were afraid would stray too far from home and become lost.

In the meantime, my Oscar was growing into a smart, handsome, resourceful young man. He was the only man I needed in my life, so I wasn't interested in dating. Even when he told me I should go out, and that he wouldn't be bothered if I found someone, I realized none of that sounded exciting to me. I loved my job, and I loved him. Taking care of people was my calling.

When I wasn't at the hospital, I did small favors for the neighbors, visiting them when they were feeling sick, patiently explaining how they were supposed to take their medicine, even doing the grocery shopping for an old lady down the street who suffered from diabetes and a sweet tooth, so it was up to me to make sure she didn't fill her cupboards with the wrong snacks. It was good to feel needed. I was useful to people, and in fact, I was a better nurse than Jessica. My young neighbors with babies and toddlers always asked me to babysit for them. No one had ever asked Jessica to babysit. How did I know that? I was always watching.

Oscar went to high school in Hinesburg. It was a twenty-minute drive from home, and it cost me nothing to drop him off and pick him up. Since he'd started school earlier than everyone, he was the youngest in his class and couldn't get a learner's permit yet. Not that he could've driven himself to school if he'd had it. But I loved driving him to wherever he needed, and I knew I had to take advantage of these last years he was still dependent on me. He was growing up so fast; soon he would demand his independence and stop asking me to do things for him. I knew that day would come, and I dreaded it. He was already making his own money, though I didn't quite understand how. He told me he was helping people with IT issues.

When he told me he wanted to go to RIT, my heart broke into a million pieces. I'd hoped he'd choose a college in Vermont, but who was I kidding? He was too good at what he did, and it would've been a shame to not let him explore it. He promised he would visit as often as he could, and he did at first, but then got so absorbed by his work and studies that I had to beg him to come home for Christmas. He got his first real job while in college.

I didn't understand half of what he explained to me he was doing, and I certainly couldn't comprehend how his part-time job brought in so much money. He was barely in his early twenties, and for my birthday one year, he told me he wanted to buy the house for me. The house I'd been renting since moving out of Charlotte's place. To him, this tiny, old house was home. To me, it was a reminder that it was all I could afford back then, and it certainly wasn't where I wanted to spend my entire life. He saw that in my eyes, in the way I hesitated when he suggested buying it. Instead of feeling disappointed, he straightened his back and told me he understood. I deserved better. We both did. He went back to college, and I stayed behind. But I knew he had a plan.

And what about Evie? I was certain she would get into a college in Vermont and stay as close to her parents as possible. The shy little thing never strayed too far from home. So, imagine my surprise when I found out she got into Columbia and moved to New York. That must've been the first time she went against her mother's wishes. I didn't think she'd have it in her.

Either way, by this point I'd accepted that Oscar and Evie were never meant to be. Oscar had forgotten about her, and Evie didn't even know he existed. I took my mind off it, hoping that one day, my son would find the right girl for him. The one.

***

Fresh out of college, Oscar moved to New York and started working for a big tech company. The money he was making was beyond my comprehension. To be honest, I wasn't sure it all came from his job. He always had a few side projects he was working on, and I wasn't convinced they were entirely legal. But he knew best, and I understood so little about IT.

He took out a mortgage without telling me and bought a house in one of the fanciest neighborhoods in New York. When he asked me to move in with him, I couldn't say no. I felt stuck in my job at the hospital, but it was more than that. I couldn't say no to my son when he was doing the exact opposite of what I'd expected him to do. Instead of pushing me away, keeping me at a distance so he could express himself in his newfound independence, he wanted me in his life. He needed his mother. I moved to New York without as much as a second thought.

It was fine. I was ready to leave it all behind. The small town I grew up in, my family that I didn't speak to, Bill and Jessica. They were uninteresting to me now that Evie wasn't living with them anymore. Bill was bald and fat, and Jessica had shrunk as if he'd been feeding off her all these years. She was always with her nose in a book, reading the most ridiculous romance novels. As for me, I didn't have time to read. My life was full.

Oscar was at work all the time. I got a job at a hospital in the city that wasn't too far from where we lived, and I had plenty of time to take care of the house and cook for my boy. I just wished we could spend more time together. I couldn't complain, though. He was doing everything right. It was hard to believe a young man like him had come out of the one-year marriage between a woman with no future – me – and a deadbeat, good-for-nothing abuser – Kirk. I knew Jessica believed to this day that Oscar was Bill's son, but he wasn't. My genes and Kirk's had been the winning combination – one of God's mysteries.

Oscar got tired of his corporate job. I would've said burned out, but he didn't want to admit it. I knew he loved his job, but he was working too much. So I was glad when he told me he'd quit. Now I could dote on him to my heart's content.

And once again, my son surprised me. I thought he'd get bored at home after a week or two, but instead, he found projects to do around the house. He turned one of the rooms upstairs into an office, then remodeled the basement. There was plenty of space down there that was wasted, he said, so he went to work. I was more than happy to help him decorate it.

The next job he took was with a start-up. The salary was more modest, but somehow, Oscar made plenty to pay the mortgage, bills, and ensure a comfortable life for both of us.

Everything had turned out so well, there were days I could hardly believe it. Now all he needed was a woman worth his time and generosity. I wanted to raise grandchildren soon.

***

I was resistant to social media at first. Oscar tried to teach me, but I was a lost cause. Until I discovered Pinterest and went down the rabbit hole of dessert recipes. The next logical step was to make a Facebook account because that was where the best groups were.

A few people from my hometown added me – patients and colleagues from the hospital I used to work at. I hadn't been thinking about Bill and Jessica Davis for years, busy living my best life with my son in New York. When their profile popped up because we had mutual friends, I felt a sense of nostalgia. What had Bill and Jessica been up to? They seemed to share the profile, like some couples did, and if I had to guess, Bill was managing it.

Mostly, he shared sports and politics – boring things I couldn't care less about. There were a few photos from when they were both young, and I recognized the building of the police station, where he and Jessica posed together, Bill in his cop uniform, and her in scrubs, his arm around her waist. That was before he came to me to bemoan his unhappy marriage. And then there were a few photos with their daughter. Evie on her first day of school, Evie riding a pony, Evie behind the wheel of her dad's car, Evie graduating high school, and then Evie graduating college.

Where was Evie now?

It turned out I shouldn't have resisted social media when Oscar had tried to teach me how to use it. Facebook was giving it all away. Apparently, Eveline Grace Davis had decided to stay in New York after finishing college, and she was working as a freelance writer. In two clicks, I found her profile, and it only took a few more to make a new, fake profile for myself, so I could send her a friend request and get access to her private posts. It was too easy to find out everything about her.

She'd dyed her brown hair caramel blonde, and it suited her. She couldn't start her day without coffee and a packet of Biscoff cookies, but then it was just tea all day. She didn't seem to go out a lot. No, actually, she didn't seem to go out at all, and when I looked through her friends list, instead of finding the boys and girls – now turned young men and women – she'd been to school with, I found hundreds of strangers from all over the world, most of them from the US, and a lot of them... writers. Not just any kind of writers. Erotic writers.

Sweet, innocent, isolated Evie Davis, the puppy Jessica had guarded with the fierceness of a lioness, was into dark romance books. What a blow that was. If I felt disappointed, it was hard to imagine how disappointed Jessica and Bill must've been. It was all Jessica's fault, I was certain. Evie must've found her filthy books, then graduated to the next level. Bill was probably furious with them both.

Even so, there was still something about Evie. She was prettier, gentler, and more educated than the girls and women I knew Oscar had pursued through the years. Yes, I knew about each of his interests and conquests. There had been many, and none had been good enough for him to bring home.

The passion for dark romance was unfortunate, but Evie had qualities that could easily make me look past it. After all these years, I still believed she was right for my son.

Was it because she was Bill's daughter, and I couldn't have him years ago, when he'd made all the promises under the sun to me, then bailed? Maybe. I could have part of him through Evie. Or maybe I wasn't trying to get revenge on him, but on his wife. Jessica had taken Bill from me, so now I wanted to take Evie from her.

I went as deep as I could, sent friend requests to Evie's friends, found the groups she frequented. I wanted to learn everything about her, and it only took a few days. But then I realized I'd hit a wall. I wasn't savvy enough to find out where she lived, so I could go check her out in the flesh. For that, I was going to need Oscar's help. That was, if he didn't want to take over. And why wouldn't he? She was perfect for him. All I had to do was draw his attention to her.

***

The first time I discovered my son liked to watch girls was when he was in elementary school. I was picking him up, and while all the other children were pouring out of the school building and into their mothers' cars, Oscar was nowhere to be seen. I went looking for him and found him inside, his nose stuck to the window of one of the closed classroom doors. He was on his tiptoes, craning his neck to see. I called his name in a whisper, and he turned to me, waved, then went back to what he was doing. I moved behind him and saw he was watching a pretty girl with mousy hair and big, brown eyes, who was bouncing on the balls of her feet, impatient while the teacher talked to her mother.

I asked Oscar, "Are they talking about you?" He said, "No." I let out a breath of relief. For a second, I'd thought Oscar had done something and the girl was turning him in. I knew he was a gentle soul. Too gentle. In fact, my son was so unproblematic that I sometimes worried about him missing out on things that were a staple of a fun childhood. Like pranking other students or the teacher. Wasn't that what kids did? I knew I'd done it when I was his age. At the same time, I wasn't going to complain. Many boy moms had told me I was blessed. I asked if he was ready to go, and he said, "One more minute, please. I think Cynthia is cute. I like her." And he continued to watch the little girl.

I gently pulled him away and explained to him that he had to be more careful. Either the teacher or Cynthia's mom could've turned their head and seen him. He asked me, "Did I do something wrong?" and I immediately assured him he hadn't. So, he liked a girl. Watching her from a distance was a natural thing. God knew I'd been doing it for years with Jessica and her family. I wasn't going to scold Oscar over something that didn't harm anyone.

This continued through elementary school and middle school, with various girls, most not in the same class as my son. He listened to my advice and was careful. I never heard a word from the teachers, and with time, I relaxed and didn't feel as anxious during parent-teacher meetings.

Sometimes he told me who they were. If he liked a girl strongly enough, he'd bring her up over dinner and tell me all about what she did that day, week, or month. Until he lost interest and moved on to another. Even if he didn't tell me about them, I knew who they were because I was watching him watching them. It was only a safety measure, though I trusted Oscar. He was too smart to get caught. Smarter than me, for sure.

When he was in high school, I found pictures of a girl in his desk drawer. They seemed to have been taken with his phone, then printed out. The girl was on the second floor of a house – presumably her parents' house – surprised in various stages of undress. The sheer curtains barely concealed her nakedness. I shook my head at how irresponsible the parents of girls could be. I wasn't a girl-mom, and still my windows were covered by thick, dark-colored curtains, which I made sure to pull as the sun went down and we turned the lights on inside. It was basic common sense.

I confronted Oscar about the pictures and asked him if he was being careful. He was. That was why he'd printed them out and deleted them from his phone. He explained that it was safer this way, since he could lose his phone, or it could get stolen by someone who knew how to get into it. My son was into IT already, and just learning about cybersecurity. He didn't yet feel confident that he could protect his digital files a hundred percent, so he'd decided to go analog until he figured it out. I was proud of him. I didn't understand half of what he told me about cybersecurity, but I was happy to see him so passionate about something that could provide a great future for him.

Also, the girl, Delilah, was beautiful. My son had good taste. He didn't bring her home, though. When he moved on to the next, he showed me the pictures himself.

***

During his first semester in college, Oscar came home every two weeks, and every two weeks, he told me about a different girl. He would show me pictures and tell me all about her friends, family, hobbies. He knew them almost as well as he knew himself, and I couldn't help but think how lucky these young women were. He invested so much time, passion, and attention in them. Eventually, he saw they fell short and moved on. I was glad he could move on so easily. He deserved the best, and as his mother,

I didn't want him to waste himself on someone who wasn't enough. Who wasn't right.

Bill had done it, hadn't he? That someone was Jessica. She wasn't worth it, and when he found me, it was too late. His leaving me had pushed me to make the same mistake as he had. I wasted my time and sanity with Kirk. The only good thing I got out of that relationship was my son.

Then college absorbed him completely, and Oscar only came home for the holidays. I missed him dearly, and we talked on the phone every day, but it wasn't the same. It was as if we couldn't truly connect over the phone. It got to a point where he started making excuses – he was busy, had to study, he was on his way to a party, he was tired. Every and any excuse under the sun. I began to feel worried.

It was the first time my son was pushing me aside, leaving me in the past. It was normal, I told myself. It was a good thing, really. He was asserting his independence, carving a life for himself away from home. But I couldn't help wanting to be a part of it. I wanted it so badly that it hurt sometimes, and I would lie in bed at night feeling physically ill, checking my phone every five minutes to see if I'd missed any texts from my son, and checking his social media to see if he'd posted anything.

That year, when he came home for Christmas, bringing a girl with him for the first time, it all started to make sense. He'd pulled away from me because he was investing so much energy in her.

To be frank, I don't remember her name. Which is no loss, because she was wrong for him, and I knew it the minute I saw her. She was trying too hard. Pretty, perky, smiling all the time, purring when he as much as touched her arm. She looked at him like he was her Prince Charming, but at the same time, she always seemed to have demands. Trivial things, like "Won't you get me a glass of orange juice, please?" And my Oscar would spring to his feet and get it for her. This wouldn't have bothered me. Not at all. My son was polite and liked taking care of people. Like me. That was why he worked so hard on knowing them and what they liked, so he could serve them better. What bothered me was the look on this girl's face when he went and did whatever she asked him to. From a perky, purring kitten, she turned into a sly fox. I didn't like the grin she gave me every time he wasn't in the room, as if to tell me that she owned him now.

I pulled him aside, and we had a serious talk about it. I told him, "Oscar, she is not the right girl for you," and to my surprise and delight, he listened. I thought he was going to defend her to me, that he was in love and couldn't see the kind of person she really was, but as we sat just the two of us in the kitchen as she slept upstairs, he confessed that he knew something was off, but didn't know what, and that was why he'd brought her over. For me to assess her!

All the times he'd rushed me on the phone because he was presumably busy were forgiven.

It was up to me to explain what was off with this girl, so on the spot, I made up a theory. And this is what I taught my son about women:

There are three types of women. Type one is the woman who is interesting, fascinating, but too independent. It's worth watching her for a while to see what you can learn from her, to see how she behaves around men, and what her social life is like. She will reveal things about a world that, as a man, you don't know very well. She's not worth pursuing, though. She'll only cause trouble.

Type two is the woman who's more open to being led as she takes a back seat. She might rely on the people around her because they make her life easier, and in return, she is easy as well. But deep down, she's still looking out for number one. In my opinion, this was the category Oscar's girlfriend fit in. And easy wasn't good. Not like that. An easy woman who's in on the game and happily plays it isn't worth it in the end. What she has to give is as shallow as her attitude.

And then, there is type three. Introverted and misunderstood, she has no clue about the games people play, and lives in a bubble of her own making where she feels safe. She's independent, but not in the way that a type one woman is. She lives alone because she has no friends and she's cut ties with her family. She has little to no social life because she doesn't know how to navigate it.

I told my son that was the woman he had to look for. That was the woman who deserved his time and attention, the woman who would offer him the most in exchange for what he provided. Only a type three woman could truly appreciate him. Like I appreciated him. She would give him no sass and no headaches. She would be grateful to have him in her life, and he would love taking care of her.

Because the best feeling in the world is to provide for and take care of someone who will thank you for it.

This type of woman, if he ever found her... Well, he had my blessing to snatch her right off the street and put her somewhere safe.

***

Eveline Grace Davis was a type three woman. Ever since she was a child, I knew she had potential, and that was why I'd tried to push her and my son together. Because of Jessica and her machinations, the two of them didn't even know each other. I didn't think Oscar remembered her from that unfortunate incident in the park, when Evie had knocked him on his bum, and he'd pulled at her pigtail. But now that I'd discovered her once again in New York, so close, yet still out of my reach, I was certain she was a type three – the only type of woman that deserved my son's full attention.

Her addiction to dark romance novels was regrettable, but it wasn't a deal-breaker. It would've been too much to expect she'd come out pristine from the mess she'd endured at home, trapped between two very unhappy parents.

I showed her to Oscar. One evening, when he got home from work, I asked him to sit down next to me as I opened my laptop and navigated to her Facebook page. He didn't react at first. There was no recognition in his eyes. I asked him, "What do you think?" and he said, "She's pretty." I said to him, "She's more than pretty. She has a beautiful, kind soul, she's gentle, sweet, and has had a hard life." Like me. I didn't say that part out loud.

He leaned over, took the mouse from me, and started scrolling through her pictures. She didn't have many, so he clicked back and went through her recent posts. I watched him become more and more engrossed, and I smiled to myself. This was going to work.

"If you like her," he said after a few minutes, "Then I like her."

"She lives in the city," I said, "She studied English Literature–"

"Don't worry," he cut me off, "I'll find out everything about her."

He was good at that. With my limited knowledge, I'd only scratched the surface.

"She's a type three," I said then. He raised his brow, and his black-framed glasses slipped down his nose slightly. I lovingly adjusted them back into place. "I know you're tired of having to deal with the likes of Miranda." Miranda was a type two woman for whose sake he'd taken a cooking class. She was tacky, easy, and worst of all, unpredictable, and I didn't like her. "Evie is the woman you've been preparing for all this time," I said. "Trust me."

Of course he trusted me. I was his mother. I also had the perfect plan and the perfect place to safely tuck Evie away before the world could disappoint her more than it already had. Oscar only had to do as I said.

***

A lot of things went right, especially in the beginning. Not all, but most. Evie turned out to be a tough nut to crack, which I hadn't expected, but I'm getting ahead of myself.

The basement was Oscar's project. He'd turned it into a small apartment with all the amenities, and he'd let me decorate it as I pleased. We'd started working on it way before I re-discovered Evie and told him about her, and even though we hadn't talked about it, we both knew why we'd poured so much energy into the remodel. The finishing touch was a metal door that Oscar installed himself, along with a keypad.

When the time came, I prepared a syringe with a special cocktail. Given Evie's negligible weight, it knocked her out within seconds. And then she was finally under our roof, where she belonged. Oscar installed an app on my phone that gave me access to all the cameras in the basement. For a while, it was enough for me. To see her, make sure she was safe and eating well. Oscar spent time with her twice a day, at least, and seeing them finally together and bonding filled my heart with joy. She was reluctant and not always grateful for my son's gifts, like the expensive dresses and shoes he'd bought her, and the books he'd stocked her library with. But I kept telling myself she'd get there.

After a few days, I decided that maybe she needed a nudge. A friendly face to tell her how lucky she was. Watching her through the cameras was nice, but I wanted to see her in person. However, Oscar told me she wasn't ready, but that he had an idea.

He found Rita online and deemed her perfect for what we needed. He brought her in to clean the basement, and what an exciting experiment that turned out to be! It ended up with us burying her in the tool shed behind the house, which did a number on my back, but I had nothing to complain about. I knew that to see some progress, we had to make sacrifices. And Evie had to make sacrifices too, so when Oscar suggested she should be punished, I didn't argue. She was going to lose a pound or two by being tied to the bed for two days, but I was going to make sure she put them back on after, when I finally got access to her.

Evie was a sweetheart. I was so glad I'd chosen her for my son. My instinct had been spot on since she was in diapers. After Rita, we became fast friends. She didn't suspect for a second that I was more than the cleaning lady who also did the grocery shopping and cooked. Oscar had insisted on cooking for her before, and I was proud of him for wanting to do everything by himself, but I wanted to help. Between work and Evie, he barely had time to rest. I was more than happy to do what I could for them both.

Evie passed all the tests. When Oscar unshackled her so she could help me clean, she behaved brilliantly, coming up with a believable explanation for the metal door trapping us in. Of course I didn't let her lift a finger. When he brought her Bobbi and ran back upstairs, leaving the door open, Evie put the child's safety before her own needs. That told me she was going to be a great mother. Not at all like Jessica, but like me. And I was going to help raise my grandchildren. Judging by how we were getting along, Evie and I were going to be on the same page.

But then she said she wasn't ready. Instead of triggering her motherhood instinct, the experience with Bobbi had triggered a sense of fear. No, terror. I didn't like at all the conversation we had afterwards.

Another thing I didn't like was seeing Oscar starting to pull away. Not only from her, but also from me. When I was at the hospital, working shifts, sometimes double because we were understaffed, Oscar would forget to feed Evie. She lost so much weight, she started looking like a different person, not at all like a healthy young woman who could get pregnant and carry a baby to term. Not that Oscar was doing anything in that direction. Thinking he was embarrassed by me, I assured him I never checked the cameras at night. But that wasn't it. He was becoming disenchanted with Evie, and for good reason. I couldn't blame him when she refused to do the most basic things to ingratiate herself to him.

She wasn't grooming herself properly, put off bathing or showering for as long as she could, didn't brush her hair, didn't fix her face in the morning. She wasn't even reading, so at least she'd have something to talk about when my son visited her. I could see that he was hurt when he saw he'd put in so much work, so much effort to get her all those books, some of them not even available in paperback, only for Evie to not spare them a second glance. Oscar never said that he was hurt, but I knew him. He was my only son, the best thing this world had given me, so I knew exactly what he was thinking and feeling.

Evie was wasting away. Oscar was back to chasing that flighty Miranda woman. I had to turn this ship around.

On the days when nothing seemed to be right, at least there was one thing that made me feel better – seeing Jessica's pain in the news. I followed Evie's case religiously, read all the articles, all the speculations, and all the drama that had ensued on the forums where true crime addicts thought they were so smart, but were in fact getting it all wrong. The first few days after Oscar brought Evie, I thought the police would come knocking on our door. I thought Jessica would instantly think of me when she realized her daughter had gone missing. But in all the interviews I read, she didn't mention me once. When asked if Evie or her family had any enemies, both Jessica and Bill had said no.

From atop her high horse, Jessica had missed so many things – Bill cheating on her with me, his disdain when she trapped him back into their marriage with her pregnancy. She'd missed how her poor parenting skills had pushed her own daughter away, how this was all her fault. And of course, she'd missed the fact that I never gave up. When I wanted something, I got it, even if it took years. I'd wanted Evie for Oscar, and now they were together, building a future.

It delighted me that Jessica was so blind. Not as smart as she thought she was. Clearly not better than me and my son. But at the same time, I kind of wanted her to know that I was doing this to her. It was something that I fantasized about, but I had enough self-restraint to keep it to myself. I wasn't going to do anything to jeopardize this.

Not when the situation was in jeopardy as it was.

***

Then there were the things that went wrong.

I thought... maybe Bobbi was too young, and all Evie had seen when she'd played with her was how hard it was to take care of a small child. I remembered that with Oscar, too, the first few years had been the hardest. She needed to get a glimpse of what joy a child could bring later, when they were more autonomous.

Bobbi lived across the street, and both her parents worked, so they sometimes asked me to babysit. They offered to pay me, but I refused. What kind of woman and nurse would I be if I asked two overstretched people with a huge mortgage and bills piling up to pay for watching their adorable toddler for a few hours? I'd babysat plenty in my hometown, and I'd never asked the parents for a penny.

Another family that sometimes asked me to babysit were the Weatherfords, who lived next door. The husband was often away on business, and the wife had just had her second baby. She needed all the help she could get, and on days that were especially taxing for her, poor dear, she asked me to help her seven-year-old daughter, Celeste, with homework.

So, I thought Celeste would cheer Evie up. I told Oscar my plan, but he didn't like it. He said Celeste was too old, and we couldn't predict her reaction to seeing the basement – with no windows and the metal door. I suggested we keep the door open, and he said it was risky.

I thought he would've had more faith in Evie by that point. The door had been left open before with Evie unrestrained, and she hadn't tried to escape. I believed she was ready to be tested further, but Oscar couldn't see it because he'd been distracted lately. I'd noticed he wasn't checking the cameras as often as he'd used to.

I brought Celeste in when he was at work. He'd started spending more time at the office and less at home. I hoped it was just a phase, and once I got Evie to act more alive and engaged, his interest in her would reignite.

Men are simple creatures. All they want is to be around women who make them feel good.

Evie was taking a bath, and that was my cue. I knew the code to the door and could let myself in and out any time, without Oscar's assistance. She didn't know that. She didn't know who I really was, and I had to keep up the façade. Once the door was open and I was certain Evie was still in the tub, I went to get Celeste from the kitchen. When Evie emerged from the bathroom, she was greeted with a scene that looked perfectly normal and believable.

Her eyes darted to the open door a few times, but I was convinced she wasn't going to do anything. I let her believe that Oscar was upstairs, when in fact, he was at the office. I had this under control. He was going to thank me later. Evie was the kindest, most compassionate soul I'd ever met. The incident with Rita had happened a long time ago, but it was still fresh in her mind. She wouldn't risk causing me or Celeste harm, even if it was at the expense of her freedom.

Though, she was comfortable here. She had everything she needed and more. Why would she want to be free?

How different my life would've been had I had a man to provide for me like my son was providing for her!

Things were going great. Celeste had accepted the explanation about Evie being Oscar's wife and living in the basement because she was feeling ill, and Evie seemed more than happy to help Celeste with her math homework. Then in the blink of an eye, everything got turned on its head.

Celeste went to the bathroom, and Evie wrote that dreadful thing in her workbook.

"He kidnapped me. I'm a prisoner."

She looked at me with hope in her eyes, and I didn't know how to react. I was frozen in place, not believing that I'd been wrong about her. She bolted out the door before I could get a hold of myself.

Thank God Oscar had checked the cameras from his office and come straight home. He arrived in time to catch Evie as she was darting up the stairs. What followed was chaos. Celeste ran home, and Oscar dragged me out of the room, making it look like I was about to have the same fate as Rita. My plan had failed, but in the end, Evie was still with us, and nothing had been majorly broken.

Except I couldn't see her anymore. She had to believe that I was dead.

At first, I thought Oscar was faking being mad at me, but it turned out he was actually mad. Furious. I'd never seen him like that. It didn't help that I assured him that between Evie running out and Celeste returning from the bathroom, I'd erased what Evie had written in Celeste's workbook. I told him that no one was going to believe Celeste. Her parents knew she had a wild imagination. Just a few months before, there'd been an incident that had led to her parents not believing a word she said. I didn't know the details, but I didn't need to. Her lost credibility was all that mattered.

Now Oscar wanted space to do things his way. Since I couldn't let Evie see me anymore, couldn't clean her rooms or cook for her, I felt like I was useless. I told him so, and that calmed him down. He hated this situation too, but maybe it was better this way. He needed to get back to being responsible for her, and I needed a break.

As it happened, there was a nursing conference in Philadelphia that I'd initially passed on, but now there was no reason for me not to go. I was going to be away for one weekend. Oscar insisted I took a few days off work – I rarely took vacations – and spend more time in Philly. He wanted me to rest, and promised to hold down the fort.

So, I went.

***

Finally, the things that went horribly wrong. The beginning of the end was marked by the appearance of Sydney Murphy.

Oscar didn't tell me about her. He'd told me about all the girls and women he'd ever had an interest in, but not about her. I didn't know who she was, where he'd met her, how long he'd been watching her.

The morning of the first day of the nursing conference, I woke up and reached for my phone – as I always did – and brought up the app that showed the feeds from all the cameras in the basement. It was my routine – to check how Evie was doing. I almost had a heart attack when I realized that the woman cuffed to the bed wasn't Evie. Evie was sitting on the floor with her knees hugged to her chest, rocking back and forth, staring at the newcomer.

I called my son immediately. He answered after a few rings and had to wait for me to calm down before he could get a word in and tell me the woman's name was Sydney, and that she was Evie's new friend. He'd brought her into the basement for Evie. He said she'd been lonely without me, and he couldn't risk bringing in another cleaning lady. Sydney was a permanent solution.

There was something in his voice. An inflection I'd heard before when he was very young and trying to lie to me, unsuccessfully. He was a grown man now, and I was two hours away from home, so I held off on confronting him. I was almost out the door of my hotel room, car keys in hand, when Oscar firmly told me I had nothing to worry about, that everything was under control, and I shouldn't even think of cutting my vacation short. I begged him to reconsider his plan. This Sydney woman was a bad idea. A bad omen. I didn't know her. Why hadn't he told me about her? Was he sure he knew her well enough? He remained unmoved.

As I drank my coffee – black – I went through the recording from the night before and saw Oscar had carried Sydney in around midnight. He hadn't told Evie more than he'd told me. Now, Evie and I were both waiting for her to wake up. I wondered how Evie felt. I felt apprehensive, jittery. I knew I had to give my son space and the opportunity to do things his way. Without meaning to, maybe I'd made him feel smothered by insisting on being part of Evie's life. I was going to take a step back and trust him.

I forced myself to go to the conference. The last thing I wanted was to be surrounded by people, but Oscar had made me promise. Sydney woke up during the second panel, and I had to apologetically sneak out of the room. I rushed to the bathroom, locked myself in one of the stalls, and used the fancy earbuds my son had gotten me to listen in on Evie and Sydney. I was stuck in that stall until lunch.

But Oscar did seem to have things under control, so I allowed myself to relax. For the rest of the day, my attention was split between my phone, panels, and superficial socializing. I relaxed even more later in the evening, when

I saw that Oscar had locked Sydney in the library and was once again sleeping next to Evie. I didn't understand his plan. Keeping one woman in our basement was one thing, especially when that woman was sweet, gentle Evie who was afraid of her own shadow. There wasn't enough space for two women! And Sydney didn't strike me as a helpless soul. I barely slept that night, tossing and turning, imagining the worst.

The next day, Evie and Sydney seemed to be bonding. It was what Oscar wanted, but I wasn't sure it was a good thing. Evie had been terribly lonely lately, but bringing in a random stranger to be her friend didn't make sense to me. It should've been someone we trusted. It should've been me, but I'd burned myself when I made the wrong call with Celeste, and there was no going back.

Then Sydney made Evie cry, and Oscar taught her a lesson. Given there were no cameras outside of the rooms in the basement, I only saw him drag Sydney out, then shove her back in with her brow bleeding.

He didn't care about her. That was good. For a minute, I'd been worried he might've been thinking of replacing Evie. But that wasn't possible. Evie was the one for him. She needed a little more time, and she'd come around. She'd only been with us for three months. Women disappeared and didn't turn up for years! If they turned up at all. What Oscar and Evie had was in the early stages, still. Sydney wasn't going to last long. If she kept upsetting Evie...

The ring and the ultimatum, I didn't see coming. I couldn't get out of the conference fast enough. I ran straight to my car, leaving my things in the hotel room. A suitcase filled with clothes was the least of my worries. Oscar had given Sydney and Evie one hour to decide who stayed and who went, and I was almost two hours away from home. I drove like a madwoman, taking the fastest route.

I was going to be too late, I was going to be too late... "Please, please, please" was my mantra as I drove and switched between the navigation app and the cameras over and over.

I was too late. They were still in the house, but Oscar... I was too late for my son.

***

What's truly grim about prison is that every day is the same. I wake up and stare at the ceiling for minutes on end before I can make myself get out of the bed and into the wheelchair. For the past few months, writing my life story has kept me busy. Distracted. The book is done, though. This is the last chapter, and after I write "The End", I'm not sure what I'll do with myself.

I'm not used to being passive. I think the word is "useless". There are few things I can do on my own, and for the rest, I need help. Both the correctional officers and the other inmates regard me with pity while I gnash my teeth and try to smile, because there's nothing that I hate more than being in this humiliating position. I'm a nurse! A caretaker. All my life, I've been in service to others. It's given me meaning, and that meaning was taken away from me when I fell down those wretched stairs.

Sydney ruined everything. She killed my son, then took Evie too, turned her against me. I was going to punish her, like she deserved, when Evie came out of nowhere and hit me on the head with something heavy. Something that broke into a thousand pieces and left me bleeding and concussed. One of my beloved snow globes. In a daze, not believing that Evie would do such a thing, I tried to follow them. I couldn't see straight. Pain exploded in my head, my vision went blurry, and the next thing I knew, I was lying at the foot of the stairs. I had no feeling in my legs.

Two spinal surgeries couldn't save my legs. I was going to spend the rest of my life in a wheelchair. My diagnosis didn't impress the judge, nor the jurors, so to add insult to injury – quite literally – on top of life in a wheelchair, I was condemned to life in prison.

Now you know my story. The story of a single mother who dedicated herself to the happiness and well-being of her only son. That's who I am. That's who I'll always be. I wanted the best for Oscar, and I did everything I could to get it for him. He deserved the world. Now he's six feet under, and I'm rotting in a cell. Tell me how that is fair. I was dealt a poor hand, I made mistakes, but I rose above my circumstances. I gave more than I took.

Why couldn't Evie just love him?

Like Bill. Why couldn't Bill just love me?

Maybe it runs in the family. Maybe I was wrong all along, and Eveline Grace Davis wasn't the one.

Epilogue

One Year Later

Sydney places the tray of perfectly shaped chocolate chip cookies in the oven and sets the timer for ten minutes. She's pretty sure they will have to bake for longer than that, but she doesn't want to risk it. For one, she's never baked chocolate chip cookies – or any kind of cookies – before, and two, she doesn't know the capabilities of this oven. It's new. Her mother bought it right before she...

"Oh God." Evie slams the book closed, pushes it away from her, and drops her head on the table, atop her folded arms, burying her face in the crook of her elbow. "Dear God, why did I have to read it?" She starts sobbing quietly.

Sydney rubs her back soothingly. They do this for a few minutes – Evie sobs, Syd rubs her back – then Evie reaches for the paper towels and blows her nose. Sydney takes the book that Evie has just finished reading and weighs it in her hands, wondering what she should do with it.

The title reads: Unbreakable Bonds, A Memoir.

The author: Nora Miles.

They can't keep it. This book has tortured Evie enough. Syd can't imagine sliding it on the bookshelf in the living room, among her mother's books, as if it were just another title waiting for a re-read. She opens the cupboard under the sink and drops it in the trash.

"What are you doing?" Evie asks.

"Take it as a symbolic gesture. We can burn it in the backyard if you want."

Evie manages a crooked smile. "I like that idea."

"Of course. I have the best ideas."

Sydney checks on the cookies while Evie bemoans having to call her mother now that she's finished reading Nora's memoir, and then having to talk about it in therapy next week.

"You don't have to do anything," Syd tells her. "You didn't have to read the book either."

"They insisted. Both of them! Dr. Garland said it would help me see that what happened to me was not my fault, and mom said it would give me closure."

Sydney listens to Evie patiently while keeping one eye on the cookies. Evie has read Nora's memoir in one day, not wanting to draw it out, and Syd wants to reward her with something sweet and homemade, hence her foray into the baking arts. Syd is of the opinion that Evie should've never picked up that cursed book. She disagrees with Dr. Garland, and she is certain Evie's mom, Jessica, actually wants closure for herself.

"Dad doesn't want to budge. He wants to keep the money from the sales of the book, says it's our right as the victims to be compensated. I asked him to donate it, but he won't hear about it. And I know what you're going to say. I shouldn't even listen to him, just do whatever I want since the money will be transferred to my bank account, but he keeps reminding me that he spent a fortune to keep me in private school, from preschool till I went to college, all because Nora was a stalker, and my mom was afraid of what she might do."

"It was all for nothing," Syd says, rolling her eyes. "All that money went down the drain, Nora still got her hands on you, and this is his chance to get compensated for all his sacrifices."

Evie cringes. "My parents never went anywhere, never traveled, never... I don't know, bought a nice car. What they had, they spent on my education."

Syd shakes her head. "You put yourself through reading Nora's word vomit that she calls a memoir so you could learn nothing? It's not your fault, Evie! It never was. If anything, your dad had it coming. He cheated on your mom. With a crazy woman! Repeat after me." The oven dings, and Syd is going to check on the cookies right after she gets this one thing through her best friend's pretty, but thick skull. "It. Is. Not. My. Fault. Come on, say it."

Evie pulls her shoulders back and takes a deep breath. "It. Is. Not. My. Fault."

"Good girl," Syd smiles. The cookies are almost there. Three more minutes. She sets the timer.

"I don't get it, though." Evie deflates in exactly half a second. "Why did Oscar lie to me? He said he found me on Facebook, randomly. He made such a big deal out of my reading preferences. The whole thing... the basement, the library, the clothes he bought me, the handcuffs... They were all to mimic what was in the books."

"Oscar was a psychopath, Evie. He wanted to make you think it was your fault. That you got yourself in that situation because you were reading romance books."

"Dark romance," Evie says, studying her hands. "And a lot of people agree with him online."

Sydney sighs. "I told you to stay off Reddit. It's full of sanctimonious pearl-clutchers and trolls."

"Okay."

"I need you to stop trying to understand Oscar and Nora. Psychos don't make sense. Their brain is wired differently than ours. I think I read that somewhere."

Evie looks up at Syd and smiles feebly. "I'll try."

"Good girl."

"I'll go take a shower," Evie says, standing up. "Maybe I can wash off the ick."

Syd laughs. "Scrub extra hard."

Evie leaves, and Syd is alone in the kitchen. She wipes the counter, and when she throws away the paper towel, her gaze lingers on the book in the trash.

She's read it already. Before Evie, probably before Evie's mother and Dr. Garland. Syd ran to the nearest bookstore on the day of release, read the book in bed that night, then hid it in her sock drawer. When Evie told her she was thinking of reading it, Syd saw no reason in lying to her. She gave Evie her copy, not before trying to convince her it wasn't worth it.

If there is one thing Sydney cannot understand, it's memoirs. Why lay it out for everyone to see and judge? She can't imagine herself writing about her life. Not even in a personal diary. There was nothing glamorous about her childhood, and the secrets she has...

It's like the world has forgotten the definition of the word "secret". According to the Cambridge dictionary – "a piece of information that is only known by one person or a few people and should not be told to others". Sydney has some of those. For instance, she's never told anyone, but even though her mother had only had bad things to say about her father, Syd remembers the time before he left them. She remembers how fun it was to be around him.

Syd's dad took her on little adventures. Like that time when they followed a stranger into the parking lot of a furniture store, and while the man was inside, her dad snuck around his car and deflated one of his tires. Then they followed him again, and when the guy stopped in the middle of the road, her dad offered to help him, gave him his spare tire, and changed it for him, too. Later that week, the grateful man came over to their house to return the tire, but Syd's dad wouldn't hear about it. He invited him in for dinner, and randomly started talking about his plan to build a patio. It turned out the man was a contractor, and eager to help. He built the patio at no cost, and Syd's dad didn't have to lift a finger.

"Always surround yourself with people who are useful," Syd's father taught her.

When Syd was in fifth grade, she wanted to be in the dance club at her school, but both her parents managed to miss the sign-up window. Her dad told her not to worry. He paid a homeless person to steal the dance teacher's purse on her way home from school, and then put on a show of running after the offender and returning the purse to her. Sydney got into the dance club.

A week after, when Sydney came home crying because she wanted to be friends with the best dancer in her dance club, but the girl was too rich, pretty, and popular to pay her any mind, her father pulled her aside and asked her what the girl's worst fear was. It was spiders. He went outside, caught the fattest spider he could find, and instructed Syd to put it in the girl's bag when she wasn't looking. Needless to say, it was easy for Syd to save the day in the locker room, when all the girls freaked out and she was the only one brave enough to kill the spider. She got her best friend, and she became a hero.

"If you want someone for yourself, just take them and make it seem like it was their idea," was another lesson her father taught her.

Sydney remembered it well in college. She saw Abbi, the most popular girl in her year, and decided Abbi was going to be her next best friend. She paid a guy to get close to her, make her trust him, then take her into a dark alley one night and assault her. She also paid him to take a light beating from Syd when she came to Abbi's rescue. Syd got carried away and broke the guy's finger. She had to pay extra.

It was harder with Finn. Syd saw him one day, on the street, entering a gym. It was random, yet it felt like it was meant to be. She was taken with his blond hair and blue eyes.

The first step was to join his gym. The second one, learn everything about him – his schedule, what car he drove, where he lived, who his friends were. All that work, and she couldn't come up with something to bring them together. She was starting to feel frustrated, when one fine Thursday morning, she saw a woman keying his car and had the presence of mind to film it with her phone.

Finn asked the front desk to take a look at their cameras, but they refused and told him to call the police. Syd to the rescue! She stepped in, showed him the recording, and saved the day. The woman who'd keyed Finn's car was his ex. Syd didn't care to know why she was so angry with him. All that mattered was that the ex was out of the picture, and Finn asked Syd out to dinner.

Sydney's father once said, "Most of the time, you make your own destiny, but sometimes, an opportunity will come up. You still have to do the work and follow through, but it will be considerably easier. Keep your eyes peeled."

Sydney's senses dulled for a while. Between Abbi and Finneas, she was content. Finn got her a job at the company he worked for, and they moved into the fanciest place Syd had ever lived in. It lasted three years, then it all came crashing down, like a house of cards.

Her two favorite people betraying her was a wakeup call. She stumbled, lost herself for a minute, picked herself back up. Met Oscar Octavius Miles.

He wasn't her type. Before he approached her, she hadn't even noticed him. He came to her as if he wanted to save her. Syd wasn't into that. She liked to be the one doing the saving. But there was something about him, there was a catch, for sure, and she was intrigued. When he offered to fix her oven, she invited him over, and they had sex.

It didn't escape her that he never took her out, never brought her to his place, and kept his distance at work. She was his sidepiece. Did it bother her? Not really. She still wasn't into him, only using him to distract herself until she found someone worth her time.

He sensed her indifference, and one weekend, took her to his place in Hollis Hills. Well, she thought to herself as she admired the two-story house of an impeccable white, with its bow windows, manicured lawn, and double garage, Oscar could afford more than Finneas ever would.

They had sex twice, and it appeared it was going to be one of those long, lazy days, spent in bed, until Oscar stepped out of the bedroom and was gone too long. She went looking for him and caught him just as he was emerging from another room, locking the door behind him. Barely paying attention to her, he told her something came up, and could she see herself out? She asked if she could take a shower first, he agreed, left her to her own devices, and rushed downstairs. Syd didn't see him pull out in his car, which meant the emergency was inside the house.

A locked door wasn't going to stand in her way. From the bedroom, she saw the window to the locked room was open. Sydney was a skilled climber. It was a no-brainer. Within minutes, she found herself surrounded by screens.

Eveline Grace Davis, the missing girl, had flooded the basement. Oscar was giving her a talking to as he was trying to salvage the pink, ugly carpet. And that was when Sydney knew – this was a once in a lifetime opportunity. She wasn't going to squander it, so she got to work.

First things first, she needed the code to that keypad, so she sat down at his computer and installed a tiny piece of software that would ping her phone with the code every time it was punched in. If Oscar changed it, she was going to know. Once that was done, she opened Notepad and left him a message – a time and place. Unlocked the door from the inside, left it wide open, called herself an Uber.

They met up late, at a bar – their first and last time together in public. Sydney told him she wanted in. She was fascinated with what he was doing, and she wanted to be a part of it. Oscar wasn't following her, but it was simple: she wanted him to put her in the basement with Evie. Syd knew she wasn't making sense, but it didn't matter. Oscar didn't have a choice. Whether he bought her crazy idea or not, he had to put her in the basement. There was no scenario in which they walked out of that bar and went their separate ways. He agreed, but on one condition – he needed to sedate her. She said yes.

Finally, she was with Evie, trapped in what looked like a creepy dollhouse. Oscar behaved exactly like she'd expected him to – erratically. He added a gun to the equation, though he hadn't used a gun before, and they hadn't talked about it. He and Syd weren't a team, but she knew that, and she was mentally prepared for it. He kept her cuffed to the bed in the beginning, so she had to bide her time and play by his rules.

Then Syd made Evie cry, though she hadn't meant to, and Oscar dragged her out, intent on killing her because, in his words, the whole plan was stupid, and it was better to end it. Sydney had to bang her head against the kitchen counter and split her brow open to convince him she was dedicated.

His stunt with the engagement ring took her by surprise. He added a ticking clock to it, and Syd realized she didn't have any more time left. She had to act within the hour. Luckily, he'd left her uncuffed, and she knew the code to the door. Oscar had changed it before meeting her at the bar. When he injected her with the sedative, he asked her if she knew what it was. She told him the old code.

He thought he was so smart. A genius. It was time for a woman to humble him. And by humble, she meant cut his life short. For her plan with Evie to work, Oscar had to go. A shot through the chest and a tumble down the stairs, and Sydney was the hero once again.

They couldn't leave the house, though. Not yet. She had to get into his office and erase the program she'd put into his computer. That was the only thing that could give away her presence there before Oscar had put her in the basement. She innocently sent Evie to explore the other rooms, not knowing what she would discover.

Oscar was dead, but he still managed to surprise her when she realized he'd spiked the tequila she'd downed for extra courage. Fighting the fog in her brain, Syd couldn't believe how stupid she'd been to drink something offered by him in such an obvious manner.

His mother was a surprise, too. A deadly one.

Sydney almost didn't make it. She was supposed to be the hero, the fighter, the protector, and there she was, crawling on her hands and knees, her brain mush, at the mercy of a madwoman with a knife and a taste for revenge.

The girl she was trying to save ended up doing the saving. In other circumstances, Sydney would've been equally grateful and turned off. But this was Evie, and it was Syd's own fault she'd rendered herself useless.

Sydney chose to adopt a different perspective. She saved Evie, and Evie saved her. They were made for each other. They were best friends. Forever.

The fact that Oscar never told Nora about Sydney was pure luck. According to Nora's memoir, her son told her everything. Except Oscar was pissed off with his mother around the time he and Syd met. Or maybe Oscar saw Sydney vulnerable after the breakup, thought she was a type three, then Sydney promptly slept with him and got herself demoted to a type two. Oscar couldn't go to his mom and tell her he liked someone who was inferior to Evie.

And now Syd is doing what she asked Evie not to do – understand two diagnosed psychopaths.

The chocolate chip cookies are cooling on a plate, and Syd hears the shower turn off upstairs. The universe works in mysterious ways, she thinks.

Not that Syd didn't love her mother. She did and still does. But it was convenient to get out of that basement and find her mother had died of a heart attack. With her health issues, she really shouldn't have taken all those new clients. Being a massage therapist was a demanding job for someone with a heart condition. Now the house in White Plains, which Syd's mother got in the divorce, was hers.

Sydney made sure the funeral was tasteful and that she cried a lot, so Evie would see how much she needed her. Evie moved in to help and support her. What was meant to be temporary turned permanent, and Sydney let Evie believe it was her idea.

Syd pours milk into two glasses and places the glasses and the cookies on a tray. She takes it into the living room, where she turns on the TV, waiting for Evie to come down.

Eveline is a far superior best friend than Abigail ever was. Unlike Abbi, she's sweet and malleable. Her universe is small – she works from home, doesn't have friends, is on bad terms with her family. And after what happened to her, she's as scared as a fawn stumbling on wobbly legs in a world that's too dangerous for her. Unlike Abbi, who has dreams of her own, Evie is content to simply exist. And Sydney is content to take care of her.

Like a true provider.

Note from the Author

Thank you for reading my book! I hope you enjoyed it, and if you did, a positive review would make my day. I read every single review (which is not very healthy, but I do it anyway), because I know the reviews will tell me how to make my next book better.

One important thing I wanted to mention: I wrote a bonus epilogue for **The Provider** called **The Visit**, and it's free to read here:

https://joannamargot.eo.page/thevisit

Eveline's mother, Jessica, visits Nora Miles in prison. It's high time the two women had a real talk.

About the Author

Joanna lives in Romania and splits her time between writing twisty psych thrillers and rescuing feral cats. When she's doing neither, she plays the piano badly, reads well past her bedtime, or dreams about taking up a dozen more hobbies. One day, she'll be a mediocre painter.

Also by Joanna Margot

The Woman in the Shed

https://joannamargot.com

Made in the USA
Middletown, DE
07 September 2024